A Question of Country

A Question of Country

Sue Parritt

Contents

The Letter

*Anna remembered arriving home that drab December day with all the
clarity of freshly washed glass, details of those long-ago hours embedded
deep in her blood and bone. They marked the birth of a tempestuous
relationship that, after fifty years, still coloured the palette of her life.*

A pile of Christmas post greeted her sleet-sodden shoes, precipi-
tating a clumsy dance away from new doormat to threadbare carpet.
After depositing her handbag and shopping bag on the hall stand, she
picked up the letters and skimmed through the small envelopes, smiling at the still unfamiliar address written by friends and relatives. At
the bottom of the pile, a brown foolscap envelope caught her attention
and her smile broadened as she noted the typed delivery details and
London postmark. Gripping the envelope between gloved fingers, she
made no attempt to retrieve the seasons' greetings that fell like giant snowflakes over the faded floral carpet. A draught from the open
door prompted swift action from her right foot, while her left hand
reached for the light-switch, positioned for some unknown reason at
least three feet from the door. Spread-eagled, she slid on Aunt Maud's
Christmas greetings, smudging the spidery fountain pen script, then
tilted towards the hall-stand. Grateful for heavy Victorian furniture,
she grabbed the polished edge to prevent a fall. Bird-light, the brown
envelope fluttered down to join paler varieties on the carpet.

Balance restored, Anna kicked off her shoes and bent to pick up the
scattered post. There seemed little point in holding the brown enve-

lope up to the light; the hall was too dingy to see anything useful at this hour of the winter afternoon. Besides, they had agreed one shouldn't know before the other; they must open it together, share the welcome or unwelcome news. Unfortunately, she knew Joseph would be late home, as his area manager's monthly visit was bound to culminate with drinks in the pub on the Friday before Christmas.

* * *

Two hours and ten minutes later, dinner ready and kitchen cosy from gas cooker and paraffin stove, she was still waiting to slit the thick brown paper. Propped on the kitchen bench next to salt and pepper, the envelope seemed to mock her deliberate busyness, its glued-down flap and unknown contents never far from thought or eye.

Suddenly, she heard the front door hit the wall with a thud. A second thump and footsteps pounding up the narrow hall confirmed Joseph's arrival.

'I'm home, darling,' he called as usual, entering the lounge.

From the kitchen doorway Anna watched him toss his coat onto a lounge chair and walk sleet-softened leaves across the cracked kitchen linoleum. Chilled lips kissed, whisky breath warmed, wet hair dripped over her candy-striped apron.

'What's for dinner?' he asked, releasing her and walking over to the cooker.

'It's arrived,' she answered breathlessly, steering him away from saucepans and frying pan.

'What?' he asked, then noticed the envelope.

Side by side, they perched on the yellow kitchen stools he had made just weeks before, their heads close together, the letter held taut between winter-pale fingers.

'Yes!' he cried.

'Yes,' she echoed.

He lifted her lightly, twirling her away from kitchen claustrophobia. Elated, they danced through sparsely furnished lounge and across narrow hall to cluttered bedroom. In the kitchen, boiled potatoes cooled, baked beans congealed, sausages stuck to shiny aluminium. The letter from Australia House lay abandoned on the kitchen bench.

No Turning Back

A taxi transported the young couple from station to docks, depositing them opposite a series of tin sheds that leant against one another for support. Anna could just make out the word *Customs* on the peeling sign above a half-open door. After unloading their two suitcases, the driver wished them good luck and sped away in a cloud of black exhaust fumes.

Behind the customs shed, the ship loomed large against a hazy summer sky, her sleek white lines punctured by portholes. Anna noted the yellow funnel, the lifeboats strung like lanterns along the starboard deck, and had to look away, not from regret at leaving homeland, family and friends, but to restore her identity. The ship overwhelmed her, snatching her insignificant life, all her dreams and fears reduced to numbers typed on a blue shipping contract. *Last minute nerves,* she presumed, recalling her parents' barely concealed tears at the station, their forced smiles as the train pulled away from the platform. They had declined a dockside farewell, her father maintaining it would be too upsetting for her mother.

Joseph's parents lived more than a hundred miles from the port and didn't own a car, so coming to Southampton docks wasn't an option. In-law goodbyes had been made weeks earlier, at the end of a difficult weekend cramped in a small terraced house along with Joseph's three siblings and a smelly dog. Since their engagement a year before, Anna had tried to become friends with Alan and Stella, but it proved an uphill battle, her mother-in-law in particular making no secret of the fact she disapproved of Joseph's choice.

At first, Anna had been miffed by the snide comments on her lack of style, her penchant for reading serious literature, her parents' Methodism, but as the wedding day drew near, she had taken refuge in the clandestine appointment scheduled for the second day of their brief London honeymoon. A late November wedding offered limited locations for newly-weds keen to preserve their savings, so they had booked three nights in a modest London hotel, their primary objective being ease of travel to Australia House in the Strand. Months earlier, they had completed emigration forms in the privacy of Joseph's bedroom – he shared a flat with two friends – and, following a swift response from Australia House, attended a specified doctor's surgery for medicals. A letter advising that both of them met Australian health standards followed soon after. By mid-October, the would-be migrants had progressed to the final hurdle, according to the cheerful young man Joseph had spoken to on the telephone when arranging the obligatory interview to coincide with their honeymoon.

Anna anticipated a formal atmosphere, stuffy civil servants sitting behind a desk firing questions, but the two immigration officers – youthful and genial – had spent most of the time enthusing about life in the 'lucky' country, their speech peppered with enticing descriptions of beach and bush. Joseph's queries about job prospects were answered with a casual, 'No worries, mate, plenty of work for those willing to work hard,' followed by friendly advice to 'learn Aussie ways quick smart' and 'don't whinge.' Listening to subsequent dialogue, Anna surmised that 'whingeing Poms' were a despised breed, destined to be ostracised at social events and in the workplace.

'Just remember, comparing Australia with Britain is a futile exercise,' the younger officer declared towards the end of the interview. 'In my book, the two countries represent opposite ends of the spectrum. Britain is an old, overcrowded nation that has had its day. Empire in tatters, high unemployment, industry in decline, grim-faced people struggling to make ends meet. Australia, on the other hand, is racing up the achievements ladder, a vibrant new nation destined for greatness.'

Although Anna admired his enthusiastic patriotism, she couldn't help feeling his views were somewhat biased. Thousands of Britons might be seeking a life elsewhere, but fifty-five million remained. Prudently, she remained silent, playing the role of compliant new wife that the officials appeared to require. There would be time later, in the privacy of their hotel room, to chew over the interview, laugh about over-embellished language and, if necessary, express long-held feminist views. The final question almost proved her undoing and it took immense effort to remain serene and respond to what she considered downright impertinence.

'How many children do you plan to have?' the older man asked, leaning towards her.

Anna and Joseph exchanged glances. Babies were not on their immediate agenda. They had discussed children but agreed that starting a family could wait for some years, with Anna being just twenty-two and Joseph twenty-four next birthday.

'Three at least,' Anna replied, in what she hoped was a convincing tone.

'Sooner rather than later?' A supercilious smile sauntered over the official's thin lips. 'Populate or perish, you know.'

'Give us a chance,' Joseph retorted. 'We've only been married for two days!'

* * *

Waiting in the customs queue, Anna recalled the officials' laughter and thought of the packets of contraceptive pills safely stored in her capacious shoulder bag. The previous week, a visit to her local doctor had secured a prescription for three months' supply, to cover the travel period plus give her time to register with an Australian GP. There would be no unplanned pregnancy in the Fletcher household.

The queue shuffled forward, the occasional suitcase opened for inspection, passports scrutinised, or, in some cases, the documents of identity supplied by Australia House at no cost to those without a current passport. *One-way ticket,* Anna mused as Joseph handed over the document, their particulars hand-written and two unsmiling faces glued inside black-bordered boxes at the bottom. It had taken Anna several attempts to acquire suitable photographs. Cramped in a photo booth, her sombre expression twice dissolved into giggles as the camera snapped. 'What the hell are you doing in there?' Joseph had asked, standing on the other side of the curtain clutching his strip of four acceptable snaps.

'Make your way to the ship now,' the customs official instructed, indicating a door to his left.

Joseph reached for her hand. 'This is it, my girl.'

Anna grinned. 'No turning back now, we're signed and sealed.'

* * *

Once on board, they shuffled along narrow, crowded corridors, searching identical doors for their allotted cabins. B deck contained mostly four-berth cabins; families were housed on lower decks. Married couples without children were segregated, four wives in one cabin, four husbands in the next. A ten-pound assisted passage didn't cater for the appetites of newly-weds. In the heady days of mass migration, it was a case of cramming in as many as possible. Every week, a ship carrying hundreds of hopeful emigrants left Southampton for the long journey south.

They didn't linger to meet cabin mates, preferring to be on deck when the ship sailed. According to Anna's much-travelled Aunt Maud, departure would bring ceremony and celebration. Streamers, a brass band, ship's horn booming, crowds on the wharf waving, cries erupting the moment a tough little tug began to tow the huge ship away from the dock.

A sailor pressed a coloured streamer into Anna's free hand as Joseph pulled her along the deck. An unbroken line of passengers stood by the rail waiting for the signal to throw. Anna would have to toss her streamer high and hope the wind carried it down to the dock, not into some stranger's backcombed tresses.

'In here!' Joseph shouted, pushing her through a tiny gap.

She clutched the rail and glanced at the upturned faces gathered for farewell. Thank God her parents had decided against coming to see them off. Uninhibited, she could relish the moment, punch the air in triumph, jump for joy, yell until her lungs were fit to burst. 'Goodbye, goodbye! Off with the old, on with the new, Australia, here we come!'

Yachts shared the liner's passage down Southampton Water, heading for the Isle of Wight or out into the Channel for a run down the coast. The island slipped by; patchwork quilt fields edged with high white cliffs. Open water from now on, first port of call the Canary Isles, specks of rock in the wide Atlantic. No cruise through the Mediterranean for their batch of migrants, as the Suez Canal had been closed to shipping since the 1967 Arab-Israeli War. Nowadays, the voyage to Australia took five weeks instead of the pre-war four, heading down the west coast of Africa, around the Cape of Good Hope and across the Indian Ocean, with only two stops before reaching the western Australian port of Fremantle.

The first few days passed in a blaze of sunshine, the hours between meals occupied with swimming in the pool, deck games and exploring the ship. During the brief visit to Tenerife, largest of the seven Canary Isles, Anna and Joseph, along with others from the ship, took advantage of a cheap coach tour to view Mount Teide, the third largest volcano in the world. Other passengers opted to walk the streets of Santa Cruz de Tenerife, admiring well-preserved colonial buildings.

One week into the lengthy voyage, many passengers remained afflicted with seasickness and on several occasions Anna and Joseph sat alone in their section of the dining room, much to the disappointment of waiters trying to offload five courses. For the first time in their lives, they ate grilled steak, relishing each succulent mouthful. Joseph demolished four pieces at one meal, delighting the Italian waiter. '*Troppo sottile*,' he said, indicating Joseph's thin arm. 'Eat, eat!'

Crossing the Equator brought fun and celebration, Anna volunteering to be one of half-a-dozen young women dressed in grass skirts, bikinis and floral garlands, cavorting on deck for the 'crossing the line' ceremony. Her reward was an ornate certificate written in Latin, featuring Neptune astride a horse, trident in hand.

But three days into the Southern Hemisphere, the Lord of the Sea shook his three-pronged spear, scattering passengers to the safety of bar and coffee lounge. Cold rain lashed empty decks and sun and stars retreated behind dark storm clouds as the ship ploughed through huge seas.

Barriers appeared around the dining tables as the ship neared the Cape of Good Hope, but food, especially soup, still had to be consumed quickly to avoid spillage. Once again, beanpole Joseph enjoyed copious portions.

Cape Town harbour provided two days respite from the wild seas, yet for Anna, the majestic Table Mountain and beautiful coastal scenery were marred by the ever-present injustice of apartheid. From the moment she stepped onto South African soil, the consequences of racial segregation smothered her like a malevolent cloud. Twenty-two years of living in a prosperous seaside town had not prepared her for the sight of children begging in the streets.

In the doorway of a large department store, a young black woman clad in a ragged cotton dress sat on the ground, holding out a tiny baby swaddled in sackcloth. Behind the woman, fluorescent lights illuminated rack after rack of tailored coats, sleek jersey dresses and jaunty hats. Shocked, Anna stood staring, unable to raise her eyes from the infant's puckered face. Wind gusted up the street from the harbour, lifting the veil of her youthful naiveté, tossing it high into the charcoal clouds shrouding city and flat-topped mountain.

'Not this shop,' Joseph said, unaware of her distress. 'We need a supermarket for washing powder.'

Still focused on extreme poverty, she allowed him to lead her down the street, remembered too late her failure to augment the few coins in the woman's begging bowl.

In the supermarket, it took some time to locate laundry products, as the first shopper Anna approached muttered, 'No speak white woman,' before scurrying away. Joseph said perhaps the woman hadn't understood the question, but Anna thought this unlikely.

Back on board for lunch, the young couple from Yorkshire whom they had befriended didn't seem to share Anna's horror and bewilderment. Small boys begging in the street had annoyed rather than upset Clive and Janette, as had the sign in the post office, which prevented them joining the shorter *Blacks Only* queue.

Later that evening, the absence of a similar sign caused further irritation when the two couples tried to enter a city nightclub and were refused entry by a scowling doorman of gigantic proportions. Through the windows, crowds of brightly dressed people could be seen dancing to a jazz band. 'Pity about that,' Joseph remarked as they retreated, 'the music sounded fabulous.'

'Bloody stupid rules,' Clive retorted. 'Thank God we're not moving here.'

Janette slapped his wrist. 'Keep your voice down, we don't want to upset him.'

By contrast, the *Whites Only* venue further up the road had recorded music – a poor selection, the English couples considered, having grown up on the Beatles and Rolling Stones. Bored, they left after an hour and decided to walk back to the ship, rather than take a taxi.

As they neared the wharves, the distance between streetlights widened, traffic diminished, and shop windows became grey shapes in the dim moonlight. They walked briskly, jacket collars turned up against the cold night air. Not far from the ship, a group of young men stood talking and smoking in a darkened shop doorway. The English foursome passed by without giving them a second glance, half-a-dozen youths congregating on a Saturday evening being a not uncommon sight in their respective hometowns. Footsteps quickening behind them were barely discernible above friendly chatter; within minutes, they were surrounded.

The men were tall and thin, dark faces and clothing melding with the shadowed street. Black hands clutched the white men's lapels, pulled them apart, plunged deep into inside pockets. Anna saw Clive tense in anticipation of a blow that never came; Joseph stood immobile, his face a mask of stoicism. Expletives sliced the night sky when hands surfaced empty of coin or note. Anna stood to one side, staring straight ahead, the handbag containing their cash and identity document slung across her chest. Cursing intensified, becoming vivid descriptions of what the men wanted to do with white women's bodies. *Only words,* Anna told herself, letting them float over her head. Beside her, Janette blanched, fear flooding her blue eyes like white-hot tears.

Still swearing, the young men retreated, leaving the four British migrants shaken but unharmed. Later, leaning on the ship's rail gazing at a star-filled sky and twinkling city lights, Anna found it hard to reconcile the beauty of place with the ugliness of manmade prejudice and privilege. But greater than fear, shock or sadness was the sense of indignation she experienced during a coach trip around the city the following day. Halfway through the tour, the coach slowed to allow tourists a good view of Groot Sur Hospital where Doctor Christian Barnard was performing the first heart transplant operations. After gazing at the white monolith for a few moments, a middle-aged woman sitting in the aisle seat opposite Anna asked the driver several questions about the long-term prognosis for transplant patients. The driver supplied only vague answers, unwilling or unable to deviate from his set spiel.

The coach moved on past grand houses surrounded by high walls topped with barbed wire, then descended a steep hill to a group of buildings reminiscent of the customs sheds on Southampton docks. Slowing a little, the driver explained proudly, 'This is the hospital we have provided for the blacks.'

The woman opposite leapt to her feet. 'It's a dilapidated tin shack! You should be ashamed of yourselves. How can you condone this appalling apartheid?'

'You English don't understand the situation here,' the driver retorted, putting his foot on the accelerator.

The woman began to speak again, but this time the man beside her placed his hands firmly on her shoulders and, pushing her back down in the seat, said softly, 'Now is not the time to be a good Quaker, Ruth.'

Other words burned in Anna's mouth. She wanted to jump up and congratulate the woman for saying what was surely on all their minds, but something held her back. It was not fear of the driver reporting inappropriate remarks to the authorities, or risking an accident by flying around sharp bends, but rather the embarrassment of standing out and causing a scene. So instead, she reached for Joseph's hand, squeezed it and swallowed hard to dislodge the impotent words stuck in her throat.

Discussing the incident later over coffee in a bar on A deck, Joseph remarked that while there was a need for action, there was also the need to know the right time for action. Anna agreed, little knowing his words would return to haunt her in the Nineties' post-apartheid world.

* * *

Boredom set in after the Cape Town interlude, with the vast Indian Ocean needing to be crossed before they reached land. They had to endure two weeks of bad weather, the swimming pool closed, walks around the deck reduced to brief, wind-jarring forays. Alone at night in her narrow top bunk, Anna longed for Joseph's arms, lingering kisses, fingers fondling soft breasts.

One evening, they struck up a conversation with an Australian couple who were returning home following a year working in England. After the usual pleasantries and discussion of the apartheid regime in South Africa, talk turned to the ship in general and cabin accommodation in particular. As paying passengers, the Australians had a cabin to themselves and offered to lend it for an hour or two, following Joseph's remark on shipboard separation. He accepted the unusual offer without hesitation, forcing a blushing Anna to flee to the nearest bathroom.

* * *

Naked on a top bunk – they didn't like to use the lower bunks inhabited by the Australians – Anna and Joseph giggled like adolescents snatching sex behind absent parents' backs. Limbs became entangled, Joseph's feet kept hitting the cabin wall and Anna couldn't get comfortable. It wasn't a total waste of time, but they decided not to request the cabin again. Making love to order in the cramped confines of a top bunk lacked appeal.

Next morning, the Australian couple approached them on deck. 'Have a good one, mate?' the husband asked, digging Joseph in the ribs.

Mortified, Anna looked at her feet, wishing the wind would whisk away Joseph's reply.

* * *

The port of Fremantle provided the migrants' first glimpse of Australia. Busy wharves, ugly warehouses, sea gulls cawing; it could have been Southampton docks all over again, except for blue sky of a brilliance seldom experienced during an English summer, let alone winter.

Along with numerous other passengers, Anna and Joseph caught a train to Perth, rattling through pockets of industry and rundown houses to the city centre. The shops were similar to those they'd left behind, although Anna was bemused to find "Manchester" meant sheets and towels. In Kings Park, they sat on a bench eating egg and lettuce sandwiches for lunch, the plain fare enjoyable after weeks of rich shipboard meals. Admiring tropical flora occupied the remainder of the afternoon, Anna revelling in the lush foliage. Foolishly, she ignored the gravel paths, staining her white canvas shoes as she ran across freshly watered lawns.

Returned to confined ship space, Anna wished they had disembarked permanently, like the passengers they observed standing on the wharf with suitcases at their feet. Impatient, she wanted to embrace Australian life without delay. 'Two more stops before we can begin our new life,' she moaned to Joseph, as they tramped the deck. 'Why do days at sea pass so slowly?'

'Patience is a virtue,' he began, reciting the first line of a poem Anna had once quoted to him. 'Besides, as far as I'm concerned, our new life began the moment we stepped on board.'

'We could have come by air,' she muttered, recalling Joseph had been the one to insist that travelling by ship would be the better option because they could bring all their belongings, rather than one suitcase each. Not that they possessed a great deal. Their first home had been fully furnished, a set of yellow kitchen stools the only addition.

'And leave our wedding presents behind?' he countered.

She thought of the hideous dinner-set Stella had given them for Christmas: thick china, gaudy colours, odd-shaped cups and bowls. 'I'm pleased we could bring that beautiful little table your uncle made,' she said, choosing tact over criticism. 'All the same, I'll be glad to reach our final destination.'

'Me too.' Joseph slowed his pace. 'My main concern is employment. Our savings won't last long if we don't find work quickly.'

Anna reached for his hand. 'Don't worry, I'm sure we'll land something within a couple of weeks. There were plenty of vacancies listed in that newspaper we read this morning.' During breakfast, the purser had announced that Australian newspapers from several states were available in the main lounge and advised passengers to peruse the relevant publication.

Joseph looked over her head at interminable blue water. 'I know, but I can't apply for a job from the middle of an ocean.'

Anna almost quoted the patience poem, thought better of it and said instead, 'Don't forget that chap behind the counter at Australia House said Brisbane is a city on the move.'

Joseph squeezed her hand. 'I love your cheerful optimism, darling.'

* * *

Brisbane, located halfway up Australia's eastern seaboard, had been chosen as the Fletchers' new home not for climate or job prospects, but because their sponsors, Roger and Mary Gittens, lived there. In 1970, childless married couples who migrated to Australia needed a sponsor to vouch for their good character and provide accommodation on arrival. Families were sponsored by the Australian government.

After completing his electrical engineering apprenticeship, Joseph had secured a position in the small company where Roger worked. The two soon developed a good working relationship, so Roger's announcement that he was emigrating to Australia with his family had been disappointing. Interested in working abroad at some future date, Joseph had asked Roger if they could correspond. Two years later, Roger and Mary had readily agreed to sponsor the Fletchers, even though they hadn't met Anna.

Rough weather buffeted the ship as it crossed the Australian Bight and Bass Strait, sending all but the hardiest hurrying below decks. Passengers breathed a collective sigh of relief on leaving the heaving Southern Ocean behind at the narrow entrance to Port Philip Bay. Winter rain squalls swept the exposed decks, the sky gunmetal grey, but at least the water remained relatively calm. For Anna and Joseph, the day in port – the city of Melbourne was located at the head of the bay – turned into almost a repeat performance of Perth. After taking a train from the docks into the city, they looked around the shops, munched sandwiches in the Botanical Gardens, then clattered past factories and small brick houses back to the ship. The weather proved the exception, showers and a cold wind bending the bare-limbed trees that lined the city streets. *More like England than sunny Australia*, Anna thought, thankful their sponsors didn't reside in Melbourne.

After leaving the expanse of Port Philip Bay, the ship headed east, travelling parallel to the Victorian coast. Whatever the weather, Anna ventured on deck for hours, marvelling at golden beaches, wild surf and grey-green forests stretching as far as the eye could see. How she longed to leave her footprints on those pristine beaches, dive into foaming waves, hike through unfamiliar trees. Admittedly, she felt a little apprehensive at the sight of immeasurable eucalypt forests. Oak, ash, elm and birch were the trees she knew, the solid legacy of a tenth-century Norman conqueror desiring a place to hunt. The New Forest of childhood picnics, wandering ponies and timid deer had held no fear for her, its roads and paths leading to thatched-roofed cottages, old stone churches and cosy pubs. However, the dense Australian forests appeared to have no beginning or end; a tangled labyrinth she felt sure would foil even the most intrepid adventurer.

Before long, the ship turned the corner and made its way up the east coast towards Sydney. Small towns and what looked from a distance like farmland, dissected the previously endless forests. The beaches remained the same, miles and miles of sand fringed with white surf. Every now and then, a headland jutted into the ocean, breaking the line of surf. Anna leaned on the rail, drinking in details of the immense continent she soon would call home.

* * *

Fast asleep in their separate cabins, Anna and Joseph missed the ship's passage through the heads into Sydney Harbour and would have also missed the Coat-hanger bridge if the captain hadn't announced its approach as they ate breakfast. There was an immediate mass exodus from the dining room, every migrant wanting to be on deck when the ship steamed under the famous bridge.

Just before they reached the bridge, the woman standing beside Anna at the rail pointed out the controversial – in her opinion – opera house under construction on Bennelong Point, a mass of scaffolding, exposed concrete beams and unusual shapes. Anna nodded and smiled, unwilling to comment on a structure she knew nothing about. Beyond the bridge, tower blocks stood sentinel as ferries scurried over blue water, transporting workers to offices and shops. Then, as the ship approached its Circular Quay berth, the same woman squealed with delight and began waving. 'That's our Eric down there!' she exclaimed. 'Come all the way from Parramatta to meet us.'

Long after the engines had ceased their relentless throb, Anna and Joseph waited impatiently for the signal to disembark. Officials organised the migrants into three groups: those destined for Sydney hostels, those being met by family or friends at the quayside and those travelling beyond Sydney. Last to leave were migrants destined for Queensland. Following disembarkation and customs processing, they were crammed into an ancient bus and driven to a migrant hostel, there to while away the hours until the overnight train for Brisbane left Central Station.

Villawood was a rude awakening. Anna's romantic dreams of the new land began to crumble as she carried her suitcase to the Women's accommodation – the shipboard separation order remained in force – one of half-a-dozen rusting Nissen huts dotting dusty ground. Metal-framed bunks lined the walls and metal chairs with torn vinyl seats leaned against a shabby Formica-topped table. Most of the bunks were occupied by older, grey-haired women who stared at the newcomers with grim expressions. No one spoke or raised a hand in greeting, so Anna dumped her suitcase in a corner and fled the sorry scene.

Joseph was waiting for her outside the Men's hut, his face a picture of misery. 'I feel like an enemy alien interned for the duration,' he said, as she took his hand.

Anna leaned closer and said quietly, 'Just now, I saw some in-mates sitting outside a hut. Stout middle-aged women wearing frumpy dresses, thick black stockings and headscarves, jabbering away in a language I didn't even recognise.'

'Probably Eastern European or Russian.'

'How long do you think they have to live here?'

'Dunno. Weeks, months maybe. I suppose it depends on available accommodation and whether they've got a job.'

'Thank God for your friend Roger. If I had to stay in this dump, I'd head straight for the airport and catch a plane out of here.'

Joseph smiled and mussed her hair with his free hand. 'We've got to stay for two years, darling, that's part of the deal. If we return home before then, we have to pay back the fare for the outward journey.'

'I know, I know.' She pouted. 'But I do think we could have been taken to a less depressing place. Villawood doesn't exactly give a positive first impression of Australian life.'

'Cheer up, it's only for a few hours.' Joseph squeezed her hand. 'Let's check out that large hut. Might be a chance of a cup of tea over there.'

'We should be so lucky,' Anna muttered.

The ruddy-faced official who'd escorted their group emerged as they reached the building. 'Good timing,' he said, holding the door open. 'Lunch is on now. Bit stodgy, but I guess you Poms are used to that sort of food.'

Anna stiffened and was about to utter a curt response when Joseph pushed her forward. 'Bloody cheek,' she said through clenched teeth, as they entered the dining area.

Long and narrow, with few windows and furnished with two rows of rectangular tables separated by an aisle, the room reminded Anna of the hut left over from the war where she'd endured school dinners at secondary school. Almost all the tables were occupied, but, after collecting their meals from a couple of sour-faced women standing behind a stainless-steel counter, Joseph located a space at the end of a table near the kitchen.

Several headscarves nodded in their direction as they took their seats and an elderly man offered a toothless grin. Anna smiled back, then turned her attention to the mess of food fast congealing on a thick white plate: grey-tinged mashed potato, slices of fatty meat, peas and a bright orange item of unknown origin. Gingerly, she scooped up some potato and peas, swallowing without tasting. The food was bland and overcooked; she toyed with a piece of meat but baulked at the orange mash. Soon, defeated, she put down her knife and fork and sat back in the seat to wait for Joseph to finish his meal.

Suddenly, a woman on Anna's left snatched the discarded plate and flashed a smile before hoeing into the leftovers. Anna tried hard not to stare at the loaded fork shovelling food into fleshy lips. Several loud belches followed the final mouthful. Fortunately, Joseph responded without delay to a tug on his shirt sleeve, ensuring a quick exit.

Late in the afternoon, the same ancient bus transported the new migrants from Villawood to the central railway station, where they boarded shabby wooden carriages resembling museum pieces. The train travelled north through unknown, unseen territory, uncomfortable seats and crying children making the night seem endless.

Dawn brought a modicum of relief, pale light revealing vistas of grey-green trees, brown grasslands and grey road ribbons. It looked to Anna as though someone had shaken a giant feather duster over the entire countryside. Devoid of primary colours, the land appeared worn, a crumbling continent locked in ancient ways. The promised golden future faded like a Polaroid photograph left too long in the sun.

Called to the dining car for breakfast, Anna dismissed her pessimistic thoughts and turned her tired eyes to toast and tea. Standing in a long queue, jostled by weary parents with fractious children, she counted the hours that lay ahead of them on the drab cattle-truck train and hoped Brisbane would present a brighter picture. She had just reached the head of the queue when the woman behind the counter knocked a jug in her direction, sending milk cascading over her blue linen coat. Almost in tears – the coat was brand new – Anna dabbed at the sodden linen with a handkerchief.

'Please could I have a cloth to wipe this up?' she asked.

A dirty dishcloth flew over the counter without an apology in tow.

Back in her seat, Anna tried to ignore the smell of drying milk, pressed her face against Joseph's chest and closed her eyes.

* * *

The next thing she knew, Joseph was shaking her awake. 'Nearly there, darling. Have a look at our new home.'

She peered out at cloudless sapphire sky, swaying green palms, red iron roofs, white fences. Turning to face him, she smiled her relief.

South Brisbane Station continued the vibrant colour scheme. Baskets filled with exotic blooms hung from an iron roof, palm trees in large pots dotted the platform, huge tropical ferns clung to wooden posts. Delighted and amazed, Anna lingered in the train doorway, much to Joseph's annoyance as he'd spotted Roger on the platform.

Warm greetings further revived Anna's spirits and she followed Roger and Joseph, already deep in conversation, out of the station to a large estate vehicle she would learn was known by the initials HG. Roger, clad in a bright open-necked shirt, tailored shorts and socks to the knees, made Anna feel overdressed in her linen "summer" coat. If this was Brisbane winter attire, what did Roger wear in summer?

The final segment of their interminable journey across the world, entailed a forty-minute drive north through the city centre and sprawling suburbs. In the back seat, Anna craned her neck to observe the vagaries of Brisbane architecture. Most of the houses were raised above ground level on wooden or concrete piers – "stumps" in Australian, Roger said. Some were high enough to store a car underneath while others sat close to the earth. Verandas varied from large structures with fancy wrought-iron edging, to narrow strips barely wide enough to hold a chair. Painted steps with handrails led from front gardens to verandas; at the top of older dwellings stood a pair of doors supported by large posts. A fence surrounded each house, top and bottom wooden rails painted white with wire mesh in between. Occasionally, a brick wall broke the pattern.

Front gardens – she couldn't see into the rear – were a bit of a disappointment after the station's tropical flora. Lawn predominated, with a few shrubs dotted about or a single tree in the middle. Concrete or gravel paths led straight from gate to steps; in some instances, two adjacent strips with grass in between served as tracks for a car parked under the house.

Roger and Mary's front garden was a welcome surprise: flowering shrubs behind a low brick wall; two squares of grass each containing several trees and a mass of bright green ferns peeping out from under the veranda and steps. Mary, slim and tanned, stood leaning on the veranda rail, her smile and sleeveless summer dress radiant as the garden foliage.

After brief introductions – neither Joseph nor Anna had met Mary before – the new arrivals were ushered into a large, open plan room, comprising a lounge with a dining area behind. 'Make yourselves comfortable,' Mary said, gesturing towards the two armchairs placed opposite a settee. 'I'll go and make tea.'

'Thanks. I didn't go much on train tea.'

Mary smiled and disappeared behind a short wall, into what Anna presumed was the kitchen.

The two men remained standing, having resumed the conversation begun at the station, so Anna took the chair furthest from the front door and sat quietly surveying her surroundings, like a potential house purchaser. Unlike most British homes, the front door led straight into the living room and, from the distinct sounds of tea-making coming from behind the wall, no door separated kitchen and dining area. The layout reminded Anna of the holiday house in Cornwall her parents rented year after year; a flimsy structure designed for summer living. From her chair near a side window, she could see a hallway leading, she imagined, to bedrooms and bathroom. She remembered that Roger and Mary had two children and wondered if they had a spare bedroom.

'Tea's up,' Mary announced, interrupting her thoughts of sleeping arrangements.

Anna accepted the proffered mug and slice of cake with well-meant thanks.

'I'll show you to your room when we've had this,' Mary said, sitting in the adjacent chair after distributing her wares. 'It's downstairs. You'll be the first visitors to use the rumpus room. Roger's only just finished it.'

Her mouth full of delicious moist orange cake, Anna could only nod.

'It's a good thing you were coming to stay,' Mary confided, leaning towards her guest. 'Otherwise the room still would be a bare concrete floor covered with piles of fibro sheets and timber.'

Anna's eyes widened. 'Roger actually built the room?'

'Oh yes, everyone's building under the house these days. It's a great way to gain space without spending a fortune. The bed folds up, so when we don't have visitors, the kids can use the space as a playroom.'

'What a good idea.'

'I've built a padded bench seat on one wall,' Roger added. 'Lift up the seat and there's storage underneath for the kids' toys.'

'Brilliant,' Joseph remarked. 'I had no idea you were into DIY.'

Roger grinned. 'I've learned lots of new skills, mate, since living in Australia. Over here, neighbours muck in to get a job done. Share a few stubbies and put on a barbie afterwards, that's all they ask.'

'Sounds like real community spirit.'

Roger nodded. 'The Aussies are good sorts, pretty laid back. They love a beer and a yarn. It doesn't take too long for them to accept newcomers, although you must be prepared for a bit of teasing, especially about your accent. And for God's sake don't criticise the place or you'll get tagged "a whingeing Pom".'

'Thanks for the advice.' Joseph turned back to his tea.

Mary patted Anna's arm. 'You're looking tired. I don't suppose you got much sleep on that ancient train?'

'No, what with children crying, people coughing and terribly hard seats.'

'You sat up all night? Why didn't you pay for a sleeper?'

'We didn't realise you could,' Joseph replied. 'Besides, we've got to be careful with our money. Who knows how long it'll take to get jobs?'

'Talk to you about that this evening,' Roger remarked, rising to his feet. 'I must get back to work now or the boss will be spitting chips.'

'Thanks for everything, Roger. I don't know what we'd have done without you. That migrant hostel in Sydney where we spent the day was pretty grim.'

'No worries, and it's Rog here, mate. You'll be Joe, Aussies abbreviate everything!'

Anna smiled, but secretly hoped she wouldn't become Ann. It would remind her of a fat girl in sixth form: clammy hands, greasy hair and terrible BO. Poor thing. No one ever wanted to partner Ann Levin during dance lessons.

* * *

The newly built room under the house served the visitors well during their two-week stay. The only snag was the lack of insect screens – the room wasn't quite finished – but they soon learned to apply a spray called Aerogard before going to bed. Apart from the occasional mosquito – swarms in summer, Roger maintained – there were few insects, much to Anna's relief. Adopting the Aussie penchant for teasing those once-termed "new chums", over succeeding days Roger regaled his visitors with stories of dangerous snakes hiding in piles of timber and huge spiders lurking in shoes, waiting to pierce unsuspecting Pommy skin. Never again would Anna put on a pair of shoes without shaking them first.

Learning Australian Ways

Spring arrived on the first of September, according to the local radio, but as far as Anna and Joseph were concerned, the season remained the same: warm sunny days with only occasional rain and cool nights. Each morning, on opening the Venetian blinds in their first-floor flat, they exclaimed anew at the brilliant blue sky and golden sunlight.

Weekdays allowed scant time for sky-gazing. Dawn meant quick showers, a hurried breakfast and dressing in clothes suitable for their respective work places. Their visions of pounding city streets day after day looking for work had proved erroneous, Joseph filling a vacancy for an associate engineer in Roger's office immediately, and Anna slotting into an administrative position at a city college two weeks later.

Finding a flat to rent was also accomplished without angst. Blocks of flats known as "six-packs" were being constructed throughout the suburbs within a five-mile radius of the city centre to cater for the burgeoning population and most were affordable. Roger – Anna couldn't bring herself to call him Rog – had taken them flat-hunting on the Saturday after they arrived and, apart from one decidedly grotty place in an older block, all seemed suitable.

They chose a one-bedroom furnished flat at the rear of a recently completed block. The kitchen was poky, with only a couple of cupboards above and below the sink, a cooker and a huge white refrigerator that looked ridiculous in the small space. The furniture was basic but sound: a vinyl-covered lounge suite, a Formica-topped kitchen table with four metal-legged chairs and a Formica bedroom suite. But far more important to Anna than style, or even comfort, was the fact that everything was brand new. No one had slouched on the chairs or settee, no one had slept in the bed, the tiles around the shower gleamed and the linoleum floor tiles were clean and bright.

Back in Britain, their first home together, a two-bedroom flat on the ground floor of a formerly grand nineteenth-century house, had reeked of age and neglect. The bathroom walls ran with condensation, the lounge suite was so filthy and worn that Anna's mother had insisted on buying loose covers, and underneath peeling wallpaper, a previous tenant had pasted strips of aluminium foil in an attempt to keep out the damp. The rent had been exorbitant, almost half of Joseph's wages, but they'd had little choice, rental accommodation being scarce in the town. The alternative, beginning their married life in her parents' home, had been dismissed as unworkable.

Roger thought the rent for the new flat rather steep and urged them to look around a bit longer, but Anna insisted it was worth every dollar and Joseph concurred, as the large garage underneath the flat was an unexpected bonus for a practical man. Anna was more intrigued by the dual concrete washing tubs located at the rear of the garage behind a concrete block screen. The letting agent referred to this space as 'the laundry' and advised that washing clothes in the bathroom or having a washing machine in the kitchen were forbidden. The landlord, a cheerful, rotund Italian who owned the entire block, didn't seem the type to instigate such a rule. Later, Anna learnt from a neighbour that state regulations stipulated a separate laundry room in every dwelling. At the rear of the block, two large metal rotary washing lines, an Australian invention known as a Hill's Hoist, stood in the middle of a patch of grass.

Like the Gittens' home, the flat's front door opened directly into an open plan living room and lacked the familiar letter slot. The post, referred to as "mail", was delivered to a brick wall studded with numbered metal boxes located to one side of the driveway, by a "postie" on a motorbike. *Such a different world over here,* Anna mused, as she hung out washing or collected mail from their box.

Although the bus stop for the city route was only five minutes' walk from the flat, Anna and Joseph soon realised that a car, far from being a luxury, was an absolute necessity in a sprawling city where, apart from small blocks of flats, detached houses set on quarter-acre blocks were the norm. The few shops within walking distance supplied only meat, bread, and newspapers; the nearest supermarket involved a ten-minute bus ride.

Transport to work was also a consideration. Buses, although frequent, took their time to reach the city centre, meandering through numerous suburbs instead of taking a direct route. The friendly chap in the neighbouring flat, Davo, suggested they use the suburban rail, as the nearest station was only a short drive away and the train would have them in the city in half the time. He offered them a lift to and from the station in his gleaming Holden Monaro until they acquired their own car. Anna accepted gratefully, but the times didn't suit Joseph, so he continued to take the bus.

Several weeks after moving into the flat, they set off by bus to visit the car yards that displayed their merchandise on both sides of the main road a few miles north. Excited by the prospect of owning a car at last and, if she was honest, influenced by rides in Davo's magnificent Monaro, Anna wanted to buy something sporty, preferably red, but as usual Joseph had more sober ideas, reliability and value for money being his primary concerns. The first major argument of their married life took place on the pavement outside Value Vehicles, with Anna extolling the virtues of a red convertible and Joseph defending the suitability of a grey Holden sedan. Eventually, after she had flounced off, threatening to catch the bus home and Joseph had shouted after her that acting like a spoilt adolescent would get her nowhere, they both apologised and, hand in hand, crossed the road to Mighty Motors, "home of Brisbane's best car deals".

After inspecting numerous cars and test-driving two, they settled on a 1965 white two-door Vauxhall Viva with red seats. Joseph handed over the hundred-dollar deposit and arranged to bring the balance of three hundred the following Monday after work. 'It's no trouble keeping the office open late,' the salesman assured them. 'Good to have an excuse to miss the kids' bath time.'

Isn't that just typical of a man? thought feminist Anna.

The car purchase put a dint in their Commonwealth Bank savings account, but at least they knew the money could be replaced quickly. Their initial wage packets had astounded them, containing almost twice what they'd earned in England and living costs, especially groceries, were cheap. For their first Sunday dinner in the flat, Anna had walked to the local butcher and purchased an enormous leg of lamb for a ridiculously small sum. It had taken all week to eat the leftover roast meat, so she made a mental note to invite Roger, Mary and the children to share a meal on the next occasion she purchased a joint of meat.

Fruit, vegetables, meat, fish, everything grew to enormous proportions in Queensland, the result, she assumed, of a sub-tropical climate. The same seemed to apply to the Australian people, as most of the passengers on the train, or those seen during the occasional lunchtime spent sitting on a bench in the Botanical Gardens, were well above what Anna considered average height and weight. Sharing her observations with Joseph one evening, she felt rather foolish when he gave a rational response that should have been obvious. 'Not climate, silly, diet. Cheap top-quality meat, cheese, fish, plus fresh fruit and veg guarantee healthy growth. Don't forget *we* grew up on post-war rations.' He grimaced. 'Remember overcooked cabbage, mashed potato and a single slice of stringy meat if you were lucky?'

'As if I could forget!'

'And we were fortunate,' he continued, wagging his finger at her as though addressing an ungrateful child. 'Think of the thousands of displaced people stuck in camps all over Europe after the war. What they would have given for *our* rations.'

'A Jewish family moved into the flat up the road when I was eight,' Anna said quietly. 'When I asked why Mum was giving them clothes and taking them the vegetables Dad had grown for us, she said they had survived years of harsh living in camps, so they needed help. I couldn't understand why living in a camp was so bad until Dad explained.'

Joseph glanced at the discarded piece of steak – a bit tough – on his dinner plate. 'A friend at school came from Holland. He told me his parents had survived the war by eating tulip bulbs. I didn't believe him at first.'

Anna reached across the table to take his hand. 'We're fortunate on two fronts. Firstly, to have grown up never knowing hunger, and secondly, to have been given the opportunity to come to Australia.'

Joseph nodded, stabbed the meat with his fork and began to chew thoughtfully.

* * *

The small Vauxhall Viva looked lost in a garage built for the sizable Fords and Holdens favoured by most Australians. Nevertheless, Joseph proudly showed it off to Davo and ignored his comment that it was a sheila's car. Anna named the car Vivienne after an old school friend, but Joseph referred to her as Viv, in deference to the Australian penchant for abbreviation.

The Saturday following her arrival, Viv inadvertently caused an embarrassing incident when Joseph decided a wash and polish would improve her appearance. By ten o'clock, the temperature had already climbed to twenty-eight degrees Celsius, so he donned a pair of the brief shorts known as "stubbies", a confusing label for a Pom who had just learnt that small bottles of beer went by the same name.

Already sporting a decent tan, Joseph looked appealing as Anna emerged from the garage carrying a full laundry basket and made her way to a Hill's Hoist. In between pegging clothes and towels, she watched his firm brown body bend and stretch over the white car, noting the way the sun had bleached his thick curly hair, and the line of pale skin revealed when he leaned over the bonnet.

Balancing the empty laundry basket on her hips, she sauntered towards the car. A moist kiss on the base of his spine sent the sponge flying and the bucket of soapy water rolling down the driveway. Twisting around, his frown evaporated when he saw Anna standing close by, dressed in her Saturday morning cleaning outfit of brief shorts and singlet top with no bra underneath. She gave a seductive smile, stepped forward and ran a warm hand over his chest. 'I should go and get the camera, you look gorgeous!'

He took her face in his wet hands and kissed the tip of her nose, her forehead, her laughing mouth.

'Not just gorgeous,' she murmured when he released her, 'but good enough to eat.' His cheeks reddened, and she wondered why, since no one else was about. Then she saw the reason for his embarrassment. The tight shorts did little to disguise his erection and the landlord was fast approaching up the driveway!

'Can you hold this for a minute?' she asked, pushing the empty laundry basket into his arms. 'I've just remembered something else I meant to wash.' Barely stifling a giggle, she fled across the concrete driveway and up the steps into the flat.

'*Buon giorno*, Joe,' she heard Mr Martelli call. 'Nice car you are having but basket, she no good for cleaning, mate, too much holes!'

Anna crept out of the flat and stood by the balcony rail, determined to hear Joseph's response.

'I was just going to retrieve the bucket.' Joseph dumped the basket on the bonnet and pointed to the bucket lodged against the driveway wall halfway down.

'She is *bella*,' Mr Martelli remarked.

'Yes, not bad for a first car.' Joseph stepped away from Viv.

The landlord laughed, a deep-throated rumble that shook his round belly, making it strain against already taut shirt buttons. 'No car, Joe, I am talking wife!'

Anna retreated inside, loath to be caught eavesdropping.

The Good Weekend

The acquisition of Viv the Vauxhall Viva enabled not only travel beyond local shops or city centre, but also allowed the new migrants to embrace that sacrosanct Australian tradition, 'the good weekend.' The first question Anna was asked at work on a Monday morning was, 'Did you have a good weekend?' the words slurred together into a string of barely comprehensible syllables. Without exception, her colleagues lived for the weekend, spending Friday morning tea break and lunchtime discussing what they had planned and Monday's breaks relating what they had accomplished. There appeared to be various categories of good weekend, with sport – watching it, mainly – being number one and visits to the coast coming a close second. "Coast", Anna soon learnt, was a general term applied to both the Gold Coast south of Brisbane and the Sunshine Coast to the north.

Viv, gleaming in spring sunlight, transported her owners north for their initial good weekend to a small island connected to the mainland by a bridge. According to Anna's colleagues, Bribie Island was a popular destination and not too far for a first venture into the unknown. As they drove over the bridge, Anna could hardly believe the magnificent vista unfolding before them. Sparkling turquoise water lapped a lengthy strip of white sand, while behind the beach stood a tangle of trees, interspersed at intervals by the linear lines of small holiday houses. Sailing boats skimmed over the water, fishing dinghies bobbed beside the bridge, children splashed in the shallows.

Anna wanted to find a parking spot the moment Viv reached the island, but Joseph had other ideas. 'This is the passage side,' he said, in an authoritative tone. 'Families favour this side, it's safe for children. We're going to the other side, the ocean proper. Surf's good over there.'

'I hope it isn't too rough.'

'You'll be fine. Anyway, we'll be swimming between the flags today. I wouldn't want to take any risks on our first day at the coast.'

Anna considered asking the significance of flags but kept quiet, reluctant to show her ignorance. Conversation turned to suntan cream, hats and the need to purchase a beach umbrella before their next visit.

Soon, they were striding along a wide beach, the fine white sand tickling their bare toes. Umbrellas of varying sizes and colours dotted the beach; beneath each one a polystyrene or metal box, an "esky" in Australian parlance. Packed with ice, eskies kept beer and food cool and were deemed essential for beach or bush outings. Umbrella owners reclined on beach towels or low folding chairs within arms' reach of their eskies, their faces tilted to the warm spring sunshine.

The waves looked promising but, apart from a few surfers, hardly anyone was in the water. Two lifesavers, sitting beside one of the flags, appeared bored and were keen to chat when Joseph wished them good morning. They recommended not venturing too far into the surf as there was a strong rip and the water was bloody cold. At work on Monday, Anna would discover that only visitors from the state of Victoria and Poms swam in the ocean during September!

Undeterred by cold water, Anna stripped off her shorts and tee shirt the moment they had bagged a vacant patch of sand near the flags. Her new black and orange bikini, rather brief, evoked a wolf-whistle and a pat on the bottom. Side-stepping Joseph's wandering hands, she ran towards the water. Foam swirled around her feet as a breaker pounded the sand. Shrieking with delight, she waded in and dived into the next wave. The water was cool and clear, the current strong. When she surfaced, the beach seemed far away, the water deeper than she'd envisaged. Turning around, she noticed Joseph ploughing through the surf towards her.

'What the hell do you think you're doing?' he shouted. 'Didn't you hear what the lifesaver said?'

'I'm a good swimmer.' She flipped onto her back.

Strong hands gripped her shoulders, pulling her into a watery embrace. 'In the bloody English Channel maybe, but you should be careful in this surf.'

She silenced him with a salty kiss.

After their swim, they sat on towels and let the sun dry their cool bodies. Sandwiches, dried-up from hours in a paper bag at the bottom of the beach bag, were washed down with tepid lemonade. An esky was a definite priority; a beach umbrella would have to wait.

The afternoon sun threatened to burn, so they dressed and were about to leave when an older man, who was sitting by himself under a neighbouring umbrella, offered them shade. They accepted thankfully, little suspecting that he and his wife would become good friends for the next twenty years.

His name was Ian. He had recently retired and moved to the coast from southern Victoria. 'I wanted to spend the last years of my life warm,' he explained. 'I couldn't stand the thought of another freezing Victorian winter.'

Anna found it difficult to imagine a freezing winter in Australia and was amazed when Ian said he often went skiing in the Victorian Alps.

* * *

As they drove into the garage, their neighbour Davo, sitting on the narrow veranda that ran in front of the three first-floor flats, waved and called out a greeting, so after dumping the beach bag on the kitchen table, Joseph went to join him. A need for man talk, Anna supposed; perhaps an issue with the car. Viv had made a few unusual noises during the return journey. She headed for the bathroom, needing a shower to wash off the sand trapped inside her sun-dried bikini.

Later, sitting at the table jotting down details of their outing in her diary, Anna remembered the damp beach towels and the rinsed bikini left dripping on the shower taps. Downstairs in the laundry, she dumped the towels in the twin-tub washing machine purchased second-hand from one of Mary's friends and hung her bikini on the rope washing line Joseph had installed to one side of the car. Mary had advised her not to hang washing on the Hills Hoist at night in case there were fruit bats in the area. 'Bats are nocturnal creatures and the fruit they eat passes through them in record time,' she'd explained, in response to Anna's puzzled expression.

So many things to remember, Anna thought as she filled the washing machine. Life in Australia was proving far from the easy transition she'd envisaged. The population might speak the same language and were predominately white-skinned – she'd noticed a couple of Indians and Chinese on the train – yet the lifestyle felt almost alien. Do this, don't do that, learn colloquialisms or face derision and never, ever complain! She indulged in a few moments of self-pity, then reminded herself that a complete change of scene had been her greatest desire. It wasn't as though life had been difficult pre-Australia; quite the contrary. Her parents were comfortably off, her younger sisters congenial most of the time and a tribe of friendly cousins lived nearby. Yet she had yearned to leave her known world from an early age. She had envisaged running away to sea at age nine, something which Aunt Maud, in whom she'd foolishly confided, had considered a silly idea. 'Far better to be a passenger on a luxury cruise liner,' her aunt had advised. 'Marry a rich man like I did, then you can holiday in exotic locations.'

Anna wondered what had gone through her aunt's mind when Joseph came on the scene. Although he had a good job, he was far from rich, having grown up in what Anna privately thought of as "a Micawber family". Like Dickens' fictional character, most years her in-laws spent more than they earned and had borrowed from their eldest son on several occasions.

Leaving the washing machine to its endeavours, she walked out of the garage and glanced up at Joseph, who was still leaning on the railing chatting to Davo. How fortunate she was to have such a laidback, some would say compliant, husband. Joseph had readily agreed to her suggestion that they join his former colleague Roger and family on the other side of the world, although his initial response had nettled her. There had been no mention of the vibrant descriptions of Australian life filling Roger's intermittent letters, just a shrug of narrow shoulders and the comment, 'Don't care where I live, so long as there's food on the table and a comfortable bed.'

Newly engaged, Anna would have preferred a romantic 'so long as you're beside me, darling,' but Joseph spoke as he thought, in plain language unencumbered by what he deemed 'soppy sentiment.' His proposal of marriage had been unexpected and straight to the point, delivered in a no-nonsense tone as they sat in his grandmother's dining room, waiting for her to bring in the pot of tea and fruitcake she always produced during their Sunday afternoon visits. 'Don't know how you feel about it, but I would like us to get married one of these days.'

Anna smiled at the memory, recalling the lengthy pause before she felt able to give him an answer, her mouth a gaping goldfish, her eyes staring as though he had just confessed to a criminal past. At least she always knew where she stood with Joseph. Witness the day she had shown off a new summer suit purchased for work. Teamed with a navy and white blouse, she'd considered the outfit smart, but when asked for his opinion, Joseph had said, 'It makes you look like a middle-aged spinster.' The following day, she'd returned the white jacket and skirt to Marks and Spencers, thankful she'd only worn it for a few minutes.

At the top of the concrete steps leading from driveway to veranda, she looked across at Joseph, hoping to catch his eye. Instead, *her* eyes were drawn to the row of brown bottles standing parallel to Davo's doorstep. Empties, she presumed, remembering Australians' preference for ice-cold beer. Forget the film she wanted to see that evening; after several beers, Joseph would be snoring on the settee by eight! *Lounge,* she corrected herself, thinking how silly it was to call a piece of furniture by the same name as the room it occupied.

Bush, Scandal and the Vagaries of Language

The new migrants decided to go bush for their second good weekend, venturing further up the Bruce Highway to the Glasshouse Mountains, a group of thirteen volcanic peaks that rose abruptly from the coastal plain. At first sight, Anna found these so-called mountains bizarre, their odd shapes and sizes sticking out of the bush as though a giant had inadvertently dropped a handful of rocks. Eager to explore, they turned off the main road onto a dirt track. Poor old Viv bounced and skidded over sun-hardened corrugations, but Joseph thought it great fun and didn't seem to mind that the car was covered with red dust by the time they arrived at an assortment of vehicles parked haphazardly amongst trees.

A nearby signpost indicated a short walk through the surrounding bush to Tibrogargan, meaning "old man" in the local Aboriginal language, so they followed a narrow dirt track that petered out at the base of a sheer slab of naked rock. Several hikers were visible on the upper slopes, but Anna baulked at the thought of climbing without the safety of ropes and stood peering up at a rock-face pocked with cave shadows, while Joseph climbed to the first ledge.

After a lunch of sandwiches and lemon cordial – kept cool and fresh in their new yellow esky – they headed back down the track, turning off before the main road onto a narrow but sealed road that ran parallel to a railway line. Road and railway cut through miles of pine plantations to a small place called Beerburrum before re-joining the Bruce Highway. The manmade forest felt too regimented. Anna preferred natural bush, eucalypts growing higgledy-piggledy, strips of bark hanging untidily from branch and trunk. Sunlight failed to penetrate the closely planted pines; they resembled the deep, dark forests depicted in childhood fairy stories, gloomy, menacing, alien trees out of place in a wide-open land.

* * *

Two days into the new working week, Joseph was unlocking the door when their neighbour Davo's door slammed shut and the landlord stomped towards their flat, a scowl on his usually cheerful face. 'Hi, Mr Martelli, something wrong?'

'He gone. Owe me three week of rent,' Mr Martelli said indignantly.

'A midnight flit,' Anna remarked, from the top of the steps. 'Who would have thought it? He seemed such a pleasant chap.'

Mr Martelli looked puzzled. 'What is chap, please?'

'Guy,' Anna said quickly, blushing as she recalled the girls at work dissolving into fits of laughter when she'd used the English term. She did so want to assimilate; it was hard being different.

Confiding her mistake to Joseph that evening, she suffered further humiliation when he advised her to get rid of the plum in her mouth if she wanted to fit in. Anna stormed off, clattering down the steps to take refuge in the laundry. Worse than the off-hand remark was Joseph's failure to understand why she'd taken offence. It wasn't the first time he'd been blunt to the point of rudeness in recent weeks; witness his remark to Mary that her cake was a darn sight better than the burnt offering Anna had served up the previous Saturday. Didn't he realise how far his voice carried in an open plan living room? Sometimes, Anna felt the marriage certificate should come with an instruction manual.

* * *

New neighbours arrived the following week. Late in the afternoon, Anna invited them in for a cup of tea and slice of cake – unburnt. They were newlyweds just back from honeymoon. Julie, petite with long blond hair, was about nineteen or twenty, Anna thought. Husband Phil seemed much older, good-looking in a weather-beaten sort of way. He spoke in a slow drawl, calling his wife 'hun', which Anna assumed was short for 'honey.' Apart from initial greetings, Julie failed to contribute to the conversation and sat at the kitchen table, head bowed, eating cake and sipping tea like a Victorian-era child required to be seen and not heard.

Disappointed – Anna had looked forward to meeting someone more her age – she hoped Julie would soon conquer her shyness and become a friend. Thirty-two-year-old Mary was kind and pleasant, but Anna had no intention of settling into what one of her colleagues had described as 'dull suburban married life' in the foreseeable future. She favoured intense emotions, discovering the dual delights of a new husband and an adopted land, both akin to falling passionately in love over and over again.

Sex, or lovemaking as Anna preferred to call it, had improved beyond her wildest expectations since their arrival in Brisbane and she often found herself longing for the end of the day when they could retire to bed and lie naked, limbs entwined. A thoughtful lover, Joseph always put her needs before his own, making certain she was sufficiently aroused before he entered and, apart from the odd occasion, taking his time to ensure she, too, experienced orgasm. It was so different from their snatched pre-marriage fumbling, when concern over her parents' return from an outing had resulted in what was described as "wham, bam and thank-you, ma'am".

Anna remained convinced that the climate played an important role in their burgeoning love-life, with lack of night clothes and heavy blankets stimulating already potent desire. As November approached, the nights grew warmer, so they invested in a pedestal fan and lay on their backs after making love, sweat drying with every oscillating sweep. Early morning brought breezes drifting through half-open

Venetian blinds, prompting Joseph to rise, switch off the fan and pull up the sheet when he returned to bed. Half-awake, Anna would turn to face him and snuggle into his cool back, one hand curved around his neat buttocks.

Scant summer clothing also contributed to sexual desire, the sleeveless mini-dresses or brief shorts and singlet she changed into after work leaving suntanned limbs and the swell of warm breasts on display for hours. She failed to understand why tights – pantyhose to Australians – were mandatory for female administrative staff. The college office might be air-conditioned, but students enquiring about loans or accommodation always left the door open on entering and departing. On particularly busy days, Anna's tights stuck to the vinyl office chair, leaving red marks on her thighs, as skirts and dresses were worn shorter in Australia, even at a workplace where bare legs were forbidden. Most of her female colleagues favoured the thick cotton uniforms approved of and partially paid-for by the college: short-sleeved shirt-style, with buttons down the front and a mini pleated skirt falling from the hips. Unwilling to be conspicuous, Anna had ordered her uniforms within a month of commencing work, although she possessed more than enough work wear. Uniforms weren't mandatory, but Anna soon appreciated their primary advantage – the elimination of early morning indecision over what to wear.

For his part, Joseph quickly abandoned heavy English clothing for the tropical outfits favoured by male white-collar workers: tailored shorts, short-sleeved shirt and the long cotton socks known as "walk-socks". Naked male knees weren't an issue in Brisbane offices.

Another office regulation – female staff were not allowed to wear trousers under any circumstances – although irritating, paled into insignificance when Anna considered the advantages of her new job. It was well-paid, with an automatic pay rise once she had completed six-months' probation, and the bonus of friendly colleagues and a pleasant supervisor meant she looked forward to coming to work – a rare occurrence in her previous occupation, where the office manager, a dour middle-aged spinster, had made the working week miserable. It seemed Miss Johnstone's mission in life was to patrol the office, pointing out minor mistakes ad nauseam, in a shrill voice guaranteed to embarrass the offender. She also insisted staff raise their hands when wishing to leave the office to use the toilet and forbade talking unless it was work-related.

'Sex starved, that's her trouble,' her colleague June had whispered, following a particularly difficult morning, a comment that had almost led to a reprimand as Anna struggled to suppress a fit of giggles. When Miss Johnstone approached their shared desk, frowning, June had come to the rescue by asking, 'Can I fetch a glass of water for Anna? I think she's having an asthma attack.'

Anna smiled at the recollection and closed the library book propped against her handbag. Only two stations before she reached her destination and Joseph's hello kiss delivered when she entered the car. *Poor Miss Johnstone,* she thought, empathy possible from a distance of twelve thousand miles; *sex wasn't the only activity lacking in her life.* According to June, the supervisor lived with a demanding aged mother who insisted her daughter spend every evening at home and accompany her on an annual holiday to Bognor Regis.

Turning from past to present, Anna watched the passing parade of old wooden houses on stilts and lengthy rear gardens where a Hill's Hoist took centre stage. Occasionally, a palm tree or a cluster of banana plants broke the monotony of grass and vegetable patch, where pumpkin vines trailed among tomatoes and zucchini. Despite the revulsion experienced in the Villawood dining hut, Anna had come to enjoy the orange vegetable, both roasted and mashed with potato. One day, she would make a batch of pumpkin scones; Mary insisted they were delicious and had copied out the recipe for her. Naively, Anna hadn't envisaged so many different foods would be available in Australia, assuming an English-speaking country would grow English produce. At first, shopping for fruit and vegetables had proved time-consuming, the vast selection making choice difficult. When confronted with items labelled "custard apples" or "Queensland blue", she had been tempted to stick to the familiar, although the delicious taste of lady finger bananas had prompted her to try other tropical fruit.

Unlike many British migrants, Anna resisted the urge to make comments beginning with, 'Back home we…', or 'In England we…' Believing in the proverb, "Home is where the heart is", within months she had moved on, the past becoming another country which she looked back on with fondness but had no desire to compare with the new land. The flora and fauna might be unfamiliar and the vernacular difficult to comprehend at times, but Australia was her home now; a place where she and Joseph could build a life together.

They were saving hard for a house; not one of the old, often dilapidated weatherboard dwellings visible from the train, but a pristine new brick veneer home in one of the estates being developed on the fringes of the city. Along with the majority of young couples in 1970s Brisbane, Anna and Joseph favoured the new and considered a longer journey to and from work a small price to pay for modern amenities. Soon after their arrival, Anna had been shocked to learn that many suburbs remained without sewerage, residents being forced to use an outside toilet known as a "dunny", located inside a small wooden shed in the back garden. 'How primitive,' she'd exclaimed to Mary. 'Even my grandparents' Edwardian house had an inside toilet!' Fortunately, the newly-constructed flats came with proper plumbing.

The train slowed to a crawl as it approached Wooloowin Station, the nearest one to their flat, giving Anna ample time to gather her belongings and wrestle with the window above the door. For some reason, there were no handles on the inside of the doors. Instead, passengers had to lift the wooden-framed window using a metal handle barely large enough to grip, then drop it into a slot without crushing their fingers and reach out to turn the handle on the other side. There seemed to be a definite knack to what Anna considered a dangerous manoeuvre, judging by the muttered swearing that sometimes arose, and during the first few weeks of train travel, she had wondered how on earth she would open the door if left alone in the compartment.

When the inevitable happened, she contemplated climbing over the high-backed bench seat into the next compartment where a middle-aged man sat staring into space, but an unwillingness to risk revealing tight-tops and lacy black knickers, forced her to attempt the window.

'I did it, I did it!' she exclaimed, running towards the car, where Joseph sat reading a library book.

'Did what?'

'Opened the train window.'

'Bloody ridiculous idea. The engineer who designed it should have been shot.' And forgetting the hello kiss, Joseph turned the key in the ignition.

Lunch and an Unexpected Development

December brought heat, the occasional tropical storm and pre-Christmas workplace gatherings designed to celebrate the end of a profitable year – or, in Anna's case, the departure of hundreds of often irritating students for the long vacation. Student Administration joined with the college library for the lunch, each staff member being asked to 'bring a plate', a phrase Anna had learnt meant take food to share. Shortcrust pastry being one of her culinary successes, she made a cheese and onion flan. Decorating her "plate" with slices of tomato prior to the lunch, she glanced at the dazzling dishes on display and felt inadequate until she discovered that the library staff – a veritable United Nations with seventeen nationalities represented – were responsible. Her own colleagues, all Australian born and bred, contributed a range of salads and, in one instance, lamingtons, still in their Coles' supermarket container. A favoured item served at the morning teas celebrating staff birthdays, Anna had yet to develop a taste for these sponge cakes dipped in chocolate and then desiccated coconut, mainly because every mouthful made her cough.

Travelling home on the train, an empty Tupperware container balanced on her knee, Anna felt relieved that there would be no need to cook dinner as Joseph was dining out with colleagues. An enormous steak, chips and salad at the Breakfast Creek Hotel, she imagined, washed down with copious amounts of beer. She must find something to occupy her evening; falling asleep over a library book or in front of television wasn't an option when she had to pick him up from the station at eleven.

* * *

Mid-evening, following an hour's ironing, she sat at the kitchen table intending to write a letter to her parents, but, following a description of the previous Sunday's visit up the coast to Dickie Beach, she felt disinclined to continue. Chatty text concerning the day's culinary delights seemed banal when compared to the curious phrases rolling around her head, demanding release. Pushing the unfinished letter aside, she dipped her pen towards the notepad used to cushion the wafer-thin aerogramme and entered a sphere overlooked since school-days.

By ten-thirty, Anna had written ten stanzas of what promised to be a lengthy poem – free verse rather than the rhyming couplets insisted upon by an old-fashioned English teacher. At first glance, her lyrical lines extolled romantic love coupled with the bliss of intimate delights, but a second reading confirmed a bizarre choice of lover. An entire continent had become the object of the poet's desire; she yearned to explore every undulation and crevice, run her hands over every inch of vastness, penetrate the land's very soul – a profundity of sentiment that alarmed the nascent writer and sent her running to the bedroom, intent on concealing her extraordinary creation between layers of commonplace clothes.

* * *

Driving towards Wooloowin station, Anna focused her attention on traditional relationships and found herself reflecting on the angst experienced during her late teens, when she had raced headlong into intimacy with scant regard for consequences or suitability. Had she feared rejection, or did she want to rebel and flout the rule espoused by a mother determined to get a daughter to the altar in one piece?

'No sex before marriage' had become a mantra repeated so often, it had failed to register in Anna's mind. *There but for the grace of God,* she thought, thankful that the route from flat to station did not take her past the Holy Cross Home and Laundry where unmarried mothers toiled while awaiting the births of their babies. Whatever the reason for her youthful disobedience, she had come to her senses in her twentieth year, proceeding cautiously with the relationship that would lead to marriage.

Rain spattered the windscreen as Anna turned into the station car park, empty at this late hour. She coasted to the entrance of the single station building without turning on the windscreen wipers, then switched off the engine.

A train pulled into the station, dismissing her uncomfortable recollections and critical self-analysis. She watched Joseph emerge from the shadowed building and glance at the pouring rain before making a dash for the car. 'Bloody awful weather,' he said, slipping into the passenger seat. 'We got soaked walking to the pub.'

'Good meal?' she asked, turning the ignition key.

'Yep, they always do a great steak at the Brekkie Creek. What did you do with yourself this evening?'

'Nothing much. Bit of ironing… started a letter to Mum and Dad.'

* * *

Anna had been sitting at the kitchen table for hours, scribbling in a school exercise book purchased at the local newsagent. Writing, crossing out, sucking the end of the pencil as though it was a sweet – *lolly,* she corrected herself, determined to override her ingrained English vocabulary. Unforeseen time alone – that morning, Joseph had decided to accept neighbour Phil's offer of a fishing trip – had provided an opportunity to indulge her new-found creativity without having to explain what she was doing.

There was something intensely liberating about having a secret, especially one kept from a husband. This wasn't a reflection on the state of their one-year marriage – she adored Joseph and knew he felt the same about her – rather, the desire for something entirely hers, something she didn't have to share. Since her teens, she had kept a journal, recording thoughts and feelings, hopes and fears in a series of notebooks with attractive covers, although she had to admit the entries had been sporadic since her marriage. Journal writing might be a private activity, but she made no attempt to hide the notebooks and would have shown them to Joseph had he expressed interest in their contents.

The poems – four in two weeks – were a different matter entirely, an authentic secret, the manifestation of a gamut of emotions experienced since the first time she had stepped on Australian soil. Passion, deep love, gratitude, desire, even irritation and anxiety on occasion; those were the sentiments she endeavoured to articulate yet refrained from sharing with Joseph. Her reasons were many, self-preservation the primary aim. Her intense adoration of this country had all the hallmarks of an illicit love affair and, as such, she was afraid exposure would lead to her undoing. An odd conclusion, she admitted, but one she felt unable to alter.

On the other hand, she was quick to respond when asked how she felt about her new country, echoing in her own words the view she'd heard expressed on numerous occasions: 'Australia's the best bloody place on earth.' Simple statements such as, 'I love it here', or 'Brisbane's a fantastic place', appeared to satisfy her questioners, the conversation quickly moving on to other topics. From what she'd experienced so far, Australians were an easy-going people, intent on enjoying life rather than delving into a migrant's psyche. Conversations with the young couples she and Joseph had befriended were usually focused on weekend activities, what sort of house to build, or sport. No one mentioned unemployment, inflation or bemoaned the country's place in the world, subjects often discussed in British homes, pubs or workplaces.

At the farewell party given by Aunt Maud and Uncle Edgar just prior to their departure, a distant cousin had said he didn't blame them for leaving the sinking ship, a statement that had surprised her given his large country home and the sleek Jaguar parked in the garage. Anna had immediately thought of the Titanic, the band playing as the ship slid beneath the freezing north Atlantic waters. Another cousin's appearance had put paid to further comments on Britain's imminent demise and she'd moved on, grateful for rescue. Negativity had no place at a party; besides, she'd felt no need to justify leaving her homeland. Unlike her parents, who had lived all their lives in the same small town, she and Joseph were embarking on an adventure, seizing the opportunity to experience a different way of life. As for Joseph's family, she could only guess at their motives for leading such a limited life. Thank God Joseph had escaped that crowded house where bickering seemed the norm and had taken advantage of his natural intelligence and a free education to pursue his goals.

A question wormed its way into her mind but, disinclined to contemplate a creative future, she stopped staring into space and returned to secret scribbling. Anna Fletcher's short and long-term aspirations could wait; she must seize the day!

Christmas Day Australian Style

Christmas cards depicting snowy scenes seemed out of place in glorious sunshine and the morning breeze sweeping through wide-open windows repeatedly scattered them over the floor. Tired of retrieval and repositioning, Anna left the cards in a pile on the bookcase Joseph had made the previous weekend and returned to preparing fruit salad, her contribution to Mary and Roger's Christmas lunch. The invitation to join the family had been welcomed, as Anna had been apprehensive about asking them to the small flat for an entire day. Their children, Judy, seven and James, five, needed space to play, and a concrete driveway and patches of grass beneath washing lines were no substitute for an extensive garden complete with swings, sandpit and playhouse. There would be other children present, too, Mary had said; another English family with two daughters and a baby son.

'Christmas is difficult for Maureen,' Mary had explained. 'She misses her parents and siblings so much at this time of year.'

Anna had thought of her own family celebrating the season on the other side of the world and, despite looking forward to her first Australian Christmas, she experienced a twinge of homesickness. 'I do understand,' she'd said, sincerely.

Chopping pineapple into bite-sized chunks, Anna felt a wave of guilt flush her face as she recalled Christmas lunch with her parents the previous year. How could she have been so insensitive, so wrapped up in her own plans that she'd stated the obvious and then wondered why her mother had left the dining room hurriedly in the middle of lunch? Aunt Maud, Uncle Edgar and cousin Christopher had kept their heads down, thinking no doubt that the absence of tactless Anna and her rough-around-the edges husband would be advantageous in coming years. The atmosphere had further deteriorated when her mother had returned, dabbing her red-rimmed eyes while her father resorted to reading out the awful jokes found in Christmas crackers, her sisters responding with forced laughter.

Drops of blood dripped from her left index finger, staining the yellow fruit. 'Damn,' she said aloud, dropping the knife and rushing over to the sink. The cut skin stung as she turned on the tap to rinse away the result of her wandering thoughts. *Why the intense guilt a year after the event?* she pondered, walking into the bathroom to retrieve a plaster. Later that afternoon, she had apologised to her mother for the remark that should have remained unspoken, giving the lame excuse of excitement about the future. The response had been unexpected; a fierce embrace from a mother not known for overt displays of affection, followed by a comment that sometimes it was difficult being a frustrated traveller. 'I never knew,' Anna had said quietly. 'I thought you liked renting a cottage in Cornwall every summer.'

Returning to the kitchen, Anna endeavoured to concentrate on the fruit salad, but her mother's wistful expression kept intruding, a reminder that nothing more had been said on the subject of unfulfilled journeys on that day or any other. But a truth had been spilt and, in the months that followed, Anna couldn't help thinking about her parents' marriage and whether other cracks had been papered over to preserve the appearance of harmony. 'Always present a cheerful face to the world,' was another of her mother's mantras, given whenever a daughter expressed discontent, a frequent occurrence during the years all three girls were moody teenagers. In the absence of explanation, Anna and her sisters had assumed the advice was simply an extension of their mother's insistence on tidy rooms, good manners and writing Christmas thank-you letters to relatives on Boxing Day.

Joseph's bleary-eyed appearance put paid to uncomfortable memories and pointless speculation. 'I need coffee,' he announced, heading for the electric jug.

'And Happy Christmas to you, too.'

'Sorry I was so late home last night.' Dry lips brushed her cheek. 'I had no choice. I could hardly refuse the boss's invitation to celebrate the season.'

Anna continued arranging pineapple, pawpaw and rock melon in the glass dish purchased from a shop near her work. 'A couple of drinks I can understand, but you passed out on the settee five minutes after walking in the door!' She sniffed, recalling the wasted meal tipped into the pedal bin. Leaving him sprawled on the yellow vinyl, she had retired to bed soon after his arrival and taken solace in a library book. During the night, she'd stirred when he slipped in beside her, but no words had been exchanged and she'd pushed away his caressing hands.

'Aussie beer's the problem.' He filled the ceramic electric jug with water and switched it on. 'It seems much stronger than the brown ale I drank in England. Guess I'll get used to it.'

'Drinking less would be the more sensible option.' She hurried into the bathroom to shower away sticky fruit juice and still simmering irritation.

* * *

The noise of children's excited play with Christmas toys made up for both Joseph and Roger's subdued behaviour. Still hungover, the pair sat side by side on a garden bench, sipping lemonade, wincing should a child venture too close. Mary served lunch in the room under the house – a selection of salads, cold chicken, ham and crusty rolls, followed by fruit salad, ice cream and trifle. Adult diners carried plates and glasses into the garden, where they sat on canvas chairs shielded from hot sun by beach umbrellas, while the children settled themselves on a picnic rug spread out beneath a shady tree, orange plastic plates resting on suntanned legs.

Picnic-style food and a garden venue meant parents could relax, unconcerned by spilt lemonade or a slice of tomato squashed underfoot. Sensible solutions for Christmas in the sub-tropics, Anna considered, relieved she didn't have to plough through roast turkey and hot vegetables, while trying to ignore the perspiration running down her neck. Clothing reflected the informal atmosphere, the three little girls wearing bright sundresses, James, shorts and a cotton shirt, baby Timothy, blue gingham pants over his nappy, with a matching shirt. The adults were similarly attired, the only difference being footwear. All the children were barefoot, their sandals having been discarded hours earlier.

Anna wore a new summer dress sewn by her mother – white cotton bodice, red and white gingham skirt trimmed with lace that once had adorned a grandmother's 1920's blouse. The gift had been welcomed, as Anna had found that the summer dresses she'd brought from England were unsuitable for Brisbane's summer. Nylon and polyester clung to skin that was damp from high humidity. She had intended to buy a couple of cotton dresses, but a glance at the price-tags in Queen Street shops prevented purchase. Saving up for a deposit on what Australians called "a house and land package" made her more thrifty than usual; she couldn't justify buying new dresses when existing ones were hardly worn.

Sewing of any kind was a chore she had always detested, her homemade garments always turning out vastly inferior to those produced by her mother. 'Don't worry, I'll fix it, dear,' was her mother's catchcry whenever Anna reluctantly modelled a completed dress or skirt. There had been no such problems with her younger sisters, as both had inherited their mother's expertise with needle and thread.

'James pulled my new dress,' a plaintive voice declared, 'and now it's all broken. I hate boys.'

Anna looked up to see Maureen's four-year-old standing in front of her mother, holding one end of a shoulder strap. A pout distorted the child's pretty face and tears mingled with the lunchtime detritus around her upper lip.

'Don't worry, darling, I'll soon mend it,' Maureen remarked, rising slowly to avoid waking the baby asleep in her arms. She turned to Anna. 'Would you mind holding Timothy while I sort this out?'

'Not at all.' Anna held out her arms to receive the chubby six-month-old. He stirred, uttered a tiny cry, then snuggled into unfamiliar breasts. 'Nothing for you in there,' she murmured, as a rosebud mouth began to nuzzle the white cotton. She stroked the downy head and smiled down at her charge. It had been years since she'd held a baby and that memory was far from pleasant, as her cousin's squalling red-faced infant had wriggled in her arms before puking over her skirt – a worst-case scenario for a seventeen-year old who had been forced to attend a family gathering instead of going ice-skating with her friends.

Something bit her ankle, but she dared not move lest the baby wake and start crying again; Maureen had had trouble settling him after the post-lunch feed. Tentatively, she rubbed the sore spot with the toe of her other sandal, hoping it wasn't a bite from one of the giant ants that roamed Australian lawns and even the patch of thin grass beneath the flats' Hill's Hoists.

'You look right at home,' a voice declared, and she looked up to see Roger approaching, a beer can clutched in his fist.

'Yes, the picture of maternity,' Joseph said, from somewhere behind her.

'Don't get any ideas,' she countered, recalling their decision to wait until they had moved into their own house before starting a family.

Joseph tweaked her ponytail, then bent to kiss the back of her neck.

'Don't leave it too late,' Roger advised, taking the empty seat beside her. 'It's preferable to be young parents, then you've more energy to cope with the hassles.'

'I agree,' Joseph answered, as he stroked Anna's shoulders. 'My parents seemed to lose the plot when the youngest arrived. Mind you, he can be a little sod at times, but in my book that's no excuse for spoiling him rotten.'

Head bent over the baby, Anna smiled at Joseph's second-hand parenting knowledge and, for a moment, felt sorry for her mother-in-law. It couldn't have been easy finding herself pregnant with a fifth child at the advanced age of forty-one. The moment passed as Anna reflected that Stella could have prevented an unwanted pregnancy, if that's what it had been, as the Pill had been available to married women since the early '60s.

Loud wails erupted from inside and under the house. Garden dwellers heard Mary's raised voice scolding her son, followed by sandalled feet stomping down the steps leading from the rear patio. Halfway down, Maureen leant over the railing to shout at her husband who was busy gathering toys scattered over the lawn. 'Leave that, Clive, I need you up here. That girl will be the death of me. I've fixed the bloody dress, but she won't stop crying!'

Joseph and Roger exchanged glances as diligent Clive straightened up and hurried to join his harassed wife. 'Three is too many, I reckon,' Roger said quietly. 'Everything's geared to two children these days: three-bedroom houses, cars built for four passengers. Poor old Clive had to trade-in his lovely Cortina once Timothy arrived. No room in the back for two child seats and a bassinet.'

'I suppose they wanted a boy,' Joseph remarked.

Roger nodded and turned his attention to his beer.

'What's wrong with girls? Anna queried, wondering if her parents had hoped for a boy third time around.

'Nothing,' Joseph was quick to answer.

'Then why do men always want sons?'

The question remained unanswered as just then Mary emerged from under the house, calling out, 'Cup of tea and a mince-pie, anyone?'

Roger held up his beer can. 'I'll stick with this, thanks, love.'

'Me too,' Joseph echoed.

'I'd love to, but...' Anna indicated the baby asleep on her lap.

'Put him on the picnic rug.'

'Maureen won't mind?'

'Of course not. He'll wake soon and enjoy wriggling around.'

* * *

But Maureen did mind. She glared at Anna as though she'd discarded Timothy like a piece of rubbish, before scooping him up and checking every inch of exposed skin for traces of those 'bloody awful Australian ants.' Satisfied the baby remained unscathed, she walked briskly to the stairs, muttering something about wanting a proper Christmas next year.

'There goes an unhappy migrant,' Roger declared, placing his empty beer can on the grass. 'Poor old Clive, he loves it here.'

'Do you think they'll go back?' Anna asked.

'Yep. Maureen has been on about it for years.'

'How long have they been in Australia?' Joseph asked.

'Six, seven years. All the kids were born here.'

Joseph nodded. 'You would have thought she'd be settled after that length of time.'

'Lovely house, too and a huge garden,' Roger added. 'Last year, Clive even had an in-ground pool installed 'cos she complained constantly about the heat.'

'Perhaps she's just missing her family,' said Anna, echoing Mary's earlier remark. 'I'm really enjoying my first Aussie Christmas, but I must admit I have been thinking about my parents and sisters today.'

Roger glanced at his watch. 'That reminds me. I mustn't forget to phone my parents this evening.' He turned to Joseph. 'When are *you* going to have a telephone installed?'

'I'm not sure it's warranted. The installation fee is steep, and we don't intend to stay in the flat for more than another year.'

'Saving going well then?'

'Very well. We hope to have enough for a deposit soon.'

'Good on you, mate, there's nothing like having your own home. Helps you feel completely settled.'

Anna bristled. 'We are completely settled, Roger. Australia's a wonderful place to live, great climate...'

'Brisbane, you mean,' Roger interrupted. 'It's different down south. Four seasons in one day in Melbourne and bloody cold winters.'

Joseph laughed. 'That's what a guy we met on the beach said. He and his wife came from Melbourne to retire up the coast. They've built a house overlooking cane fields not far from the beach. Can't remember the name of the place.'

'Bli Bli,' Anna said, relieved the men had moved on from the topic of Maureen's failings. It seemed unfair to pass judgment without hearing her side of the story. Perhaps she hadn't wanted to emigrate; perhaps Clive was so tied up with work – he was an industrial chemist working for something called the CSIRO – he didn't notice his wife felt lonely. Being at home with three children under school age wouldn't be easy, especially as Maureen had said they lived far from shops or public transport.

The men began to discuss the merits of retiring up the coast, leaving Anna to contemplate a life confined during the working week to house, garden and the company of small children. From Roger's comments, she gathered the family only possessed one car and assumed Clive needed it to get to work, transport being miles away. Anna would never agree to living on acreage out in the sticks, as Maureen had described it. A modest house and garden would be preferable, neighbours to engage with, shops and transport within walking distance if they couldn't afford a second car by the time a baby arrived.

'Tea's up,' Mary announced, from the rear patio that led into the dining room. 'Shall we have it inside, Anna? I'm sure the guys are boring you with talk of cars and football!'

'Coming.' Anna rose from her seat and hurried to join her friend. 'Where are the others?' she asked, surprised to find Mary alone.

'Gone home. Clive said the children would benefit from a swim as it's so hot this afternoon.' Mary raised her eyes heavenward. 'Them and their pool. They only had to ask and I would have turned on the sprinkler. Our kids love running through the spray.'

'Sounds fun. Pity I didn't bring my bikini.'

'Still a kid at heart, eh?'

Anna smiled, then added in low voice, as though the departed guests might overhear, 'Bit rude not to say goodbye to their hostess.'

'Never mind. Perhaps they'll invite us to their place next year, then we can all swim.' Mary reached for the teapot, leaving Anna to reflect that conflict always arose over Christmas, a period often described as the most stressful time of the year.

Later, munching a second delicious home-made mince-pie, she recalled a long-ago Christmas lunch when her six-year-old eating habits had irritated Uncle Edgar to such an extent that he had crawled under the table to retrieve the peas she'd tried and failed to spear with her fork. Emerging red-faced, the knees of his best trousers creased, he had glared at her before carrying the offending vegetables at arms' length into the kitchen. Tears had fallen onto her new dress as she contemplated her failure to prove she was old enough to sit at the adult dining table, rather than the small table for children positioned on polished parquet well away from pristine beige carpet.

* * *

'Lovely end to a lovely day,' Anna mused late that night, resting a hand on Joseph's firm stomach. He lay on his back, legs stretched out, feet hanging over the end of the bed. She would have preferred to prolong their close contact, but the last time they'd made love, he'd declared that the summer humidity was too high for lengthy hugging.

'Still seemed odd to me, celebrating Christmas in a garden.'

'Different, not odd.'

'Don't be pedantic.' Joseph turned on his side and propped himself on one elbow. 'That Maureen was a bit of a killjoy, fussing over the kids all the time and moaning about the heat. I felt sorry for Clive.'

'I felt sorry for her. The poor woman looked worn out.'

'And whose fault is that? She didn't have to have three kids so close together.'

'She might not have had a choice. Some men want a son at any cost.' Anna turned away from him. 'And the word is "children"; "kids" are young goats.'

'Children, kids, what does it matter?'

Anna sighed. 'Let's not argue about it.'

A hand stretched out to stroke her arm. 'Sorry, hun.'

'I am not your hun.' She removed his hand. 'Or your darl.'

'Why not? I thought you loved everything about Australia?'

'Everything except the tendency to abbreviate,' she muttered.

'Suit yourself.' He rolled over and resumed his usual sleeping position. Snores soon punctured the thick night air.

Wide awake, Anna lay beneath the sheet, her muscles tightening with his every breath. *Bloody men, they have no idea what parenting involves for women,* she thought, recalling Joseph and Roger sitting under a beach umbrella quaffing beer while Mary and Maureen dealt with the children. At least Clive had assisted when asked to, or rather screamed at. As she tried to relax her rigid limbs, she made a mental note to leave a decent gap between her own children.

Wild Weather

They woke to torrential rain pounding the corrugated iron roof and beating against the bedroom window with such ferocity, Anna felt certain the glass would crack. Conversation proved impossible, so she padded into the kitchen to make cups of tea. Peering through the Venetian blinds while the jug boiled, she watched rivers of rain race down the driveway, muddied by soil that was spilling over the low wall separating balding grass and concrete. Below, in the neighbouring garden, palm fronds had shredded like flimsy flowers and thin trunks bent at odd angles. Mango missiles from an enormous tree behind the palms flew over the dividing fence and splattered against rapidly rotating Hill's Hoists, creating swirls of green. Mesmerised, Anna ignored the jug's frantic jig across the draining board and turned around only when a crash announced its tumble into the sink.

Steam clouds obscured the sink and overhead cupboards, so it was several minutes before Anna could assess the damage. Fragments of yellow ceramic dotted the shiny stainless steel; the black plastic lid hooded one tap. 'Stupid design,' she muttered, wishing they had continued to use the whistling kettle they had brought from England, instead of consigning it to the back of a cupboard because it took longer to boil than an electric jug. Tentatively, she reached into the sink to retrieve the broken pieces, noting with dismay that the base was pitted in several places. Should she confess to the landlord, or hope he wouldn't notice when the time came for them to leave? Undecided, she tossed the evidence of her negligence into the pedal bin and returned to the bedroom to confess.

Joseph seemed unperturbed. He mumbled something about 'no worries, darling, accidents happen' and, reaching for her hand, he drew her back to bed. Outside, the tropical storm continued to cause havoc in surrounding streets, but failed to attract the attention of lovers consumed by moulding malleable flesh. And when their own interior storm erupted, neither party gave thanks for the claps of thunder and driving rain that had prevented close neighbours from overhearing their exclamations of delight.

* * *

Eventually, satisfied that the storm had ended, Anna and Joseph emerged from their flat and leant over the veranda railing to survey the destruction below. Smashed mangoes, leaves and small branches littered the concrete driveway; on the grass above, a Hill's Hoist lay on its side, one arm bent and broken. The neighbouring garden resembled a war zone with its fallen trees, upended table, chairs flung against a fence, soil and plants spilling from toppled terracotta pots.

'Bloody hell, that was a storm and a half!' Joseph exclaimed. 'I've never seen anything like it. Even that huge mango tree has copped a battering.'

'All that fruit spoilt. What a waste.'

'It'll take forever to clear up the mess.' He peered at the old wooden house, paint peeling on sagging weatherboards, rust stains dotting the corrugated iron roof. 'No sign of life over there. We should check the old couple are all right.'

'Gone to their son's place down the coast for Christmas, Phil said the other day. I wonder if he has a contact number for them?' Anna realised she didn't even know the couple's names.

Joseph moved away from the railing. 'I'll see if Phil and Julie are home.'

Still standing by the railing, Anna watched him knock on their neighbours' door and, receiving no response, move on to the next.

'I'll check around the front,' he called from outside the third door.

Unlike many of the contemporary apartment blocks dotted around Brisbane suburbs – rectangular brick boxes, two-storey, six living quarters above six garages or open car-ports – their building was L-shaped. The front flats, two up, two down, lacked any space for a car, so residents parked their vehicles in the street. Anna assumed these flats attracted a lower rent but had no wish to move into what appeared from the outside to be even smaller living spaces than their own.

Although she had loved the flat at first, appreciating its large windows, clean lines, unmarked white walls and unchipped floor tiles, six months of shoebox living had soured the joy. The cheap furniture provided by the landlord, particularly the bedroom suite made of chipboard covered with a thin layer of Formica, had already lost its sheen. The wardrobe doors refused to close completely and the dressing-table drawers stuck, mostly on workday mornings when she was in a hurry. Attempts to rectify these deficiencies had failed, resulting in Joseph being concerned when the Formica split as he hammered in nails for extra support. By contrast, the bookcase he'd made from thick pine planks sourced from the local hardware store looked as though it could withstand any amount of wear and tear. His second project, a sturdy, free-standing cabinet with sliding glass doors, stood beside the fridge and housed crockery, there being limited space in the small cupboard under the sink. Bookcase and cabinet would move with them to a new house; no longer a distant dream, but almost within reach.

At the end of each month, Anna would open their Commonwealth Bank passbook and calculate how much longer it would take to save the required amount for a deposit on one of the houses mushrooming in the new estates. During a Saturday afternoon drive around the northern fringes of the city, they had observed numerous dwellings in various stages of construction. These "spec houses" were constructed by builders who owned parcels of land and were of similar but not identical design. They were predominately high-set, having three bedrooms, bathroom and open plan lounge, dining and kitchen on the upper floor, with laundry and space for cars underneath. The more expensive dwellings had brick-veneer exterior walls, concreted garage floors and tilt-doors. Access to the upper floor was via a door at ground level that led to a tiled foyer and interior staircase. At the rear, exterior stairs led to a small patio.

The cheaper houses were clad in weatherboards and perched on concrete stumps surrounded by hard-packed earth, the exception being a narrow strip of concrete at the rear for laundry tubs and washing machine. Exterior stairs led to both front and rear doors. Anna had decided to aim for a brick-veneer house, the economy variety appearing flimsy and half-finished. She couldn't envisage living in a building perched on slender concrete stumps, or parking Viv on bare dirt.

From conversations with friends, she knew that some young couples preferred to put a deposit on a block of land first, pay it off and then use the land as security for the house. Once a mortgage had been approved, a builder would be employed, and plans drawn up, taking into consideration the purchasers' budget and requirements. This was the path their neighbour had chosen, Phil having mentioned that he'd purchased a block of land several years prior to getting married.

'They've poured the slab,' he'd advised recently, as the two men sat on the veranda sharing a beer. 'We should be out of this shoebox in twelve weeks.'

'Half your luck, we're looking at a year.'

'Don't worry, mate, twelve months will soon pass. Besides, I've got years on you. I'm thirty next month, so need to get a move on, if you know what I mean.'

'Children?'

'Yep, I want a tribe of 'em!'

'What does Julie think?'

'Oh, she's used to kids. Big family, she's the third of ten.'

'Seems it's populate or perish over here,' Joseph remarked later to Anna, when repeating the conversation in the privacy of their flat.

'Don't get any ideas,' she said, feeling sorry for her neighbour. She had discovered Julie was only sixteen, virtually a child-bride.

'No worries. I agree with Rog and Mary. Two's a good number.'

'But not until we have a fully furnished house. Imagine a baby here! Where on earth would we put the cot?'

Joseph shrugged, then changed the subject.

* * *

They were standing at the end of the driveway surveying the huge tree limb blocking the exit and wondering how on earth they were going to shift it, when someone called out, 'Want a hand over there, mate?'

Looking up, they saw a skinny young man leaning against the fence opposite, smoking a cigarette.

'Thanks, mate, much appreciated,' Joseph called back.

A second man, much older than the first, appeared on the front balcony. 'Problem, Sam?'

'Branch down opposite, Dad.'

'Be right there.'

Father and son sauntered across the steaming bitumen, kicking fallen foliage out of the way with their bare feet. Each wore a pair of the brief shorts known as "stubbies", topped with a cotton singlet. They were unshaven and looked as though they had just got out of bed.

Anna stepped onto the grass footpath – no sealed pavements in suburban side streets – and held out her hand. 'Hi, I'm Anna Fletcher. Thanks for coming over, we couldn't move it on our own.'

'No worries, Anna,' Dad replied, shaking her hand. 'Trevor Brown.'

His hand felt rough against her soft skin; she visualised him wielding a pick or laying bricks during working hours. 'Pleased to meet you, Trevor.'

'Reckon we need a chainsaw,' son Sam remarked. 'Bit on the large side for three blokes to shift in one go.'

'And a strong woman,' Anna reminded him.

'Not a job for a sheila,' Trevor remarked.

Anna resisted the urge to argue, conversation and observation having taught her that Australian men liked to make a show of brute strength, especially in front of women. She found this trait childlike, as though the men needed to prove themselves worthy of manhood.

Most likely it was a hangover from frontier-society days. 'I'll fetch a broom to sweep up the leaves,' she said to no one in particular.

Trevor turned to face her. 'We'll fix it. Why don't you go over and meet my wife and daughter-in-law... have a cuppa and a chat?'

His smile was so genuine, Anna felt it would be rude to refuse the offer. 'Thanks, Trevor.' She looked down at her crumpled shorts. 'I'll go and change first.'

'No need, darl, we don't stand on ceremony here in Oz.'

Blushing, more for her homeland than herself, Anna stepped over felled timber and walked across the road.

The house resembled others in the street, 1930s' high-set weatherboard with corrugated iron roof, but, unlike some, it appeared well-cared for, even the latticework under the front steps being freshly painted. *It pays to marry a practical man,* Anna thought, as she knocked on the front door.

A hand appeared in the adjacent window, lifting a net curtain. 'Come in,' a female voice called, 'it's not locked.'

Anna turned the handle and stepped into a cool, dim hallway with closed doors on either side. 'Hello, I'm Anna,' she said tentatively, wishing someone would appear. 'Hope I'm not disturbing you.'

A door on her left opened and a grey-haired woman emerged. 'No way, neighbours always welcome.'

'I'm from the flats,' Anna said, stepping forward, her right hand extended.

'Yes, I know. Seen you out and about with that handsome hubby of yours.'

Uncertain how to respond, Anna smiled.

'Vi Brown, Trev's wife.' She took Anna's hand but, instead of shaking it, led her down the hall to the rear of the house. 'Come and meet Shirl.'

'Your daughter-in-law?' Anna queried, relieved to have something to say.

'Yes, three months now. Lovely girl. I was delighted when Sam told me they were getting married.'

Once more, Anna smiled to mask her lack of response. She couldn't imagine Stella referring to her as 'lovely' or expressing delight at Joseph's choice. Polite toleration summed up her relationship with the elder Mrs Fletcher.

'We get on so well,' Vi continued. 'Shirl's the daughter I never had. I worried at first that living with us would be a bit much, but she assures me it's not a problem. And it won't be for long, just until they have their own place.'

Anna shuddered at the thought of co-habiting with her in-laws.

'Something wrong, dear?'

'No. Must be the change in temperature from outside.'

'Yes, these old houses were designed to be cool.' Vi looked up and smiled. 'It's even cooler in Sam and Shirl's room under the house.'

'Did Trevor build it?' Anna asked, recalling the room Roger had built as a guest room and children's play space.

'Trev and Sam together. It's a combined bedroom, living room. No shower and toilet down there, I'm afraid, we couldn't run to that.'

'I'm sure they're delighted with the room.'

'At least they've got some privacy. Trev and I had to share a small house with my parents for over a year before we could afford a place of our own.' She opened the door at the end of the hallway with her free hand and ushered Anna into a long, narrow kitchen. 'Two bedrooms right next to each other.' Vi leant towards her guest and said quietly, 'You can imagine the difficulties when we made love.'

A little embarrassed by the older woman's frank and, to Anna's mind, unnecessary disclosures – apart from the 'no sex before marriage' command, her mother never mentioned sex to her daughters, let alone to a first-time visitor – she turned her head and looked out of the kitchen window to the rear balcony, where a young woman sat in an easy chair reading a magazine.

'You go and meet Shirl while I make some more tea,' Vi suggested, releasing Anna's arm.

Grateful for a change of subject, Anna nodded.

* * *

After the usual introductions, Shirley – a pretty name spoilt by abbreviation in Anna's opinion – mentioned her job as a library assistant, her serious demeanour and obvious interest in her work a surprise, given her "dolly-girl" appearance. Peroxide-blonde hair, back-combed and split into pig-tails tied with scarlet ribbons, slashes of red lipstick, excessive turquoise eye-shadow and a gaudy mini-dress, had given a less than favourable first impression. Anna had envisaged Shirley coasting through work until motherhood claimed her, but she seemed intent on climbing the career ladder and made no mention of wanting a family.

Just as Anna was about to ask what Shirley intended to study, Vi appeared in the doorway, carrying a tray. 'Here we are. Hope you like pavlova, Anna.'

'Love it.'

'Left over from yesterday,' Shirley explained. 'We were too full of turkey and roast veggies to make much of a dint in dessert.'

'A wonderful first attempt,' Vi remarked, passing a plate to her guest. 'Such a shame we couldn't do it justice.'

Anna glanced at the portion of meringue and fresh fruit that almost filled the plate. 'Let's hope I can,'

Conversation shifted gear, domestic matters replacing career and study as Anna hoed into sweet stickiness tempered by the tang of pineapple and passionfruit. If only Vi would leave, she thought, so that she and her new acquaintance could discuss what they wanted to achieve in their lives. Like Shirley, Anna favoured further study at some stage and had no intention of limiting her life to raising children and housework. These days, women had opportunities the previous generation couldn't have dreamed of and few expressed surprise should a mother return to work or train for a new career once the children had started school.

Anna thought of her mother, postponing a return to work until her youngest had left school, and then taking a part-time job in order to have dinner on the table when husband and daughters returned from work or study. Why hadn't Mum insisted they all help prepare the meal? Even at weekends, Anna and her sisters had been discouraged from helping in the kitchen, their mother insisting they enjoy themselves instead. As a consequence, cooking had been a trial and error exercise during the initial months of married life, Anna being grateful for a husband who ate everything with gusto and never complained.

'Delicious,' she remarked, laying the strange fork on her empty plate. Later, she would learn that the "splayd", a combination of fork, knife and spoon, was another Australian invention, supposedly designed because the male inventor observed women had difficulty using traditional cutlery when plates were balanced on knees at barbeques.

Vi beamed at her daughter-in-law. 'Shirl's going to knock 'em dead at the Ekka in a few years' time, aren't you, darl?'

A smile masked Anna's ignorance. Vi could have been speaking a foreign language for all the sense she could make of her pronouncement, but she noticed a blush creep across Shirley's face, followed by a sudden need to gather empty plates and mugs. 'Let me give you a hand with the washing-up,' she called, rising to her feet.

'I'll go and check on the boys,' Vi announced to their retreating backs.

The slap-slap of rubber thongs on painted wood faded as Vi reached the garden, prompting a series of sighs that floated to the kitchen ceiling like excess soapsuds.

'Are you feeling all right?' Anna asked, concerned that, like her, Shirley had a stomach ache after consuming too much pavlova.

'Oh, she means well, but sometimes I just want to scream. Such nonsense about winning a prize at the Ekka, as though that would be the pinnacle of my aspirations.'

'What's the Ekka?'

'An agricultural show held in Brisbane every August.'

Anna frowned. 'But what's that got to do with prizes for desserts?'

'Something for the ladies to show off their cooking skills.' Shirley slammed her fist against the sink. 'I'd rather win a prize for writing an excellent essay.'

'Me too. Have you mentioned study to Sam?'

'Sure, and he's really supportive. I start the first of my library papers at the end of February.'

'At university?'

'No. That would mean quitting my job and delaying our house purchase for years. This way, I can study by correspondence, one subject at a time. Exams are held at the end of each term.'

'Sounds interesting. Might even consider it when I'm fed up with college administration.'

'Where do you work?

'Queensland Institute of Technology, Administration Department. I'm a clerk-typist.'

'Do you enjoy it?'

'Mostly. Sometimes the students can be a bit annoying, but I like helping people.'

'You didn't consider teaching or nursing?'

Anna shook her head. 'I wanted to enter the workforce as soon as possible, earn my own money. I left school at sixteen, did a short secretarial course, then got a job at a local college. Short-sighted of me, really.'

'At sixteen, you don't know your own mind. I sort of drifted into library work after school because my aunt was employed as a librarian and I love reading.' Shirley smiled. 'Not that I regret it, especially now that I can further my career through study.'

Anna smiled back. 'I've been writing poetry recently. Perhaps I should study literature?'

'Why not? I'm sure there would be evening classes available in the city.'

'The trouble is, I'm uncertain what it could lead to, career-wise. I don't want to teach, at least not in a school.'

Shirley grimaced. 'The thought of trying to control a classroom full of kids appals me. I'd be up for mass murder within a week!'

'You don't like children?'

'Two would be all right, widely spaced and not for years.'

'My sentiments entirely.'

Footsteps on the stairs stalled their conversation. Looking guilty, Shirley ran hot water into the sink as Anna piled in mugs and plates. Both forgot about adding a squirt of washing-up liquid.

'Come on down, girls,' Vi called from the balcony. 'The boys have shifted the branch and Trev's got the barbie going for lunch.'

'Coming, Vi,' Shirley answered, her expression one of resigned obedience. Then, as though she'd had second thoughts, a wicked grin spread over her face and she deliberately shook her hands at Anna who stood alongside, holding a tea towel. Droplets of water glistened on summer-flushed skin as both women dissolved into giggles.

Eager to join in the fun, Anna flicked the tea towel at Shirley's legs, prompting a return to the sink, followed by a dance around the kitchen as each tried to outdo the other. Finally, red-faced and breathless, the new friends collapsed into balcony chairs, grateful that Mother-in-law had returned downstairs.

* * *

Long after midnight, Anna lay sleepless, her thoughts swirling as she recalled the wild weather and its aftermath. The storm had excited as well as alarmed her, built yet another layer into her nascent rapport with the new land. Benign one minute, malignant the next, Australia tendered the promise of a tempestuous relationship, but at least one in which boredom would figure rarely. British landscapes had become over-familiar, neat fields, hedgerows and lanes winding between ancient trees to picture-postcard thatched cottages, merely an extension of her well-ordered life. Washed-out skies, sunlight muted by cloud, an insipid grey-green sea; a colour scheme that had threatened to turn her palette into a pallid paste.

The bold colours of Australia ignited her emotions and left her spinning with sensation, adjectives crowding her mind. Phrases evolved in quiet moments – an unclouded azure sky, the golden sheen of sunlight, black velvet night flecked with silver stars, pellucid turquoise ocean, dazzling white sand – all became lines of poetry written in an exercise book. She laboured long over stubborn stanzas, determined not to resort to rhyme but aware of the need for rhythm. During time alone when Joseph was working late or sharing a beer with a friend or neighbour, she would retreat to the bedroom and stand in front of the dressing-table mirror to read her latest effort aloud, listening for cadences, observing her facial expressions.

Days, or sometimes weeks later, once satisfied with the language, structure and fluidity of her work, she would secrete the exercise book between her plastic sandwich box and library book in the large shoulder bag used for work. Lunch break would find her slipping a clean sheet of paper into the typewriter kept in the office behind the reception area. Fingers flying, she would transcribe the scrawled words into the permanence of black letters on pristine paper, grateful that those colleagues not rostered on the front desk had already adjourned to the canteen. Back home, her latest poem, dated and hole-punched, would be added to the red ring-binder concealed beneath rarely worn jumpers in a dressing table drawer.

Still musing on torrential rain and gale-force wind, Anna glanced at the bedside clock, a lump of cheap plastic stuck to a varnished wooden base alongside a cylindrical lamp that emitted insufficient light for reading. The clock-lamp was another of those wedding presents she felt obliged to use, at least for a few years. She had hoped it would break during the long journey across the world, but it emerged from the crate intact, unlike two favourite mugs whose handles lay in pieces. Reluctant to dispose of the mugs, she had placed them on the vanity unit in the bathroom, where they housed toothbrushes and toothpaste.

Cloud blanketed her "black velvet night", reducing the light from the half-open blinds to dark shadows that masked the pseudo-gold hands that were moving inexorably towards dawn. Turning away from clock and window, Anna tried to focus on mundane matters: whether the sheets needed changing, the unironed shirts piled in a basket down in the laundry, the few Weet-bix remaining in the Tupperware box. Soon after moving into the flat, a nasty surprise one morning had taught her that in Brisbane, non-refrigerated food had to be kept in sealed containers, otherwise it would be invaded by huge cockroaches. Wide-awake now, she shuddered at the thought of the vile creatures scurrying around her kitchen at that very moment.

Sighs surfaced and hung limply in the humid air like smoke rings blown from pursed lips. Kicking off the sheet, she recalled Shirley's reaction to her mother-in-law's presumption of endless domesticity. Had their subsequent juvenile behaviour marked the dawning of friendship? Anna hoped so. She needed at least one good friend to replace those left behind. Mary was pleasant company, helpful and kind, but her world revolved around the needs of children and shifts at the school tuckshop, and her friends were mostly other mothers. Work colleagues presented a different problem; the two Anna had befriended, or, rather, who had befriended her – one, a clerk-typist like herself in Administration, the other, met in the canteen, a secretary in the Architecture Department – lived south of the river, miles from their northern suburb flat.

As the pale fingers of dawn filtered through the blinds, Anna finally succumbed to sleep, hugging the image of a neighbour whose outlandish appearance belied a serious intellect.

New Year Celebration

New Year's Eve marked the beginning of another "long weekend", the phrase Australians used to describe public holidays that were added to the usual two-day break. As New Year's Day fell on a Friday that year, workers like Joseph, who hadn't accrued much recreation leave, looked forward to another short break. Anna had been forced to take three days' leave as the college closed between Christmas and New Year. They had been trying to decide how to celebrate the end of a momentous year, when their neighbours, Sam and Shirley, asked if they'd like to join them on a three-day camping trip up the coast at Peregian, about eighty miles north.

'We can set up camp directly behind the beach,' Sam explained, as the two couples enjoyed an evening drink – beer for the guys, shandy for the girls – on the veranda in front of the Fletchers' flat. The narrow space meant that all four sat in a line like birds on a telephone wire, the only difference being the men's longer legs, stretching as far as the railing.

'Sounds great,' Anna replied. 'The trouble is, we don't have any camping equipment.'

Sam smiled. 'No worries. Leave it to us. I can borrow a couple of sleeping bags from Mum and Dad. We've got the rest of the gear.'

Shirley, positioned at the end of the line, leant forward. 'It'll be a cheap trip, there's no charge to camp at Peregian. We'll take our car, so we can share the cost of petrol, which just leaves blocks of ice for the eskies, food and some champagne to celebrate the New Year.'

'Count us in!' Joseph said eagerly, from his chair nearest the door.

Anna frowned. 'But is there enough room for four of us and the camping gear?'

Sam nodded. 'I'll be borrowing Dad's trailer. Got a tow bar fitted on the Holden before Christmas.'

'He thinks of everything. He loves planning trips,' Shirley remarked, turning to Anna. 'I reckon he's missed his vocation. Should have become a travel guide, not an electrician.'

'Our friends John and Judy will meet us up there,' Sam continued, after acknowledging his wife's compliment with a grin. 'Good sorts. You'll like them.'

* * *

Leaving the so-called main road – narrow, but at least bitumen – Holden and trailer bumped over uneven ground, weaving between trees to reach the unofficial campsite which was nothing more than a patch of grass sloping down to sand dunes. 'They beat us to it,' Sam remarked, spotting John's Ford parked next to a large eucalypt.

Shirley leaned out of the open window and yelled, 'Get the billy on!' to the young man who was lifting an esky from the rear of his ute.

In the back seat, Anna remained quiet, her only concession to mounting excitement being a squeeze of Joseph's hand. During the long drive up the coast, she'd found it difficult to contain her enthusiasm at the prospect of camping only yards from a beach and annoyed her fellow passengers by repeatedly asking when they would get there.

'Got anything to silence that impatient child?' Sam had asked eventually, turning to his slim wife who was crammed into the front bench seat with a pile of beach towels. A rummage in the glove box had produced a bag of Minties, that were quickly passed around.

Hasty introductions were followed by a flurry of activity, as Sam was keen to set up camp before the brief twilight gave way to pitch-black night, a gas lantern and one torch being all he possessed for illumination.

A tarpaulin tied between the two cars served as protection from the elements. Picnic blankets and sleeping bags were laid side by side underneath, topped with heavy eskies to ensure the bedding remained in place. Sam and Joseph lugged the enormous beer esky down to the beach, while Shirley and Anna carried the boxes of sandwiches they had made earlier. Bringing up the rear were John and Judy, laden with beach towels, a box of fried chicken drumsticks and bottles of lemonade.

After dumping the gear on a smooth patch of sand, Sam announced an immediate search for driftwood. 'We always make a fire on the beach at night,' he explained, noting Anna's puzzled expression. 'Dig a pit, then build a fire. Dry grass behind the dunes serves as kindling.'

Anna nodded. 'I'll dig the pit. Got a spade, anyone?'

Sam grinned. 'Bare hands, Anna. The sand here is soft as a baby's bum.'

'Right. Where do you want the pit?'

He pointed to a slight depression in front of the beer esky. 'Might as well take advantage of that.'

* * *

An ebony sky dotted with star-diamonds, a silver moon rising, orange flames illuminating suntanned faces; in her wildest dreams, Anna couldn't have imagined such a scene. They had the beach to themselves, the only sounds beside their own voices being the slap of waves on sand and the whistle of a warm wind. In the trees behind the camp, cicadas created a high-pitched, sometimes irritating buzz, but the group on the beach remained unaware of the insects' existence. Sitting in a circle around the fire, the three couples soon munched through the sandwiches and chicken, washed down with lemonade and beer.

Anna leant away from the fire and pushed her hands into still warm sand, completely at one with the natural world and companions she hoped would soon be counted as friends. Between Christmas and New Year, she had relished the hours she had spent with Shirley, enjoying serious discussions on careers and house-building, interspersed with light-hearted chat about clothes, favourite films and records. Shirley had shown her how make lamingtons, a messy process that had left Vi's kitchen resembling a disaster zone. In return, Anna had baked a Victoria sandwich, filling the two halves with whipped cream and jam. 'You can make numerous varieties,' she'd informed her eager pupil. 'Mum's favourite is coffee and walnuts. Butter icing in the middle, topped with coffee glace icing and walnuts.'

Busy licking cream from the spoon, Shirley had nodded her approval.

'Just going to wash my sticky hands,' Shirley announced now, getting to her feet.

'Mind if I join you?'

'Of course not, Anna.' She looked over at Judy. 'Why don't you come, too? We can have a bit of a paddle.'

'Sure.' Judy stood up and stripped off shorts and t-shirt to reveal a brief bikini.

Shirley and Anna followed suit and the three ran down the beach to splash in the shallows like children. Wind blew tendrils of hair over their faces, salt spray stung exposed skin, wave-foam clung to damp legs. Judy reached down, doused Shirley with cool water, then plunged into breaking surf to escape retaliation. Laughing, Anna sprayed Shirley as Judy surfaced, mermaid tresses flowing down glistening skin.

'Come out, Jude,' John called from his place beside the fire. 'You know it's dangerous to swim at night.'

'Come and get me,' she yelled, before disappearing into dark water.

Discarded t-shirts littered the sand, bare feet pounded down the beach. Reunited, two couples embraced in the shallows, salty lips stinging, while the third met in a breaking wave, clinging to one another for a moment before swimming back to shore.

* * *

Towards midnight, Judy left the campfire and climbed back to the campsite. She returned carrying two large plastic boxes. 'Cooked prawns and slices of bread and butter,' she announced, setting her wares on a beach towel. 'We can have them with the champagne.'

Joseph got to his feet. 'I'll fetch the champagne.'

'Give you a hand, mate,' Sam volunteered. 'I need a pee, anyway.'

Anna watched the two men clamber up the sand dune and disappear into the night. She hoped they would take care not to trip over bedding or tree roots; both had drunk a considerable amount of beer during the evening. Shouted expletives proved otherwise, but ensuing laughter reassured her no lasting damage had been done to either bodies or belongings.

They drank a toast to 1971 with champagne poured into tin mugs, then joined hands to dance around the diminishing fire. After numerous circuits of the fire-pit, a rousing chorus of *Auld Lang Syne* led to kisses all round, until legs collapsed onto towels and hands reached into boxes for prawns and bread.

A night breeze rustled leaves on nearby Wallum Banksia as Anna slipped into a lightweight sleeping bag. Beside her, Joseph lay with his mouth open, snoring and snorting like a pig. Reaching out, she grasped his right shoulder and tried without success to turn him on his side. 'What's the matter?' he mumbled, shaking her off.

'You're snoring,' she said in a fierce whisper.

'Sorry.' He turned away from her and buried his face in the top of the sleeping bag.

Grass and earth proved an inadequate mattress; and Anna wriggled around in an attempt to get comfortable. Lying on her back with her legs slightly apart seemed the best position, although it still felt as though she would slide towards the dunes before long. Gazing at the tranquil beauty of a night sky untainted by ambient light from street-lamps or houses, she offered a silent prayer of thankfulness, despite professed non-belief.

It had been a disappointment to her parents, who were faithful worshippers at the local Methodist church, when she'd announced at the age of seventeen that neither service nor minister held her interest. For a year or two, she'd tried other denominations; Congregationalist, Anglican, Baptist, none had appealed. An exploration into Buddhism followed, but she'd fallen asleep during meditation, the hall overheated, the other participants' quiet breathing soporific. Since then, she'd put aside regular worship, having decided that religious belief and all its connotations had no place in her adult life.

Sharp pains in her stomach dismissed her drowsiness, alerting her to imminent vomiting. Clutching a hand to her mouth, she pushed the sleeping bag downwards, then half-crawled, half-staggered away from the campsite. Just as she reached a small stand of trees, she retched and emptied the contents of her stomach. Retreating from the stinking mess, she leant against a tree trunk to catch her breath. A second spasm gripped her, but before she could remove her shorts, a stream of diarrhoea ran down the inside of her legs. Alarmed and embarrassed, she made her way down to the beach, eyes focused on the ground in front, moonlight guiding slow steps. At the water's edge, she stripped off her soiled clothing, then plunged into the cool ocean. Cleansed, she returned to shore, picked up her clothes and began to rinse them.

'What's up, Anna?' a voice called.

Turning around, she saw Shirley standing a few feet away. 'Vomiting and diarrhoea. Must be something I ate.'

Shirley stepped forward. 'A contaminated prawn, most likely. They have that effect.'

'I've never experienced spasms like it and so sudden. Thank God I wasn't asleep.' Anna gave her clothes a final rinse before wringing them out.

'Come on, I'll help you back to bed. You should be all right now.' Shirley extended a hand and together, they walked slowly back to camp.

For the remainder of the night, Anna slept soundly and woke to the sounds of breakfast preparation. Her stomach gurgled, demanding sustenance, but felt tender to the touch, so she decided not to risk a repeat performance. A breakfast of water and a slice of dry bread would have to suffice. Reluctant to call out, she lay dozing until she became aware of someone sitting beside her. 'Joseph?' she asked, without opening her eyes.

'No, Shirley. How are you this morning?'

She half-opened her eyes. 'A bit sore.'

'I'm not surprised. A contaminated prawn always causes a violent reaction. It happened to me once at a friend's place. I didn't think I was going to reach the toilet in time, and when I did, I worried that it would overflow! Luckily in my case, only one end was affected.'

Anna managed a wan smile. 'Would you mind fetching me some clean clothes from the bag in the car?'

'Sure, and I'll tell Joe what happened.'

'Thanks. Was anyone else affected?'

Shirley shook her head and headed for the Holden.

* * *

Saturday passed without incident. Anna still felt washed out, but was able to join in with ballgames on the beach and swimming. She ate sparingly, confining herself to freshly prepared salad and fruit. By evening, she felt almost back to normal, so she readily agreed to Joseph's suggestion that they take a walk along the moonlit beach. Conversation remained sporadic as they strolled hand in hand, each conscious of the other's proximity, the tang of sun-dried salt on their warm faces, the balmy breeze caressing their exposed skin. Both wore their swimming togs and Joseph carried a rolled-up beach towel under one arm – 'In case we fancy a swim'.

'Good idea,' Anna had answered, understanding his ulterior motive. Late at night, she'd heard familiar movements in other sleeping bags, heard familiar exclamations quickly silenced by moist lips. Food poisoning and inhibition had kept their own intimacy at arms' length.

Peregian Beach seemed to go on forever, like a white border sewn to an unravelling bolt of deep blue fabric. The low ridge of dunes offered scant refuge, but eventually they came to a larger bank, shadowed by wind-sculptured trees. 'I need a rest,' Anna announced, unwilling for some reason to mention her intended purpose.

'Stomach playing up again?' Joseph asked, releasing her hand to stroke the smooth skin below her navel.

'No, I'm fine.'

A smile replaced his worried frown. He guided her up the beach and into the dune, then spread out the towel.

Lovemaking proceeded without a word, as though neither party wished to break the spell of solitude. Sea-wind ruffled salt-stiffened hair, sang in branch and grass, melding with surf sounds and the dribble of dying waves on wet sand.

Afterwards, they lay on the towel, relishing the sensation of a cool night breeze on over-heated flesh, the inhalation of salty air. Toes burrowed into talcum-powder sand; suntanned faces tilted to a star-filled sky.

Despite the morning discovery of mosquito bites on body parts that were normally kept covered, dune-sex became a favourite pastime during subsequent camping trips, the lovers eager to replicate their initial magical experience.

Late Summer Shock

January and half of February passed in a haze of work weeks, interspersed with either Saturday or Sunday and the occasional weekend spent on Sunshine Coast beaches with new-found friends. Lack of spare time meant Anna paid little attention to mundane matters, a quick flick sufficing for flat-cleaning, washing being done in the evenings and hung in the garage to dry. Ironing was abandoned, except for work clothes; she shopped for food during lunch breaks, then stored meat and her few frozen products in the lunchroom refrigerator, transferring them to a small polystyrene esky for the train journey home.

Unaware of the risks of excessive exposure to harsh sunlight, both Fletchers acquired almost all-over tans, pale skin visible only when naked. On days when the three couples had a long stretch of beach to themselves, Judy and Shirley sun-baked topless, but Anna felt reluctant to expose her breasts. The other couples also went skinny-dipping at twilight during camping weekends, but never put any pressure on Anna and Joseph to join in. Long conversations around the fire, shared meals and walks along the beach cemented a variety of friendships, six proving a suitable number. Anna and Shirley, both prone to waking at dawn, would slip out of their sleeping bags and run to the water's edge, splashing in the shallows as they discussed light-hearted or serious topics. Aware that the imminent commencement of library studies would occupy Shirley most Sundays, Anna made the most of their early morning conversations, delighted she had found such a compatible friend.

The men seemed to prefer a threesome if engaged in what they termed 'men's business', such as cutting up firewood or fetching extra beer from the nearest bottle shop and would speed away from the campsite in John's ute, leaving tyre tracks on grass and bitumen. The girls laughed at their antics, more suited to late adolescence than mid-twenties, before retreating to a shady spot to chat or read. Judy, a primary school teacher, sometimes had homework marking to do, so would sit apart from the other two, head bent over Grade Three exercise books.

When forecast wet weather thwarted beach plans for the third weekend in February, Anna felt grateful for an opportunity to catch up on chores and sleep. Two months of non-stop activity had left her exhausted and she longed for a lie-in, followed by a leisurely breakfast. As expected, Saturday was spent in a whirlwind of shopping, food supplies having run extremely low, plus washing and cleaning, so she promised herself a restful Sunday.

An overcast sky ensured they woke late, but Anna still felt tired, so Joseph offered to bring her breakfast in bed. 'A treat for my sun-kissed darling,' he said, springing out of bed and pulling on a pair of shorts before heading for the kitchen. Lying back on the pillows, Anna listened to the sound of heavy rain but felt too lazy to get up and close the window. No damage would be done to the rendered brick windowsill or tiled floor, should rain blow in.

A gust of wind sent spray through the dusty insect-screen; she sat up and saw dirty spots decorating the freshly-washed top sheet. 'Damn,' she said aloud, pushing the sheet aside and swinging her legs out of bed. Reaching a hand through the half-opened blinds, she quickly closed the window and flopped back on the bed.

In preparation for the breakfast tray, she sat up and was about to pull up the sheet when she noticed smudges of blood on her inner thighs. Leaving the comfort of bed, she padded into the bathroom. Perched on the toilet, she waited for more blood to appear, but none came.

Automatically, she touched her breasts, sensing the slight soreness and heaviness that always accompanied her period. *Stomach ache any minute,* she thought, standing up and pressing the flush button. After washing her hands, she rummaged in the vanity unit for a Tampax and inserted it gently.

When she returned to the bedroom, a tray containing two mugs of tea, a bowl of cereal and a plate of toast sat in the middle of the bed. Joseph lay on top of the sheet munching a piece of toast, crumbs falling onto his tanned chest. She slipped in beside him and picked up the bowl.

'Feeling better now?' he asked, reaching for a mug.

'Not really.' She grimaced and muttered 'Period', before looking down at Weet-bix and sliced banana.

'Never mind, at least you can take it easy today.'

She nodded and lifted her spoon.

* * *

Waking from the luxury of an after-lunch nap, Anna reached out to open her bedside drawer and retrieve the small diary she used to note social activities and other important dates. Flicking through the pages, she located Sunday February the twenty-first and looked for the cross that indicated her period's due date. Nothing marred the page. She searched seven subsequent days, then turned to the previous week, but failed to find the reassuring symbol. Anxious now, she turned back the pages and learnt to her dismay that her period had been due on *January* the twentieth. Seven weeks since her last period. There was no need to retrieve the previous year's diary from the back of the drawer; she could remember the date, December 27th. She had been thankful her period wouldn't coincide with the camping trip to Peregian Beach.

How could she have been so caught up with "good weekends" that an entire month had passed without her noticing the absence of a habitual event? Since taking the Pill, her period had always been regular, four weeks to the day, over and done with in four days instead of the pre-marriage seven. Images flashed through her mind: the spacious house they hoped to build within a year; the furniture needed to make it into a home; the planned winter holiday driving Viv north to the southern end of the Great Barrier Reef; camping on a beach, snorkelling amongst schools of brightly-coloured fish. Dreams banished to some future date, eclipsed by an unplanned event. She thought of the cramped flat, trying to envisage a cot tucked into a corner, nappies flapping on the Hill's Hoist and pushing a pram up the hill to the shops.

Wild speculation diminished as she reasoned there could be other reasons for a missed period: hormonal imbalance, illness, stress. She would have to visit the doctor and discover the truth without delay. There was no point in worrying Joseph at this stage. She would feign illness on Monday morning and ask him to call the college when he arrived at work.

* * *

An almost sleepless night ensured that Anna looked far from healthy when the alarm clock emitted its tinny ring. There were bags under her eyes and her tan seemed to have faded overnight, giving her face a washed-out appearance. After bringing her a glass of water, Joseph showered and dressed for work and told her to phone him from Vi and Trev's place if her condition deteriorated and she needed him to come home early.

'Take care of yourself, darling,' he said, dropping a kiss on her damp forehead. 'Let's hope it's just a twenty-four-hour bug.'

She managed a small smile and lay back on the pillows, thankful Joseph always slept soundly, so hadn't questioned her fictional tale of vomiting and diarrhoea during the night. In fact, she *had* visited the toilet several times, insomnia inducing the need to pee every couple of hours, but despite her rising agitation there had been no other physical reactions, not even a single drop of blood.

The all-clear signal – Viv reversing slowly out of the garage, then dashing down the driveway – filtered into the flat, prompting a swift exit from bed and bedroom. Anna couldn't risk falling asleep. The surgery opened at nine and she wanted to be first in the queue to ensure an appointment that day. She would have to keep herself occupied for the next hour and a half. No sitting in a chair with a book, or listening to the radio. Baking seemed a suitable alternative, so she hurried into the kitchen, opened the cupboard Joseph had made and reached for the painted tin box containing her favourite recipes, written on 5 x 3 cards and filed in appropriate sections.

Gingerbread, Fruitcake, All-Bran loaf; which one to choose? Her fingers hovered over the Cake section, before she decided all three would take too long to cook and flicked to Biscuits. First in line, Australian biscuits, her mother's recipe typed on a blue aerogramme, along with family news. Instead of copying the recipe, Anna had cut it out and stuck it on a card, the sight of the old Olivetti's uneven type somehow reassuring. Australian biscuits resembled the Anzac biscuits she had eaten over the road, although Vi's were always thinner and crisper than her own.

* * *

A delicious smell wafted from cooling rack to sink, but Anna ignored her mounting hunger and continued with the washing-up. An hour remained until the surgery opened; sufficient time to finish clearing up the kitchen, have a shower, dress and walk up the hill to the imposing old house perched on a large, sloping block overlooking her street. From the surgery door, accessed via a flight of steep concrete steps, it was possible to see the flats and most of the houses in the street, although the creek at the bottom remained out of sight. Vi had mentioned that the creek overflowed its banks periodically, flooding low-lying gardens and houses. 'Not that it worries us. Halfway up the hill, we're safe and sound, but.'

'But what?' Anna had wanted to ask, then remembered this addition to the end of a sentence was a frequent occurrence in Queensland-speak.

Dressed in a floral summer skirt, skimpy top and sandals, Anna made her way up the hill, slowly at first, then increasing her pace as if speed would deliver the outcome of her doctor's visit faster. The surgery door was already open when she arrived, so she lingered in the hallway to catch her breath before approaching the receptionist, who was holding court behind a counter to the right of the waiting room.

'Morning,' said a voice behind her. 'Everything all right, dear?'

Anna turned her head and saw an old woman leaning on a walking stick. 'Yes, thank you. I just walked too fast up the hill.'

'It's them bloody steps up to this house that do me in. I'd go elsewhere if there was another doctor within walking distance.'

Anna smiled and stood aside to let the woman pass.

'No, dear, you were here before me.'

Reluctantly, Anna entered the waiting room and walked over to the counter, where she stood with her hands clasped in front of her to stop them shaking.

The receptionist advised her that Dr Jameson could see her within half an hour. It wasn't worth going home, so Anna picked up a magazine from the pile on a low table and took a seat. Months old and tattered, the *Women's Weekly* offered little of interest. She flicked through the pages, trying to ignore photographs of plump babies and grinning toddlers entered for some competition and an advice column for young mothers. Discarding the magazine, she stared at the wall opposite, willing the minutes to pass.

'Mrs Fletcher,' the receptionist announced at last as she got to her feet, clutching a slim folder.

Startled, Anna rose quickly, tripped over a child's toy and almost lost her balance.

'No need to hurry, we allow ample time for each appointment.' The receptionist, an older woman with sharp features and thin hair pulled back into a bun, frowned at Anna before ushering her into the surgery.

Dr Jameson, forty-something, with kind eyes and a caring expression, listened to Anna's carefully constructed speech without interruption, then reached into her desk drawer for a specimen jar. 'Well,

Mrs Fletcher, from the dates you've given me, I'd say you're pregnant, but to be certain, I'll need a urine sample.' She handed Anna the jar. 'The toilet is at the end of the corridor. Come straight back and I'll test your sample.'

Anna could only nod, the doctor's use of the word "pregnant" rendering speech impossible.

* * *

Dr Jameson smiled. 'Congratulations, Mrs Fletcher, you're going to have a spring baby.'

'But that's not possible! I'm on the Pill. And I've never missed a day.' Anna looked down at the floor as tears threatened.

A hand reached out to touch her arm. 'The test is conclusive, but tell me, have you had any illness in the last couple of months – vomiting or diarrhoea, for instance?'

Anna recalled stomach pains and rinsing away embarrassing evidence in cool salt water. 'Yes. I had a violent reaction to some prawns on New Year's Eve.'

'Then that's the explanation. If you vomit within two hours of taking the contraceptive pill, it won't have been absorbed by your body, so you need to take another one straight away to ensure you're still protected against pregnancy.'

'I didn't know that.' Anna wiped her eyes, then raised her head. 'Bloody prawns. I'll never eat one again.'

'That's probably wise. You could have an allergy to shellfish.'

'I doubt it. I ate all kinds of fish at home and didn't have any adverse reactions.'

Dr Jameson nodded. 'I'd like to see you in a month to check that the pregnancy is proceeding normally.'

Anna shuddered at the thought of her stomach swelling, concrete proof of ignorance and error. Then she remembered the bloodstains. 'There was a bit of blood on my thighs yesterday morning. Is that a problem?'

'Any since?

'No.'

'In that case, there's no cause for concern. It's what we call spotting and it often happens, especially during early pregnancy.'

Crestfallen, Anna sighed loudly, the hope of a miscarriage eliminated.

'Don't worry,' the doctor said brightly. 'You have months to get used to the prospect of motherhood and I'm sure your husband will be delighted.'

Anna shook her head. 'He'll be furious. We're saving up for a house. No chance of that now!'

Mid-winter Woes

Anna would be eternally grateful for Joseph's sensitive response to her news, his arms around her neck, his soothing words as she sobbed bitterly, his refusal to blame her for the forthcoming change in their circumstances. 'Conceived in a sand dune,' he mused, once her crying ceased and she was seated at the kitchen table, drinking the mug of tea he'd made. 'That'll be something out of the ordinary to reveal at his or her twenty-first birthday party.'

Despite her fear of the future, a smile surfaced as she acknowledged that his devotion remained undimmed; they would work together to overcome the obstacles an unplanned pregnancy had created. Money would be tight once she gave up work, but in the interim they could save more, cancel the holiday – at least they hadn't booked anything – find a larger flat to rent. One of Joseph's colleagues and his wife rented a two-bedroom flat in Wooloowin. It was a bit shabby and had no garage, but something like it would suffice until they could afford to purchase a house.

* * *

During the succeeding months, Anna hugged this knowledge to her expanding stomach, intending to discuss it with Joseph when the right moment arose. He still maintained they would be able to buy a house a few months after the baby's birth; not what they'd planned, for sure, but adequate for a few years. 'Better than paying a landlord,' he declared, when Anna grimaced at the thought of a weatherboard house on stumps, with tiny rooms.

By mid-July, Anna felt too tired to visit local real-estate agents to enquire about larger flats, or the temporary sales offices erected at the entrance to new estates on the fringes of the city. Work had become a chore, hours to get through from Monday to Friday. She couldn't wait to leave at the end of the month. Once her pregnancy began to show, the recently appointed supervisor, middle-aged, unmarried and extremely old-fashioned, had promptly adjusted the staff roster. There were no more shifts on the front desk for Anna, which was the best part of the job. Instead, she was confined to the back office, as though the sight of her pregnant body would offend students and the occasional parent that accompanied them. The supervisor had asked her to stop work a month earlier – 'It's important to rest, dear' – but Anna refused, conscious of the need to save as much as possible and confident she remained productive. Other colleagues, particularly those around Anna's age, supported her stance, one even threatening to call in the union if the supervisor persisted.

'Anyone would think we were living in the nineteen-fifties,' said Marie, feisty and often in trouble for speaking her mind, as they discussed the issue over lunch in the canteen. 'It's high time we had maternity leave in this country. Losing your job because you're pregnant is downright wrong. Not every woman is in a position to stay at home for years, looking after children.'

Anna thought of Joseph's adolescence, his mother working the four to midnight shift in a factory, leaving him in charge of three younger siblings and preparing the evening meal until their father returned from work. It was nothing short of a miracle that he'd managed to do well at his Secondary Technical School and subsequently gain an electrical engineering apprenticeship. How fortunate she and her sisters had been, with their mother always at home when they returned from school and no chores to complete during the week because homework had priority.

'You're absolutely right,' she remarked to Marie. 'But even if I could stay at home for years, I don't think I could cope. Surely there must be more to life than bringing up a child and housework?'

'It wouldn't suit me,' Marie replied, 'but then I don't plan to get pregnant.'

'Neither did I,' Anna admitted ruefully, patting her stomach. 'At least, not for several years. I wanted to study, gain a qualification so I could get a better job.'

'No need to give up your dream, Anna. Why don't you study by correspondence? Babies sleep a lot, don't they?'

'I suppose so.'

'Cheer up. At least you won't have to deal with Miss Tight-lipped Prude anymore.'

At last, Anna smiled, grateful for a colleague who always looked on the bright side, despite what must have been a difficult childhood, with her mother having married three times and given birth to seven children, and a step-father who drank most of his wages. At fifteen, Marie had left home and school to live with an older sister, then taken evening classes to complete her schooling while working full-time in a supermarket.

* * *

The possibility of study by correspondence occupied Anna's mind as she sat in bed, finishing the mug of tea Joseph had brought her prior to leaving for work. It was her second day alone at home and the new role was proving uninspiring so far. The previous morning, she had begun with good intentions, by asking Joseph to lift the sewing machine, an ancient Singer loaned by Mary, onto the kitchen table so she could hem the cotton sheeting that was already cut into lengths. She had tried to generate enthusiasm, but the cot sheets remained unfinished. Sitting at a table bent over a machine had proven a difficult and uncomfortable task with a huge stomach in the way. Why had she listened to well-meaning Mary, who advised that making the baby's bedding would not only occupy her time, but also cost less than half of that on sale in Myer?

Seven months into her pregnancy, Anna still hadn't come to terms with her changing shape. She hated her distended stomach, the breasts that had grown to such an extent they resembled melons and dreaded the appearance of stretch-marks or varicose veins. A parcel of home-sewn maternity dresses had arrived from England two months earlier, voluminous garments that, to Anna's mind, only emphasised her condition. Like Mary, her mother meant well, but the accompanying instructions not to wear trousers or shorts while pregnant and never to expose an inch of her burgeoning cleavage, had irritated her to such an extent, Joseph thought she was about to burst a blood vessel. Forced to wear the shapeless dresses during her last six weeks of work – 'it's time you stopped wearing your uniform, dear, taut fabric looks rather unsightly' – Anna had discarded her tent-dress on arriving home and donned one of Joseph's old t-shirts, adding a pair of his pyjama pants when the weather cooled.

In bed, increasingly wary of exposing her unattractive body to Joseph's gaze, she insisted on wearing a one-size-fits-all nightdress bought in a sale and turned her back the moment he slipped in beside her. Making love became sporadic, something to be endured rather than enjoyed, a radical transformation considering the delight she'd taken in it before. Joseph made no mention of this change of heart, but he did express concern at her increasing unhappiness and total lack of interest in their coming baby. Her response that it was all right for him, his life hadn't been completely ruined, only intensified his anxiety.

* * *

A knock on the front door forced Anna to abandon her contemplation and face the new day. 'Won't be a minute,' she called, easing herself out of bed and grabbing her dressing gown from the wardrobe. Draping it around her shoulders – there was no way the fitted garment would fasten around her stomach – she hurried to answer the door.

'Morning, Anna,' Mary said brightly. 'I don't blame you for having a lie-in while you can.'

'Come in, I'll make some tea.'

'Thanks. I just wondered how you were getting on with the cot sheets?'

Anna grimaced and ushered her inside.

'Problem with the machine?' Mary asked, as Anna switched on the electric jug and set out mugs.

'No. Problem with my bloody stomach.'

'You don't like being pregnant, do you?'

'I hate it.' Unwilling to face her friend, Anna fiddled with the tea towel hung over the sink. 'The sooner I'm back to normal, the better.'

'What about the end result? Have you accepted that yet?'

Anna shuddered and grasped the edge of the sink to steady herself.

'Come and sit down, love.' A hand reached out to stroke her arm. 'Don't worry about tea, what you need is a sympathetic ear. I do understand your situation.'

'How could you?' Anna muttered, but nevertheless allowed Mary to lead her over to the sofa where they sat side by side in silence, staring at the cream Venetian blinds shading the lounge and kitchen windows.

After a few minutes, Mary got to her feet and headed for the door.

'Please don't leave!' Anna cried. 'I'm so sorry, I didn't mean to be rude.'

Mary turned and tossed her a smile. 'I know. I'm just going to open the blinds. It's a bit cold in here.'

'Sorry, I didn't think.'

Brilliant winter sunshine spilled onto the cheerless vinyl tiles, filling the room with light. Anna looked down at her pale hands. Summer's warm hue had diminished along with the season's high spirits; she had become a wishy-washy creature, unworthy of a second glance.

'That's better,' Mary declared, returning to the sofa. 'Strange to think this would be considered a warm summer day in England.'

'Is that why you emigrated, to live in a warmer climate?'

'No, it was Roger's idea. He thought a fresh start would help me get over...'

'Sorry if I've brought up sad memories.'

'Stop apologising, Anna. It's not necessary and frankly quite irritating.'

Anna bit her lip to prevent the escape of a further apology.

'Now it's my turn to apologise for snapping at you.' Mary turned and smiled. 'Guess I should explain.'

'Only if you want you.'

Mary nodded. 'I lost my first baby to what's known as cot death.'

Anna looked puzzled. 'I've never heard of it.'

'It refers to unexpected and unexplained death in a baby under a year old. Clare was nine months old, a perfectly healthy baby who was developing normally. Then, one morning she just didn't wake up.'

'Oh God, how awful!' Anna stroked her swollen abdomen, an action she had deliberately avoided until that moment.

'I blamed myself. I saw Clare's death as my punishment for months of resentment and negativity.' Mary sighed. 'My first pregnancy was unplanned, like yours.'

Anna shuddered at an exact description of her own state of mind.

'We had been married for just three months and were living in a caravan in my parents' back garden, so we could save up for our own home. I felt I'd let Roger down, spoilt all our plans. House, furniture, then baby – that had been our intention.'

Anna's fingers touched the ridge of a tiny foot and wonder surged through her veins. The warm feeling passed as Mary shifted her position. Perhaps she needed to distance herself from the all too obvious results of another woman's mistake.

'I was shattered by Clare's death,' Mary continued, locking her fingers together so tightly, her knuckles turned white. 'Nine months in my care and I had failed her. Nothing would shake my belief that I alone was responsible for her death. Despite my delight in her, experienced from the moment I held her in my arms, I considered that the negative feelings generated during pregnancy had doomed my baby from the start. There was no way she could survive such overt re-jection.'

Shocked and frightened of future failing, Anna embraced her un-born child. She had two months in which to make amends and inject love and warmth and joy into the developing human being she and Joseph had created. A life created in love; a life that deserved to be loved in return. Would eight weeks suffice to reverse seven months of adverse emotion?

The question remained unanswered as Mary's voice, less fraught than before, invaded Anna's mental space. 'Two years passed before I came to terms with Clare's death and accepted that I was in no way responsible.'

'Is that when you came to Australia?'

'Soon after. We were sponsored by Roger's distant cousin who lives north of Brisbane. I'm not sure of the exact relationship, but I believe they share the same great-grandparents.'

'Second cousin?'

'Probably. Anyway, after discussing the possibility of emigration with me, Roger contacted Louisa and asked her what it was like liv-ing in Australia. Louisa and her husband had emigrated in the Fifties. She's much older than Rog, late forties now, I think.' Mary's expression lightened. 'I loved Louisa's letters. They were so positive, so fascinat-ing. Her descriptions of the Australian bush, the beach and even their old wooden house that she said stood on tree trunks, made me realise I needed a complete change of scene.'

Anna reached out a hand to touch Mary's arm. 'I'm so glad you came. We wouldn't have been able to emigrate if you and Roger hadn't sponsored us.'

'I said the same to Louisa and Ted.'

'I dreaded the thought of staying in England, buying one of the boxy little bungalows being constructed on the edge of town, Sunday lunch with Mum and Dad, nothing ever changing. I wanted adventure, dif-ferent landscapes, different way of life. A new land with new oppor-tunities, space to move and endless sunshine!'

'Success stories all round, then.'

Anna smiled ruefully and patted her stomach. 'Not much chance of adventure now.'

'Why not? Having a baby doesn't mean the end of adventure. We took Judy camping on Stradbroke Island when she was six weeks old. We bathed her in one of the freshwater pools every day.'

'Heavens, you were game!'

'Not really. She had her bassinet to sleep in, milk on tap and cuddles from one or other parent all week long. What more could a newborn want?'

'I see your point.' Anna fiddled with the edges of her dressing-gown. 'The trouble is, I'm so scared I won't cope, especially being cooped up with a baby in this tiny flat. Nowhere to store baby clothes and nappies, let alone a cot.'

Mary glanced around the sparsely furnished room, then appeared to be contemplating the small space between the linen cupboard and the wall separating kitchen and tiny hallway.

'Hardly suitable,' Anna remarked, before her friend could mention a solution. 'No window and no sunlight even in the middle of the day.'

'But fine until baby needs a cot. You could buy a bassinet with a stand on wheels and move it around as you wish.'

'Sounds expensive.'

'I'll have a look in the second-hand shop near our place. I got a portable cot there when Judy was six months. Bit of a shabby old thing and washing didn't improve the filthy netting, so I dyed it navy blue. We used it for years. Strapped it to the car roof-racks when we went on holiday.'

Anna tried to envisage a large folding cot perched on top of Viv. No way would Joseph agree to roof-racks spoiling the appearance of his beloved car.

'Hang on a minute, I think it's still up in the roof. I kept it in case a friend needed one. It's all yours.'

'Thanks. Perhaps I could use it permanently, save buying a cot?'

'Up to you.' Mary got to her feet. 'Enough talk of baby furniture. Go and get dressed, I want to take you out for a drive.'

'Where?'

'Surprise destination.'

Hopeful Horizons

Anna envisaged lunch at a nearby café, or a drive to the bayside suburb of Sandgate where Mary and Roger had taken them the day after their arrival. If she remembered correctly, there was a flat, grassy area dotted with benches running parallel to the water. A walk followed by a sit beside the sea in warm winter sunshine would do her good, blow away the cobwebs created by recent lethargy. So it came as a complete surprise when, after winding through suburban streets to the main road leading to Sandgate, Mary drove towards the city. After a few miles, she turned right into a wide street comprising a strip of bitumen in the middle, bordered by broad swathes of grass.

'Are we going to visit one of your friends?' Anna asked, as Mary pulled up outside one of the old wooden houses on stumps known as Queenslanders that lined either side of the street.

Mary silenced the engine. 'No, and don't worry, it's only a short walk.'

Curious, Anna exited the car with as much gracefulness as she could manage and stood waiting for Mary to retrieve her handbag from the back seat and lock the car. Coarse grass poked into her sandals, scratching the soft skin on the top of her feet. Looking down, she noticed an army of ants scurrying across a patch of bare dirt towards a discarded apple core and smiled at a Christmas Day memory of Maureen being horrified lest giant Australian insects invade the rug where her baby son lay.

'Ready for the surprise?' Mary asked, taking Anna's arm and leading her across the grass footpath to an easement that led down the side of the house to a building site.

Beneath their feet, furrows created by heavy machinery made walking a little difficult, even though heat and sun had dried the churned soil. On their left, a recently built fence, its top and bottom rails gleaming white, enclosed the front house and its modest rear garden, where the obligatory Hill's Hoist took centre stage.

'According to a friend of mine who lives in this street,' Mary advised, 'the elderly owners didn't want to move, but were finding the large garden too much to manage, so they decided to sub-divide instead.'

Anna found herself staring at concrete stumps and a half-laid wooden floor rising from scraped ground. In front of the structure stood a concrete mixer surrounded by bags of cement and a pile of sand. There were no builders in sight, although a rusty ute was parked to one side.

'Lunchbreak probably,' Mary said before Anna could think of an appropriate comment. 'Gone to the corner shop for pies or burgers, I expect.'

'Is it going to be a house, or a garage?' Anna asked, trying to imagine anyone actually living in such a small building.

'A house, of course. Three bedrooms, bathroom, kitchen, living area upstairs, laundry and space for a single garage underneath.'

Anna nodded. 'It's very small.'

'Agreed, but it would be a start. All the basics, plus a good location and a decent backyard.'

Being tucked at the rear of an old house wasn't Anna's idea of a "good" location.

'Walking distance to shops and a station,' Mary persisted.

'I doubt we could afford it,' Anna remarked quickly, unwilling to offend her friend. 'Our savings don't amount to much.'

'It might be worth finding out the price, though. I imagine this house will be cheap, tucked in here. Most young couples prefer to buy in a new estate where the roads have kerbing and channelling and decent street lighting.'

Despite her initial response, Anna took a second look. The concrete stumps varied in height as the land dipped on the left-hand side, a disadvantage if one wanted to build a rumpus room at a later date. However, the stumps were widely spaced, so Viv would fit between them on the high side. 'Do you think the builders would mind if we looked around the back?'

'No, but I'd better stay here in case they return. I can explain you're in the market for a house.'

'Thanks, I won't be long.' Stepping onto muddied, flattened grass littered with off-cuts of wood and discarded food wrappers, Anna headed for the fence that ran along the side boundary, figuring the ground would be less disturbed there. Long grass wove through rusty wire and paint peeled from the rails, but further down, a line of flowering hibiscus had been planted parallel to the fence and their glorious, buttery blooms fluttered in the breeze. Anna loved the huge hibiscus flowers with their splash of scarlet in the centre, so she continued to follow the fence, pausing every few yards to glance at the neighbouring garden. A paved path led to trees laden with citrus fruit and raised garden beds planted with neat rows of vegetables.

Reluctantly, she turned to survey the land behind the emergent house, anticipating a broad expanse of overgrown grass with the remains of a concrete path and a rusty lop-sided Hoist, but saw instead mown lawn and a stand of mature trees that stretched the entire width of the block. Apart from glimpses of green between the trees, the house and garden backing onto the property were hidden from view. The privacy appealed to her. The land that surrounded houses in new estates was generally devoid of trees or shrubs, a thin lawn the only concession to the natural environment. She turned to look up at the house, trying to envisage steps leading to a balcony and curtains framing the windows.

'Want to see the drawings, darl?' a voice enquired from somewhere nearby.

'Yes, please.' She glanced around, but failed to see anyone and was about to walk away when a man wearing work-boots and the heavy drill shorts and shirt she'd seen advertised on TV as "Hard Yakka", backed out from the low part of the house. 'Sam!' she cried, recognising their friend. 'What are you doing here?'

A grin split his face and a grubby hand pushed an errant lock of thick black hair away from his forehead. 'Working, darl. More to the point, what brings you to a building site?'

Anna explained the impromptu drive and its surprise destination.

'It's not bad for a starter. You and Joe in the market for a house?'

'I wish. The trouble is, I don't think we've got enough for a deposit and there's not much chance of saving now I've had to give up work.'

'I reckon it's worth a try all the same. The bank manager won't bite your head off.'

Anna smiled and pointed to the roll of papers tucked under Sam's right arm. 'Can I have a look?'

'Sure.' Sam knelt on the grass and unrolled the house plans, positioning the external views on top instead of the wiring diagram he'd been studying. Taking a hammer and pliers from the leather belt slung around his waist, he used them as weights to secure the paper. 'Decent size living area, bedrooms a bit on the small size but who cares, you only sleep in 'em.'

Anna bent forward, peering at front, rear and side elevations. The dimensions remained a blur, but she didn't want to make an exhibition of herself by trying to manoeuvre her heavy body into a kneeling position.

'Hang on, I'll fetch the chair.' Sam turned and disappeared under the house, returning with a folding canvas chair that had seen better days. 'Boss uses it for smoko,' he explained. 'He's getting' on a bit, must be sixty at least.'

'Thanks. I find kneeling rather difficult at the moment.'

He gathered up the plans and passed them to Anna. 'When's the bub due?'

'End of September.'

'House could be finished around then.'

'Bad timing. I don't fancy moving and dealing with a newborn at the same time.'

'The completion date's not set in stone. It depends on weather, availability of tradesmen, materials. We've got half a dozen houses on the go at the moment.'

'The boss must be pleased.'

'He's not the only one. Plenty of overtime sure suits me. The sooner we get our own place, the better. Mum still thinks I'm a kid, gets on my nerves.'

Anna nodded, reluctant to enter into a discussion of maternal shortcomings. Last week's aerogramme from mother-in-law Stella had really annoyed her – a page of complaints about their thoughtlessness in moving to what she termed *the arse-end of the world*, especially now that she was going to be a grandmother. 'Is there an internal drawing?' she asked, looking up at him.

'Yep.' He leant over her and flipped through the drawings. 'Here.'

She peered at a rectangular diagram divided into squares, marked with what she presumed indicated doors and windows. The dimensions meant little; she couldn't visualise size. 'It doesn't make much sense to me, I'm afraid.'

'No worries. I'll bring 'em round one evening to show Joe. That's if you're interested?'

For the first time in months, Anna sensed a flicker of light shining through the darkness that surrounded her world. 'Thanks, Sam, that would be great.'

* * *

A succession of sighs followed by the puckering of thin lips did not auger well for a positive outcome. Seated opposite the dour bank manager – he had yet to offer anything resembling a smile – Anna and Joseph exchanged worried glances as his fountain pen scratched figures on a notepad. Their Commonwealth Bank savings account passbook lay open on the desk, its meagre record of transactions testament to an insufficient deposit.

Long, pale fingers placed the pen parallel to the notepad before shifting their mortgage application form a little to the right. 'Mr and Mrs Fletcher,' he began, fixing them with glacial blue eyes.

Instinctively, Anna wrapped her arms around the baby bump, a gesture intended to shield foetal ears from unwelcome news. Beside her, Joseph tensed, increasing the stiffness of trousers pressed earlier that morning. Since leaving Britain, his winter-weight wool suit, purchased for their wedding at Stella's insistence, had hung in the wardrobe alongside his tailored gabardine raincoat, both taking up precious space yet rarely worn. In Brisbane, a lightweight jacket sufficed for meetings with important engineering clients, while the raincoat, designed for fog and drizzle, had proven totally impractical. During tropical downpours, most city workers unfurled umbrellas, or sought shelter beneath shop awnings. A dash to the station might result in a soaking, but clothes dried quickly in the muggy atmosphere of a packed train, its windows closed to prevent rain entering the compartment.

'I am inclined to refuse your application for a ten-thousand-dollar mortgage,' the manager continued, picking up the pen and passing it from hand to hand as though embarrassed by his decision. 'However, in view of,' he gave a slight cough, 'in view of Mrs Fletcher's condition, I am willing to overlook your inadequate savings in the interests of a new Australian family.' The glimmer of a smile surfaced but was quickly quashed by pursed lips. 'We can't have migrants rushing back to England with one of our own, can we?'

Anna bristled at his patronising tone. She had no intention of rushing back to England, despite a recent offer from Aunt Maud to pay for both their outgoing and return journeys should they decide that a supportive network of family would be beneficial during, in her words, *this difficult time*. On first reading the letter, Anna had presumed her aunt was referring to the imminent birth, then remembered that Uncle Edgar, with his wife's approval, had packed their only son off to boarding school at the earliest possible age. Perhaps Aunt Maud had meant the baby's entire childhood. Her cousin Christopher, now a successful stockbroker based in London, rarely visited his parents and remained as aloof as he had been as a child.

'Born middle-aged, that one,' her mother had remarked, following a Boxing Day lunch during which Christopher pontificated about the stock market and refused to engage in "normal" dinner table conversation, much to her father's chagrin.

'Thank you for your understanding, sir,' Joseph said, his tension deflating like a pricked balloon.

Anna pushed thoughts of her stuffy cousin to the back of her mind. 'We're most grateful, Mr Bradley. A house will provide security for our family.'

At last, the smile won through and a hint of warmth tinged a sombre face. 'My pleasure, Mrs Fletcher, and may I wish you all the best for the coming, er, event.'

Anna returned the smile, envisaging a bachelor flat in the city, heavy, old-fashioned furniture inherited from elderly relatives, an overfed cat the only one awaiting Mr Bradley's return from work.

* * *

Outside in the street, the successful applicants hugged and kissed like young lovers snatching precious minutes together, oblivious to the obstruction they were causing lunchtime crowds eager to make the most of a limited work break. One woman tapped Joseph on the shoulder with her umbrella, while another remarked that it was disgusting the way young people behaved these days, but neither managed to dislodge the exuberant pair. Eventually, the city hall clock chimed the hour, prompting Joseph to declare that he'd better get back to work.

'I'll make your favourite dinner tonight,' Anna called to his receding back, but he pressed on through the crowd, unaware of the promised delights.

Hungry now – she hadn't thought to bring a sandwich or even an apple – Anna set off towards the station, intending to purchase a bar of chocolate from the platform kiosk. She was halfway down Ann Street when someone called out her name. Turning around, she searched for a familiar face and almost lost her balance when Marie embraced her.

'Sorry, I didn't mean to startle you,' her friend remarked. 'Everything all right? You look a bit flushed.'

'Excitement,' Anna replied and quickly shared her news.

'Wonderful! I'm so pleased for you. Better send me an invite to tea when you're settled.'

'It won't be for a few months. The house hasn't got a roof yet.'

Marie smiled. 'Want a bite to eat? There's a café around the corner?'

'Just something light. I can't eat a big meal these days,' Anna replied, unsure how much cash remained in her purse. She would have to call at the butcher's on the way home, to buy meat for dinner. A new household budget based on a single wage had been discussed but not yet implemented, their spare time over the past fortnight having been taken up with poring over house plans, arranging a holding deposit with the builder and filling in forms for the bank.

The Best Laid Plans...

The next few weeks passed in a blur of activity: weekend visits to the building site, weekday shopping expeditions with Mary – Anna couldn't believe how much one newborn needed – searching second-hand shops for a few pieces of furniture. Apart from the small bookcase, kitchen cupboard and television unit Joseph had made, they lacked basics such as chairs and a bed. As well as transporting her to numerous shops, practical Mary also sewed cot sheets and the oddly named "bunny rugs", which Anna learnt were used to wrap up new babies.

They soon located a heavy, old-fashioned double bed base, but finding a decent second-hand mattress was proving difficult. Anna wrinkled her nose at the thought of sleeping on the evidence of strangers' emissions, prompting Mary to tell her not to be so sensitive, just buy a mattress protector to disguise the stains. Anna ignored the advice. After spending the first seven months of married life sleeping on a disgusting mattress, she had vowed never again. A generous gift from Aunt Maud solved the problem, enabling the purchase of a new inner-spring mattress. Anna blessed her aunt every time she entered the bedroom and saw the plastic-wrapped mattress leaning against the wall.

The remaining dollars and Anna's holiday pay were used to buy a large refrigerator, an essential item in Brisbane's sub-tropical climate, where even jars of jam and sauce bottles had to be refrigerated to prevent ants or cockroaches seeking out the slightest spill coating the glass. On the advice of the delivery man, the new Westinghouse fridge, encased in a protective layer of cardboard, was placed in the garage to await transportation to its new home.

With the bedroom and kitchen organised, Anna now turned her attention to a living area that encompassed a decent-sized lounge and small dining area. The folding canvas chairs purchased for picnics and camping would suffice until they could afford a lounge suite, while the yellow stools – dismantled so they would fit in a small shipping crate and stored in the garage ever since – could be used to sit at the breakfast bar for meals. That left the baby's room. Anna refused to call it a nursery, with its connotations of aristocratic mansions and Norland-trained nannies. She had escaped the rigid class system that dominated British life and now lived in an egalitarian country, where hard work and assisting one another counted far more than inherited wealth. When they had settled in, she would throw a party – BYO chairs – to thank all those that had given time, energy and the myriad items stacked in the garage to help them handle a first baby and a first house.

The space labelled 'second bedroom' on the plans and situated at one end of the house opposite the main bedroom, had a built-in wardrobe, but, according to Joseph, lacked any shelves to store nappies or other baby paraphernalia. In the continuing absence of stairs, either front or rear, he would climb the builders' ladder weekly to check on progress, while Anna, standing on hard-packed earth, would gaze upward, wishing she could see more than the gap where the front door would be and six inches of kitchen wall. Sometimes, when diminishing footsteps indicated Joseph had moved to the bedroom end of the house, she would climb a few rungs to obtain a better view, but fear of being caught out and the subsequent lecture on reckless behaviour, would send her scurrying back to earth. In recent months, Joseph had become over-protective to such an extent that Anna wanted to scream. He insisted on carrying even the lightest package, or moved things out of her way as though walking through their sparsely furnished flat without tripping was beyond her ability.

Despite her recent acceptance of what Mary termed the 'end result,' Anna couldn't wait for her body to return to normal. Articles in the *Women's Weekly*, read in the doctor's waiting room, might rave about the joys of pregnancy, but she continued to find the whole process, if not totally abhorrent, at the very least unpleasant. She did not look or feel radiant. Her back ached, her ankles had swollen, and her breasts were growing to such an extent that they already spilled out of the new bra which she had purchased less than a week before leaving work. Sleeping through the entire nine months, or going to a laboratory to pick up one's fully-formed baby – an option Anna imagined women would have in the future – seemed preferable to her current condition. As for giving birth, she dreaded the prospect and would be requesting any medical intervention on offer. Thank God husbands weren't encouraged to attend the birth. She would hate Joseph to see her in the state shown in the film she had viewed at a recent ante-natal class.

* * *

Childbirth was far from Anna's thoughts as she stood in the garage, painting the pine chest of drawers she had purchased a few hours earlier. After an unsuccessful search for second-hand, Joseph had suggested she try the shop selling raw pine furniture located near the station. 'I had a quick look yesterday as the bloke was closing up,' he'd added as they sat at the kitchen table finishing dinner. 'Cheap stuff, but it looks well made. Why don't you drive me to the station tomorrow and take a look? I reckon a small chest of drawers would fit in Viv's boot.'

And it had, once the plump, cheerful shopkeeper, who assured her he made all the furniture, had removed the drawers and put them on the back seat, before picking up the frame and placing it in the boot. He'd even supplied a short length of rope to tie the open boot door to the bumper bar and said not to worry about returning it.

Impatient to begin transforming her purchase, Anna detoured on the way home to buy a can of white paint at the hardware store. Back at the flats, she parked on the driveway, opened the garage door, then untied the rope and managed, albeit with a great deal of huffing and puffing, to lift the frame out of the boot and carry it into the laundry. Returning to fetch the drawers, she decided it would be easier to leave Viv on the driveway while she painted. The landlord preferred his tenants' cars to be garaged, maintaining the place looked untidy if they were left outside, but she considered it unlikely he would visit, with the grass newly mown and no one in the process of moving in or out.

She had almost finished the first coat when the sound of a vehicle reversing up the driveway made her drop the paintbrush and rush to the garage door. Mr Martelli's ute had stopped only inches from Viv and his face looked like thunder as he descended from the cab.

'*Disordinato, disordinato*,' he muttered, his expression altering to one of pleasure when he noticed Anna standing just inside the garage.

'*Buon giorno*, Mr Martelli,' she called, adding quickly, 'I've just got home from shopping.' Too late, she realised that a paint-spattered t-shirt reaching to her knees and bare feet made a mockery of her statement.

'*Buon giorno*, Signora Anna.' He stepped towards her. '*Bambino* good?'

She patted her stomach. 'Growing fast.'

Mr Martelli beamed. 'Big boy for sure, like Joe.'

Anna smiled back. 'We'll have to wait and see.' She stepped forward. 'I'll move the car in a minute. First, I need a...' She hurried to the steps, leaving the landlord to complete her sentence.

Mr Martelli was nowhere in sight when she returned with the car keys, so she manoeuvred herself into the driver's seat and turned the ignition key. Driving that morning had been challenging, with her stomach almost touching the steering wheel and her arms stretched to their full capacity. She hadn't driven for weeks and acknowledged ruefully that putting Viv in the garage would be her last attempt for a while. Glancing in the rear vision mirror, she realised she had parked too close to the block wall separating the flats from the adjoining property. The driveway sloped downwards and, with Mr Martelli's ute close by, she would need to execute a flawless hill-start.

With her bare feet balanced on clutch and brake, she slowly released the handbrake. Viv crept forward and stalled after a few feet. 'Damn,' Anna muttered, braking hard to prevent the car sliding backwards. After numerous attempts – for some reason Viv kept on stalling – she managed to garage the car and sat hunched over the steering wheel, her breath coming in loud gasps. The wheel dug into her stomach, but she lacked the energy to push the seat back or even open the door.

When her breathing finally returned to normal, she summoned sufficient strength to exit the car and half-staggered into the laundry. A second coat would have to wait until tomorrow, as right now she would be hard-pressed to put the lid on the paint can and rinse out the brush. As she reached up to retrieve the old coffee jar used to store paintbrushes, warm liquid trickled down her legs.

'Bugger!' she exclaimed, wishing she'd gone to the toilet before shifting the car. Lately, she'd had to pee more often; the baby must be pressing on her bladder. But when she looked down at the puddle forming at her feet, it seemed the wrong consistency for pee. Anxious now, she stepped sideways and grabbed the edge of the concrete lattice screen that divided garage from laundry. Hand over hand, she slowly sank to the floor and, leaning forward, sniffed the clear, slightly yellow fluid.

Definitely not urine. Advice tendered the previous week at the antenatal class suddenly became relevant. 'Once your waters have broken, ladies, you must get to hospital quickly in order to protect your baby from infection,' the stern-faced woman, who reminded Anna of a harassed school teacher, had declared, wagging an index finger at her pupils.

Anna lifted the t-shirt and watched in horror as more liquid gushed from between her thighs. Shit, this wasn't a false alarm. She must go upstairs and pack a bag. As it was still four weeks away from her due date, what to take to the hospital hadn't entered her head. She reached for the concrete screen, wincing as its rough edge jabbed her palm and hauled herself upright. At the garage door, she paused to check that

Mr Martelli was nowhere in sight before fleeing to the sanctuary of an empty flat.

In the shower, she rinsed away the sticky evidence, trying not to think about the coming ordeal. First-time labour was supposed to take an age, so apart from the loss of protective fluid, there was no rush to reach the hospital. Better to take her time and try to remain calm. The absence of any pain reinforced her decision to pack an overnight bag before venturing across the road to use Vi's telephone.

Satisfied nothing had been overlooked, Anna zipped up the bag and sat on the bed to rest for a moment before getting dressed. At least the baby's early arrival would mean she no longer had to wear maternity dresses, or suffer the indignity of a further increase in the size of her stomach. The dreaded stretchmarks hadn't developed; with daily exercise and a sensible diet, she would resume her usual figure quickly and be able to wear her bikini, confident of a flat, unmarked stomach. Gaining weight had never been a problem for her; she enjoyed the occasional chocolate bar or googy cake, but rarely over-ate and had avoided the temptation to eat for two during her pregnancy.

Interior movement – the baby shifting its position, she hoped, rather than a contraction – drew her attention back to the immediate issue. What if Vi had gone out? How would Joseph get home from the station without the car? There was no direct bus from the station and Anna couldn't recall if she'd ever seen a taxi in the vicinity. Although husbands were not allowed to remain in the labour ward when birth was imminent, she wanted Joseph nearby. Simple geography provided the solution to the latter problem. Royal Brisbane Women's Hospital was situated a short bus ride from the city centre; she would ask Joseph to meet her in the labour ward. A second phone call would secure a taxi for herself.

As she pulled a creased tent-dress over her head – why iron the bloody thing when she looked terrible, anyway? – Anna decided not to bother Vi or any other stay-at-home neighbour. Instead, she would carry her small bag to the doctor's surgery and ask the receptionist to phone for an ambulance. She might as well make use of the ambulance service they paid for, along with private health insurance. Soon after their arrival in Brisbane, Roger had advised them to take out health and ambulance insurance, explaining that the public health system in Australia left much to be desired. Brought up with the NHS, Joseph and Anna had baulked at the amount of money involved, but acquiesced after learning about Mary's experience of a public ward. Admitted to hospital with pneumonia during her first Brisbane winter, Mary had spent a disheartening week lying in a narrow bed on an enclosed but still draughty veranda – overspill from the main public ward – surrounded by elderly women suffering from dementia.

In the maternity wing, Anna would be occupying what their health fund brochure described as an Intermediate room, which meant sharing with one other woman. Babies resided in the Intermediate nursery and were wheeled into rooms at feeding times only, as rest was considered of prime importance for both newborns and mothers.

* * *

Nothing untoward happened during Anna's slow walk up the hill to the doctor's surgery, in the ambulance, or during the first few hours spent at the hospital. It was as though, despite ejecting the amniotic fluid, her body had decided the baby wasn't ready to be born for another month. Nurses prodded and poked, called the resident obstetrician, who listened to the baby's heartbeat, said, 'nothing to worry about, baby will arrive in due course,' and Joseph arrived as breathless as if he'd run all the way from his office.

After a further hour, Joseph left her bedside to fetch a sandwich and a coffee from the hospital cafeteria. Thankful for the opportunity to rest undisturbed by his blatant anxiety and endless questions she couldn't answer, Anna settled back on the pillows and closed her eyes. A thick mantle of sleep shielded her from neighbouring maternity moans and the squeak of crepe-soled nurses' shoes scurrying across polished linoleum sent her deep into an alternate world, where dreams suffused body and soul. Floating in a surreal scarlet sea, she made no attempt to swim back to shore, or raise an arm to attract attention or utter a cry for help. Instead, convinced of the ocean's benevolence, she waited for waves or a change of tide to carry her to solid ground.

When something brushed past her, she envisaged a sea-creature disturbed by her presence and offered an apology so soft, the words lay unspoken on her pallid lips. Seeking respite from the sunlight that heated her exposed skin, she slipped beneath the surface and hung suspended in its salty embrace. Her skin continued to burn, so she sought dark depths where translucent organisms paid her no heed. At peace with her new environment, she failed to sense her journey's imminent end.

* * *

A hand felt for swollen skin, but touched instead a wound dressing and a small plastic tube. Alarmed, Anna quickly withdrew her hand. Her eyelids fluttered, prompting unwelcome sound and action. A white figure loomed over her; an unfamiliar voice spoke her name. She shivered, tried to reposition her other hand under the warm bedclothes and felt the tug of something embedded in her skin.

'Where am I?' she asked, afraid to open her eyes lest she find the surroundings uninviting.

'In the recovery room,' came the reply from somewhere above her.

Anna licked dry lips. 'Why am I so thirsty?'

A warm hand stroked her brow. 'I'll bring you some ice to suck in a moment.'

'Water,' Anna pleaded, 'I want water.'

'Later, dear. You've only just come round and you were very sick prior to the C-section.'

'No, I wasn't. Pregnancy isn't an illness.' Her eyes opened, swivelled from side to side, saw nothing but pale green walls and starched white fabric. 'Where is my...?' Her voice trailed off, as though she was afraid to utter a word she had once tried to ignore.

'In the premmie nursery. He's doing well.'

Anna's still-drugged brain struggled to decipher the abbreviation. 'Premmie?'

'Premature, dear. He's small, like most pre-term babies, so he needs to spend a few days in a humidicrib. Nothing to worry about.'

'No, he's enormous. I have to wear tents instead of dresses.'

'Four pounds, six ounces is small, dear. Now, just relax while I fetch the ice.'

Confused, Anna closed her eyes and tried to re-enter a soothing sea.

'Here we are, dear.'

Anna opened her eyes to clasp the proffered plastic beaker.

'Make sure you only suck one ice-cube at a time.'

Obediently, Anna tipped a single cube into her mouth.

'Good girl.' The nurse smiled. 'I'll be round again soon to check how you're getting on.'

Footsteps faded and a door closed. Left alone, Anna savoured the welcome moisture, rolled the cube around her parched mouth with her tongue, sucked, swallowed. Subsequent cubes seemed to melt at a faster rate; she yearned for a jug of water to top up the tiny beaker. Consumed by her task, she managed to ignore the unwelcome thoughts mustering like storm clouds in her head, but when the empty beaker slipped from her hand onto the white blanket, her fears could not be denied. Would she be left with only an abdominal scar to re-mind her of what might have been? Premature babies often died or had severe respiratory problems due to under-developed lungs. Grieving for a baby's unfulfilled potential, or watching an innocent child strug-gle to breathe, would be her future tasks; just penalties for months of anger, indifference and disgust. Tears rolled down her pale cheeks and seeped into her moist mouth, their saltiness mocking her welcome return to shore.

... of Mice and (Wo)men Often Go Awry

After three days, although Anna still felt exhausted and the slightest movement caused sharp pains to shoot from her wound, she summoned sufficient spirit to challenge the nurses' insistence that she remained too weak to get out of bed. Moving from bed to wheelchair demanded both energy and fortitude, the pain almost unbearable when she tried to stand up straight. Biting her lips, she fought down rising giddiness and, grateful for a helping arm around her shoulders, lowered herself onto a black vinyl seat. Slippers and dressing-gown were quickly extracted from the bedside locker. 'I'll be fine in just my nightdress,' Anna remarked, as the nurse tucked thick, quilted fabric around her. 'It's awfully hot in here.'

'Maybe so, but we can't have patients roaming the corridors half-dressed.'

Suppressing the urge to give a sardonic response, Anna lifted each foot in turn to receive sheepskin slippers.

The journey from Intermediate room to Premmie nursery seemed endless: a long corridor, a lengthy wait for a lift that juddered so much she thought her stitches would burst, followed by another insipid green corridor with squeaky linoleum underfoot. Wheeled into position in front of a nursery containing half a dozen humidicribs and assorted equipment, Anna waited with gathering impatience while the nurse tapped on the door to alert the gowned and masked individual leaning over a crib in the middle of the room. A whispered exchange followed through a door that was opened only a fraction, as though breath from unmasked faces would damage the tiny patients enclosed by plastic walls. When a gloved finger pointed to a humidicrib half-covered with a white cloth, a wave of anxiety surged through Anna's veins. Then, as she was about to rise from the wheelchair and demand access to her dead infant, the words, 'No, nurse, I said baby Fletcher,' reached her ears.

Her exhaled breath left a white mark on otherwise spotless glass as Anna watched the nursery nurse wheel an uncovered crib towards the window. Straining to see through the thick glass, she stared at the scrap of humanity a surgeon had lifted from her slashed womb during the emergency caesarean section. Her baby, lying on his back and wearing only a nappy, resembled an elf with his pointed ears and thin face. Wrinkled fingers fluttered around his head, searching for a rosebud mouth, but settled instead for the folded skin at the top of his ears. She wanted to tap on the window and tell him that pulling on his ears would only compound his elf-like features, but remained silent, unwilling to risk a reprimand from the poker-faced nurse who had left her post reluctantly to transport an anxious mother to the Premmie nursery. Denied the possibility of having her baby wheeled into the Intermediate room she shared with an over-exuberant fourth-time mother – a boy at last, thank God – after three days, Anna had threatened to get out of bed and make her own way to the next floor unless someone took her to see her son.

Joseph had already viewed their so far unnamed baby, but, when plied with questions during the previous evening's visiting hour, said he looked like all the other newborns, red-skinned and wrinkly. No mention had been made of long fingers and toes, or the black hair sticking up all over his head.

'Time's up,' the nurse declared, after what seemed less than a minute.

'Why isn't he wearing the nightdress I packed?' Anna asked, hoping for a lengthy response.

'It's easier to deal with premmies when they're wearing just a nappy.' Hands grabbed black rubber handles, white lace-up shoes shifted position, the wheelchair was turned away from the plate glass. 'You'll have to buy some smaller clothes now, Mrs Fletcher. That nightdress would swim on him.'

The tone implied failure, sending her confidence plummeting. 'I'll ask my friend to get the right size when she comes tonight,' Anna murmured, remembering Joseph had mentioned Mary's forthcoming visit.

'No rush. Your baby won't be leaving hospital with you.'

'Why ever not?'

An extended sigh inferred a further transgression. 'Surely you realise we can't release our premmies until they have reached an acceptable weight?'

'What's an acceptable weight?' Anna asked, wishing she could say what was really on her mind. 'Our premmies', indeed! He belonged to *her*, not the hospital!

'Six pounds.'

Anna pondered the significance of that particular weight but lacked the courage to ask another question. She had suffered more than enough withering looks from Nurse Bevan.

The previous morning, Anna's post-breakfast nap had been disturbed when Bloody Beatrice Bevan, soon abbreviated to Triple B by room-mate Ellen, had entered the room armed with a clipboard, marched over to the bed and demanded, 'Breast or bottle?'

Struggling to surface from sleep, Anna had asked her to repeat the request.

'I said, breast or bottle?

Anna had looked down at the swollen mounds threatening to burst out of her nightdress, noted the damp patches staining the pink cotton and promptly answered, 'Bottle.'

'Just as well. Save me time teaching you to use the breast pump.'

Anna had shuddered as images of new mothers attached to farm milking machines danced before her eyes. Nevertheless, she felt guilty denying her son what some deemed 'the best start in life.' Attitudes had changed since her mother's day, when most believed that only the uneducated lower classes breastfed their babies.

'Waste of time and energy, anyhow,' Nurse Bevan had continued, as she annotated the list on her clipboard. 'We give our premmies special formula. Only the best for them.'

Totally confused, Anna had slumped back on the pillows and, closing her eyes, ignored the final remark about a breast binder that Triple B flung over her shoulder as she left the room.

* * *

Back in bed following her brief excursion, Anna turned her face to the wall and wept. A single word defined her present condition: failure. Not only had she failed to see her pregnancy through to full-term, she had needed extreme medical intervention to produce the premature baby she was forbidden to touch or even look at without a barrier of thick glass between them. She had failed Joseph as well, for, according to Triple B, it would be six weeks before she could drive, hang out washing or even make the bed! Joseph would be forced to take holiday leave to tend an invalid wife, a wife who now bore the permanent disfigurement of a lengthy scar.

Every painful movement conjured up images of the wound still concealed beneath a thick dressing. She dreaded the thought of revealing red, raw skin; it was bad enough seeing the spiky pubic hairs and red nicks, evidence of hurried pre-surgery shaving, on visits to the bathroom. Painful breasts, bound so tight she felt like an Egyptian mummy, only contributed to her desolation, reminding her of yet another failure. Stupid hospital regulations might deny her baby breast milk for a few weeks, but the decision, made almost without thinking, meant he would never suckle.

Immersed in a state of absolute misery, it didn't occur to Anna that most of what she termed 'failures' were the result of matters beyond her control. On several occasions, she'd asked nursing staff what caused premature birth, or why she'd haemorrhaged, but none had supplied a satisfactory explanation, fobbing her off with statements such as, 'It just happens sometimes,' or 'No need to worry, it's unlikely to happen next time.'

Lying awake during noisy hospital nights – trolleys clattering down the corridor, blood pressure machine being wheeled into the room – Anna analysed her actions during the hours before her waters broke, convinced that she alone was responsible for her subsequent bodily malfunction. There were three possible explanations: lifting a lightweight pine frame out of the boot, difficulty parking the car, or reaching for a paintbrush, although none had involved excessive or strenuous exercise. She tried to remember if Dr Jameson had mentioned curtailing activity during late pregnancy. She could recall only the advice to carry on as normal – no special diet, have a few drinks, reduce smoking to a minimum but don't give up entirely if it helps relieve stress. Anna had never smoked, apart from trying it once in the school playground for a dare, and rarely drank more than two glasses of wine, so adhering to these guidelines had been easy. The woman taking the antenatal classes had echoed the doctor's words, adding in recent weeks the importance of gentle exercise such as walking to the shops, and not, in her words, 'lying about at home all day like a beached whale'.

Three days into a ten-day hospital stay, she found the mornings brought the relief of daylight and heightened nursing activity, but the pangs of guilt that threatened to overwhelm her resurfaced once Anna was left to her own devices. Neighbour Ellen had regular feeding sessions to break up her day and, apart from the compulsory post-lunch rest, she was allowed to get out of bed and make use of the sitting room at the end of the corridor, where mothers gathered to chat or watch television.

As her tears continued to soak the pillowcase, Anna was so focused on her own misery that she failed to notice that Ellen had slipped out of bed and crossed the small space between their beds. Plump arms encircling her shoulders and a kiss dropped on her damp forehead, were the first indications she had that someone really cared and they caused a fresh burst of sobbing rather than the intended calm.

'Nothing wrong with a good cry,' Ellen remarked, 'whatever Triple B says. Too obsessed with routine, that one. Feed every four hours on the dot, whips him away after twenty minutes, saying he'll get bloated and won't sleep if he has too much milk. What a load of shit! No wonder my boy's yelling in the nursery. He's ten pounds, for God's sake. He needs a damn sight more than ten minutes each side.'

'Ten pounds?' Anna exclaimed, shock stalling her tears. 'Labour must have been agony.'

Ellen shrugged. 'No, pretty quick fourth time around. This is the last one, mind you, whatever Pete says. I've had more than enough of washing nappies and being deafened by screaming kids. I'm not getting any younger, either. I'm thirty-one tomorrow.'

'Happy birthday for tomorrow.'

'Thanks. I doubt Pete will remember. He'll be too busy celebrating his son's arrival down the pub with his mates. When it comes to kids, men get a good deal, don't they? Fun making 'em, bounce 'em on their knees when it suits, hand 'em over when they're crying or stinky.' Arms slid from Anna's shoulders and plump lips pouted. 'Oh, what the hell. Let's forget about men and have a laugh.'

'How?'

'It's time to compare post-baby tummies, even though I'm bloody sure who's going to win the chocolate Pete brought in last night.' Ellen stepped away from the bed and flung up her nightdress.

Astounded, Anna could only stare at the mass of loose flesh quivering like a bowl of Aeroplane jelly.

'Come on, girl, get out of bed.'

Anna shifted her legs over the edge of the bed and, taking care not to stretch her abdomen, slid to the floor. Encouraged by her room-mate's complete lack of embarrassment, she lifted her nightdress.

'No doubt about it, you win!' Ellen announced brightly, adding in a more serious tone, 'Jeez, girl, you don't half look skinny. Are you starving yourself or what?'

Anna glanced down and, for the first time, looked beyond the wound dressing to the pale skin that stretched over her hip bones and a flat, almost concave stomach. 'You're right, Ellen. I've lost more than baby weight.'

'Must be the shock of having surgery.' Ellen turned on her heels and headed for her bedside locker. 'Here we are, Cadbury's dairy milk.'

Anna looked up and smiled. 'Why don't we share it after lights-out... pretend we're children having a midnight feast?'

'Right-o. I reckon we should wash it down with a beer, but.' She tossed the chocolate to Anna before grabbing her dressing gown from the end of the bed. 'I'll just go and ring Mum, ask her to bring in a few stubbies tonight.'

'Good idea. Could you ask her to bring a can of lemonade as well? I like a shandy.'

'Sure thing.' Ellen swept from the room, trailing acres of quilted pink nylon.

A Surreal Homecoming

Ushered into the flat by an over-attentive Joseph, Anna wanted to wander through rooms rather than sit in a chair. During the journey from hospital to home, he'd asked every few minutes if she was all right and offered to drive even slower if bumps in the road were causing her pain. Ten days away had engendered in her a kind of love for their small flat with its cheap mass-produced furniture and bland floor tiles.

'Cup of tea?' Joseph asked, releasing her arm as she sank onto yellow vinyl.

'Yes please, and a biscuit, if there is one.'

'Arnott's Monte Carlo, I bought them specially.'

Anna beamed. 'Thanks, darling, you're so thoughtful.'

'No more than you deserve. You've been through hell.'

'Tough for you, too, worrying about me and the baby.'

'Yep.' He stood shifting his weight from one foot to the other. 'I didn't want to tell you while you were in hospital, but when the surgeon came out of the operating theatre, he spotted me sitting in the corridor, came over and said, "Congratulations Mr Fletcher, you have a son. However, I'd advise you not to celebrate until we're certain he's out of the woods."'

Anna gulped back tears. 'Did he say how long that would be?'

'Couple of days.'

'So, there are no permanent problems?'

'Not according to that bossy sister.'

'Triple B,' Anna muttered.

'Isn't that what they call those enormous trucks?'

Anna shrugged. 'No idea. My room-mate came up with the nickname.'

'Thinking of names, we should decide what to call our son. Any more thoughts?'

'I'd prefer a name that can't be shortened.'

'Why am I not surprised?'

Anna pouted. 'I can't help it if I hate the way Australians abbreviate everything.'

Joseph leaned over and stroked her cheek. 'How about Ian?'

Anna shook her head.

'Adam?'

'Not bad, but he needs two names. I always resented the fact that my parents only gave me one.'

'Adam Joseph.'

'Sounds good.'

'Decided then.'

'Are you sure it won't be abbreviated to Ad?'

'Don't be daft.' He smiled down at her. 'Let's toast our firstborn with tea and a Monte Carlo or two.'

* * *

Asleep in the confines of the Premmie nursery, Adam Joseph Fletcher, now weighing almost five pounds, remained unaware of either his naming, or his mother's dislike of abbreviation. Until he was discharged at the appropriate weight of six pounds, he would be known only as 'Baby Fletcher,' the name written in blue biro on a tiny rubber label tied around his right wrist with white string. As a precaution, a second label – a square of unbleached calico annotated with surname, gender and birth weight – was pinned to his hospital-issue nappy.

* * *

Once Joseph had departed for work the following morning, Anna sensed a rewinding of time, the tedious months of pregnancy becoming nothing but a protracted dream. A dream from which she had emerged scarred but otherwise unchanged. With her breasts almost back to normal size and shape and her stomach firm, she bore no resemblance to the new mothers she had observed in the hospital sitting room during the last few days of her stay. Anticipating a slow return to her pre-pregnancy figure, she had asked Joseph to bring her peasant-style mini-dress into the hospital for the journey home. In the event, it looked as though she'd borrowed the dress from a much larger friend, as her arms and legs protruded from the embroidered white cotton like paddle-pop sticks.

The flat remained as she had left it, with no trace of an addition to the family apart from the towelling nappies, bunny rugs and baby clothes stacked on top of towels in the linen cupboard. The folding cot offered by Mary remained stored in a dusty loft, Anna ignorant of its appearance, while details of the pram seen weeks earlier in Myer had faded from her consciousness. The purchase of other equipment, such as a baby bath and change table, had been postponed due to lack of space rather than cost. The kitchen sink and bed would be utilised for bathing and changing until they moved into the new house.

Anna had no difficulty envisaging the house's progress and looked forward to the weekend, when Joseph had promised to take her to the building site. The front steps and veranda had been installed during her hospital visit and at last she would be able to examine every detail of upstairs, rather than rely on Joseph's observations. Particulars of timber thickness, plumbing and electrical wiring held no interest for her. She wanted to stand in the various rooms and plan the placement of future furniture, carpet and curtains. There were still four weeks and four days to get through until she could drive. There would be no restrictions then on visits to the site, even if she had to park outside in the street for a few minutes until the builders had left for the day. In Brisbane, the working day for tradesmen, according to Joseph, began at seven in the morning and ended just after three, so there would be plenty of time to look around before she had to prepare and cook the evening meal.

Content with her future plans, she sat on the sofa dreaming of her new Australian home, clutching a duster employed earlier in an attempt to ward off boredom. Wooden houses perched on stumps of varying heights had looked so alien when she had driven through the suburbs with Roger on that first day; now, though, they were a natural part of her environment. The open plan design and large windows in contemporary suburban properties enabled light and air to fill the rooms. She would not feel hemmed in as she had in England, where doors were always closed to retain the heat and windows opened just a fraction, whatever the outside temperature. Her youngest sister had been an absolute pain before and after meals, almost slamming the dining room door in their mother's face to avoid draughts from the unheated hall.

She shivered at the thought of an English winter, layer upon layer of thick clothing, an umbrella a constant companion. Waking to frost patterns on the inside of the bedroom window; bringing in washing snap-frozen on the line. Another world, a place she thought of only when reading pale-blue aerogrammes, or glancing at the calendar sent at Christmas by a cousin "to remind you of the English countryside". She didn't need reminding. She had no desire to reminisce about muddy country lanes or picnics spoilt by cold summer showers. Present and future were all that mattered; a vibrant life filled with brilliant sunshine, wild tropical storms and a people bursting with optimism.

How she loved the heightened exuberance of the Australian environment, the emphasis on generous dimensions embodied by names like the Great Barrier Reef. The preference for substantial size extended to the creation of tourist attractions, witness the Big Pineapple that had opened on the Sunshine Coast only days earlier. Did the hillside farm produce the biggest pineapples in the world, or was the TV news presenter referring to the enormous ice-cream sundaes served in the adjoining café? It didn't seem to matter so long as the items on show were larger than normal, the sign in a local shop proclaiming

Brisbane's biggest cauliflowers. She recalled the huge leg of lamb she had purchased soon after moving into the flat, the standard portions she'd served occasioning numerous similar dinners, plus sandwiches for lunch. Not that she had repeated the exercise. She'd had no need to, as Joseph had adopted the Australian penchant for large helpings of meat within weeks of that legendary roast. After sampling many a steak at the Breakfast Creek pub, nowadays he felt hard done by if the home-cooked variety didn't stretch from one side of the plate to the other.

Reminded of the need to prepare dinner, Anna rose from the sofa – a noun adopted in place of both the English "settee" and Australian "lounge" – and walked slowly into the kitchen, trying to stand ramrod straight as directed by nursing staff to ensure correct wound healing. Other rules, she obeyed almost without thinking, leaving the bed un-made and the Hoover unused. She had also ignored the overflowing laundry basket; Joseph could carry it downstairs later and load its con-tents into the twin-tub.

Sizzling steak and boiling vegetables masked the sound of his ar-rival, so Joseph's loud greeting caught her unawares. 'Hi there,' she answered, thankful she'd had the presence of mind to avoid twisting around.

'Good day?' He hurried across the lounge into the kitchen and dropped a kiss on the back of her neck.

'Yes. I managed a bit of dusting and a lot of daydreaming about the new house.' She turned slowly, disguised a wince behind her smile.

'I'm so pleased. I was worried about leaving you alone. I thought you might feel a bit depressed.'

'No way. It's fine now I'm home. Everything's back to normal.'

'How can you say that when Adam remains in hospital?'

Shit, she'd forgotten about the baby! 'He's in safe hands,' she replied, adopting a serious expression. 'No point in fretting about the situa-tion.'

'I guess that's the right attitude.'

'Would you prefer it if I sat here crying all day?'

'No, of course not. It's just... well, I thought you might be missing him.'

How can I miss what I've never had? 'I'd rather not dwell on that,' she said aloud and turned back to the stove.

The rest of the evening passed without incident, their conversation light-hearted with no further mention of their absent baby. Sleepy but no longer exhausted, Anna prepared for bed with high hopes for a similar tomorrow. The pain from her wound was diminishing with each passing day. Before long, she would be able to bend and stretch as usual. She had forgotten about the washing, but that didn't matter, Joseph could carry the laundry hamper downstairs in the morning. If she took care to lift only a few items at a time, there was no reason why she couldn't load and unload the machine. Shirts could be put on hangers and hung on the garage washing line, no stretching needed down there, while underwear could be pegged on the small folding airer kept in the laundry. Satisfied with what seemed a sensible solution, she slipped under the covers and closed her eyes.

She'd almost succumbed to sleep when Joseph announced he had telephoned the hospital that afternoon to arrange visits to the Premmie nursery. Fortunately, her immediate reaction, 'Why waste time and energy visiting a baby who has no notion of our presence?' remained unspoken. 'What did they say?'

'Twice a week is fine, so tomorrow I'll leave work early and come home and pick you up.'

Anna thought of the casserole she'd planned, slow cooking to complement a slow-moving day. 'I could catch the bus and meet you there.'

'That's not an option, silly girl.'

'Why not? It's only a short walk to the bus stop.'

'Do I have to spell it out?'

She pouted. 'I am not an invalid.'

'I didn't say you were.' He turned away from her, his back a barrier to conflict resolution.

'Sorry, I didn't mean to snap,' she said, after a lengthy silence. 'It's just...' She couldn't complete the sentence, at least not in the way he expected. It would be easy to blame her hormones – they were supposed to wreak havoc after giving birth – but in truth, she just wanted to resume normal life as soon as possible and catch a bus without asking permission.

'No need to explain, I understand.' He rolled over and stroked her cheek.

* * *

Next day, arm in arm, they stood outside the Premmie nursery, peering through the glass at their slumbering baby. Newly released from the confines of a humidicrib, Baby Fletcher lay on his back in a plastic box perched on a wheeled metal stand that, to Anna, resembled her laundry trolley. Wrapped in a white blanket with his black hair and elf-ears hidden from view, he looked like one of the dolls Anna had played with as a small child, hard plastic mass-produced in a factory.

'I wish he'd open his eyes,' Joseph said. 'He doesn't look real.'

Her mind focused on childhood, Anna almost replied that the eyes open only when the baby doll is held upright. 'I don't even know what colour they are,' she said instead. 'He's been asleep every time I've visited.'

'They're probably blue.'

'How did you work that out?'

'I read somewhere that all babies have blue eyes at first. They change after a few weeks, apparently.'

'Can't say I've heard that one.'

Joseph released her arm and looked beyond the plastic cots and humidicribs to the closed door at the rear of the nursery. 'No sign of that nurse. How about tapping on the glass to see if we can rouse him?'

Anna turned slightly to glance up and down the corridor. 'Go on then, I dare you.'

His fingers tapped the thick glass. Several babies stirred. 'We have movement,' Joseph whispered, as though a nurse was standing behind him.

'Wrong ones. Ours hasn't budged.' A mischievous grin spread over Anna's face. 'Let's both try.'

Eight fingers proved successful; eyelids fluttered, a pink mouth opened.

'Oh shit, he's going to start crying.' Joseph stepped back from the window. 'That'll bring the nurse running.'

But Baby Fletcher remained quiet, oblivious to the cacophony behind him, his only concern the pursing and relaxing of his tiny lips.

'We should leave.' Anna tugged Joseph's arm.

'No. I've had enough of inhumane hospital rules. I'm going to ask the nurse on duty to bring Adam out to us.'

As if on cue, the rear nursery door opened to admit a stern-faced nurse.

'Oh no,' Anna cried, 'it's Triple B!'

Joseph grinned and, heading for the door to the right of the window, made a fist with his right hand. His loud knocking evoked an Olympic-style sprint. After opening the door a fraction, Nurse Bevan spat a reprimand.

Joseph paid no attention to her words. 'Good evening, Nurse. I'm Adam Fletcher's father.'

Nurse Bevan frowned. 'Adam?'

Joseph pointed to the cot closest to the window. 'Adam was born nearly two weeks ago but my wife and I still haven't held him. I would like you to wheel him out to us now.'

'And I would like you to leave immediately, otherwise I shall call security.'

Joseph stood firm. 'Five minutes is all I ask.'

'Certainly not, Mr Fletcher.' Still frowning, Nurse Bevan looked over at Anna, who was cowering nearby. 'Your wife will be able to hold the baby when she comes in for a trial feed next week. Tell her to ring and make an appointment.'

The door closed in Joseph's face.

Trials and Other Tribulations

'Failed, Mrs Fletcher. Come back in two days.'

Alone in the flat, the pronouncement made by a dour middle-aged nurse, returned to haunt Anna hour after hour, a perpetual reminder of her continued incompetence. Her one mistake had been crossing the black line drawn on a tiny bottle. There was no possibility of remaining in the room adjacent to the nursery for another three hours to try again. But how could she have known Adam would guzzle the formula so fast, and why fill the bottle if he was only supposed to drink a certain amount?

The feeding instructions had been delivered in a no-nonsense tone by a nurse so stout, she could have balanced even full-term babies on her shelf-like bosom. 'At home, warm the formula to room temperature and check the temperature by dripping several drops onto the inside of your wrist. Give small amounts every three hours. Burp frequently – we can't have baby uncomfortable with wind in his tummy. Change the nappy after the feed, then pop baby straight back into the bassinet. Remember, premmies need plenty of cot rest.'

Bottle had followed baby in such quick succession, Anna had had little opportunity to savour the first moment of contact. She'd hoped to loosen the blanket, examine the tiny fingers, stroke the downy cheeks. Instead, in her attempt to hold Adam as directed, she had almost dropped the bottle, provoking a sharp reprimand. Then, with the nurse looming over her, blocking the light from a nearby window,

Anna had failed to disguise her shaking hand and might have missed her baby's mouth altogether had it not been wide open in readiness.

A nappy-changing lesson had followed the trial feed. Anna had been so nervous that she'd feared stabbing Adam's abdomen with the enormous pin. At least she'd had a chance to view his lower half, although his swollen testicles came as a shock. Too afraid to ask the nurse if this was normal, she had decided to mention it to Mary on the journey home.

As usual, Mary had supplied a reassuring response, but Anna's spirits remained low, despite her friend's subsequent attempts at light-hearted conversation and an offer to detour via the building site. Apart from brooding on the feeding failure, Anna had been preoccupied by the presence of a wicker bassinet on the back seat and kept glancing over her shoulder as though Adam would suddenly materialise. Roger had discovered the old bassinet when climbing into the loft to retrieve the portable cot and suggested to Mary that, cleaned up, it would serve Anna well for a few months.

* * *

Anna had been delighted with the unexpected gift and effusive in her praise of Mary's handiwork – a new white cotton lining and pale blue sheets – but the following day, her feelings oscillated between pleasure and pain as she tried to fill the empty hours between Joseph's departure and return. The bassinet, tucked into the small space between the linen cupboard and the kitchen's rear wall, resembled an item in a shop window labelled: *For display purposes only, please do not touch.* In the bedroom, a further reminder of her indeterminate state lay propped on the pillows. Sam and Shirley had brought the soft toy into the hospital, labelling it a substitute baby, much to neighbour Ellen's amusement. Anna knew they meant well, but a large orange dog wearing tartan trousers and waistcoat seemed an odd choice of gift.

Other presents remained piled on the dressing table: a small blue teddy bear, a yet-to-be-assembled mobile to hang above cot or bassinet, a lacy shawl, baby clothes. Gifts from England still languished mid-ocean, their arrival timed for September, although numerous cards had been received via air-mail. Out of a sense of duty, Anna read every one of the sickly-sweet sentiments espoused by greeting-card manufacturers but had no desire to repeat the exercise, so she quickly added the latest arrivals to the collection arranged on bookcase and television unit.

Flowers evoked a different response and were admired whenever she entered the kitchen or living room. The bouquet purchased by Joseph from a vendor standing outside the hospital walls was the first to expire, Anna experiencing a wave of sadness as she swept fallen petals from the kitchen table. Doomed, once cut, to a brief existence, the brittle stems and faded flowers reminded her of dreams cast aside only seven months into her first antipodean year. The promise of Australia remained – no bare winter limbs on the trees planted either side of the street or in neighbouring gardens, no leaves crunching underfoot – yet she struggled to envisage a new season's turning, focusing instead on past blooming, brilliant but transitory. She thought of the red folder buried beneath winter clothing, untouched since late summer; there were no additions to swell her small collection of poems, no inspiration.

Submerged in self-pity, she had abandoned the written word, supposing her present and immediate future unworthy of creative effort. Then she had a change of heart. Why hadn't she made use of the poetic form to express frustration, anger, disgust? Powerful emotions teamed with potent language could have produced more creditable work, worth sharing. A woman railing against the body that had betrayed her might be viewed as repugnant or even unbalanced, but her bold candour could appeal to others in the same situation. Goaded into action, Anna abandoned dustpan and brush and headed for the bedroom, averting her eyes from the empty bassinet as she passed by.

* * *

Sweaters spilled from a dressing table drawer; a scarlet cardigan lay in a heap on the bland vinyl tiles. Propped against all four pillows, her thin legs bent at the knee, Anna opened the red folder and began to read. Language spoke to her, drew her deep as she read about her first vision, her first rejoicing, her impassioned responses to a chosen land. Once more, she experienced the exquisite ardour of new-found love, danced across gleaming white sand, plunged into sparkling turquoise water, gazed with awe at a black velvet sky studded with innumerable diamond stars. 'With my body I thee worship,' she murmured, thinking not of wedding vows repeated in a rarely-visited church, but unexplored territory waiting for her caress.

A stabbing pain pierced her abdomen; she winced and shifted her position, trying to ignore her continuing discomfort. A second twinge caught her unawares and it took her several moments to realise a corner of the folder was sticking into her still tender scar. Distraught, she threw the offending item at the wall and watched it fall to the floor, leaving behind a thin red line. It was too late to retrieve her lost emotions and transform them into meaningful language. The angry young woman had metamorphosed into an incompetent, timorous mother once more. Turning away from the scarred wall, Anna reached for the orange and tartan dog and held it tight as she dissolved into a blubbering mess.

* * *

She woke to the sound of noisy myna birds squabbling in the flowering bottle brush outside the window and recalled her mother calling for an end to sibling conflict. A strong, no-nonsense woman, confident in her ability to discharge the role that fate, or God, to use her mother's preferred language, had assigned, her mother had never complained, automatically putting her husband and children first as women had done since time immemorial. As a teenager, Anna had embraced a different ideology, as obedience to an unseen deity was regarded as old-fashioned and irrelevant in a Swinging Sixties world. Cutting the apron strings had been a priority, as Anna was determined to become an independent woman making her own decisions. Marriage had been entered into as a union of equals, division of household labour along gender lines being thought of as unnecessary and unacceptable. That is, until a woman-only venture had taught her otherwise.

Lying on her bed in the middle of the day with a stuffed toy in her arms, twenty-three-year-old Anna was forced to acknowledge a yearning for maternal guidance. Having her mother close by would make a difference, or at the very least restore balance to her topsy-turvy mind. The decision to emigrate had been easy and was in no way regretted, but motherly hugs would be most welcome. If only she could pick up the phone and have an unhurried conversation! But with calls to England costing one dollar a minute and no telephone in the flat, the prospect seemed remote. She hadn't spoken to her mother since Christmas – Joseph had relayed the news of Adam's early arrival from Mary and Roger's house – and she longed to hear the familiar voice, be reassured instead of reprimanded, share a laugh if the moment arose.

* * *

Light faded as the afternoon drew to a close, bringing a chill to suburban homes designed for nine months of summer temperatures, rather than three cooler months given the misnomer of winter. Inside the neighbouring house – old weatherboards with tongue and groove timber interior walls – the elderly residents donned nightwear, dressing-gowns and slippers following their customary five o'clock showers, closed the curtains and settled down to an early tea, grateful for the warmth of an oven.

The blinds in one of the cavity-brick flats opposite remained open, the occupant being absorbed in a task begun hours earlier that showed no imminent sign of completion. Sitting at the kitchen table, Anna wrote out her heart on a pad of flimsy paper. The lengthy narrative, if not a cure-all for troubled times, was at least providing a sense of, in her mother's words, 'relief at getting things off your chest.' Buried beneath several other completed pages, the initial effort began with a deliberately curtailed greeting which Anna believed was essential, given the subject matter that followed. It was a letter for a mother's eyes only; a mother who would empathise with her daughter's fears and failings. The bond between them had been loosened rather than severed, as Anna had once believed necessary. The distance between them now was a fact, not a reason for rupture.

* * *

When the letter had been delivered to the street posting box, Anna felt a lightness of being that bore little resemblance to getting things off her chest. Her confidence, battered by the overbearing nurse less than twenty-four hours earlier, returned with unexpected vigour, combined with a righteous determination to remove her son from the hospital's clutches whatever the result of a second feeding trial. Joseph, rather than Mary, would be her ally in this endeavour as Anna acknowledged, against her feminist principles, that a male presence would carry more weight with the old-fashioned nursing staff.

After dinner, she would ask him to accompany her to fetch their son. She would speak to him in a calm, considered manner rather than the weepy, irrational style she had found herself employing since the baby's birth. In control at last, she would walk into the hospital with her head held high and Adam's own clothes and baby blanket packed in a bag. She would be the model of maternal efficiency, feeding and changing as though such tasks came naturally to her, and she would be top of the class.

* * *

Top of a class of one, Anna mused as she walked through sanitised corridors the following day, carrying her sleeping baby. Beside her, Joseph still wore the expression and carriage of male dominance that he'd adopted on arrival at the Premmie nursery. Success had been assured from the moment a nurse answered Joseph's knock on the door.

'Good morning, nurse. As I explained earlier on the phone, we're here to collect our son, Adam Fletcher,' he'd announced, in a no-nonsense tone. 'Naturally, my wife will feed Adam before we leave the hospital, so please bring him and his bottle to the adjoining room without delay.'

'Of course, Mr Fletcher,' the young nurse had replied, and bustled away, no doubt eager to escape from a demanding father whose eyes seemed to bore into her skull.

On entering the 'training' room, Joseph had reacted with obvious distaste to the uninspiring space. 'When you consider how much money we pay for private health insurance, you'd think they could provide decent chairs and a picture or two on the walls to detract from the sickly-green paint. God almighty, it's worse than the NHS, my dear.'

Trying not to laugh at his assumed upper-class accent – the nurse had appeared in the doorway – Anna had nodded gravely before taking a seat.

'Here we are, Mrs Fletcher.'

Anna had taken the proffered bundle. She noted the closed eyes and, assuming her role, declared, 'He should be awake and ready for his feed by now. I believe he's still on a three-hourly schedule.'

'Yes, Mrs Fletcher. I woke him, but he went straight back to sleep. I'll just fetch the bottle.'

'Thank you, nurse.' After watching the nurse scuttle into the corridor, Anna had turned to her slumbering baby. 'Now listen here, my boy. Wake up and play your part.'

As if on cue, Adam Joseph Fletcher, just six pounds, had opened his eyes and mouth simultaneously.

The perils of Efficiency

The role of competent mother proved impossible to discard. By eight each morning, Anna had completed the bulk of her morning tasks and wondered what on earth to do until Adam woke for his next feed. Washing was up to date; nappies were pegged on the airer positioned on the veranda, clothes hung in the laundry on a second line Joseph had fixed at a lower height so she didn't have to stretch. She longed to reach the six-week post-operation date when driving and other currently forbidden activities would be permissible. Even the thought of shopping for more than a few items at a time seemed attractive, which she knew was a sad reflection on her current state.

Tethered to a small space for most of the day by a baby who slept and fed without variation, Anna failed to understand why the other new mothers whom she encountered at the nearby maternal and infant welfare clinic on Tuesday morning, complained of total exhaustion. Mary told her to be grateful for a contented baby – Judy had screamed incessantly for the first few months – but although Anna admitted she was fortunate, it didn't diminish her sense of wasted hours. There was a limit to how many books one could read, or how many biscuits and cakes one could bake. She could have reworked the poems she had written earlier in the year, or attempted new creations, but the red folder remained undisturbed in its nest of winter knitwear, her birthday present Parker pen lying unused at the back of a kitchen drawer. Boredom had smothered creativity, rendering her incapable of writing anything apart from letters to far-away family, thank-you notes for baby presents, or short shopping lists.

Sometimes, Anna thought of her friend studying librarianship in the room built under the old house opposite the flats. Shirley worked full-time as a library assistant, yet was prepared to sacrifice half the weekend and several evenings a week to achieve her career goal. A planned life with no deviations, the route marked with milestones she intended to reach in the correct order, with the full support of husband Sam. Work, study, save for a house, no thoughts of a family until she held the coveted certificate and they could provide a fully-furnished home in a good location for their offspring. Not for them a tiny house furnished with a second-hand bed, fold-up canvas chairs and a half-painted chest of drawers. Slumped on the cheap vinyl sofa, Anna felt a surge of envy electrify her limbs. 'Why, why, why?' she raged, jumping up and stamping across the tiled floor to the door.

Downstairs in the garage, she vented her frustration with the brisk strokes of a paintbrush, completing the task she had begun weeks earlier. Standing back to admire the shining paintwork, she acknowledged that jealousy was a futile emotion and dismissed her lingering regret for steps not taken while she had the opportunity. Her immediate prospects might be lacklustre, but the future could hold exciting possibilities.

* * *

By the fifth week, Anna had reached screaming point, so she abandoned the suffocating flat after the ten o'clock feed, not caring if Adam complained at being disturbed from the cot rest deemed essential for premature babies. He opened his eyes as she carried him down the steps and into the garage where the pram was stored, but made no sound other than a burp, and soon fell asleep again when tucked into warm bedding.

Late September sun shone from a cloudless sky, lifting her spirits as she walked past old weatherboard houses, noting glossy spring growth in narrow front gardens. A metal barrier marked the end of the street.

Beyond it, long grass and overgrown bushes screened any view of the creek named Kedron Brook that flowed through the northern suburbs. She was about to turn around when a large dog emerged from tangled vegetation, leapt over the barrier and crashed into the pram. Horrified, she wrenched the pram away from the stunned animal and began to run back up the street. Thank God she'd raised the pram hood to shield Adam's face from the sun, otherwise the dog would have landed on top of him.

Halfway up the street, she became aware of shouting but resisted the urge to glance over her shoulder. Footsteps alerted her to an imminent arrival. In panic, she sped up, ignoring the pain in her newly-healed abdomen, the ache of untoned muscles.

'Hey, missus! I want a word,' a man's voice yelled.

Anna heard heavy breathing not far behind her. Maternal fury prompted a sprint into the nearest garden. Leaning over the pram, she grabbed her baby and held him close as she powered up wooden steps to a wide veranda.

'Stop, or I'll set the bloody dog on youse.'

Loud barking erupted as she hammered on the door.

No one answered.

She tensed, waiting for jaws to snap. Adam began to cry, his tiny body shuddering against her chest. His cries became screams as rough hands grabbed her shoulders and twisted her around.

'Youse deaf, or what?' The man removed his hands and stepped back.

Determined to appear unfazed, she stared at the red-faced stranger and noted a bristled chin and matted shoulder-length hair. 'Your dog is upsetting my baby,' she declared, lowering her gaze to the enormous stomach brimming over skimpy shorts like ice-cream over the rim of a cone. 'Would you mind shutting it up?'

'Course I bloody mind. He's more than upset, missus, he's hurt. You should look where you're going with that bloody pram.'

Anna raised her head. 'I'm sorry he's hurt but he almost overturned my pram. You should keep him on a lead.'

'Don't you tell me what to do!' Red cheeks blazed. 'Keep your distance in future, you bloody toffee-nosed Pom!' And with a shake of his stomach, he shuffled over to the steps. 'Come over here, taking our jobs and buying up our land. Go back to where you come from, missus, we don't need your sort 'ere.' Grabbing the rail, he descended slowly, the dog running ahead.

Shaken, Anna watched until he turned into the last house on the right-hand side before making a move. After retrieving the pram, she continued to hold Adam, his screaming now reduced to a whimper, and headed for home.

On both sides of the street, front doors began to open and residents, mostly older females, stepped onto verandas, eager to exchange comments on the fracas, a rare event in the quiet street. Head bent, Anna passed by unnoticed, hearing only the tail-end of conversations called from house to house. By piecing fragments together, she deduced that the dog owner answered to the name of Bruce and was a perpetual drunk, best avoided. As she turned into the flats' driveway, she made a mental note to turn right on future walks. Better still, she would wait a few days, then put the pram in Viv's boot and drive to a park or the seafront.

* * *

Although unnerved by the encounter with the dog and his owner, she tried to make light of it when relating the details to Joseph, lest he rush down the road to confront Bruce the Bully. 'Leave well alone,' she advised, when he suggested phoning the police. 'Only a few more weeks and we'll be out of here.'

'That doesn't mean we should ignore what happened. Chasing you up a flight of steps and shouting at you is harassment, Anna.'

'I know, but I don't want to make a fuss.'

'All right, no police, but I'm going to warn Sam and Trev about him. We wouldn't want Shirl or Vi harassed.'

'No,' she murmured, and almost laughed as an image of petite but feisty Shirley kicking Bruce in the balls filled her mind. 'We must invite them all to dinner before we leave,' she added, wanting to change the subject.

'Are you sure you can manage it, with Adam to care for?'

'With your help,' she answered, preferring a tactful response. At present, any distraction would be welcome, but telling Joseph that motherhood bored her to tears might provoke an argument, which was something she could do without after a stressful morning.

* * *

Freedom Day dawned dull, drizzle threatening to spoil the planned picnic. Undaunted, Anna flew through her early morning tasks, her only regret being the need to hang washed nappies indoors rather than on the Hill's Hoist. She had looked forward to seeing them spin around in the sun, brilliant white squares testimony to enduring maternal competence. The resumption of normal activities meant she could forget the tedious months of pregnancy and its unexpected aftermath, and focus on the positive. Her body had already reverted to its usual shape: flat stomach, rounded hips and decent-sized breasts. The 34-22-35 measurements taken that morning following her shower were reassuring. Standing in front of the bathroom mirror, tape measure in hand, she had managed to ignore the evidence of the emergency surgery – an untidy job according to the gynaecologist she'd visited the previous week for a check-up – and smiled instead at the overall picture.

Dressed for the outing in a favourite pair of soft cotton trousers, red-checked shirt and red sandals, she paused in front of the bassinet and, noting the wide-open eyes, asked, 'So what do you think, my boy?'

Tiny arms emerged from beneath the blanket and a milk bubble arose from pursed pink lips.

'I'm glad you approve.' She scooped him up and held him level with her face. 'Right, off we go. Everything else is already in the car, I just need you.' She returned him to the bassinet, lifted it from the stand and headed for the door.

* * *

Huddled on a wooden bench in a corner of the bayside shelter, Anna felt foolish but decided she might as well eat the food she had prepared earlier, rather than take it home. Beside her, oblivious to weather patterns – the drizzle had turned to light rain since her arrival – Adam slept on, snug in his blankets. 'Not much company, are you?' she said, wishing she'd called on Mary instead of pursuing her original goal.

Sandgate foreshore failed to inspire at low tide on a rainy day, grey mud and grey sky melding to become a drab blanket that quickly smothered her earlier bright spirits. 'Mudgate,' she muttered, peering at the exposed seabed, its rippled surface broken by clumps of black mangrove roots. Even the seagulls appeared lulled into a somnolent state, standing on the mud staring at the distant sea, rather than checking out the sandwiches arranged on a plastic plate in front of her. She didn't blame them; cheese and lettuce were hardly gourmet fare. Washed down with lemon cordial – she hadn't wanted to waste time earlier making a flask of tea – the first of the sandwiches sat in her stomach like a lump of lead. Sighing, she carried her plate over to the rubbish bin and tipped the contents inside.

A walk along the foreshore path had been part of her plan, but that idea was abandoned now as she packed up belongings and returned to the car which was parked nearby. Leaning over the back seat to secure the bassinet, she felt cold rain penetrate her thin cotton shirt and sandals, unsuitable wear for a showery day. Why on earth had she been so inflexible? The picnic could have been postponed. Bad weather in Brisbane rarely lasted long. Tomorrow and the next day and the next stretched out before her, blank squares on a calendar awaiting annotation. No one cared whether she went for a picnic, read a book, or spent the day staring into space like a seagull marooned by the tide. Weekdays, once filled to the brim with workplace activities, had become hours to be endured until Joseph came home. No wonder she had clutched at the prospect of leaving the flat for a few hours. She had never felt so lonely, so invisible.

Driving away from the foreshore, she decided to visit the building site on the way home, a detour certain to improve her mood. The house had reached what Joseph called "lock-up stage", meaning only the relevant tradesmen had internal access, so she hoped someone would be present and accede to her request for a quick peek. Halfway down Sandgate Road, Adam began to cry, and a glance at her watch revealed it was way past his lunchtime.

'Hang in there, my boy,' she called, hoping the sound of her voice would deflect his attention from hunger pangs. 'I can't stop on the main road. Just one more set of traffic lights and I can turn right into our street, park on the grass verge and get out your bottle.'

The crying stopped, as though he had understood every word.

'Good boy,' she said, relieved her strategy had worked. 'Won't be long now.' Before changing lanes, she glanced in the mirror, then, looking over her shoulder, caught a glimpse of tiny fingers pushing through the net covering the bassinet. 'Yes, I know you don't like that net, but it's a necessary safety measure in case I have to brake hard. Bouncing up and hitting the roof wouldn't be good for you.'

He answered with a gurgle, followed by a hiccup.

'You can have a proper baby seat soon,' she added, as the car sailed across the intersection seconds before the light turned red.

There was no response save a sucking sound, perhaps a hint to accelerate.

'No speeding at this point,' she advised. 'I'm preparing to turn.' Amused by the persistent monologue, she thought of the mothers she met at the Maternal and Baby clinic, young women who appeared incapable of addressing their infants in a normal voice. Anna couldn't abide baby-talk. No way would she revert to juvenile vocabulary, or bill and coo like a dove engaged in a mating ritual. Such behaviour would be an affront to both Adam's intelligence and hers. He would be taught to speak clearly and correctly, as she had been; no "bow-wow" or "piggy-wiggy" for her little man.

A decade later, an embarrassing incident in a restaurant would cause Anna to question her insistence on correct terminology, at least momentarily. The conversation went something like this:

Adam: 'Mum, guess what I saw in a magazine at Auntie Joan and Uncle David's house?'

Anna: 'I've no idea. Why don't you tell me?'

Adam: 'I saw a lady's pubic hair and her vagina.'

Stunned silence. Other diners turn to stare at the child.

Anna: 'We'll talk about it later. Eat your dinner now, love.'

Joseph (under his breath): 'What the hell was David thinking, leaving a magazine like that lying around? I'm going to have words with him.'

* * *

Parked on the wide strip of grass opposite the old house that occupied the front of the divided block, Anna was sitting in the passenger seat, Adam in her arms sucking greedily, when an elderly woman approached the car and rapped on the window. Lowering the window, Anna said politely, 'Good afternoon. Hope I haven't parked in the wrong place?'

'What do you think you're doing?' the woman replied, her lower lip curled in disgust.

'Feeding my baby.'

'I can see that. But in the street?'

'It's bottle, not breast.'

The woman recoiled at the last word, covering her mouth with a gloved hand.

'He won't take long,' Anna continued, bemused by the woman's reaction but determined to keep a straight face. 'I'll move the car then, if it's in your way.'

The gloved hand shifted to a wrinkled cheek. 'I don't drive.'

Anna nodded, silenced for a moment by the thought that the woman could be her new neighbour. 'Do you live near here?'

'Top of the street.'

Anna smiled. 'Then we'll be near neighbours soon.'

'Near neighbours? No one's selling but.'

'But what?' Anna said, looking down at Adam to hide a mischievous grin.

'I said no one's selling round here.'

'Sold, not selling.' Anna looked up. 'See the new house down the easement? 'We'll be moving in soon.'

'Silly idea, putting a house in a backyard.'

'Seems sensible to me,' Anna countered, irritated by the woman's tone. 'Saves a great deal of gardening.'

'I couldn't agree more,' a second woman called, from somewhere behind the car. 'Better than working yourself into the grave trying to keep up a big yard. Me an' Ted got better things to do with our time these days, Miss Jones.'

Anna looked in the wing mirror and saw a plump elderly woman stomping over the footpath towards the thin spinster. Ignoring Miss Jones, the woman bent towards the open car window. 'Well, who have we here?'

'Anna and Adam Fletcher,' Anna replied, reluctant to mention the imminent move.

Smiles creased a rosy face as the woman bent to gaze at Adam. 'What a beautiful baby. What brings you to our neighbourhood?'

'I've come to see how our new house is coming along. We hope to move in soon.'

'Well I never!' The mass of white curls quivered in excitement. 'I'm Mrs Wootton. Me 'an Ted live opposite.' She pointed to the old wooden house sitting smug behind its brand-new fence. 'Welcome to Harrow Street, dear.'

'Thank you, Mrs Wootton.'

'Oh, you can call me Nell, dear. No need to stand on ceremony when we're going to be such close neighbours.'

Anna smiled. 'Pleased to meet you, Nell. I can't wait to move. There's not much room in our flat now that Adam's arrived.'

'Not much room in a car to feed a baby, either. Why don't you come inside with me and have a cuppa before looking at the house?'

'Thank you so much, I'd like that.'

Harrow Street

Prior to the Fletchers' arrival, Ted Wootton had grown a selection of plants in pots from cuttings to assist in the regeneration of land he had nurtured for decades. A backhoe had of necessity ripped up the lawn to prepare the site, but numerous tradesmen had shown little regard for the environment, throwing off-cuts of timber framing and plasterboard on top of shrubs and crushing smaller plants with their heavy work boots.

On moving day, Anna was appalled to discover their new home still resembled a building site. She had imagined that the rubbish would be removed and the earth levelled, at the very least. Picking her way over ridges of sun-dried soil, trying to avoid the sharp edges of abandoned roof iron and the odd puddle, she almost cried at the thought of negotiating such a degraded landscape with a pram. The sight of freshly painted steps lightened her spirits, until she reached the veranda and realised that mud from her shoes had sullied their surfaces. She would have to wear her wellington boots until a concrete path or grass had been laid. Perhaps her father had had a premonition when he insisted she pack the pair she had worn for years on winter walks through sodden woods.

Despite her protestations, Joseph insisted on carrying her over the threshold and deposited her in the centre of the empty living room, following a lengthy embrace. 'Our first real home!' he exclaimed, grabbing her hands to twirl her around. 'No more landlords with their petty rules. Here, we can do as we please. Hang pictures on the walls, repaint walls if we don't like the colour.'

Releasing her hands, he rushed over to the French doors that were permanently locked because they led nowhere. 'Our own piece of Australia! I'll soon knock the garden into shape and get a few mates to help me build a back veranda and steps.' He turned to face her. 'Come on, let's explore the rest of the place.'

Her muddied shoes had been abandoned on the veranda and sawdust from the unsealed floorboards had stuck to the soles of her bare feet, but, enlivened by Joseph's optimism, she ignored it and padded after him on an inspection of the rest of the house. There had been no spare money for carpets, or even the shiny polyurethane surface known as Estapol that was popular in many new Brisbane homes; apart from bathroom and toilet tiles, every floor comprised raw hardwood boards.

The blue carpet square they'd purchased months earlier to introduce a little colour into the flat's bland living room, soon embellished the lounge area and, together with the TV unit plus the two folding chairs, made the space seem more like a home than an unfinished house. The new fridge, positioned against the wall separating kitchen from living room, dominated the small space, its pristine white surfaces gleaming in the sunlight pouring through the uncurtained window.

Delighted with her new kitchen, Anna rushed around opening cupboard doors, admiring the spacious pantry, glossy benches and shiny stainless-steel sink. 'At last I can unpack all our wedding presents!' she declared, gesturing towards what seemed like unlimited storage space.

Puzzled, Joseph scratched his unshaven chin. 'I thought we'd done that months ago.'

'Have you forgotten the cardboard boxes we stored in the laundry?'

'Never took much notice of what was in there. Just used the tub to wash my hands when I'd been working on the car.'

'And didn't clean the tub afterward. Typical man! Why can't you...?'

He silenced her with another lingering kiss, then led her down the hallway to re-inspect the main bedroom, now furnished with the second-hand, old-fashioned double bed. Still in its plastic wrapping, the new mattress lay on top of the heavy wooden base that had triggered a torrent of curses from two burly removalists as they endeavoured to manoeuvre it down the narrow hallway. The grumpy men had departed in a flurry of earth and dust, van tyres slipping on the churned-up easement that one day would be levelled and strips of concrete laid to create a driveway.

'We can use cardboard boxes covered with small tablecloths for bed-side tables,' Anna declared, after surveying the room. 'And a sheet pinned to the window-frame will do for a curtain.'

'Plenty of time to worry about details,' Joseph countered, falling back on the mattress. 'It's comfortable. Come and try it.'

'Shouldn't we take the plastic off?'

'Later. We don't want to mess it up before we've even slept on it.'

Anna giggled, not at the prospect of making love on slippery plastic, but because she recalled her mother's request, made with obvious embarrassment, a week before their ship sailed from Southampton. After packing their few belongings in crates to be collected by a lorry and driven to the docks, she and Joseph had moved in with her parents for their final weeks in England. One afternoon, while helping to fold clean laundry in the kitchen, Anna had been handed a small towel. In response to her puzzled look, her mother had explained that certain stains were difficult to remove from sheets. Mischief had bubbled in Anna's throat. She wanted to shout the word "semen", hear it bounce around the walls. Instead, unwilling to cause further discomfort to her mother, she'd muttered apologies and, rushing upstairs with the towel, had flung herself on the twin beds Joseph had tied together with string on their first night. Pillows had muffled her unrestrained giggles.

* * *

In subsequent days, emptying boxes, lining cupboard shelves with paper before arranging belongings, plus dealing with a new baby, kept boredom at bay. At last, Anna sensed a return to her old self, the exuberant young woman who was delighted with her adopted country and determined to succeed in her role as a New Australian. Physical activity toned her body and sunlight tanned her exposed skin as she hung out washing on the new Hill's Hoist positioned in the centre of what remained of the back lawn, or watered the pot plants Ted had handed over the fence dividing the two properties. She planned to create gardens beds once the indoor tasks had been completed and would seek Ted's advice on where to plant. Sun or shade seemed the only alternatives, but, unaccustomed to both gardening and a sub-tropical climate, Anna had no idea how to organise the garden.

A few months after moving into the house built in what Ted Wootton referred to as 'my old backyard,' Anna abandoned the English word 'garden' in favour of the Australian vernacular "yard", even though she disliked the term. The colourful displays of flowering shrubs and neat lawns surrounding the old house and the embryonic plants growing in freshly turned soil around the new dwelling, bore no resemblance to the untidy stacks of timber and bricks stored behind builders' premises, or the heaps of coal filling a coal merchant's yard.

Rather than a further attempt to assimilate, Anna's choice of vocabulary reflected her appreciation of the elderly couple who had gone out of their way to help them settle in. Nell had taken care of Adam while they unpacked. She had provided numerous casseroles and homemade cakes during their first weeks and offered to teach Anna how to make curtains, while Ted, energetic despite his seventy-five years, had helped Joseph clear up the builder's detritus.

* * *

As her baby grew from sleepy newborn to lively four-month-old, Anna spent extended hours outdoors, planting, weeding and watering. When he wasn't asleep upstairs, Adam wriggled and gurgled on a bunny rug, shade from the beach umbrella protecting his delicate skin from harsh summer sun. Clad in nothing but a nappy and a Bond's cotton singlet, he learnt to roll over, grasp toys and pluck fistfuls of grass, which he crammed into his mouth, chewed, then spat out. Fresh air and constant movement ensured he continued to sleep well, rarely waking at night after the age of four months. Apart from a short period during the evening, he remained a contented baby – Anna flatly refused to adopt the Australian nouns "bub", "bubby" or "bubba" – but cuddles from Joseph usually helped restore his equilibrium.

However, despite a good appetite, Adam remained underweight and small for his age, factors that had the Maternal and Child Health nurses tut-tutting whenever Anna took him to the clinic. Plump babies were greeted with purrs of approval, their round cheeks admired, the rolls of fat on arms and legs gently squeezed. Smug satisfaction spread like a rash over some mothers' faces, while others cast pitying glances at Anna's thin offspring when they thought she wasn't looking. Undeterred, Adam continued to smile and laugh at all present, pumping his skinny limbs as though training for a marathon.

'What a happy little guy,' a mother remarked one morning, as she attempted to sooth her fractious heavyweight. 'Is he always like that?'

Anna beamed. 'Oh yes. He rarely cries.'

'Half your luck. Mine whinges more often than not.' She frowned at the baby grizzling in her arms. 'Why can't you smile like him, Gregory?'

Grumpy Gregory let out a howl.

'See what I mean.'

Anna nodded but remained silent, reluctant to offer advice. No wonder the baby looked miserable. Anyone would, if constantly greeted with a grim expression. A smile could work wonders; babies loved to mimic. How she'd laughed the previous night when Adam had copied Joseph, smacking his lips as though he, too, had just taken a satisfying swig of cold beer.

'Mrs Fletcher!' the nurse called, preventing further contemplation.

'Time for the weigh-in, my boy,' Anna announced, lifting Adam to his favourite position, with his head bobbing over her shoulder. She rose quickly and tossed Grumpy Gregory a brilliant smile. As she walked over to the nurse, she felt certain that gurgles were replacing grizzles.

Following the weigh-in, conducted with the usual comments on below average weight gain, the nurse suggested introducing solids. 'But make sure you dilute the infant cereal more than the packet instructions advise, as he's rather young. And only a few teaspoons to start with.'

'Yes, nurse,' Anna answered obediently.

Still lying on the scales, Adam began to wave his arms around and opened his mouth wide as though delighted at the prospect of a more varied diet.

'Oh, who's a happy bub!' the nurse exclaimed, lifting him out and handing him over. 'Well, Mrs Fletcher, you must be doing something right. He's a contented little soul.'

'He takes after his father,' Anna replied, and couldn't help adding, 'he looks like him, too, skinny as a rake no matter how much he eats.'

Solids were accepted with enthusiasm, Adam swallowing each spoonful with glee. In quick succession, three teaspoons become four, then five. The thin substance called to mind the watery gruel described in Dickens' novels, standard fare for abandoned or orphaned children forced to endure the rigors of a Victorian orphanage. *No wonder Oliver asked for more,* Anna thought, as she spooned cereal into Adam's mouth.

* * *

Weeks passed and both front and rear garden began to take shape. Viv the Viva glided along smooth concrete strips on her journey to the road, with its broad grass verges and narrow bitumen centre. Joseph had hired a concrete mixer and, with Roger's help, managed to complete both strips in a weekend. Inside the house, polished floors gleamed in strong December sunlight and the view from the French doors now encompassed the bare bones of a balcony, due to be completed when Joseph took holidays after Christmas.

Bright curtains now adorned all three bedrooms. The cheap but cheerful fabric had been purchased at a local shop and sewn by Nell, Anna having been afraid to use her neighbour's ancient Singer in case her ineptitude damaged it. As a token of gratitude, she took Nell out for the day, driving her to the bayside suburb of Sandgate, where they lunched on fish and chips and, following a walk beside sparkling water – high tide on this occasion – had afternoon tea in a tiny café wedged between a department store and a florist. The purchase of a large bunch of flowers completed the day's events, Nell protesting that Anna had spent too much but obviously delighted with the gift.

Although the house remained sparsely furnished, Anna felt content with their progress so far. Only one room bothered her – the tiny third bedroom, now equipped with an old wooden desk and chair found abandoned in the street. Designated a study by Joseph, the room had yet to see any evidence of creative activity other than letters written to parents, sisters and aunt while sitting gingerly on the rickety chair. On the odd occasion Joseph answered his mother's letters – usually Anna was left with the task – he perched on one of the yellow stools at the breakfast bar, an incorrect label given that all meals were eaten there in the absence of a dining table and chairs.

Anna refused to eat dinner from a tray in front of the television, having been taught from an early age that consuming meals in this manner was permissible only when sick. 'To do otherwise is uncivilised,' her mother had maintained. 'It is a behaviour pattern observed in council houses, not in the homes of the well-mannered middle class.' Wisely, Anna did not repeat her mother's words to a husband brought up in a succession of council houses, maintaining instead that she found it difficult to cut up food when a tray was balanced on her knees.

In one corner of the study, Anna had stacked cardboard boxes containing items for which she still hadn't found a permanent home. These included the red folder, small enough to be housed in one of the desk's three drawers but still languishing beneath large brown envelopes stuffed with baby and wedding greeting cards. The adage, "out of sight, out of mind", with its connotations of deliberate avoidance, had so far refused to register in Anna's brain, her thoughts being pre-occupied with practical matters.

I'll write some poetry after Christmas, she promised herself, *when the weather's too hot and humid for gardening.*

* * *

Before long, they were celebrating their second Australian Christmas in Mary and Roger's backyard. This time, there were just two couples and their children, Clive and family having flown 'home' for what his unhappy wife called a 'real Christmas.' Immersed in the Clark Rubber out-of-ground pool Roger had recently erected, Anna shivered at the memory of frost, or the snow that sometimes fell in southern Hampshire. She recalled the long walk to her aunt and uncle's home on pavements littered with piles of dirty slush when it was their turn to host Christmas dinner, her father being unwilling to risk the car skidding on icy roads.

As the eldest child, it hadn't taken Anna long to learn the real reason for her family's bi-annual perambulations. Throughout Christmas lunch and into the evening, both parents embraced the generous offerings from Uncle Edgar's jam-packed drinks cabinet with an enthusiasm not seen on other days of the year, when adherence to Methodist principles prevailed. The journey home had been mortifying for an adolescent, due to her parents' tuneless renditions of Christmas carols as they shepherded their flock through darkened streets, interspersed with gales of laughter and the odd hiccup. Anna, with a younger sister either side of her complaining of weariness and cold, had kept her head lowered in case someone she knew emerged from the houses they passed along the way. The recollection caused her to shiver.

'Get out if you're cold,' Joseph called from the opposite side of the pool, where he held a wriggling Adam in his arms.

'I'm not. It was just a passing thought.' She swam over to join him, noting Adam's wet hair and wrinkled fingers. 'He doesn't seem fazed by the water.'

'He loves it. I've dunked him several times to test his reaction. A few splutters when he surfaces, then he's flapping his arms as though asking for more.'

A smile dusted Anna's cool lips. 'Let's take him to the beach tomorrow. Bribie, perhaps?'

Joseph shook his head. 'Too crowded. A guy at work mentioned a beach at a place called Bokarina, halfway between Caloundra and Mooloolaba. He said it's never crowded.'

'It's a long drive up there.'

'True, but Adam's good in the car. He falls asleep almost as soon as we're out of the driveway.'

'Yes. How lucky we are to have such a contented baby.'

Joseph reached out to stroke her cheek. 'No regrets, eh?'

Reluctant to answer, Anna ducked beneath the surface.

* * *

Boxing Day dawned bright and sunny with a breeze keeping summer humidity at bay. With baby and beach paraphernalia taking up half the back seat plus the entire boot, Viv coughed and spluttered on leaving the driveway, but proved up to the task once she reached the Bruce Highway. Traffic remained light, as most Brisbanites were spending the second public holiday with family, or were already established for the Christmas break in tents and caravans at one of the many camping areas dotted along the north coast.

Halfway to Bokarina, contented Adam woke and began yelling for a feed, so Joseph pulled up outside the general store in Landsborough, which they had visited on numerous occasions the previous year with Sam and Shirley. Back then, the four friends had entered the shop to buy hamburgers, then sat outside on rough benches, eagerly devouring juicy beef and salad, the ubiquitous "mayo" smeared on suntanned cheeks and chins.

'Think I'll go and buy a hamburger,' Joseph remarked, as Anna extracted Adam's bottle from a polystyrene container. 'Do you want one?'

Anna shook her head. 'I have packed a picnic, you know,' she called to his retreating figure, but Joseph either didn't hear or chose to ignore a statement delivered in a caustic tone. Not that eating a hamburger mid-morning would spoil his lunchtime appetite; this she knew from experience. Beanpole Joseph could eat ten times a day and not put on weight!

The remainder of the journey passed in near silence, Anna gazing out of the window, Joseph delighting in speed as he pushed Viv to her limit on the quiet road. Pine plantations gave way to cane fields and a smattering of houses. Before long, they had turned off the highway and were driving towards the small seaside town of Caloundra. After winding through the town and passing Dickie Beach, they headed north along a road bordered by scrubby bushland, some of which was fenced off. If they had stopped to read the faded signs fixed to the fence at regular intervals, they would have discovered the low-lying strip had been used by the military as a firing range during World War II. Twenty-six years after the war, development had begun in the area, and houses in various stages of construction were visible from the road.

Joseph slowed when he saw a turning to the right a short distance ahead. 'Perhaps this leads to Bokarina?' He glanced at a sandy track winding through bush in the direction of the beach.

Anna shrugged. 'Doesn't look very promising. No signs.'

'No, but Len said it was a right turn off the Nicklin Way. Let's take a look.'

'Okay. I need to change Adam, anyway.'

Joseph wrinkled his nose. 'So that's what the smell is. Why didn't you tell me to stop before?'

'You were too intent on breaking the land-speed record,' she countered and turned around to address her son, who was beginning to squirm in his seat. 'We'll be stopping soon, Adam. Then you can experience the beach for the first time.'

'I just hope he doesn't eat sand. Wouldn't do his innards much good.'

She turned to face forward and poked Joseph in the ribs. 'Don't worry so much, it wouldn't do him any harm. Babies put everything in their mouths. He's been sampling grass for weeks in the backyard. Spits it out after a while.'

'Are you sure he doesn't swallow any? It could explain the foul smell.'

'If you changed ten to twelve nappies a day, you'd recognise the smell.'

'Touché,' he muttered as they turned right.

At the end of the track, they discovered half a dozen cars parked haphazardly, some nose-in to the bush, others abandoned in the middle as though their owners had been desperate to reach sand and surf. Viv took up a position next to an orange panel van, its high roof providing a little shade as Anna changed Adam on the front seat.

'Panel vans are popular with the young guys, according to Len,' Joseph remarked from his downwind position. 'I expect the owner's got a mattress in there. Len refers to panel vans as "shaggin' wagons".'

'Too late for you,' Anna called, lifting Adam onto her hip. 'Three's a crowd. Besides, I prefer a firm double bed.'

Joseph laughed and moved to open Viv's boot. 'Christ, how the hell are we going to carry all this clobber to the beach?'

'Don't swear in front of Adam,' Anna admonished, stepping towards the boot. She peered inside, noting its bulky contents, which didn't include the two bags lying on the back seat. One contained suntan cream, hats and two pairs of togs – bikini and swimming trunks in English parlance – the other, nappies, plastic pants, nappy liners, a plastic rattle and a soft cloth dog Adam favoured. 'I can manage the beach bag and baby bag, if you can take the esky and umbrella. Fortunately, Adam is still a lightweight.'

'Good thinking, 99,' he answered, quoting from the television series, *Get Smart*, an American spy spoof he enjoyed watching.

'Don't get sand in the shoe-phone, 86,' she answered, recalling the bumbling spy Maxwell Smart's hidden device.

Oblivious to television programmes of any genre, Adam nonethe-less joined in his parents' laughter, his tiny hands and feet drumming on Anna's ribcage.

Shangri-La Shocks

Porterage apportioned, the family set off along a sandy path that wound through low coastal scrub towards what they hoped was Bokarina Beach. After a few minutes, they reached a ridge of dunes stretching as far as the eye could see and climbed up to survey the scene. Some distance from where footsteps led onto the sand, beach umbrellas of varying sizes created a multihued tapestry bordered on one side by turquoise waves trimmed with white lace. Swimmers bobbed beyond the breakers, some clutching polystyrene bodyboards, others engaging in a lazy crawl.

'Such a beautiful place!' Anna exclaimed. 'And not crowded.'

'What are we waiting for then?' Joseph lifted the heavy esky – he'd dropped it on the sand – and, with his shirt flying in the breeze, careered down the other side of the dune.

Sandals sank into powdery sand, so Anna descended warily, Adam clinging to her t-shirt as though he, too, understood the need for caution. 'Nearly there,' she murmured, stepping onto the beach. Ahead, Joseph stood staring into the distance, one hand raised to shade his eyes despite his new sunglasses. 'Anywhere will do,' she called, longing to relinquish her load. Four bag straps and a bra strap had created a trench in her left shoulder.

Joseph remained rooted to the spot, the umbrella tucked under one arm, the esky at his feet.

'I said, anywhere will do,' she repeated, taking slow steps towards him. He jumped when she touched his arm. 'Everything all right?'

'That bloody Len!' he said, turning to face her. 'He took a chance I wouldn't ask Rog if he'd ever been to Bokarina. This is a bloody nudist beach!'

Anna blinked, then stared open-mouthed as a young man and woman emerged from the ocean, yards from where they stood. Bronzed bodies glistening in summer sun, the pair appeared completely at ease with their nudity, raising hands in greeting before running off down the beach.

'No harm in trying it,' she said, remembering a colleague in England who had invited her over for a weekend. Staying in a tenth-floor apartment overlooking the bay had been a new experience for Anna, who had enjoyed sipping drinks on the balcony as the summer sun set over distant cliffs. High-rise conversation had comprised commonplace topics until Ebba, tall, blonde and Swedish, had casually mentioned that she and her husband, tall, blonde and Danish, belonged to a local nudist club. Reluctant to appear shocked, Anna had politely asked what facilities the club provided, at which point a photograph album was produced, revealing a well-kept country retreat with clubhouse, swimming pool and tennis court. Apart from bare bodies of all shapes and sizes, nothing had seemed out of the ordinary until Anna turned to the last page and had to suppress a giggle at the sight of a small group wearing see-through plastic raincoats during inclement weather!

'Well, if you're sure you don't mind?' Joseph asked.

'I'm game if you are!'

Joseph grinned and bent to pick up the esky.

Trailing behind him, her shoulder sore and Adam heavy as lead, Anna looked straight ahead, her eyes focused on the sand rather than other beachgoers.

Joseph chose a spot near the first of the beach umbrellas, about halfway down the beach. Here, the sand was firmer, making it easier to anchor their blue and red striped umbrella. Next, he unfolded the large beach towels, so that Anna could deposit their wriggling baby in a patch of shade. Eager to embrace a different environment, Adam quickly rolled onto his tummy and squirmed to the edge of the towel like a newborn seal seeking its mother's nipple. Head and shoulders raised, he surveyed the beach for a moment, then lifted one hand, resulting in total collapse. Saved by an attentive mother, he appeared none the worse for his adventure, fending off Anna's attempts to brush his face clean with her handkerchief and spitting out sand as though this were an everyday occurrence. Released from her arms, he immediately rolled over to examine the wooden umbrella pole, lost interest and head-butted the esky before executing several rolls in order to reach the sand again.

'I'll take him down to the water,' Joseph said, lifting his sand-encrusted infant. 'He can splash about for a bit, tire himself out.'

'Let me take his clothes off first.' She reached for the squirming baby, deftly removed the terry-towelling jumpsuit and nappy, then handed him back.

Joseph held him at arm's length. 'What if he pees, or worse?'

'What does it matter? You're nude! Just wash it off.'

Grinning sheepishly, Joseph cradled Adam in the crook of one arm and got to his feet.

After removing her own clothes, Anna lay on the towel, relishing the waft of a cool sea breeze on her sun-heated skin. Freed from a tight embrace – despite burgeoning Women's lib, she hadn't had the courage to burn her bras – her full breasts relaxed against her chest. She risked a glance at her abdomen, noting with relief that the scar had begun to fade. Pregnancy had left her with a slightly rounded stomach, not unattractive, she thought, and Joseph preferred her less angular body, or so he said during intimate moments. He had always admired her breasts and disliked the current trend for a boyish figure, the "fried-egg" chests of willowy models.

Shifting her gaze, she watched husband and son playing at the ocean's edge. Half-turned towards her, Joseph sat with Adam wedged between his outstretched legs. She envisaged a photograph: strong brown limbs protecting delicate white ones, a father bent over his baby, shoulder-length black hair brushing a downy head, work-worn fingers dribbling water over a soft stomach. A study of contemporary fatherhood; 1970s man, comfortable with his role, unlike previous generations with their overt masculinity. She couldn't imagine her father changing a nappy or pushing a pram. At first, Joseph had been afraid to handle such a diminutive infant, but soon conquered his nerves, even volunteering to give Adam the ten o'clock bottle so that she could have a few hours of uninterrupted sleep during the initial months of three-hourly feeds.

Reflecting on her good fortune, Anna got to her feet and made her way down the beach. 'I thought you might want a swim,' she said, kneeling beside her family.

Joseph shook his head. 'You go first. Adam's loving it here.'

'Okay, but I'd better get him a shirt and hat or he'll get sunburnt.'

'No worries there, I'm shielding him from the sun.'

'I'll make it quick.' She rushed into the water and flung herself into a foam-tipped wave. Surfacing into a gentle swell, she lay on her back, savouring bodily liberation, feeling a sensuous stream of cool water between her thighs and buttocks, her erect nipples seeking hot sunlight. Overhead, breeze spun cloud into cottonwool, white wisps suspended in a sapphire sky. Closing her eyes, she imagined floating forever, travelling wherever wind and tide directed, unencumbered by the onerous responsibilities of marriage and motherhood.

A splash nearby quickly terminated her fanciful thoughts. Wary of sharks – there were no observant lifesavers scanning these waters – she rolled over and was powering towards the beach when another swimmer surfaced beside her.

'I thought you were in trouble,' the bearded young man declared. 'Strong currents out here, you know.'

'I'm fine, thank you.'

'You should take more care,' he persisted, indicating the beach with a wave of the hand. 'Look how far you've drifted.'

She peered at the faraway sand. 'I see what you mean.'

'Can you make it to the beach?

'I'm a good swimmer,' she said, more to convince herself than him.

'That's as maybe, but I'll swim alongside just in case you need a hand.'

'Thanks.' Increasing her pace, she pushed ahead to hide her growing embarrassment. What on earth would Joseph think if she emerged from the water held in a stranger's arms? A naked stranger!

Once safe in the shallows, she stood up and scoured the beach for Joseph, but saw nothing but a sea of umbrellas rippling in the wind. Which one was theirs? Had she drifted north or south? She turned to ask the young man, but he had vanished and for a moment she wondered if she'd dreamt his appearance. A sudden movement to her right brought relief as she spotted him scrambling to his feet a few yards away. Unwilling to waste time on further conversation, she began to run, the sucking sand impeding her progress. Retreating to firmer ground, she was making her way along the beach, trying to distinguish one naked body from another without appearing to stare, when she almost collided with an older man.

'I'm so sorry, she murmured, averting her eyes from his sea-shrivelled genitalia. 'I'm trying to find my husband.'

'Anna Fletcher?' he queried.

She stepped back, reluctant to confirm her identity.

'Ian McBride. We met months ago at Bribie.'

She glanced at his face. 'Ian, oh yes. Sorry, I didn't recognise you.' Colour tinged her cheeks; how could she have made such a silly statement?

'Joe's over there.' Ian indicated two umbrellas further along the beach, slightly apart from the others. 'We met when I pitched my umbrella near yours. Bub's having a sleep now, so when I said I was going for a swim, Joe asked if I'd look out for you.'

'I didn't realise I'd been gone so long.'

'He just wanted you to know he'd returned to the umbrella. Said you hadn't responded to his wave.'

'I drifted a bit with the current, that's all.'

Kind grey eyes smiled down at her. 'It's best to swim near others on an unpatrolled beach.'

'I'll remember that in future.'

He smiled. 'It's a beautiful beach. I discovered it a few months back. Shangri-La, the regulars call it.'

She was tempted to ask if Ian would consider himself a regular and whether his wife ever accompanied him, but felt reluctant to quiz someone she hardly knew. 'I'd better get back and give Joseph the opportunity for a swim,' she said instead.

'I'll join you.'

'I thought you wanted a swim?'

'Later will do. It must be time for lunch.'

Together, they walked up the beach, both waving as they approached the red and blue umbrella.

Over lunch, unspoken questions were answered, Ian explaining that he and Elizabeth had been nudists for years and once had attended what he called a naturalists' convention. 'Friendly people,' he told them, 'but the place was too primitive for us. Tents and caravans perched on a dusty slope near a creek. The whole place turned to mud when it rained on the second day. Facilities were a bit basic – bush toilets and showers no more than buckets rigged up on a pulley.'

Anna pulled a face. 'Wouldn't suit me, either, but I do like nude swimming and sunbathing.'

'Me too,' Joseph concurred. 'It's always seemed stupid having to put togs on to go for a swim.'

'So, I'll see you here again?' Ian smiled at the sleeping baby, wrapped in a bunny rug. 'Good kid you've got there.'

'Have you got any grandchildren?' Anna asked.

'Boy and a girl, but they live down south, so we don't see them often.'

'Perhaps they'll come up for a holiday soon.'

'Next year. In-laws' turn this last Christmas, my daughter said. We're going down at Easter before it gets too cold.' Ian looked thoughtful. 'Why don't you come up to our place for a weekend? We've got plenty of room and Elizabeth would love to see the baby.'

Anna looked to Joseph for a response, but he remained silent, no doubt debating whether it was worth carting so much baby gear for a two-day stay.

Ian appeared not to notice their deliberation. 'We've still got the portable cot we bought for the grandkids, even though they've outgrown it. Elizabeth must have had an inkling we'd need to use it again when she insisted we bring it up from Melbourne.'

Joseph looked up and smiled. 'Thanks, Ian. We'd love to accept your invitation.'

'Good. I'll just have to check with Elizabeth to see when we have a weekend free. She's our social secretary. I'll get your phone number before you leave.'

Joseph nodded. 'Don't you have a swimming pool, if I remember correctly?'

'Sure have. We love swimming, especially late in the evening when you can see countless stars overhead, unblemished by ambient light from the city.'

'It sounds wonderful,' Anna murmured, wondering if the couple swam nude at home.

'And what a spectacle it is when they fire the cane in the paddock opposite, before harvesting! Flames shooting into the sky. We can even hear the leaves crackling.'

'Why do they burn it?' Joseph asked.

'Gets rid of the leaves and any other trash, plus it flushes out snakes and mice.'

Anna shuddered. 'Aren't you worried about snakes getting into the garden?'

Ian shook his head. 'Birds pick them off long before they get to our place.'

Anna tried to envisage an entire field burning and saw only wild creatures evicted from their homes, scrambling to reach safety before flames or birds consumed them.

Conversation turned to the more mundane, with Joseph and Ian discussing gardening in the sub-tropics. Anna was only half-listening, as she was dealing with a baby who, despite his hunger, insisted on flailing his arms, almost knocking the bottle from her hand. 'Hold still, will you, or we'll end up with sand in the milk,' she admonished him.

Grey-blue eyes widened. The teat slipped from slack lips.

'Now what are you doing?'

Feet pummelled her breasts.

'Ouch! Stop it, you little beast!'

'Problem over there?' Ian asked mildly, from the sanctuary of his uncluttered towel.

'Yes. Mister Wriggle thinks it's fun to kick his mother.'

Joseph, who was sitting on the edge of the neighbouring towel, facing away from his fractious wife and baby, refrained from comment.

'Bring him over here. Let's see how he likes my bony old chest.'

Keen to offload Adam, Anna quickly dismissed the assumption that Ian had been looking at her breasts and rose to her feet. 'All yours,' she declared, dumping baby and bottle in the grandfather's arms.

'See? All good,' Ian remarked moments later. Adam lay quiet in his arms, sucking contentedly, mesmerised by the unfamiliar face smiling down at him.

'Thanks. You must have the knack. I'm afraid I don't have much patience.'

'None,' Joseph mouthed to his neighbour. 'I'm off for a swim. We'll have to be going soon.'

'Why don't you join him?' Ian said, watching Joseph race down the beach.

Anna surveyed the detritus around her – empty lemonade bottle, discarded sandwich drying on a plastic plate, crumpled packet of crisps. 'I'd better clear up. He hates getting stuck in traffic.'

She gathered up plates and beakers and tossed them in the esky along with the rubbish. The sound of the sea reached her ears, waves slapping sand on an incoming tide, the rush of water as they retreated.

She longed to revisit her tranquil place beyond the breakers, float beneath a summer sky without a care in the world.

'All done,' said a nearby voice, drawing her back to domestic tasks.

She fastened the lid on the esky before extending her arms to receive her child. 'Thanks so much, Ian.'

'No problem. Glad to help.' He took a step towards his umbrella, then stopped and turned back to her. 'Tell me it's none of my business, but I sense you're finding it difficult to adjust to motherhood.'

She reddened and looked down at Adam, now half-asleep. 'I feel so guilty.'

'Why? No one said parenting was easy.'

'No, but overall it's supposed to be fulfilling.'

'Not for you, eh?'

She shook her head. 'I loathe being at home with a baby. It's so boring, nothing but repetitive tasks all day long. Worse than working on an assembly line, I reckon. At least in a factory I'd have someone to talk to and I'd get paid.'

'Elizabeth was climbing the walls with our Mark,' he said evenly, 'what with the broken nights, endless crying and living in a poky flat, miles from a tram or train. Each night when I returned home from the base, she would thrust him into my arms before I'd hardly got in the door! No grandparents to help out, either. All back in Melbourne. We were living in Brisbane then, my last wartime posting. Elizabeth joined me after a few months, as we'd already spent much of our married life apart. Brisbane was swarming with Yanks, so finding decent accommodation was nigh on impossible.' He paused and smiled down at her. 'Still, it was a big improvement on the jungles of New Guinea, I can tell you.'

Anna shivered. 'How did you get through it?' she asked, knowing her domestic issues were trivial compared with jungle warfare.

'Local vicar and his wife called round one day and told Elizabeth about a mother and baby group held weekly in the church hall. It saved her sanity, meeting other women in the same boat.'

'I meant New Guinea.'

Ian looked down at his sand-dusted feet. 'King and country and all that. We didn't want the bloody Japs taking over.'

'Or the Germans,' she said quietly, recalling comments overheard in her grandparents' sitting room years after the war's end.

'Enough talk of the past. I'm having a grand retirement and I predict a bright future here for a smart pair like you and Joe. You're just the sort of migrants this country needs.' He bent to stroke Adam's hair. 'You too, little man.'

'I hope so. We love Australia.' Anna looked up and smiled. 'I'm looking forward to our weekend in Bli Bli and not just for the swimming. I trust Elizabeth won't mind if I pick her brains about child-rearing?'

Ian shook his head. 'She'll love getting to know all three of you. Neither of us regret moving up here, but she misses the family down south.'

'I miss my family, too,' Anna admitted for the first time.

Ian reached out to touch her shoulder. 'Understandable. It can't be easy leaving everyone and everything behind. Don't reckon I could have done it.'

'You would have managed just fine. Besides, it must have been much tougher when your ancestors emigrated.'

'Grandma almost died on the ship. Imagine giving birth somewhere in the Indian Ocean in the middle of a storm! Least that's what my father told me.'

'You two still talking?' Joseph called, as he ran towards them. 'I thought you would have everything packed up by now, Anna. Time to go if we're going to beat the traffic.'

Anna and Ian exchanged knowing glances.

'No worries, Joe, we're all sorted here,' Ian called back.

A flurry of sand announced his arrival. 'Fabulous swim! I managed a bit of body surfing, too.'

Anna moved away from the towel, resisting the urge to remind him not to shake it in her direction. 'Ian, could you hold Adam while I collapse the umbrella?'

'How about I do it instead?'

'Thanks.' She bent to retrieve the two bags positioned on either side of the umbrella.

'Leave them, too. It's time this old man went home. Elizabeth will be back from visiting her sick friend and wonder where I've got to.'

'Thanks again. It was a bit difficult carrying everything down that track.'

Ian nodded and set to work.

* * *

Back at the makeshift car park, Ian dropped his own gear beside the orange panel van, before helping to load the Vauxhall Viva.

"Thanks for everything, Ian,' Anna called, leaning out of the window as Joseph started the engine.

'I'll be in touch about the weekend,' he called back and, to her surprise, turned to unlock the van's rear doors.

Resurgence

Anna had no idea what triggered the return to writing poetry. At first, she thought it was the experience of Shangri-La that had enabled her to cast off the pall of despondency that had descended on her since learning of her pregnancy. Shedding her clothes, albeit only for a few hours, had evoked a sense of freedom lacking in her everyday life. She had envisaged awkwardness, huddling under the beach umbrella, too inhibited to risk a walk to the water. Instead, once she realised that neither female nor male beachgoers paid her any attention, she'd moved with the confidence of a seasoned nudist.

Months later, following a third visit to the house perched on a hill overlooking cane fields, she assumed it was the burgeoning friendship with Elizabeth and Ian that had prompted her to remove the red folder from its cardboard hideaway and place it centre stage on the study desk. The retired couple had happily taken on the role of Australian grandparents in the absence of the English variety, even coming down to Brisbane on one occasion so that Anna and Joseph could go away for a romantic weekend. Adam adored them both and, as if to show his appreciation, not only sat up unaided for the first time beneath *their* beach umbrella, but also took his first steps in *their* living room, tottering from one to the other, laughter bubbling on his lips.

Later still, when an Olivetti Lettera 32 portable typewriter replaced pen and paper, Anna felt certain this unexpected birthday present from Joseph had set the scene for resurgent creativity. Joseph didn't pretend to understand poetry, especially the odd-shaped pieces she labelled "concrete", but always showed interest in her latest effort and suggested she should try to get some published.

Whatever the reason, life at 69a Harrow Street acquired a different hue, more in keeping with the brilliant sheen of Brisbane skies. Adam, although displaying the usual irritating toddler traits, remained a good sleeper and went willingly to his afternoon nap, giving Anna a daily two-hour writing slot during the week. She gained further writing time when Joseph worked late or spent the evening playing squash, a sport he'd taken up to keep fit. However, she remained aware that too many hours pursuing separate goals could damage the fabric of their marriage, so she made a point of joining Joseph in the garden most Saturday mornings, with Adam playing nearby in his sandpit or "helping" with planting and weeding. Hosing her child clean following a particularly energetic gardening period, Anna blessed the warm Brisbane climate.

If rain prevented outdoor pursuits, the family retired under the house, where Joseph was in the process of constructing a workshop and enclosing the laundry. Anna played apprentice to Joseph's tradesman, passing tools and holding lengths of hardwood framing while he sawed them to size. She also provided endless cups of tea. The remaining family member amused himself in ways befitting his age group: tipping up trays of nails and screws, grabbing tools and hiding them around the garden, or, his favourite, bringing wet leaves and twigs into the workshop as gifts for his parents.

Sundays were reserved for pleasure, unless a household task required immediate attention. Visits to beach or bush took priority, although on occasion the family enjoyed barbeques with friends at one another's homes. During the short winter months, these shared meals were held indoors: huge joints of meat with mountains of roast vegetables, followed by apple pie and custard. Anna found she missed the summer pavlovas crammed with fruit and cream that were enjoyed when the barbeque flames had turned to glowing coals, but she always politely accepted a slice of pie.

Their old neighbours, Sam and Shirley, were frequent visitors to Harrow Street, Sam delighting Adam with rough and tumble play, Shirley bringing welcome talk of higher education and her working world. Sometimes, Anna would catch Sam looking longingly at Adam, but she knew Shirley had no intention of embracing motherhood until the last of her library papers had been completed.

Sensible girl, Anna thought as she picked up toys late each evening. There was no way she could consider further study until Adam went to school. A few hours here and there writing poetry might keep her sane, but lengthy periods were needed to pursue the Australian equivalent of the A-levels she'd refused to embark on at age sixteen; a qualification she believed essential for gaining more satisfying employment. She had no intention of returning to work as a clerk-typist and fantasised about going to university and graduating with a degree in literature, or the drama she'd loved at school. A teaching career was out of the question. Like her friend Shirley, she couldn't imagine dealing with an entire classroom of children, but other options would be available.

One steamy night when sleep eluded her, she mused on interesting careers: editor for a publisher, journalist at the *Courier-Mail*, stage director, film producer. Apart from the first option, none seemed possible for a married woman with a small child. 1973 might have dawned weeks earlier, but young women were still expected to embrace the traditional careers of nursing and teaching, work that could be undertaken part-time to fit in with the demands of family. How she hated the words "fit in" and "demands", with their connotations of conformity and compromise. Why couldn't *fathers* work part-time and put *their* career on hold for a few years?

The following day, she wrote out her frustration, embarking on a short story entitled *Cage Birds*, which drew on childhood memories of a blackbird that had flown into church during the service and couldn't find its way out. Aunt Maud had rescued it, ignoring the pained expressions of other worshippers as she clattered over stone pavers in high-heeled shoes to open the double entrance doors. It had taken several minutes of whispered encouragement for the bird to realise freedom lay within its grasp, but by the time it sailed over her head and out into the street, the hymn had finished and Aunt Maud's whoop of delight disturbed a congregation who were preparing for prayer. Adam woke from his afternoon sleep before the fictional rescuer, a married woman of thirty with two children, achieved her goal, so, with cries of 'Mumma!' ringing in her ears, Anna abandoned authorship for a less appealing role.

During subsequent days, she completed the first draft, granting her protagonist an hour's liberation following the bird rescue. Instead of hurrying home from church to make lunch for her family, the woman headed for a bayside café where she relished a solitary meal washed down with a glass of white wine; just reward for assisting one of God's creatures.

Further drafts followed, Anna working late into the night to hone her first attempt at prose since school essay writing. Rather than risk a negative reaction from Joseph – the piece expressed strong feminist views – she posted a carbon copy to Shirley with a request for honest criticism. A response was soon forthcoming as her friend called in after work to give verbal encouragement.

'Have you thought of entering it in a short story competition?' Shirley asked, as she perched on a yellow stool at the breakfast bar while Anna made Adam's dinner.

'No. I was going to send it to a magazine, maybe *Women's Weekly*.'

'Not the sort of thing they'd publish. I would try a literary journal. I could look up some possibilities in the library, if you like?'

'Thanks, that would be great.'

· 'I'll look up competitions as well, in case you want to go down that track.'

'I guess it's worth a try.'

'Got to be in it to win it! For what it's worth, I think you write well.'

'Really? You're not just saying that because we're friends?'

'No.' Shirley smiled. 'Any plans to write more short stories?'

'I've got a couple of ideas.'

'Then my advice is to develop them. Writing is a great occupation. You can do it anywhere, anytime. Who knows, one day you might write a novel!'

Anna gave a wry smile. 'I'd need a great deal more free time than I've got now to attempt a lengthy manuscript.'

Shirley looked over at Adam, busy emptying the Tupperware cupboard. 'He'll be off to school before you know it.'

Anna sighed. 'The trouble is, Joseph wants another one.'

'Surely that should be a joint decision?'

'I agree, but he doesn't see it that way. He keeps harping on about only children being lonely and finding it difficult to mix with others.'

'That's not necessarily the case. My cousin is an only child and she's perfectly well-adjusted. Dawn once told me she loved coming home from friends' places to the sanctuary of a bedroom she didn't have to share.'

'I never asked my younger sisters if they minded sharing. Being the eldest, I got a bedroom to myself.'

'Me too, thank God. My little brother was a pain. Still is, if I'm honest.'

'Is that why I've never met him?'

'No. He lives in Sydney. Plays trumpet in a band. Never got any money, always hoping for the big break. Mum says he should get a proper job.'

Anna shrugged. 'So long as he's happy.'

She turned back to the sink, drained the steamed vegetables and tipped them into a plastic bowl alongside cooked chicken breast, chopped into bite-sized pieces and covered with apricot sauce. She would reheat the Apricot Chicken dish later, adding steamed rice and vegetables for herself and Joseph. From an early age, Adam had insisted on eating the same food as his parents, a trait that had induced more than one reprimand from the Maternal and Child nurse, until Anna learnt honesty wasn't the best policy when asked what her son had eaten for dinner the previous day.

'Chilli con carne?' the nurse had repeated, one afternoon soon after Adam's first birthday. 'What on earth were you thinking, Mrs Fletcher?'

Anna's response that he spat out baby food had caused further concern, the nurse reminding her that a mother did not give in to a child's demands. 'Fussy eaters are created, not born that way, Mrs Fletcher.'

Wisely, Anna hadn't pointed out that Adam's mature tastebuds made life much easier for her. Cheaper, too, there being no need to purchase separate food, apart from the occasional tin of the Heinz baby chocolate custard he adored.

Shirley slipped from the stool. 'I'd better get going. Sam will be home, wanting his tea. Thanks for the tea and cake. I'll be in touch about the writing opportunities.' She moved into the kitchen, gave Anna a goodbye hug and patted Adam's head. 'Hooroo.'

'See you later,' Anna murmured, still unable to adopt the odd farewell employed by many Queenslanders.

* * *

Autumn arrived, signalled by the absence of frequent afternoon storms, rather than the turning of leaves experienced in more temperate climates. Anna welcomed the lower temperatures, especially at night. Sound sleep was rare during times of high humidity when, despite a pedestal fan, perspiration dampened her face and her hair stuck to the back of her neck. Insect screens on windows and doors kept mosquitoes at bay most of the time, but periodically, one or two would invade the bedroom and buzz around her face and ears, driving her to distraction. The inevitable bites would itch like crazy, sending her into the bathroom for calamine lotion and cottonwool. Some mornings, her face and arms resembled her pink spotted sun-dress and a shower would reveal bites the size of a twenty-cent piece, fire-red and swollen. Unjustly in her opinion, Joseph remained untroubled by insect bites, a tiny red dot on his skin the only evidence of a mosquito's thirst.

A second advantage of the changing season soon became apparent during her afternoon writing sessions. The cooler weather conjured fresh bursts of creativity as she sat at the old desk, her fingers poised over the typewriter keys. Dressed in calf-length peddle-pushers or jeans, rather than summer's skimpy shorts, her thighs no longer stuck to the chair and frequent interruptions to fetch a cold drink could be replaced with a single after-lunch cup of tea. Poems emerged less frequently now and were often the result of strong emotions, the conduct of an ultra-conservative state government providing topics more often than not. Prose – short stories and the occasional article – became her favourite form of expression, giving her scope to develop characters, expound ideas, hone dialogue and experiment with tense and structure.

Her confidence increased as autumn turned to brief winter, but still she lacked the courage to submit her work to magazines or competitions, despite the lengthy list provided by Shirley. Visits to the local library gave her the opportunity to borrow collections of short stories and poetry anthologies, but these works of well-known authors, although inspiring, only highlighted her own inferior talent. Shirley suggested she undertake a writing course that could be completed at home, with assignments posted to a teacher and returned with constructive criticism. Unfortunately, Anna discovered that these correspondence courses were conducted by private colleges and commanded a hefty fee. Enquiries at the library uncovered an affordable evening class in English expression and Anna became excited at the prospect, until she discovered it was held in the central city branch. Joseph never knew when he would be asked to work overtime and couldn't afford to turn it down, as their modest home was still sparsely furnished and Viv the Viva was getting on in years.

The remaining option, a part-time job, would be possible once Adam started kindergarten, but that was still eighteen months away and, as a three-year-old, he could attend only four hours a day twice a week, which was insufficient time to offer most prospective employers. Disappointed, but resigned to waiting until he started school – or, at the very least, four-year-old kindy, as it was called – Anna decided on a teach-yourself approach, with assistance from books on grammar and a thesaurus purchased second-hand.

'After all, practice makes perfect,' she told Shirley, as they chatted on the back veranda, spring sunshine warming their winter-pale skin. 'One of these days, I'll write something worth publishing.'

Shirley sighed. 'But how will you know if you don't give it a go?'

'I'm not good enough yet.'

'Who says?'

Anna hesitated, unwilling to admit that stalling the submission process suited her for the present. Rejection slips could undermine her fragile confidence, triggering a return to the endless procession of dark days that had haunted her both during and after pregnancy. Writing had helped her reclaim the still centre... enabled her to focus on the positive. 'I can't take the risk,' she said, aware how pathetic that sounded.

'Did you know that the Brontë sisters had to pay to have their first book of poetry published?'

'I'm hardly in their league.'

'Maybe not, but everyone has to start somewhere. Think about it. A competition, at least. No one need know you've entered, not even Joe or me.'

'I suppose not.'

'Promise me you'll consider it?'

'Oh, all right, anything to shut you up.' Anna got to her feet. 'Now, to change the subject, when are you free to go to the movies?'

Rejection

Weather dominated every conversation at the start of 1974, with south-east Queensland experiencing its wettest January in a century. The entire state was already water-logged from three weeks of continual heavy rain, when the remnants of cyclone Wanda dumped 642 millimetres on the Brisbane area in just three days. The resulting flood, which inundated the city centre and surrounding suburbs as the Brisbane River broke its banks, occurred during the Australia Day long weekend. Sixteen lives were lost, hundreds were injured, and thousands of homes destroyed or badly damaged.

Areas of higher ground became islands, cut off from shops, railway stations and main roads. There was no electricity for days, resulting in householders losing the contents of fridges and freezers in the hot, humid weather; a minor inconvenience when compared to the loss of an entire house. At 69a Harrow Street – no flooding, but Viv the Viva was marooned on an island of mud under the house – Anna remained glued to the transistor radio, while Joseph, his city office under water, gained first-hand information as he, along with hundreds of other volunteers, assisted authorities in clean-up operations. His nightly reports both shocked and amused her: houses wrenched from wooden or concrete stumps, lying lop-sided in mud-covered gardens; an entire shopping centre submerged; men paddling an improvised raft laden with cartons of beer down a flooded street.

As the floodwaters receded, their friend Sam joined an army of electricians reconnecting power, a hazardous exercise that saw him standing in damp city basements, drying out switchboards he trusted had been correctly turned off.

City offices, most housed in brick or concrete buildings, began to re-open once power had been restored and cleaning completed, but some weatherboard dwellings were declared beyond repair, so had to be demolished. Others, built close to overflowing rivers and creeks, had floated off their stumps and ended their days as flotsam in Moreton Bay. Day after day, extensive media coverage communicated graphic details and images of the disaster, inducing a mixture of horror and fascination amongst readers and viewers. News bulletins broadcast overseas, although briefer and less frequent, alarmed distant relatives and friends, resulting in overloaded telephone lines as thousands sought to connect with loved ones.

Anna would have liked to play an active role in the post-flood operations, but she couldn't imagine any of the relief organisations wanting a helper with an overactive toddler in tow, so she took refuge in the written word. Initially, she wrote a short story from a child's point-of-view; a child whose home had been badly damaged, focusing on both the trauma and excitement of rescue by boat from a flooded street, followed by relocation to an emergency shelter. The conclusion presented problems. Should it be positive, with the child being reunited with a Christmas gift bicycle retrieved from the mud a week later? Or should the story end on a more sombre note, with the realisation that the family would not be returning to their street as their house was declared uninhabitable and demolished?

Undecided, Anna typed both endings on separate sheets of paper and shoved them in a desk drawer, intending to revisit the piece after a week. During the intervening days, she planned to write an article exploring the sense of helplessness experienced in the face of a natural disaster, coupled with the realisation that no amount of advanced technology could have prevented the events of the Australia Day weekend as nature, not humanity, had been in control. In the event, the story remained unfinished for months and the article was never written, a delicate personal issue taking precedence over the authoring process. Like the January floods, tropical weather played its part.

Late one February evening, when humidity cloaked the house like a thick wool blanket, Anna joined Joseph on the back veranda, risking mosquito bites for the slightly fresher air available outside. Her nerves were frayed already by an irritable child who had taken hours to settle, despite wide-open windows and a newly-installed ceiling fan, so Joseph should have known better than to raise a contentious subject. His assertion that they should definitely try for a second baby that year, induced an eruption rivalling that of Vesuvius in 79 AD!

'Are you drunk or just bloody insensitive?' she retorted, eyeing the empty beer bottles arranged around his canvas chair. 'I've just got Adam to sleep and you want to talk about another one? And in case you hadn't noticed, it's thirty degrees with one hundred per cent humidity; not exactly the atmosphere for rational discussion, so you can take your assertion and stuff it where it hurts!'

'No need to bite my head off just because you've had a difficult evening. I meant no harm.'

'Then you should have kept your mouth shut. Or did you imagine two years and five months of motherhood, the most boring occupation in the world, would have so worn down my brain cells that I wouldn't object to more of the same?'

'Whoa there, Anna, you're becoming hysterical.'

'That's right! Put a label on what you regard as inappropriate behaviour. A typical male reaction – blame it on my hormones!'

'For God's sake, calm down. All I said was…'

'I know what you said and it's not the first time you've raised the subject. Going on about only children being lonely and saying if we don't get a move on, there will be too much of an age difference. What about me? Don't I get a say in the matter?'

Joseph sighed and took another swig of beer.

'And while I'm at it, I hate seeing you drink straight from the bottle. It isn't as though we haven't got any glasses.'

'Standard Australian practice. I don't know why you should object. I thought you loved everything about this country?'

Anna bristled. 'I love living here, but that doesn't mean I have to embrace every single custom.'

'You're such a bloody snob sometimes.' He leant back in his chair to tip the dregs into his mouth.

'And you're showing signs of regression!'

'What the hell does that mean?'

'Back to your working-class, council house roots.'

'Better than your stuck-up family with their insistence on best crockery for Sunday lunch and cloth serviettes at every meal.'

'What's wrong with cloth serviettes?'

The beer bottle hit the timber deck.

Lightning flared in her wide-open eyes. 'Pick it up before it rolls down the steps and smashes on the concrete.'

'Do it yourself.' He kicked over another bottle with his bare foot.

She leapt from the chair and stomped across the deck to retrieve the bottles. 'It's lucky for you that I possess good manners.' She stood over him, a bottle clasped in each hand. 'Otherwise I might hit you over the head to try to knock some sense into you.'

'I could say the same to you,' he countered, getting to his feet. 'But how about we call a truce and go to bed?'

She nodded, unwilling to answer and risk further dissent.

* * *

The atmosphere at 69a Harrow Street remained strained throughout February and March, continuing high temperatures and humidity contributing to household tension. On weekday mornings, Anna felt like a pot about to boil over until Joseph departed for work, leaving her free to turn down the heat. Then, she would go about her domestic tasks as though nothing was amiss, humming popular tunes as she swept and dusted, washed and ironed. Summer lunch was eaten in the shade under the rear veranda, Adam's child-sized wooden table and chair positioned on the concrete pad Joseph had laid a few months earlier.

Anna sat on one of the folding chairs usually taken to the beach. When they had eaten, she would fill Adam's inflatable paddling pool with fresh water, remove his towelling pants – the only item of clothing he would wear during hot weather – and let him splash to his heart's content. Half an hour of water play would usually cool him sufficiently for her to attempt the afternoon sleep, which, although shorter now, at least gave her some time to herself.

One afternoon, she tried to resurrect her short story about the flood but found all the unresolved conflict had blocked her imagination. Likewise, subsequent attempts at poetry resulted in balls of screwed-up typing paper being thrown to the study floor in disgust at poorly-constructed stanzas and unsatisfactory metaphor.

Convinced her first flushes of creativity had been aberrations, the result of excitement at arriving in a new country followed by a bid to distance herself, at least for an hour or two, from motherhood, she deserted the typewriter and retreated to fictional worlds fashioned by others. Never before had she read so many library books. Never before had she embraced so many imaginary lives; lives that, in most instances, appeared intense and fulfilling when compared with her own. Part of her knew this obsessive flight from reality was unhealthy, but she couldn't abandon the precious books. They alone preserved her sanity.

Evenings brought a flurry of physical activity – preparing and cooking dinner, washing up, bathing Adam and putting him to bed – tasks that, by their repetitive nature, swallowed thought and kept unease at bay. The hours until they retired to bed would pass in a haze of black and white television, Joseph slumped on the sofa, empty beer bottles at his feet, Anna sprawled in an armchair. Conversation, limited to between programmes or during advertisements on the odd occasion they watched a commercial channel, remained cordial and centred around domestic matters or what they planned for the coming weekend. The topic of another baby never arose, but sometimes Anna felt it lurking in the shadows of Joseph's mind, waiting for the right opportunity to emerge. On those occasions, she would sit coiled in the armchair like a snake ready to pounce, even though her twisted limbs meant hot skin sticking to hot skin and associated perspiration.

Lovemaking continued as usual, several times a week, although not with the exuberance she had experienced during their first Australian summer. The new ceiling fan created a breeze that cooled their over-heated bodies but did not encourage lingering union, as sweat trickling down their respective chests was a decided turn-off for both parties. Anna presumed this was a normal state of affairs after four years of marriage, rather than the result of underlying conflict, so afterwards, she would turn on her back and go to sleep.

On days when the mercury rose to thirty centigrade plus, she aban-doned housework and drove to Shorncliffe, a bayside suburb adjacent to Sandgate, where a small beach shaded by large cotton trees offered hours of enjoyment for Adam, plus the possibility of meeting other young mothers. Although Anna liked many aspects of living in an older suburb – shops and a library within walking distance, a nearby train station and established parks – she missed the company of her own generation, as most of the old weatherboard houses in the area were inhabited by elderly people. Nell and Ted Wootton remained friendly and the sixty-something neighbours on the other side would often engage in conversation over the fence, but Anna longed for a younger friend or two to share part of her weekday world.

Shirley, a qualified librarian since mid 1973, worked full-time in her newly-acquired position at the University of Queensland library, and Mary had a part-time job now that both children were at school, so nei-ther were available during the week. A job, even a few hours a week, might have eased Anna's sense of isolation, but Joseph wouldn't hear of putting Adam in a childcare centre and so, with no family around to look after him, Anna remained tethered full-time to motherhood duties.

Visits to Shorncliffe beach proved positive experiences, with Anna getting to know several young mothers over the summer as their chil-dren played together. She particularly liked Astrid, a tall, tanned blond with a two-year-old daughter. A large cotton tree provided sufficient shade for Anna and Astrid to sit side by side, while Adam and Melinda dug in the sand, or curled on beach towels for after-lunch naps.

Initially, the two women spoke about their children, homes and husbands' occupations, safe subjects that helped to foster a fledgling friendship. Astrid lived in an old weatherboard a few streets from the beach that had belonged to her Norwegian grandparents. She and her husband were restoring the house on weekends, a mammoth task that made Anna grateful for a new dwelling. 69a Harrow Street might be poky, but at least the rooms had painted walls and sound floorboards.

Following several beach encounters, the two women ventured outside the narrow circle of domesticity and began to discuss other issues, such as emerging feminism and the reformist Labor prime minister Gough Whitlam, who had led his party to power in late '72 after twenty-three years in opposition. Astrid was particularly interested in Whitlam's push to make university education more attainable for students from working class backgrounds, by abolishing university fees within months of taking office.

'A step in the right direction at last,' Astrid remarked, 'and one I intend to take advantage of before too long.'

'Before Adam came along, I used to dream of going to university,' Anna remarked wistfully, glancing at the sleeping children.

'A child won't stop me going to uni. Helen Reddy is right. I am strong, I am invincible.'

'Great song,' Anna murmured. 'So, when do you plan to apply to university?'

'Later in the year. I want to do an arts degree, majoring in languages and literature. I hope it will lead to a teaching career. Secondary, rather than primary school.'

'I'm impressed. You've got it all planned.'

'I've discussed it with Rick and he's totally supportive. I'll be applying as a mature-age student. These days, a number of places are allocated for those over twenty-five. Life experience as well as entrance qualifications are taken into consideration in that instance.'

'Wow! How did you find out about all this?'

'It was Rick's doing. Last year, he saw a TV programme about mature-age study and suggested I follow it up, so I contacted the University of Queensland. They sent me a heap of literature about the scheme. I'd been talking about further study for ages. I always regret not going to uni straight from school.'

'Why didn't you?'

'I wanted to travel first, discover my roots. I was always asking my parents about our Norwegian and German relatives. Dad's grandparents came from Hamburg at the turn of the century, Mum's parents from Bergen in the Twenties. Anyway, to cut a long story short, they suggested I go to Europe on a working holiday. I speak Norwegian well and my German's not bad as I studied it at school, so it wasn't difficult to find jobs.'

'Did you meet Rick over there?'

Astrid nodded. 'I had visions of falling in love with a tall, blond Norwegian or German. Instead, I met a stocky redhead from Brisbane with Irish ancestry, who was also on a working holiday. Talk about ironical!'

Anna smiled. 'Love's a strange business, that's for sure. When I first met Joseph, I didn't consider him husband material. Our backgrounds were too different, for a start.' She paused, recalling her mother's reaction to the new man in her daughter's life. 'Mum didn't approve at first. She said she cringed every time Joseph opened his mouth. But, despite his broad Hampshire accent and slapdash grammar, he won her over and now she thinks he's wonderful!'

'That's mothers for you. Mine thinks I married too young and didn't know my own mind. She would have preferred a son-in-law with a PhD, so she doesn't think much of a plumber.'

'A useful trade, I would have thought, especially with all your renovations.'

'My thoughts entirely. Besides, I love him to bits.' Astrid turned to attend to Melinda, who was whimpering as she stirred from sleep. 'Hot are you, my pet? Never mind. We'll go for a swim when Adam wakes up.'

'No need to wait for us,' said Anna, aware of a sudden need to mull over Astrid's news. The mention of life experience as a criterion for entry to university had sparked a thought that she, too, could consider further study when Adam started school. Given Joseph's views on childcare and the lack of grandparents nearby – she assumed Astrid and Rick's parents would help look after Melinda – she couldn't consider applying for over two years. No matter; it would be light at the end of the tunnel, a kernel of hope to cling to during difficult days. *Mixed metaphors,* she thought, and was reminded of the unfinished poems tossed in the waste paper basket. Why had she given up so easily, allowing a few weeks of writer's block to dictate the future of an activity she enjoyed?

The answer arrived instantly, slapping her in the face like the waves that pounded the ocean beaches. Skin tingling, she decided there would be no more stalemate, no avoiding an issue that threatened the very fabric of her marriage. She would speak to Joseph that night and tell him a second baby was out of the question. No postponement until she felt more able to cope with the demands of motherhood – he had suggested that. After two and a half years, the situation remained crystal clear. She would not grow into the role. She lacked the intense maternal urge experienced by most other women and feared a second child would tip her over the edge.

There was no doubt in Anna's mind that she loved Adam, but there were moments when his behaviour so exasperated her that she slapped him harder than necessary. The resulting imprint of her hand on the back of his leg or buttocks made her deeply ashamed and afterwards, she would hug and kiss him to such an extent, he struggled to be free, as though more concerned by her remorse than the slap. She hated being stuck at home with a small child but dreaded the thought of the authorities removing Adam from her care should Joseph or anyone else discover evidence of her abuse.

Months earlier, she had almost confessed her loss of control to Elizabeth – they were discussing the difficulties of raising children without the support of family – but the moment had passed and there had been no opportunities since for candid exposure. Fear of losing the friendship had kept Anna silent; she enjoyed the visits to Bli Bli and especially appreciated the older couple's delight in Adam's presence. She recalled the day they encountered Ian on Shangri-La beach; his pleasure when nursing Adam; his attempt to reassure her by mentioning his wife's difficulties with new motherhood decades earlier. Anna couldn't imagine Elizabeth taking out her frustrations on a toddler. Whenever they met, she radiated serenity, never raising her voice when Ian knocked over his glass of wine – a common occurrence as he always gesticulated wildly when telling stories of past adventures – or Adam spilt cordial on the floor. Wisdom gained with age, Anna supposed, hoping she would acquire patience and equanimity in time.

A strong smell wafted over her, prompting a swift return to the immediate. Wrinkling her nose, she looked down at Adam, who was busy investigating his togs.

'Look, Mumma, a big poo.' He held the offending item towards her, laughing when she backed away. 'Clever boy,' he added, repeating his mother's words.

Anna resisted the urge to reprimand him, snatched him up and, holding him at arms' length, raced down the beach into the water.

Fight or Flight

Dirty dishes remained on the draining board, but Anna felt it more important to continue their conversation, so she joined Joseph on the front veranda where he'd adjourned after dinner to finish the bottle of wine provided that afternoon by a satisfied client. Rather than wait for the weekend to drink the wine – he seldom drank anything other than beer during the week – Joseph had opened the bottle at the dinner table, as Adam had been put to bed early. Weary from a day of sun and swimming, the toddler had almost fallen asleep over his dinner, giving his parents the chance to linger over *their* meal.

'According to my client,' Joseph had remarked, when Anna took her first sip, 'this wine is a first vintage from the Yarra Yering winery in Victoria and, despite its uninspiring label, is a bloody good drop.'

'I tend to agree with him,' she'd replied, glancing at the label. 'Dry Red Wine No. 1. He was right about the label, too.'

Spontaneous laughter had followed, easing the anxiety she had experienced since making her decision on Shorncliffe beach. After two glasses of wine, a good meal and with the evening breeze cooling her sunburnt cheeks, she felt sufficiently relaxed to raise the second baby question.

'I was surprised to receive a gift of wine. It's usually beer or tickets to the rugby,' Joseph remarked, as Anna's lips parted in readiness to speak. 'The only Aussies I know who drink wine are Ian and Elizabeth. The other day, one of my colleagues called me a plonkie when I mentioned drinking wine with meals.'

'Plonkie! That's a new one on me. But you're right. Quaffing wine doesn't seem part of the Australian drinking culture. Let's hope the situation is about to change. Your client obviously enjoys wine.'

'He's from southern Italy. Looks like a Mafia boss with his slicked-back hair and black suits. Told me he came over from Sicily with his parents and two sisters after the war. Ten of them now. What a handful!'

Dive in, girl, it's now or never, she thought, uncrossing her legs and sitting up straight. 'On the subject of family numbers, I think it's time we settled the issue once and for all.'

'No time like the present, as they say,' Joseph replied, leaning towards her, wine-bright eyes shining. 'Let's go to bed and make a start.'

Her chest tightened, trapping the necessary breath. 'I think...' she began, her voice as weak as the water she'd swallowed between glasses of wine. She concentrated on the breathing process, inhale-exhale, inhale-exhale, each action an effort until the band around her chest slackened. 'You misunderstand,' she said, trying to remain calm. 'There is no way I can have another baby.'

His free hand reached out to stroke her bare thigh. 'Oh, darling, why didn't you tell me? Is the doctor certain?'

She sighed. Why was he making this so difficult? 'It isn't a medical issue. At least, not in the way you mean.'

'What then?'

'Just listen will you, please?'

He removed his hand and sat back in the chair, his arms folded.

'It's a question of mental health,' she continued, having decided there was little point in mincing her words. 'No way could I cope with another baby, next year, the year after, or at any time in the future. If I had to stay at home for another five or six years, I'd really lose the plot.'

'I suppose you mean a breakdown,' he muttered.

She fiddled with the hem of her shorts, searching her mind for the right words. Words that wouldn't cut too deep and destroy the love between them that she believed remained strong, despite their recent animosity. 'I've tried to adapt to motherhood but, as I'm sure you've noticed, I haven't totally succeeded. A planned pregnancy might have helped, but I doubt it. I need....'

'What about Adam's needs?' he interrupted. 'Shouldn't they take priority?'

'Of course, and they do. I try to be a good mother. I take him on outings, play with him, read to him. It's just sometimes I...' She hesitated, sensed self-preservation kick in, pushing honest disclosure over the balcony rail and out into the warm night. 'Sometimes I feel life is passing me by and I want to scream.'

'I'm sure you're not the first mother to feel that way. What you need is more interaction with other mothers of small children. A mother's group, or something like it. Adam would enjoy meeting other children more often and you could have a good natter while the kids are playing.'

Anna couldn't think of anything worse than nattering with a group of mothers, expected to coo over babies or wax lyrical about a toddler's toilet training. Her experience at the Maternal and Child clinic had taught her most mothers had only one topic of conversation. She looked down at her feet, tanned from going barefoot most of the year, footwear only worn when leaving the domestic sphere. Not so long ago she had loved shoes: pretty sandals, elegant court shoes, colourful slip-ons. Her toenails had been neatly trimmed, nail varnish applied at least once a week, moisturising cream rubbed in every night to ensure smooth skin. Nowadays, her heels were cracked, her toes splayed, her toenails often dirty despite scrubbing them in the shower. 'What I need,' she said, half to herself, 'is a part-time job to restore my self-esteem.'

'You selfish woman!' Joseph snapped. 'Can't you even wait until he's at school?'

'I don't mean right now. I was thinking of next year when he goes to kindergarten.'

'How many hours a week do kids attend kindergarten?'

'Three part-days at age three. Nine until two, I think Astrid said.'

'Astrid?'

'The woman I met at Shorncliffe beach a few months back. I'm sure I told you about her. She's hoping to go to university next year when her little girl reaches kindergarten age.'

'She'll need more than fifteen hours a week to study at university level.'

'Her mother will help out and her husband's totally supportive.'

'Good for him.' Joseph emptied his wine glass. 'But your mother isn't around, Anna, so the situation's completely different. Besides, there aren't many jobs that would fit in with kindergarten hours. I can't see you as a checkout chick with your plum-in-the-mouth Pommy accent.'

Anna bristled, tempted to ask if a broad Australian accent was a pre-requisite for a supermarket position. Instead, she muttered, 'At least checkout chicks get paid.'

'So, I'm keeping you short of money, eh? Want a few more clothes, do you? More petrol to go gadding about?'

'No, and the housekeeping is quite sufficient, thank you,' she said, through gritted teeth.

'Good.' He bent over to retrieve the empty wine bottle. 'I admit a few more dollars wouldn't go astray, but as things stand, you'll just have to grin and bear it for a couple more years. Get yourself a hobby, go to an evening class if you're so desperate to get out of the house.' He got to his feet. 'Come on, girl, time for bed.'

* * *

Over subsequent days, Anna spent hours considering her next move. Certain Adam would enjoy playing with other children for two or three days a week, she was tempted to look for a job immediately as retaliation for Joseph's unyielding views on childcare. A sociable child, Adam often staged a tantrum when leaving playground or beach, and she had to drag him away, his small body rigid, his yells loud enough to cause head-turning and remarks about strict parenting. What would indulgent mothers say if they knew she had refused to have another baby?

Since Adam had turned two, complete strangers frequently asked when she was going to have a little companion for her son, a question she considered an impertinence and one which she always answered with a vague, 'We're thinking about it.' For all those prying women knew, she *could* be "trying for a baby" – an expression Anna abhorred – without success or have a health condition that prevented a second pregnancy. Next time anyone asked about her reproductive plans, she would alter her expression to one of melancholy and, in between lengthy sighs, describe a serious heart defect. She made a mental note to look up heart conditions in the library encyclopaedia.

The opportunity came sooner than expected, as several days of heavy rain prevented visits to beach or playground. After settling Adam with a picture book in the library's children's section, Anna hurried to the reference shelves and retrieved the H to M volume of a 1960s' encyclopaedia. Risking a reprimand from the stern-looking librarian sitting behind the loans desk, she lugged the heavy book over to the children's area and sat on a tiny chair next to Adam.

'Boat, Mumma' he announced, as she opened the encyclopaedia.

'Clever boy,' she answered, glancing at a red boat with white sails, floating on squiggles of blue sea. 'What else can you see?'

Mother and son turned pages, studied text and pictures. Adam soon became bored and, tossing his book on the floor, headed for a child-sized table where wooden jig-saw puzzles offered a more interesting activity. Absorbed in congenital heart defects, Anna failed to notice the librarian's approach. 'It's important to teach children respect for books,' the middle-aged woman remarked in a loud whisper.

Anna took a few moments to raise her head. 'Sorry, what did you say?'

The librarian pointed to the picture book that was lying open face-down on the polished floorboards.

'Oh, sorry. I thought he was still looking at it.' She shunted the heavy encyclopaedia to the seat Adam had vacated and bent down to retrieve *Johnny Goes to Sea.*

The librarian gave a small smile as Anna reached for the book.

'It won't happen again, I assure you, 'Anna whispered, sensing the need for an apology.

'Tell me, what are you so engrossed in?'

'Ventricular Septal Defects.'

'Oh dear. Not your little boy, is it?'

Anna shook her head. 'I've just learnt that a friend has a hole in the heart. I thought I'd look up the condition to learn more about it.'

The librarian nodded her approval and sat down in the empty chair to Anna's left. 'My niece had that condition. Lovely girl, but she wouldn't take the cardiologist's advice. She listened to her husband instead.'

Anna noted the past tense and assumed the niece had died.

'Five years tomorrow and I still get angry thinking about what happened. The cardiologist recommended one pregnancy only, but her husband wanted another child. It cost Nancy her life.'

Anna reached out to touch the older woman's arm. 'How dreadful. Why didn't your niece have surgery to repair the defect?'

'There was only a fifty-fifty chance of surviving the operation when Nancy's VSD was diagnosed in nineteen-sixty. It wasn't life-threatening, so the doctors advised her parents not to risk an operation. They said Nancy would have a normal life-span if she adhered to a few restrictions, such as not playing sport, having just one baby and taking antibiotics before dental procedures or surgery. Not much to ask, was it?'

'No.' Anna wanted to add, 'Men, they're so selfish,' but felt such a comment would be inappropriate.

The librarian got to her feet. 'Thanks for listening. I wish your friend well.'

Anna smiled and, thinking of Astrid, said quietly, 'Oh, she and her husband are quite content with their one little girl.'

The librarian nodded and hurried back to her desk.

* * *

When Anna next met Astrid on Shorncliffe beach, she repeated both the library disclosure and the balcony conversation. Astrid was amused by Anna's plan to thwart second baby questions, and relieved that Joseph had agreed with the decision not to have a second baby. 'I still don't understand his objection to childcare,' Anna added, as Astrid stretched out beside her on a colourful beach towel. 'I'd be so much happier if I had a job. Even one day a week would help.'

'My advice is to go ahead and find one. He'll soon get used to the idea.'

'I suppose so.' She tried to envisage Joseph's reaction and felt dismayed at the thought of becoming embroiled in an intense argument. She didn't want to risk creating a rift that couldn't be healed.

'I've put Melinda's name down at Sandgate childcare centre for next year,' Astrid remarked, glancing at her daughter, who was busily engaged in patting Adam's sandcastle. 'It's a great place, located right next to the kindy. In fact, it occupies half of the same building. A fence separates the two sections, so kindy kids whose mothers can't collect them at two are taken next door. The director told me staff call them "the fence kids". Just right for Melinda, if I'm accepted at uni. My plan is to attend part-time until she goes to school – two subjects a semester and evening lectures if possible.'

'Wish I had my life sorted like you do.'

'Not sorted, Anna, planned. If I don't get into uni, I'll have to think again.'

'A job?'

'I refuse to consider a plan B at the moment.'

'Fair enough.' Anna got to her feet. 'Fancy a swim?'

Astrid nodded. 'Sure, it is a bit hot.' She sat up and reached for Melinda's "floaties", the inflatable yellow armbands recommended for babies and toddlers. 'Come on, kids, water time.'

Two tousled heads looked up and small hands discarded plastic spades. 'Good-oh,' Adam exclaimed and took off for the sea.

'Wait for me!' Anna shouted, racing after him. 'You need your floaties.'

They met in shallow water, Anna managing to grab Adam's togs as he ran headlong over a sandbank. Skinny buttocks wobbling, he shook her off and disappeared into a deep trough. She plunged in after him, located the squirming body – he was making a valiant attempt at dog-paddle – and, seizing his waist from behind, lifted his head clear of the water. Safely back on the sandbank, she turned him around. 'What on earth do you think you're doing?'

'I swimming,' he answered, his lips parting in a cheeky grin. 'Clever boy.'

'Not clever, naughty. You must never go in the water without me.'

His lower lip trembled.

'No ice-cream for Adam today.'

He began to blubber, saline tears and water mingling on his flushed cheeks.

She carried him to shore, swallowing her own impulse to cry.

Acceptance

Summer continued well into April, with the unrelenting high humidity creating discord in many a suburban household as pedestal and ceiling fans struggled to cool overheated dwellings. The Easter holiday provided some relief, with many families departing for the north and south coasts in cars laden with camping gear. Lacking sufficient funds to hire a caravan or buy a tent, Anna and Joseph decided to take day trips to anywhere offering shade and the prospect of immersion in cold water. Mass suburban exodus meant crowded beaches, plus difficulty in finding a parking spot, so they abandoned coastal areas and headed into the bush.

Swimming in cool creeks in various pockets of the Sunshine Coast hinterland proved a delightful experience. Shaded by huge eucalypts, these less popular – even over Easter – picnic spots provided a welcome respite from suburbia. In some places, water tumbled over smooth boulders into shallow pools, giving Adam the opportunity to paddle and sail plastic boats, while his parents watched from grassy banks or deeper water mid-stream. With the near-disaster at Shorncliffe still fresh in her mind, Anna had made certain to attach floaties to her fearless son's arms the moment Joseph had silenced Viv's engine.

Four days spent in tranquil bushland finally dispelled the pall of tension that had hung over 69a Harrow Street for months, giving Anna hope for a harmonious future. There would be the occasional argument, of course – a natural occurrence in any relationship – but she believed the worst was behind them now that Joseph had accepted her baby decision. Apart from appearing more relaxed in the evenings, he refrained from switching on the television the moment he walked in the door and, after discarding his work clothes and shoes for a brief pair of shorts, would pad into the kitchen to chat as she prepared dinner. He also paid extra attention to Adam, joining his son before bedtime on the living room carpet to construct towers with wooden bricks, or build with the new Lego Duplo bricks designed for pre-school children. Energetic play frequently followed, Adam squealing with delight as his father swung him around or pretended to be a dinosaur and chased him on all-fours between the furniture. Like many small boys, Adam was fascinated by these huge reptiles from a bygone age, particularly Tyrannosaurus Rex, which he called "six-inches teeth", as the Latin classification was beyond his two-year-old ability. Over-stimulated, he would take longer to settle at bedtime, but Anna felt this was a small price to pay for additional paternal participation.

Her father had rarely played with his daughters when they were small and wouldn't have dreamt of sitting on the floor or crawling around furniture. In keeping with most 1950s fathers, on returning home from work he would head for his favourite armchair, to retreat behind the evening paper until dinner was served. On light summer evenings, he might engage in a ball game or push one or other daughter on the swing, but routinely he spent the time watering vegetables or weeding, irritating their mother by wearing his white office shirt and suit trousers, rather than changing into more suitable garments.

Sometimes, as Anna unpegged Joseph's short-sleeved cotton work-shirts and tailored shorts from the Hill's Hoist after less than two hours in the sun, she would picture her mother draping damp garments on a wooden clothes-horse in front of the fire during the long winter months. Then, whatever the temperature, she would shiver at the memory of winter in their first flat: underwear spread to dry on lukewarm radiators, heavy clothes hung on an airer positioned over the bath. Winter washing in England had been a drawn-out process, and one she hoped never to repeat.

The end of April brought cooler, less humid weather and with it, a lengthy letter from England containing welcome news. Her parents were planning a September visit and wanted to check if staying with their daughter and son-in-law for six weeks would be too much of an imposition. Anna laughed at her mother's formal language. The prospect of adult company was a delight rather than a nuisance. She replied the following day, assuring her parents it would be a pleasure to show them around her adopted land – at least the South-east Queensland part – introduce them to her friends and acquaint them with the Australian way of life. In her excitement, she forgot to mention getting to know their first grandchild, so had to screw up the first sheet of airmail paper and begin again! Thank God Joseph hadn't read her letter, as he often did before she sealed the envelope.

Since the second baby discussion, Anna had tried to appear content with her lot in deference to Joseph's understanding. She had been prepared for lengthy debate leading to bitter argument and wondered if her inference of future mental illness had been the catalyst for his capitulation. Months earlier, watching a television documentary on the increasing prevalence of psychiatric disorders, Joseph had expressed horror at the subject and had left the room.

When he returned from 'a walk around the block to clear my head', he'd told her about his late Uncle Norman, a relative Anna had never met or known existed. An airman shot down over Germany and taken prisoner for two years, Norman Fletcher had returned home in '45 haunted by his experiences and was in and out of psychiatric hospitals for decades. The year Joseph turned fourteen, he had shared his bedroom with Uncle Norman for six months while the sixty-year-old, declared unfit to work and allocated a one hundred percent war pension, waited for a council flat. On an almost nightly basis, Joseph had woken to screams and shouts of 'She's going down!' and 'The bugger's got the gunner!'

Witnessing an uncle's terrible unravelling as an adolescent might have influenced the adult Joseph, but whatever the reason for his acceptance, Anna felt grateful for a husband who had acknowledged her concerns as genuine, rather than the rantings of a bored housewife. She decided not to take Astrid's advice and deferred all thoughts of getting a job until Adam was installed at kindergarten. Her parents' visit would provide distraction from domestic matters, both during their stay and beforehand, as she planned a holiday itinerary.

A second letter received on a rain-swept May morning confirmed their arrival and departure dates, prompting more practical matters. They would need a second double bed, pillows and bedding, plus new bath towels to replace those that were faded and thin from copious washes; all costly items that would put a dent in their meagre savings. Transport was also a problem now that Joseph had decided to take three weeks' leave during his in-laws' visit, as Viv was too small to accommodate four adults and a child. Although child restraints in vehicles were not yet mandatory in every state, gone were the days when small children could sit on adults' knees. Adam had a booster seat that enabled him to see out of the window and was strapped in with a seatbelt, one of four Joseph had installed even though the current legislation covered new cars only.

'We could hire a larger car,' Anna suggested, following a lengthy discussion about the outlay necessary to host her parents for six weeks.

Joseph considered the issue, one hand resting on her knee, the other cradling a wineglass. They were sitting side by side on the three-seater sofa, rather than in the individual armchairs they favoured during hot weather. 'Bit of a waste of money. Maybe we could borrow Rog's station wagon?'

'No way. What if we had an accident?'

'Insurance would cover it.'

'But think of the inconvenience for them.'

Joseph removed his hand from her leg and scratched his chin. 'You've got a point. So, what's the alternative?'

Anna shrugged. 'I'm too tired to think, after trawling second-hand shops all day for another bed.'

'No luck then?'

She shook her head and yawned. 'I'm off to bed. Coming?'

Suddenly, Joseph slapped his bare thigh, propelling droplets of red wine from his glass to his pale blue shorts. 'One problem solved!' he declared, oblivious to the spreading stains. 'We put your parents in our room and borrow a couple of camp beds and sleeping bags from Rog and Mary. They only use them at Easter and Christmas.'

'Clever boy!' she cried, leaning towards him and planting a kiss on his tanned cheek. 'And that way we won't clutter up the study permanently.'

'All the same, that room could do with more than a desk and an ancient filing cabinet. Keep looking for another bed. We're bound to get more visitors from England and it's not as though anyone studies in there. Besides, now we don't need the space for a second child, we can furnish it as a guest room.'

Colour flooded her cheeks, threatening to betray a well-kept secret. She rose quickly, walked down the hall to the toilet and closed and locked the door behind her.

* * *

Fingertips pounded typewriter keys and the carriage return bell reverberated through the room as though an impatient salesman stood at the front door. Narrative exploded in her mind, but lack of practice meant she could barely keep up with the flow.

I'll show him what I use the study for! she thought, pulling a third sheet of paper from the Olivetti. Child-chatter from the second bedroom reached her ears. 'Bugger,' she said aloud, listening for the patter of small feet on polished floorboards. Bent over the typewriter, she sensed Adam's presence in the study doorway, so forced a cheerful inquiry. 'Good sleep, poppet?'

'Sleep all gone.' He wandered over to the desk and stood beside her, sucking his thumb, a much-loved, almost threadbare teddy clutched in his free hand.

'Drink?' she asked, her sentence stock exhausted.

He thrust the teddy onto her lap. 'Toilet first, Adam good boy,' he declared between sucks and hurried from the room.

Her irritation dissipated as she zipped up the blue typewriter cover, a necessary protection against inquisitive fingers. Adam *was* a good boy mostly, her impatience with a child who was slap-bang in the middle of the "terrible twos" – Astrid's label – being a fault she must try to overcome. The conclusion to her new short story, *The Window*, could wait until tomorrow, as the details were clear in her mind.

The following afternoon brought a second surge of creativity, plus an unexpected telephone call from Shirley giving details of a short story competition run by the Fellowship of Australian Writers, Queensland Branch. After posting her entry, Anna still couldn't fathom why one particular competition had eliminated her lingering self-doubt, but she still remained determined to write whenever the opportunity arose.

* * *

The winter months passed in a flurry of activity, both physical and cerebral. Preparations for her parents' visit proceeded apace, Anna washing curtains, wiping down paintwork and tidying cupboards as though her mother would be inspecting every inch of the house. At weekends, Joseph worked alongside her in the garden, planting, weeding and pruning, while Adam played his part by picking up discarded material and loading it into his small wheelbarrow. Sometimes he tipped the contents onto the concrete slab beneath the rear veranda, or took handfuls of twigs and flung them skyward, laughing as they peppered the lawn. On these occasions, it was Joseph rather than Anna who displayed intolerance and she had to remind him that their son hadn't yet reached his third birthday, so couldn't be expected to behave like an adult labourer.

Throughout winter, darkness descended shortly after five o'clock, offering additional time for poetry and prose. After bathing Adam, Anna tossed her good mothering intentions aside and sat him in front of the television, before retreating to the study for an hour to edit the afternoon's effort. Soon, the red folder bulged, prompting the purchase of a second ring binder, yet her creativity remained clandestine, as she couldn't risk disturbing household harmony. Wife and Mother might be the labels assigned to her by a still traditional society, but her interior world favoured a different classification, one she hoped would alter with time and practice. Unpublished, she remained loath to call herself Writer and chose instead the more accurate Apprentice Wordsmith.

September arrived, bringing warmth and cold-climate parents, a third birthday celebrated on a sunny veranda, cake and candles, plus a young mother's wish for continued inspiration. Anna rejoiced in the chance to parade her preferred country and spent the first two weeks taking her parents to favourite haunts within reasonable driving distance. Whether picnicking on the passage side of Bribie Island or walking through lush rainforest at Mount Glorious, she extolled the delights of living "down under", employing more adjectives than a verbose nineteenth-century poet.

'Swallowed a thesaurus, have you?' her father remarked one afternoon, as they sat eating ice-cream on Sandgate foreshore, a high tide ensuring a pleasing view of Moreton Bay.

'No, I just want you both to know how much I adore living here. Emigrating was the best decision Joseph and I have made to date.'

Her mother smiled. 'I'm relieved to see Australia is working out for you, dear. I have to admit I was concerned. Moving to the other side of the world seemed such an enormous step to be taking less than a year into marriage.'

'We wanted adventure, a chance to explore another country, embrace a different way of life. As for timing, we considered it sensible to take the opportunity before we settled down to parenting and a mortgage.'

Her father nodded and patted her shoulder. 'You've done well, my dear. A lovely little house and a beautiful garden.' He rose from the seat and headed for his grandson, who was now busy chasing seagulls.

'Typical of your father. He forgot to mention your most important achievement.'

Anna refrained from comment and turned her attention to a sailing boat scudding across the bay.

'Are you planning another baby soon?'

Anna sighed, a fictitious heart condition being of no use on this occasion.

'Is it proving difficult this time?'

Reluctant to risk a verbal response – her mother had always known when she told lies – Anna lowered her gaze.

'Oh, darling, I'm so sorry. I won't mention the subject again.'

Grateful for a reprieve, Anna raised her head and smiled her thanks.

* * *

An unexpected evening visit from neighbour Ted – he rarely ventured outside after his five o'clock shower – banished all memory of that awkward bayside conversation. After refusing the offer of a beer and a comfortable armchair, the old man perched on a dining chair and embarked on a long-winded exposition of the Holden Kingswood's merits compared with those of the Vauxhall Viva.

'Are you trying to sell me your car?' Joseph asked, when at last Ted paused for breath.

'No way, mate, I couldn't do without the Kingswood.'

'Then is there something I can do for you?'

Ted studied his worn slippers. 'Knew I should have brought Nell. She's so good at explaining.'

Joseph leant forward. 'Sorry Ted, I didn't quite catch that.'

'Well, it's like this.' Ted raised his head and looked directly at Joseph. 'I've watched your missus taking her folks out in the Vauxhall and I said to Nell, "Reckon it'll be a helluva squash when young Joe takes his holiday." ' He paused to take another breath. 'So, I was wondering if you'd like to borrow the Kingswood? It seats five adults easy and the seat I made for the grandkids when they were small should be just right for the littl'un.'

Anna leapt to her feet and hurried across the room. 'Oh Ted, that would be wonderful!' She planted a kiss on his stubbled cheek, much to the old man's embarrassment.

A chorus of thanks erupted, followed by insistence on a toast to Ted's magnanimous gesture. Joseph hurried to the fridge to fetch beer and wine, with Anna close behind to ensure he selected suitable glasses.

English voices rose in unison. Ted beamed as glasses clinked, a beer bottle clasped in his weathered fingers.

* * *

On the last day of her parents' visit, Anna was preparing a light lunch when Adam raced into the kitchen clutching a letter. In recent months, she had allowed him to retrieve the mail on his own, a task he enjoyed and so far, had accomplished without incident.

'Postie been,' he declared, shoving the envelope into her shorts' pocket.

'Thank you, Adam. Just the one today?'

He nodded, then held up two fingers.

'That's two.'

'Yes. Two letters for Granny Nell.'

Her parents were packing in the bedroom, well within earshot, so she dropped to her knees and said in a low voice, 'Adam, you mustn't empty other people's mailboxes.'

'Granny Nell let me.'

'Did she ask you to fetch her mail today?'

'No.' He grinned. 'I big help, she said.'

Anna sighed. She would have to run next door to check what Adam had done with the Wootton's mail. He had no trouble opening the gate leading into their front garden, so hopefully he had left it on the front doorstep.

Her mother's arrival stalled her departure. 'All packed,' she announced. 'So, can I help you with lunch?'

Anna shook her head and, getting to her feet, quickly explained the mail issue.

'Post,' her mother corrected and pointed to the envelope sticking out of Anna's shorts. 'Better leave your letter here, you could lose it running to the neighbours.'

Anna extracted the envelope and noted the sender's city address. 'Probably another bill.' She fumbled with the thick paper, her hands damp from washing lettuce.

'Here, let me open it.' Her mother slit the envelope with a polished fingernail. 'Not a bill, dear, it's from FAW, whatever that is.' She handed over the letter.

'Fellowship of Australian Writers,' Anna explained, eyes and smile widening as she read. 'Good heavens, I've won the short story competition!' Waving the letter above her head, she twirled around, prompting a similar movement from her small son.

Her father appeared in the doorway. 'What on earth's going on out here?'

'Anna's won a writing competition.'

'Well I never!' Rushing into the kitchen, he flung his arms around his daughter, an atypical gesture that saw Anna almost slip on the vinyl flooring. 'Congratulations, my clever girl. And to think we didn't even know you had taken up story writing.'

'I also write poetry,' Anna said, as he released her. 'I started soon after we arrived here. Responses to the beautiful Australian landscape.' She glanced at her bare feet, grubby as usual from gardening. 'I haven't had any published.' She looked up and smiled at her father. 'Shirley's always on at me to do something with my work, so I finally succumbed and entered the FAW competition.'

'Shirley?'

'You must remember her, Dad. We visited Shirley and Sam last weekend. Great barbeque at their lovely new house.'

'Oh yes, the girl with pink streaks in her hair.'

Anna suppressed a sigh. Why did men always notice a woman's appearance, rather than listen to what she had to say?

Her mother moved into the kitchen. 'What's the prize, dear?'

'One hundred dollars.'

'Lovely. You can buy yourself some new clothes.'

'Maybe.' Anna smoothed her creased shorts. Books would be preferable to clothes. Books on the art of writing. Her confidence had soared in the few minutes since reading the letter. Could she dare to hope the win might be the beginning of a career?

Her mother stepped forward, smiling. 'Keep up the good work, dear. Writing is a nice little hobby and fits in well with parenting and home duties.'

Beneath the surface of her smile, Anna seethed.

Consolidation

The Fletcher family spent ten years living in the house built in the Wootton's former back garden, but by 1981 it was time for a change, as the suburb was altering before their eyes. One after another, the quaint weatherboard homes were being demolished and replaced with bland brick flats that covered almost the entire length of each long, narrow block of land. Nell had moved years before, Ted having died of a heart attack one afternoon while digging his vegetable patch. A good way to go for him, as Joseph said, but a terrible shock for Nell, who'd witnessed the event from the back steps.

Soon afterwards, Joseph had purchased the Holden Kingswood – Nell couldn't drive and had no intention of learning in her seventies – providing much-needed space to transport the procession of visitors from England. Despite only having a single car space in the garage, Viv the Viva remained part of the family for several more years, Anna preferring to drive a smaller vehicle to her part-time job as secretary to a Sandgate solicitor. A second car also proved useful when Joseph had to visit building sites far from his city office.

In mid '78, Joseph changed jobs to gain promotion, triggering a search for Viv's replacement as his new company was situated in a suburb lacking decent public transport. By then, Anna had been driving the Kingswood to and from work for some months, Viv proving unreliable. Several Saturday mornings were spent trawling second-hand car dealerships, giving rise to subsequent disagreements on the footpath which recalled an earlier occasion, when Anna had wanted a two-seater sports car and Joseph a four-seater sedan.

At this juncture, Anna wanted a small Datsun hatchback, while Joseph favoured a Datsun ute, maintaining it would be handy to transport garden waste and other rubbish to the dump, as well as to use for work. The day Viv was traded in, Anna struggled to suppress tears as the family squashed into the ute's bench seat and drove away from the car yard. Viv had been a lifeline during Adam's first five years, enabling her to escape the constricting space of house and suburb. She remained convinced that, without such freedom, she would have fled both motherhood and marriage long before the lure of fictional worlds delivered salvation, albeit at intermittent intervals.

* * *

Over the years, Anna had had a modicum of success, with short stories, articles and poetry being published in magazines and anthologies, but the payment received – twenty, thirty dollars, or a free subscription – was insufficient to make a difference to the family income, so, once Adam started school, she had looked for a part-time job. Three days a week satisfied both her desire to contribute to the household and Joseph's wish that Adam continue to be her top priority. Like many men of the period, he remained trapped in a '50s/'60s mindset that regarded woman as the primary child-carer, man as the primary breadwinner. However, he should have known better than to label Anna "the cake-winner", on the day she secured her part-time job. Although delivered in a mock-serious tone, the designation failed to impress, making Anna determined that one day she would earn a second loaf.

The secretarial position paid well and a nine-to-four working day enabled her to drop Adam at school on her way to work. A woman Anna had befriended at the school gates collected him at three o'clock along with her own three children, a solution that satisfied all parties. Adam was delighted to have extended play and Narelle White was happy with the notes pressed into her palm at the end of each week. Anna imagined the family were struggling – there were three older children as well – so made certain to pay above the going rate for childcare. School holidays presented a problem if the solicitor's wife couldn't step in – she already worked the two days a week that Anna didn't – but usually someone could be found to look after a small boy described by one teacher as 'a delightful child with beautiful manners' and 'a dear little angel' by another.

With her own relationship with Adam still oscillating between intense love and frequent irritation at his disobedience and penchant for mischief, Anna found it difficult to envisage an angelic schoolboy seated quietly at his desk. Sometimes, sitting at her own desk in the study, she wondered if she had produced a changeling, a thought that eventually morphed into a short horror story.

Then, as the new decade dawned, Anna's pleasure in creating short fiction and poetry began to wane and she assumed her creative period had ended, a logical conclusion given she was no longer a bored house-wife struggling to cope with a pre-school child. At first, she felt sad-dened by the demise; unlike her friend Shirley, librarian and mother of five-year-old George, she had failed to achieve anything of note over an entire decade. The desired progression to professional author had not transpired, her limited output confirming her mother's observa-tion that 'writing was a nice little hobby'.

The hours spent hunched over a typewriter or staring into space waiting for inspiration had been therapy, nothing more, nothing less; an essential exercise for the safe release of tension, frustration and the host of other negative emotions she had experienced over many years. By inventing characters that could love and hate, rage and pacify at her whim, she had kept darker thoughts at bay. What would have hap-pened if her tendency to lash out had escalated into child abuse? The consequences were too horrific to contemplate. Since securing a job, Anna had abandoned self-analysis, convinced it led to dejection and lack of self-esteem rather than adjustment of behaviour and attitudes. She had hated being a full-time mother, that was her truth and berat-ing herself for what society regarded as complete failure accomplished nothing meaningful.

The retreat from authorship demanded more than doing extra housework or visiting the library during her two days a week at home, so she sought other activities that promised interesting interludes. Swimming held her attention for a few months, but trawling up and down designated lanes – middle for competent swimmers, either side for the mediocre – became tedious, toned muscles a meagre reward for having to wash togs, towel and hair after every session.

She had met a couple of young women, but neither showed promise as future friends, as the conversations they had held while sunbathing on the grassy banks bordering the pool were limited to children's accomplishments and grumbles about husbands' failure to fix things around the house. Winter was fast approaching, so Anna took her leave of the outdoor pool and joined a public-speaking group that met once a fortnight in the local library on Wednesday evening.

Suburban Speakers was open to men and women of all ages, its aim being to foster self-confidence and overcome nervousness by providing a safe environment in which to learn. Constructive criticism was given by the Club Critic, a recently-retired high school teacher. Beginners were encouraged to speak for no more than three minutes on a topic of their choice, eventually progressing to ten minutes on set subjects. The ultimate aspiration of many members, already achieved by a few, was to reach the finals of a public-speaking competition held as part of Brisbane's Warana Spring Festival.

The prospect of speaking in public held no fears for Anna – she had often read the lesson at school assembly and in church – so she quickly advanced from three to ten minute speeches, much to the delight of Joan Thursby, the Club Critic. Drafting the speeches proved excellent discipline, speakers having to confine their notes to headings on 3 x 5 inch cards. After annotating the cards, Anna would practise her speech in front of the bedroom mirror before unleashing her often controversial opinions on fellow members. By the end of the year, Joan had suggested Anna enter the next Warana competition, a proposal that evoked both pride and apprehension. It was one thing to be a star pupil – Joan's opinion – quite another to represent Suburban Speakers in a prestigious competition.

'Maybe next year,' Anna told the older woman, as they sat sipping tea in the library kitchen following the first meeting of 1981. 'I wouldn't want to tread on anyone's toes, particularly those with years of experience.' She was thinking of forty-something Ralph, who had come third in the competition three years earlier and contrived to mention his success at almost every meeting.

'It's time for a change,' Joan replied. 'We have more than our fair share of middle-aged members. Having a young, competent woman as our contestant would do wonders for this club.'

'Not if I was knocked out in the first round.'

'I'm confident you wouldn't be.'

Anna recalled Shirley's advice that was given years before. 'I guess you've got to be in it to win it.'

'Good on you, girl. We'll show those men!'

* * *

Joseph frowned when Anna repeated Joan's statement as they lay in bed that night. 'From the way you've described her, I hadn't figured Joan as a Women's Libber.'

'Appearances can be deceiving, you know.' Anna pushed back the sheet to reveal Joseph's evenly tanned body. 'I'm sure none of the other parents attending Adam's school concert would imagine we enjoy taking our clothes off on the beach and cavorting in the waves with other nudists.'

'Swimming and sunbathing in the nude are healthy activities,' Joseph said solemnly.

'Unless,' Anna countered, running her fingers over his abdomen, 'one is naked in private with a desirable partner.' Her kiss prevented further conversation.

* * *

Unwelcome attention from an anaemic-looking accountant dealt the first blow to Anna's public-speaking aspirations. Initially, Ralph the Finalist's offer to coach her for the Warana competition seemed harmless enough – half an hour or so after the club meeting, with library users still present on the other side of a thin wall – but his hand resting on her shoulder as they left the building, followed by a kiss on both cheeks, soon alerted her to an ulterior motive. A subsequent suggestion that they meet for an extended period at his flat, convinced her it was time to call a halt.

Joan tried to dissuade her from leaving the club, but Anna had made up her mind to join another public-speaking group closer to the area where she and Joseph hoped to purchase a larger house, later in the year. In the interim, she would concentrate on decorating, every room looking shabby from over nine years' occupation.

The painting proceeded unhindered throughout the autumn and winter months, as Anna was determined to present an attractive home to prospective buyers. At weekends, Joseph tackled the outside, hiring planks and trestles from the local hardware store when he reached the high side of the building. At almost nine, Adam offered to prepare lunches, leading Anna to remark that he would make a great chef one day.

At the end of September, with fresh paintwork gleaming and the garden blooming, they decided to put the house on the market. The real estate agent said the house could take several months to sell, being rather small and tucked away down an easement, so Anna resigned herself to weeks of keeping the house tidy – a difficult task with regard to Adam's bedroom. Meanwhile, they decided to spend Saturday afternoons driving around the new estates that were sprouting in former market gardens further north.

Anna favoured a newish but well-established house, one storey brick with double garage and two living areas, while Joseph wanted brand-new, saying he preferred to plan the garden layout himself. The third member of the family didn't care what he lived in so long as it was close to water, preferably the salty variety, although a chlorinated pool would suffice. Since starting school, Adam had become a proficient swimmer and diver, winning medals in the school swimming carnival every year.

A combination of Anna's poor navigation skills and Adam's incessant chatter led Joseph to take a wrong turn as they approached a new estate not far from Sandgate. 'Shut up, both of you!' he shouted, brakes squealing as he rounded a corner and came to a halt in front of a mountain of soil. Seizing the Refidex – Brisbane's street directory – from Anna, he flicked through the pages, trying to establish their location. 'I think we're here,' he muttered, stabbing the corner of a page where dotted lines indicated unmade and unnamed streets. 'Elizabeth Park.' He glanced at the tangle of bush opposite. 'Doesn't look much like a bloody park.'

'Early days, I expect,' Anna remarked, her gaze sweeping over tree-studded grassland to her left and white-painted pegs marking the boundaries of newly-created house blocks.

'No good to us, then. It will be months before anything's built.' He flung the Refidex at Anna before selecting reverse gear. 'A double move would be a pain in the arse.'

'Are we going to buy two houses now?' Adam asked.

'Don't be silly.' Gravel scattered like marbles as the car reversed.

'Dad means we'd have to move into a rented place first, if we were going to build a new house.'

'But we've got a house!'

'I'll explain later, love.' Anna gripped the side of her seat as the car shot forward into a new-laid cul-de-sac. A glance at Joseph's face told her it would be unwise to mention his mistake.

'Shit, fresh bitumen!' He applied the brakes and sat hunched over the steering wheel. 'God knows what it's done to the bloody paint-work!'

Anna suppressed a smile, his concern for the car reminiscent of a blustering character in the TV sitcom *Kingswood Country*. Since purchasing Ted's beloved Kingswood, Joseph had joined the ranks of

Australian men that prized their Holden above all else. 'I'm going to stretch my legs.' She unfastened her seatbelt. 'Coming, Adam?'

Mother and son explored each of the five blocks, Adam climbing several large eucalypts, Anna meandering between trees, the vision of a spacious brick home hovering above slashed grass. There was room for a pool if they could afford it, plus a ten-minute drive to work and she was sure they had passed a school just before the wrong turn. Adam didn't seem bothered by the prospect of changing schools when they moved, his reaction a nonchalant, 'Don't care, Mum, so long as there's a pool.'

A deep-throated car horn bellowed through the landscape like an enraged bull, putting paid to further rumination. 'Time to leave,' she called to her boy, who was kneeling on the ground to examine a trail of ants.

'I like it here. Can we come back?' he asked, as they skirted soft bitumen.

She smiled. 'I'll see what I can do.'

Suburban Shocks

In the weeks leading up to Christmas 1981, persuading Joseph to consider building a house in Elizabeth Park, or locating another public-speaking group, were far from Anna's thoughts, the headlines in the *Courier-Mail* and the sombre news items on local radio and television being her primary focus.

The first she knew of what became almost the only neighbourhood talking point for months, was a telephone call at work from Adam's teacher, asking her to collect him from the staffroom, as Mrs White had been unavoidably detained. Narelle White had given birth to her seventh child six months before, so Anna assumed baby Claire was sick, or there was a problem with one of the other children. As she drove away from work, she hoped this didn't mean a new after-school carer would have to be found. Adam liked the rough and tumble of the White household. He enjoyed playing ball games in the overgrown back yard, having jam sandwiches and red cordial dished up for afternoon tea – items never served in his own home – the lop-sided swing, a shaggy dog that licked his sticky fingers.

For her part, Anna considered it important for Adam to experience a slice of life in a family different from his own. He needed to learn that not every child had his advantages: a bedroom to himself, a new rather than second-hand bicycle, expensive toys and clothes sent from England by doting grandparents. Adam had been too young to notice unpolished floorboards or a sparsity of furniture, during what Anna privately dubbed "the struggle years", and in recent years, his father's promotion and mother's income had enabled them to pay off the mortgage, as well as purchase a second car. Compared with the White family, the Fletchers lived a luxurious existence.

When Narelle had announced she was expecting a seventh child at the advanced age of forty-five, Anna was so shocked, she didn't know how to respond. Congratulations seemed inappropriate; surely no one would plan a seventh child, especially as the other six were all at school?

'I thought it was the change at first,' Narelle had added, her expression one of resignation. 'No such luck, but.'

'What are you going to do?' The question was asked before Anna had considered its futility. In Queensland, a woman couldn't have an abortion unless her life was at risk. Abortion had been a hot topic that year, with ultra-conservative Premier Joh Bjelke-Petersen and his cabinet seeking to strengthen the existing law by drawing up the Pregnancy Termination Control Bill. Following emotive demonstrations, including a threat to storm parliament, the bill, described by one female MP as 'the most frightening piece of fascist legislation I have ever seen in my life', had been narrowly defeated.

'Nothing I can do except hope for a miscarriage.'

Anna had remained silent, memories of her own unspoken thoughts nine years earlier pricking her conscience like red-hot needles.

But since Claire's birth, Narelle had appeared content, the baby plump and placid, the older children happy to mind her while their mother made dinner, so the teacher's whispered comments, made while escorting Anna and Adam to the school gate, seemed more like gossip than facts.

'Cigarette burns?' Anna exclaimed. 'Surely the neighbour must be mistaken! Besides, Narelle doesn't smoke.'

'Maybe Mr White's to blame, or one of the older boys.' The teacher slowed to allow Adam to run ahead. 'But, whatever the case, when the neighbour phoned the school, she said a social worker had asked her to look after the younger kids until Mr White came home.'

Anna glanced at her son who was skipping towards the gate. 'Was Adam at the house when this was going on?'

'No. I found him hanging about by the school gate. He said you had told him always to wait for Mrs White, so he didn't go with her kids when they decided to walk home on their own.'

Anna sighed with relief. 'Thank you for looking after him. I'd better make alternative arrangements for tomorrow afternoon.'

'Don't worry about that, Mrs Fletcher, I'd be happy to mind him. Give you the chance to organise something over the weekend.'

'That's very generous, Miss Trent. I'll get here as soon as I can.'

'No need to hurry. Adam read a book while he was waiting for you. He was good as gold.'

Anna hoped her smile was convincing. It was hard to picture Adam sitting still for five minutes, let alone an hour. On the days she picked him up from school, he raced around the house and garden like a tiger just released from a zoo enclosure.

* * *

When Adam had gone to bed, Anna explained the childcare situation to Joseph, making sure to stress that she believed the neighbour had over-reacted. If Narelle indulged in the odd cigarette to calm her nerves, she might have accidentally burnt Claire's arm.

'I just can't believe Narelle would deliberately harm her baby,' she concluded. 'I've never seen her so much as smack one of the children.'

Joseph nodded. 'Well, whatever happened, you'd better find someone else to mind Adam. I really don't want him going back there. The poor woman has got enough to do with seven kids. Are they Catholics, by any chance?'

'I don't think so.'

'Well, I hope he had the snip after the last one.'

'Vasectomy is still illegal in Queensland, I believe.'

Joseph shrugged. 'No idea. Not something I've ever thought about.'

Anna gulped her shandy to smother a caustic response. Apart from using condoms on the few occasions they had made love before marriage, he had always left birth control to her. 'Thank God for the Pill,' she muttered.

Joseph raised his beer bottle. 'I'll drink to that. Didn't go much on Durex and I sure as hell don't fancy a vasectomy.'

'It's less invasive than a woman having her tubes tied. That's a major operation.'

'How do you know?'

'Read about it somewhere,' she answered, unwilling to mention the Children by Choice literature Shirley had shown her.

Parents of one by choice, both Shirley and Sam supported the organisation that offered counselling services and information to women experiencing unplanned pregnancies. 'In this day and age, every woman should have a choice about reproduction,' Shirley had said one afternoon, as her son George and Adam kicked a football around the garden. 'Queensland abortion laws are like something from the Dark Ages. Sometimes, I wonder if voters will ever toss out this regressive state government.'

Anna felt the same, but rarely had the opportunity to express her views, politics, like religion, being taboo when socialising. Before long, she would have to find a group, public-speaking or otherwise, that would at least tolerate her progressive views. 'What would you say if I wanted to join...' she began, then glanced at the wall clock. Ten-fifteen; too late to begin what could become a heated discussion.

'Wanted to what?'

'Nothing, just thinking aloud.'

'About sterilisation?'

'No, women's rights,' she said quickly and, picking up her empty glass, she hurried into the kitchen.

* * *

Over the weekend, Anna made numerous phone calls to the parents of Adam's school friends, but although most sympathised with her situation, none expressed a willingness to care for him after school. Concerned that she wouldn't be able to rearrange her working hours – the solicitor's wife played tennis and bridge three days a week – Anna turned to neighbours in the hope someone could help her out for the remainder of the school year. The six-week school holidays wouldn't be an issue, as the family were travelling to England, courtesy of Aunt Maud, who maintained it was high time her great-nephew experienced a proper Christmas.

A teenage girl dressed entirely in black answered Anna's knock on the shabby front door of the house opposite the easement. 'Yeah?' the girl asked, mascara-stiff eyelashes fluttering.

Anna was about to apologise for the interruption – she'd forgotten the house had been sold a few months earlier – when the girl suddenly smiled. 'Hi there. You live down the easement, don't you?'

'Yes, I'm Anna Fletcher. You've probably seen my son Adam riding his bike up and down the street.'

'Yep. Cute kid. Loves doing wheelies. Good at them, too.'

Anna didn't want to think about bicycle tricks on a road that could get busy, so she asked the girl if her mother was at home.

'No, it's just me and Dad. Mum pushed off years ago.'

'I'm sorry,' was all Anna managed to say in response.

'Don't be, we're fine.' She brushed strands of black hair from her face. 'Anything I can do for you, Mrs Fletcher?'

'Please call me Anna.'

'Righto.'

Anna quickly explained the reason for her visit, prompting another smile and an offer she couldn't refuse. It turned out that Cheryl was at a bit of a loose end, having just finished school. She couldn't look for a holiday job to tide her over until uni began, as she and her Dad were 'going up north to the rellies' for Christmas.

'What do you plan to study?' Anna asked, berating herself for pre-judging the girl based on appearance alone. She should have known better, having a friend like Shirley, who now sported an afro hairstyle but still wore the long, flowery skirts and cheesecloth blouses of the mid-seventies.

'Medicine.'

'Good for you! A great career choice.'

'Thanks. Most people are surprised.' She grinned. 'They find it difficult to equate Goth girls with brains.'

Anna didn't like to ask the definition of a Goth girl; obviously it had nothing to do with ancient Germanic tribes. 'Would you like to come over to meet Adam?'

'Sure, Anna. Now's as good a time as any.'

* * *

Joseph remained in his workshop while Anna introduced Adam to his new after-school minder. It was a blessing, as she felt certain he would have objected to a heavily-made-up teenager wearing black jeans, black singlet and black thongs. When Cheryl departed, Adam not only declared her 'a cool dude,' but said he liked the Goth look, a statement that had Anna wondering how on earth a nine-year-old knew about such matters. Weeks later, seeing a photograph of the White family in the *Courier-Mail*, she realised the eldest boy was dressed in a similar fashion.

Attempts to contact Narelle were less successful, with her husband Frank answering the phone on each occasion and refusing to let Anna speak to his wife. Anna decided to call round on her next day off to offer assistance, even if it was just a shoulder to cry on, or minding the baby for an hour or two. Still convinced the neighbour had over-reacted, Anna wanted Narelle to know she empathised and had no intention of judging her, whatever the truth.

The curtains were drawn when she arrived at the house and no one answered her knock at the door. Undeterred, she descended the front steps and walked around to the back, searching the garden for signs of life. Two child-size bicycles were propped against the old shed, a rusting laundry trolley stood beneath the old Hills Hoist and a pair of pink thongs lay abandoned on the pad of rough concrete in the laundry doorway.

'Narelle, are you there?' Anna called, stepping into the laundry, which wasn't a room like her own, built by Joseph to precise measurements, the sheets of fibro painted pale blue, the wide window framed by blue gingham curtains, but just a few old floorboards and a sheet of unpainted fibro laid on hard-packed earth. An ancient washing machine balanced on the uneven floor. Behind it, old concrete tubs leant against the wooden slats that filled the gaps between concrete stumps to enclose "under the house". The slats resembled prison bars, the thin strips of sunlight filtering through them illuminating nothing but dank soil. Anna felt like an intruder, so she backed out and hurried around the house to the street.

Seated in the highly-polished-inside-and-out Kingswood, she envisaged the twenty-dollar bill she had handed over at the end of each working week, her attempt to help a woman struggling with a horde of children. A token gesture, given with a smile, followed by a brief conversation before gathering her child and retreating to her neat, well-maintained house and garden.

Throughout the short journey home, images of bank notes and a dark underbelly lightened by slivers of sunshine juxtaposed in her mind; liberty for one, a confirmation of captivity for the other. Twenty dollars might buy a cotton dress or underwear for the children, but it made no real difference. Narelle continued to face days and weeks and years of washing, cleaning, childcare, feeding, all on a shoestring, never knowing whether she would have sufficient left over on Friday for the family treat of fish and chips from the shop on the corner. Her husband, Frank, gave her the housekeeping money later in the evening, when he returned from the pub flushed with beer and bonhomie.

Did Narelle ever think of a future free from money worries? A future where she could earn money of her own and thus dictate the quality of her existence? Anna had no idea. She had never asked, afraid of sounding like a feminist crusader intent on showing a down-trodden woman a way out of poverty. Instead, she had exchanged a few pleasantries, listened on the odd occasion to serious concerns and made sympathetic noises, all the while trying not to glance at her watch. 'Duty calls,' she would declare most days after about ten minutes, thinking of the lamb chops in the fridge, the school uniforms to be washed and hung on the line in the garage.

As she turned into her driveway, Anna pondered whether, despite appearances to the contrary, Narelle had reached the end of her tether and couldn't deal with a seventh baby born years after the sixth. If so, the cigarette burns had been a cry for help and the neighbour had been meant to observe the abuse.

Head bent over the steering-wheel, Anna sat staring at the garage door, wondering if she should have waited for Narelle's return, or at least asked around the neighbourhood to find out if the family had gone away. Radio voices purred beneath the hum of the engine and midday pips announced a news bulletin. She turned the plastic knob to increase the volume and listened carefully to each brief item, as though anticipating something other than political commentary, a road accident and an inclement weather forecast.

A Means to an End

Gossip greeted Anna at the school gates; gossip founded on rumour, ignorance and, she suspected, a desire to inject excitement into monotonous suburban lives. 'All seven children have been taken into care,' one mother declared in a breathless voice, while another pronounced Narelle White a disgrace to the neighbourhood, with her gaggle of scruffy kids, shabby house and useless husband who spent most of his spare time in the pub.

A few steps away from the group, Anna stood leaning against the wire fence, her agitation increasing as the accusations intensified, fuelled by so-called "evidence" of odd behaviour, such as an unwillingness to engage in school fund-raising activities.

'Too right, Janice,' said a woman to Anna's left. 'Narelle couldn't give a stuff about the school community. Or anything else, for that matter. That poor baby! Thank God the authorities have been informed. I wouldn't mind betting she's abused the other kids at times, too.'

Heads nodded in agreement as a bell announced the end of another school day.

Appalled by the women's lack of compassion and self-righteous condemnation, Anna felt unable to stay silent. 'Don't you think it would be better to know the facts before pronouncing judgment?'

Six heads turned to face her; six pairs of sandals scuffed the dry grass footpath.

'Know the facts, do you?' the woman called Janice asked, her beady brown eyes fixed on Anna's reddening cheeks. 'Suppose you would, as your kid goes to Narelle's place after school.'

Anna decided not to mention her new after-school arrangements. 'I have never had any occasion to fault Narelle's care of Adam. She's a kind woman and, from what I've seen, does her best to raise a large family under difficult circumstances.'

'Get the posh accent, eh, girls?'

'Southern English, actually,' Anna advised, standing her ground even though she felt like making a run for it.

'Whatever.' Janice bit her thin lips.

'I called to see Narelle earlier, but no one was home,' Anna continued, determined to gain something from the awkward exchange. 'Anyone know if she's gone away?'

Six heads shook slowly.

'Probably didn't want to let you in, that's all,' a plump woman muttered, in between drags of a cigarette. 'Bit embarrassed, I expect.'

'Oh dear, I hadn't thought of that.' Anna reached up to touch her flushed cheek. 'I'll go back to see her when I've collected Adam. Her children should be home then. That'll make it a bit easier.'

'Want someone to go with you?' the plump smoker asked.

'Thanks, but I think it would be better if just Adam and I go.'

Six heads nodded as Anna made her escape.

* * *

When Anna pulled up outside the house, she was relieved to see the living room curtains had been drawn back and windows opened. A detour via the supermarket to purchase a filled sponge cake had ensured her arrival would be after, rather than before, the three younger children returned from school. Leaving Adam to make his way around to the rear garden, she climbed the steps and knocked on the front door. 'Narelle, it's Anna,' she called through the open window.

No response.

'Hi there! Just called to see how you are.'

No response.

Convinced Narelle had to be home – small children would be un-likely to draw back the curtains – Anna turned the handle. The un-locked door swung inwards, so she stepped inside, noted school bags dumped on the floor and a pair of thongs leading into the kitchen as though the wearer had just discarded them. Normal post-school be-haviour. The children were probably in the garden playing with the dog. A bark reassured her and she ventured into the kitchen. Sliced white bread spilled from a plastic wrapper; a fly gobbled jam that was smeared on a knife; an opened red cordial bottle stood on the draining board. The usual afternoon snack, according to Adam.

'Narelle,' she called, moving into the hall, 'want a cuppa and some cake?'

'In a minute. I'm busy now.'

'Okay, I'll put the jug on.'

'Thanks, Anna.'

Narelle's voice seemed to be coming from a distance; perhaps the bathroom that had been tacked on to the four bedrooms like an af-terthought. Anna listened for sounds of baby Claire's whereabouts and hearing none, padded down the hall, peeping into each room she passed. Bunk beds, scattered toys, rock star posters stuck on walls with strips of Sellotape, a cot tucked in a corner of the main bedroom. An empty cot, small pillow plumped, a pink blanket tucked in, the top of a white sheet folded over. Too neat for the time of day when Claire would have woken from her afternoon nap.

Her naivety dissolved as she stifled a sigh. The gossiping women had been correct in their assumptions. The baby had been taken into care. Uncertain how to proceed, she fled back to the kitchen and mun-dane tasks: fill the electric jug, switch it on, lift two mugs from the dish drainer, locate tea, sugar and milk. Small movements to distract her, to give her space to ponder subsequent questions such as, 'Can I help?'; 'How are you coping?'; 'What happens next?'

'All finished,' Narelle called, from the other end of the house.

'Tea and cake coming up.' Anna washed the jam-stained knife, then quickly divided the cake into six pieces. Movement in the hall drew her attention to the kitchen doorway and she settled a smile in readiness for affable greetings.

'Oh, there you are,' she began, unable to complete the sentence as her eyes and brain adjusted to the sight of stained clothing and a bloody carving knife held in an outstretched arm.

Images flashed before her eyes like scenes from a TV crime series employed to amplify dramatic tension: four children playing in the garden, a telephone out of reach, a narrow hallway, nowhere to run. She felt divorced from reality, an actor embracing the role of stunned housewife. A question formed on her lips, learnt lines essential to advance the storyline. 'Are you hurt, Narelle? Let me help you.'

The other actor stared straight ahead as the camera zoomed in on a bead of make-believe blood suspended from a stainless steel blade. In slow-motion descent, a crimson droplet splashed onto a faded floorboard.

Well-rehearsed action prompted a flurry of feet and a balled hand bashing hard against wrist bones. A knife fell to the floor, tension dissolved. Exhaled breath hung in the humid air, Anna moving to a different script as adrenalin replaced dread. 'Right, back to the bathroom, let's get you cleaned up.' Her hands encircled Narelle's waist, propelling the older woman backwards down the hall. She made no resistance, resignation her preferred emotion, her tired eyes clouded.

The closed bathroom door, the paintwork around the handle bearing traces of blood, presented a barrier, but one that was quickly surmounted with the flick of a wrist. Pushing Narelle inside, Anna paused to take a deep breath before stepping onto the tiled floor. 'Clothes off and into the shower.'

Narelle complied meekly, then stood naked in front of the plastic shower curtain, her flesh quivering.

'All right, *I'll* turn on the taps.' Keeping her eyes fixed on Narelle's face, Anna reached around the curtain to twist both taps. Old plumbing groaned, water spluttered, then gushed. 'Right, in you go.'

The slack mouth tightened, the trembling lips mouthed a defiant 'No', but before Anna could react, Narelle had sprinted out of the bathroom. The slam of a door and the rattle of a bolt suggested she had locked herself in the adjoining toilet.

* * *

Anna would never know what made her draw back the shower curtain rather than hurry to the toilet door in the hope of persuading Narelle to come out, but she remained certain it had nothing to do with saving water by turning off the taps. All she could recall of the moments before a second burst of adrenalin kicked in was minute movement and wet curls plastered to a small scalp.

The policewoman assigned to interview Anna following the arrival of ambulance and police vehicles, said partial recollection was a blessing, otherwise horrific details could have been imprinted on her memory forever. Such reassurance provided little comfort as Anna sat on a cracked plastic chair adjacent to a veranda rail threaded with yellow crime scene tape. She couldn't stop shaking. Her entire body, inside and out, was a mass of quivering jelly. Beside the chair, a cup of hot, sweet tea sat untouched, as her muscles and brain lacked the ability to coordinate hand-to-mouth movement. It was shock, an inevitable aftermath, quick action and self-control being no longer necessary.

Fragments of the first-aid she had learned at school had surfaced as Anna lifted Claire free of the gushing water. The closeness of bath towels proved an advantage in terms of staunching blood flow and concealing wounds. Cradling the tightly-wrapped baby, she had run to the living room, dialled 000 and somehow managed to give a coherent account of the situation.

'What did you do next?' the policewoman asked, leaning towards her.

'Locked the back door leading to the garden to stop the children coming in, then left the house via the front door, locking it behind me. I took refuge in my car.'

Others had taken care of the four children engaged in after-school garden games, although whether they had been neighbours or police, Anna couldn't say and hadn't been told. 'They're safe, no need to worry' was all the policewoman had disclosed when Anna had asked. Relieved of any added responsibility, Anna concentrated on answering questions, hoping a comprehensible account would negate the need for further interviews.

A doctor had been called to check her over but had yet to arrive – another blessing, as Anna had already decided to refuse any offer to put her to bed with a tranquilliser. At this juncture, masking her feelings wasn't an option. She needed to express herself clearly to both police and Joseph, who was on his way home by taxi, to ensure that only the facts remained at the forefront of her mind. She had had enough gossip for one afternoon.

'One last question, Anna and then you can rest.' The policewoman offered a small smile. 'When you confronted Narelle White in the hall, did she make any attempt to hurt or threaten you?'

'No.'

'But you had to knock the knife out of her hand?'

'As I said before, it was a reflex action. I thought she had tried to kill herself.'

'Because she had harmed the baby?'

A seed of irritation lodged in Anna's throat. How did she know whether Narelle felt remorse? It wasn't her place to speculate on a disturbed woman's state of mind. Let a psychiatrist work that one out. She coughed to eject annoyance. 'As I said before, I didn't think the baby was in the house. All that concerned me was checking out Narelle's injuries and stopping her inflicting more.'

'Thank you, Anna.' The policewoman sat back in her seat, also white plastic. 'That's it for now, but we'll need you to come down to the station in the next couple of days.'

'Why?'

'We require a written statement.'

Anna sighed. So, despite her best efforts, the facts had to be retained for a second interrogation. No fade to black as the episode ended and the credits rolled. Reaching down, she picked up the mug of tea.

* * *

Subsequent days passed as though time had absorbed the early summer humidity, each hour seeming suspended in the cloud-streaked sky and unable to advance at its usual pace. People and places merged to become a single entity, a distorted version of the Australia promoted in British newspapers, the Australia Anna loved. The suburb that had been her home for nine years looked unfamiliar, its houses shuttered, garden fences a barrier against the unwelcome intrusion of malevolent forces. Mothers held their children close, streets reverted to their original purpose, cricket or football now being confined to backyards. Outside the supermarket, housewives exchanged brief greetings rather than lingering to gossip, an undercurrent of suspicion rendering every woman a possible child abuser.

Sought out by journalists, Anna could no longer go about her everyday life with anonymity. She had morphed into a series of newsprint headlines: Heroine, Courageous Brisbane Mother, Suburban Saviour. Compelled to shop further afield, she kept her head down when pushing a supermarket trolley and refused to meet the gaze of checkout girls, scuttling back to her car as though pursued by hordes. She wore dark glasses whenever she drove and avoided library, newsagent and chemist. Goth-girl Cheryl collected Adam from school five days a week, Anna feeling unable to face questions or even complimentary comments from the knot of mothers gathered in front of the school gates.

Weary of the intense scrutiny, Anna almost envied Narelle, secure in her prison cell, three meals a day, kept apart from other inmates for her own protection, according to the *Courier-Mail*. A trial date had been set for February. A defence lawyer had been appointed, as the defendant was expected to plead not guilty to attempted murder by reason of insanity, an explanation Anna found difficult to accept. There was no doubt that Narelle had been unbalanced that afternoon, but insanity seemed too potent a label, with its inference of a lifetime's confinement to a psychiatric institution. Anna believed Narelle had been let down by the system, her initial cry for help answered with nothing but a Band-aid solution – several visits from a social worker rather than a referral to a psychiatrist who could have ascertained why she'd suddenly flipped.

* * *

November flipped into December. Journalists moved on to different news items and school gate conversations reverted to familiar topics, such as the forthcoming Christmas holidays. At 69a Harrow Street, Anna retrieved ten-year-old winter coats from storage and aired them on the back veranda, along with the padded parka purchased in July for Adam's school trip to the Snowy Mountains. Despite the prospect of a cold, damp Christmas – it rarely snowed in southern Hampshire – she couldn't wait to fly away from suburban stress. The fishbowl existence of the past few weeks might have waned, but neighbours, friends and even Joseph still treated her like an invalid, asking on a daily basis how she felt, if she was sleeping well and had she considered counselling? The imminent family reunion would restore her equilibrium. Daughter, sister, aunt and niece were easy roles to play.

A Limited Season

Thick fog blanketed Heathrow airport as the Qantas jet made its descent, disappointing a small Australian boy who envisaged getting a bird's-eye view of Big Ben and the Tower of London from his window seat, even though his parents had said they wouldn't be flying over the city. Anna realised that an old castle and a huge clock would hold more interest for him than the prospect of meeting relatives, most of whom had been seen only in photographs, so she had bought Adam a *Child's History of England* book to read on the plane. In the event, he read very little, preferring Travel Scrabble and the bag of goodies handed to child passengers following take-off. Meals divided into segments and eaten from a tray delighted him, as did the plastic cups of lemonade and Coke – drinks rarely allowed at home – that were available at frequent intervals.

The airport reunion brought an unexpected surprise. All four parents were standing behind the barrier as Joseph wheeled the luggage into the arrivals area. Adam flew into his maternal grandmother's arms, much to the annoyance of Grandma Fletcher who was waving nearby, peaks of pink-tinged hair arranged around her face like stiff meringue.

'Adam, come and meet Grandma and Grandpa Fletcher,' Anna called, above the hubbub of mass greetings.

'In a minute, Mum. I'm talking to Pop.'

Anna glanced at Joseph, sandwiched between his parents, both hands gripping the luggage trolley, his rigid posture a sure sign of discomfort. 'Let's get out of this crush and reassemble over there,' she called to him, pointing to an empty space adjacent to a concrete pillar.

The trolley wheels began to move.

Arguments over transport arrangements erupted, ending with Joseph pacifying his agitated mother by agreeing to travel, along with Adam, in his parents' car. As he handed the trolley to Anna – no room in a Mini for large suitcases – she kissed his cheek in an attempt to raise a smile and whispered, 'It's only a hundred mile journey.'

He leant towards her. 'Cramped in the rear of a Mini for hours isn't my idea of fun.'

'Don't worry. Your mother will sit in the back with Adam.'

He gave a wry smile and hurried to catch up with his parents, who were already heading for the exit.

'Did you know the Fletchers were coming to the airport?' Anna asked her parents, as the two groups made their separate ways to their parked cars.

'No,' her mother replied. 'And I suppose they'll expect lunch.'

'I'll give you a hand.'

'Thanks, darling.' Her mother smiled. 'At least there's no room for them to stay overnight.'

Mother and daughter exchanged conspiratorial glances, then linked arms to present a united front.

Seated behind her father, Anna felt like a tourist rather than a native returning to her homeland. The countryside seemed alien, the bare branches a shock, neat fields surrounded by hedgerows presenting an ordered landscape that left nothing to the imagination. Morning fog lingered over high ground. Frost speckled winter-thin grass and grey slate farmhouse roofs, a weak sun failing to disperse the general air of gloom. Apart from wisps of smoke issuing from brick chimneys, the roadside villages appeared abandoned, clusters of identical houses squatting on sodden ground. No one walked the narrow streets, no one chatted over a fence or hung out washing. Despite the car's overheated atmosphere, Anna shivered and turned away from the window. She couldn't envisage leading a shuttered existence for months on end, rushing from car to shop or office, eyes focused on icy pavements, frozen fingers fumbling with car keys.

Their increased speed on the motorway proved a welcome distraction, with heath-land and farmhouses retreating into the morning mist before Anna could indulge in lengthy and, if she were honest, biased comparison. Following the first flurry of animated conversation, talk had become sporadic, then ceased altogether as mother napped and father concentrated on driving, leaving Anna to wonder how Joseph and Adam were faring, trapped in a small car with a garrulous mother/grandmother and a taciturn, pipe-smoking father/grandfather.

No doubt the Fletchers would stop for a cuppa and a plastic-wrapped cake at a Little Chef café, as Stella was never willing to travel far without a tea break. That would be a new experience for Adam, who was accustomed to roadside rest areas where a flask of tea, a bottle of orange juice and a slice of homemade cake would be produced from the esky and carried over to a picnic table positioned in the shade of tall eucalypts.

Bundled in a heavy coat, her ankles swollen from the long flight, Anna longed to revert to Brisbane attire and feel balmy air caressing her bare arms and legs and stretch toes that were cramped from being confined in boots last worn a decade earlier. Apart from sneakers and one pair of court shoes, she only possessed sandals and found it amusing when Brisbane women trotted out in knee-high boots during the so-called winter.

Six weeks in a cold climate held no appeal; she would have preferred a summer visit, but couldn't voice her preference when Aunt Maud had paid for their tickets. Being trapped indoors for weeks would be torment, particularly for Adam, who was reared on year-round outdoor activities. *Think positive,* she told herself, and began to plan brisk walks in the woods near her childhood home, pointing out squirrels, robins and blackbirds. Adam loved wildlife, especially birds, so he would be intrigued by all the different species. Perhaps Aunt Maud, relocated to a luxury flat near the town centre, would enjoy showing him the photographs of seabirds taken by her late husband? A keen photographer, Uncle Edgar had developed his black and white prints in a darkroom built onto the back of his garage, a process Anna had observed with awe on the odd occasion she was permitted inside.

'We're almost home, Anna,' her father declared, as though she possessed no memory of her hometown streets. 'I expect you'll welcome a decent cup of tea, dear. The airline variety leaves a great deal to be desired.'

'It sure does, Dad, but I guess it's difficult to feed hundreds of passengers from a tiny kitchen.'

'You sound like an American, dear,' her mother remarked. 'It seems those elocution lessons were an absolute waste.'

'Australian, Mother,' Anna corrected without thinking.

'You're English, dear, wherever you live now.'

Anna said nothing, her thoughts turning to the citizenship ceremony she had attended the previous year. Standing alongside immigrants from diverse countries, she and Joseph had been proud to pledge their loyalty to the Commonwealth of Australia and in return, receive certificates adorned with a coat of arms featuring a kangaroo and an emu. It was confirmation that they belonged to the land they had chosen ten years earlier as a fitting place for their future.

Nationality Australian, their new passports proclaimed, but convincing Joseph's mother they had no intention of returning permanently to England would be a difficult exercise. In almost every letter and at the end of each telephone conversation, Stella asked, 'When are you coming home?' The question had remained unanswered for a decade, but face-to-face, a confrontation seemed inevitable and was one Anna had no desire to witness, let alone participate in.

Cowardice wasn't the issue. Rather, it was the need to shield herself from the drama of Stella-style hysterics. Heightened emotions would threaten the tranquilly Anna sought to cultivate during the holiday. Soon after their return home, she would have to give evidence at Narelle White's trial, an experience she was dreading. Apart from the distress of recounting the details of that horrific afternoon, she feared the intrusive media, the camera clicks as she arrived at court, the microphones thrust in her face.

'Home at last!' her mother declared, scattering her concerns.

'I can't wait to take off my boots.' Anna wriggled her toes in anticipation. 'Have you got a spare pair of slippers I can borrow?'

Mother turned around to beam at her daughter. 'No, dear, but I've knitted you a pair like the ones I always take to the holiday cottage.'

Anna recalled pale pink bootees adorned with bows, an incongruous sight when teamed with one of her mother's summer dresses. 'Thanks, that's great.'

'I've made a pair for Adam as well. Red and white stripes with pompoms. I hope they fit.'

'I'm sure they will. His feet haven't grown that much since I last sent you his measurements.'

'Good.' Mother opened the car door and stepped onto damp gravel. 'I'll go and put the kettle on.'

'There's no sign of the Fletchers yet,' her father remarked. 'I hope they haven't broken down.'

'No worries, Dad, they'll have stopped at a Little Chef for sure.'

'Right, let's get the luggage organised.'

* * *

Weeks passed in a flurry of activity: visits to relatives, the delight of a pantomime, walks on a wind-battered promenade, Adam running ahead trying to catch the foam flurries tossed from iron-grey waves. Diplomacy ensured the Christmas period came and went without argument, the Australian Fletchers spending Christmas lunch with Anna's parents, sisters and their families plus Aunt Maud, then driving thirty miles to spend the next few days chez Stella and Co.

Undeterred by icy roads and an unfamiliar car – his father-in-law's elderly Austin Cambridge – Joseph delivered his family safe and sound to an overheated house where tinsel was draped around every room and an enormous Christmas tree adorned with gaudy baubles took up most of the small lounge room. 'You wouldn't get anything like this in Australia,' Stella remarked to Adam as he gazed at the tree, eyes wide and mouth gaping like a fish. 'It's not a proper Christmas when it's hot.'

'Grandma, on Christmas Day we go in Mary and Roger's pool,' he answered, turning away from the tree. 'And we have races on pool ponies. They've got faces like horses, but I've got one shaped like a banana. I call it Cecily.'

Stella frowned. 'Cecily?'

'A woman Joseph works with,' Anna explained. 'Adam's met her a few times and rather likes her.'

'Cecily bought me a pair of goggles for my birthday. I swim under-water a lot, Grandma.'

'He's a real little dolphin,' Joseph added. 'He won first place for his year in diving at the school swimming carnival.'

Adam grinned with pride, prompting a pat on the head from Grandma. Then, looking up at her, he asked, with a child's candour, 'Grandma, why is your hair the same colour as Mum's new slippers?'

Anna had to leave the room in a hurry to prevent an outburst of giggles, so she failed to hear Stella's response.

New Decade, New Direction

Time to recover from jet-lag was a luxury Anna couldn't afford, with a new school year looming two days after landing. She rushed around shops, purchasing the items Adam required for Grade Five, the list supplied by the school running to an entire foolscap page, ridiculous for nine-year-olds in her opinion. She wondered how poor families managed, especially if they had to kit out several children. At least, with Goth-girl Cheryl having returned from the north, Anna didn't have Adam in tow, whingeing about shopping when he could have been at the beach. Still looking for a part-time job that would provide much-needed cash during her university studies, Cheryl had welcomed the opportunity to earn some money. Another after-school minder would have to be found once uni started at the beginning of March, but Anna refused to worry on that score, the imminent court case being of far greater concern.

The visit to England had helped put the events of that November afternoon into perspective. Anna would never forget the traumatic experience, but, thanks to prompt and perceptive action by the police, Adam and the younger White children had been spared the sight of both an injured baby and a distraught mother. In the days following the incident, Adam's preoccupation had been police cars, sirens and an ambulance racing down the street. Shielding him from every television news item or chattering friends and neighbours had proved impossible, but, when answering his questions, both parents stressed the positive outcome – Claire's recovery – rather than Narelle's crime.

Anna also told Adam about the court case, explaining she would have to describe what happened to a judge and jury so they could decide what to do. She emphasised the importance of telling the truth, making only vague references to verdict and sentence. Adam seemed to understand, his expression grave as he absorbed each piece of information, his usual fidgeting absent. He hadn't mentioned the suburban drama once during the holiday, leading Anna and Joseph to believe he hadn't been adversely affected.

The court appearance proved less daunting than anticipated, with both prosecution and defence lawyers asking reasonable questions and refraining from the aggressive stance depicted in TV crime dramas. Afterwards, walking through sunlit city streets to Central Station, Anna felt a lightness of being, as though more than half her bodyweight had been left behind in the Supreme Court witness box. Confident she could now focus on the future, especially their plans to move to a new house, she would have skipped up Ann Street if she hadn't been wearing high heels and a tight skirt.

Seated in the train, Anna wished she had something to read, as the familiar urban landscape was failing to dispel an unwanted image that had settled in her mind the moment she entered the carriage. Narelle White's altered appearance had been a shock. Led into the dock by a correctional services officer, the woman Anna still considered a hapless victim, rather than a criminal, was now white-haired, with sunken cheeks accentuating the deep creases on either side of her small, pointed nose. When Anna was called to give evidence, she'd wondered whether Narelle would display any sign of recognition, but her thin face remained devoid of emotion, as it had been since proceedings began. *A coping mechanism*, Anna had decided, as she rose from her seat and moved towards the witness box.

A burst of speed was followed by deceleration and a brief halt at a station; the pattern was repeated as the train headed north. The stop-start repetition soothed her, gently erasing her court room recollections. Alone in the carriage, Anna focused on the seat opposite, examining the cloth inserts which were a vast improvement on the old, cracked benches of the early Seventies. Musing on the old "rattlers", with their uncomfortable seats and stiff windows that threatened to trap one's fingers when opening them to exit the train, Anna recalled the story that had set her prose-writing hobby in motion. Like most beginners, she had drawn on her own experience, turning a twenty-something woman's irrational fears of being stuck in a carriage into a prize-winning story by creating a small boy protagonist. Her creative flow had slowed to a trickle the previous year, but now a question was forming in her head; a question she felt reluctant to acknowledge, yet alone answer.

The train pulled into Wooloowin station. She alighted with care and walked slowly along the potholed platform and out into the street. Unbidden, the question echoed her footsteps, words that demanded a response, a yes or no at the very least. Should she capitalise on the White family's tragedy and write a novel focused on a mother's inability to cope and its horrific consequences? *No, that would be unethical,* came the unspoken reply and yet she wavered, reluctant to accept the decision.

She passed a row of familiar shops, with merchandise in wooden boxes displayed on the footpath beneath corrugated iron awnings and slowed her steps. Determined not to become distracted, she averted her eyes from fresh vegetables and bargain homewares. Beyond the shadow of the shopping strip she increased her pace, conscious of a desperate need for notebook and pen. From experience, she knew concepts and characters wouldn't linger long; like bubbles blown from a child's plastic pipe, soon they would burst, their contents evaporating in the summer sun. Inhibited by her formal clothing and the afternoon glare that, despite sunglasses, forced her to look down at her feet, it took another five minutes for her to reach Harrow Street, and several more before the easement leading to her home came into view.

Her fingers fumbled in her handbag for the house keys as she climbed the wooden steps to the front veranda. Perspiration dripped from the tip of her nose and sizzled on the heated paintwork. Inside at last, she kicked off her shoes, tossed her handbag on a chair and headed for the bedroom, unzipping her skirt en route with clammy hands. Wriggling out of her skirt and blouse, she left them on the bedroom floor then peeled off her damp pantyhose and bra, ignoring the open curtains in her haste to feel the touch of cooler air on her overheated skin. Reluctantly, she grabbed a pair of brief shorts and a tank top from the dressing table drawer.

On her way to the study, Anna detoured via the bathroom to gulp some water straight from the tap, forgetting that the initial flow would be warm. Then she hurried across the hall into the space once coveted on a daily basis and found, to her dismay, that the desk was littered with paperbacks, plucked from overcrowded bookshelves, that she had meant to take to the Op shop before the holiday. Extending both arms, she swept the books to the floor with little regard for their welfare. *Librarian Shirley would be horrified,* she reflected, opening a drawer to retrieve notebook and biro. The thought lingered, becoming the career her protagonist had abandoned once her pregnancy had begun to show.

A first and only pregnancy. *Her* character wouldn't be a mother of seven and, unlike Narelle White, would be innocent of the charge brought against her. This much had become clear during the walk from station to home, Anna being aware that whatever the verdict in the real-life case, Narelle would not be returning home for many years.

The death of a child, a miscarriage of justice, lengthy imprisonment – these were the seeds from which a fully-formed novel could emerge. Years of hard work lay ahead; it would be a steep learning curve, yet Anna felt undaunted and resolved to complete the task, whatever the eventual outcome. A new decade stretched before her; she would not allow the Eighties to slip by without an achievement.

* * *

Anna confided in Shirley months before mentioning the project to Joseph, afraid he would think she was about to give up her job. Despite his pride in being the primary breadwinner, he acknowledged that, without Anna's contribution to the household, the mortgage would not have been paid off so early, or money made available for a second car. Buying a new house with a double garage, a family room and, if possible, a pool, would eat up most of their savings as neither of them wanted to take on another large mortgage.

Shirley expressed delight and offered to borrow books on the legal system or any other pertinent subject from the university library, to assist her friend's research. 'I have every confidence in you,' she declared, raising her plastic wine glass. 'To Anna the author! May she shine like Australian sunshine!'

Late afternoon sun slipped below the crest of a nearby hill. Grateful for the deepening shadow, Anna blushed. The two friends sat on cane chairs on either side of a glass-topped table, beneath their feet the tiled patio Sam had constructed around a newly-installed in-ground pool. Study, hard work and a change of career path for Sam had seen the couple's lives improve beyond expectations. Once her son George had started school, Shirley had returned to part-time study, embarking on a Bachelor of Arts degree at the University of Queensland, essential if she wished to gain promotion in the future, while Sam had moved into illuminating engineering.

At times, Anna found it difficult to manage her own multi-layered life, so she couldn't possibly imagine how Shirley juggled a job, study and a young child. Writing a novel would add another layer, one she envisaged could become all-absorbing, but at least an unknown writer wouldn't have a publisher breathing down her neck.

Or a judge and jury waiting to pronounce verdict and sentence.

Change of Scene, Change of Pace

Persistent lobbying from both wife and son saw Joseph abandon his preference for a completed new house. Sixth months after their first visit, a second trip to Elizabeth Park convinced Anna that a home built in a quiet cul-de-sac among tall eucalypts would be far superior to a spec-build. Adam didn't much care about the house itself. His focus was on climbable trees and a nearby patch of undeveloped bush!

A single builder was responsible for developing the small estate, which required purchasers to buy a house-land package, although plans displayed in the sales office provided extensive design choice. After much deliberation, the Fletchers chose a low-set L-shaped house, brick veneer with tiled roof, comprising three bedrooms, bathroom, laundry, kitchen with meals area, family room and separate lounge/dining room, plus a two-car garage. A small deposit secured their chosen block until the Harrow Street house sold, when they would pay for the land in full. Payment for the house would be made in regular increments as the building work progressed.

A subsequent visit to the bank secured a small mortgage, the bank manager delighted when learning that the entire proceeds of their existing house sale could be used as a deposit. As they left the bank, Anna shuddered at the memory of their first mortgage application; the dour manager's remarks on insufficient savings, followed by sly glances at her distended stomach and coy remarks about the coming event. 'What a difference money makes,' she remarked, taking Joseph's arm. 'Nine years ago, our application didn't stand much of a chance.'

'Only one wage and a baby on the way made us a hell of a risk. I reckon that first manager took pity on us.'

'That's for sure, but we've proved he made the right decision. I don't imagine too many couples manage to pay off their mortgage in nine years.'

'Hard work, sensible budgeting and a willingness to make do with second-hand – that's the trick,' Joseph answered smugly.

'There's more to it, I believe. As migrants, we had to stand on our own two feet. We couldn't run back to our parents when things went wrong. It was sink or swim for us. We had only one chance to demonstrate we could make it in a strange land, far from everything familiar.'

'Hardly strange. Same language, Westminster-style government, Western values.'

'True, but don't you remember standing on Zillmere station a few days after we arrived, saying how daunting it was to realise you had no idea how to get anywhere except back to Mary and Roger's?'

Joseph shrugged. 'Can't say I do, but it didn't take me long to find my way around.'

'No, thank goodness. You wouldn't want to rely on my poor navigation skills.'

She recalled the anxiety she had experienced, trying to negotiate unfamiliar streets on her way to visit Narelle in the Female Division of Boggo Road gaol. Her tension had increased on entering the prison, the sense of foreboding growing acute as the steel doors clanged shut behind her. Although Narelle had agreed to see her – Anna had written a few weeks after the ten-year sentence had been handed down, the plea of insanity having been rejected – the visit had been a complete failure. Slumped in a chair behind a glass screen, Narelle had shown no emotion. Her expression had been vacant, her eyes dull as though she had retreated to a world far from her present reality. Conversation had been strained, with Narelle limiting her responses to monosyllables.

Dismayed, Anna had made no promises to visit again, preferring to restrict communication to the occasional letter.

Joseph patted her arm. 'Don't look so sad, love, you're not alone. Most women have trouble reading maps.'

'It's not that. I suddenly thought of Narelle and her family. Unlike us, there's nothing for them to look forward to.'

'My advice is to forget about the whole sordid business.'

'Easier said than done.'

'A new house in a different suburb will exorcise ghosts of the past.'

Loath to continue the conversation, she steered him towards a coffee shop.

* * *

One year into the new decade, Anna had completed preliminary research for her novel and written three chapters of a first draft. Satisfied with her output – she managed to devote two six-hour days a week, plus the occasional Saturday to creativity – she suspended novel writing for a few weeks, to prepare for their imminent move.

They had to vacate two weeks after Christmas, the house having sold in two months, rather than the estimated four or six anticipated by the real estate agent. The move to a rented two-bedroom flat near Anna's workplace would be temporary, as the new house was due to be completed within three months. After the Christmas holidays, Adam would transfer to the school nearest to Elizabeth Park. As he was now ten years old and a sensible child, both parents felt he was old enough to ride his mountain bike to the new school, which would give him some independence, plus eliminate the need for an after-school minder, as Anna got home from work less than an hour after classes finished. Anna couldn't believe that only two years of primary schooling remained before Adam progressed to High School. Her son's once interminable childhood was vanishing before her eyes.

Occasionally, watching Adam playing alone in the garden, she felt guilty for having denied him a sibling, yet he appeared content and never asked for a brother or sister. At school, he was a popular child and often received weekend invitations to school friends' homes, Anna making sure to reciprocate. However, her one attempt to provide a companion for him during a holiday to Byron Bay had been a complete failure, as Adam had taken her aside after two days to ask why she'd invited boring Barry.

'It's not right,' he'd added, following her whispered explanation. 'It's always been just the three of us, so please don't invite anyone else to share our family holiday.'

Chastened, she'd promised it would be just the three of them in future.

* * *

The move to a new house and suburb proved more beneficial than Anna could have envisaged. Adam loved his new school, especially the pool complete with diving board and within weeks, he had joined the swimming club that was held after classes every Friday. Sitting on the grass beside the pool, Anna would cheer him on during races and applaud his diving skills. The "little dolphin" had become a competent swimmer and diver and daily practice in the family's new kidney-shaped pool was helping him win trophies for his team at inter-school sports events.

Much to Anna's relief, a smart new Ford station wagon soon replaced the shabby Datsun ute Joseph had purchased years earlier, as a further promotion package included a company car. Work took up more of Joseph's time now, as a manager was expected to remain at his desk long after other staff had left for the day.

Anna didn't mind. The extra hours enabled her to focus on possible narrative as she dusted furniture or cleaned the shower. Once the housework was completed, on hot days she would join Adam in the pool, engage in a game of tag, or throw a ball. Content with one another's company, mother and son would prepare dinner together wearing wet togs, ignoring the droplets of chlorinated water dripping onto the patterned vinyl flooring.

Summer evenings were spent in the family room, lounging on lightweight cane chairs in front of the television, or reading library books. In the garden, cicadas hung in the tall trees, their loud buzzing an irritant until one learned to ignore them. When heat and humidity lingered into late evening, Anna and Joseph would slip into the pool before going to bed, relishing the touch of silken water on their naked bodies. Mosquitoes buzzing around their heads proved detrimental to watery lovemaking, so they would retire to the bedroom and turn on the ceiling fan, entwining their cool limbs beneath its welcome breeze.

Cooler weather engendered less languid activities, such as house and garden maintenance, or brisk walks through forests with Adam leading, eagerly pointing out colourful birds and the droppings of nocturnal creatures. Sitting on a rock beside a tumbling waterfall, or racing husband and son along a deserted wind-swept beach, Anna found it impossible to imagine living anywhere else on the planet. Australia had given her the autonomy she craved. Freed from the bonds of her parents' set-in-stone world, she could embrace a heightened existence; she could dare to dream.

Month by month, her manuscript grew, a secret second child nurtured by imagination and persistence. Joseph knew she was writing a novel but had no notion of the subject matter. 'You can read it when it's finished,' she said one evening, in answer to his queries. 'I'm only on the first draft, so you would be reading unpolished work.'

'Give me a clue. Is it a mystery, a romance, a crime novel?'

'Wait and see. Even I'm uncertain how it will end.'

'How come? I thought authors wrote an outline first?'

'Not necessarily. Writers work in different ways.'

'Keep your mystery then,' he said, sounding affronted and turned back to the television.

Nothing more had been said on the matter, which suited a fledgling novelist unsure whether she possessed sufficient ability to produce publishable material. Finishing the task was her immediate goal, and the search for a publisher or agent of secondary importance. Since beginning the novel, Anna had joined the Fellowship of Australian Writers. She read their monthly magazine with interest and periodically took the train into the city to attend a Saturday afternoon meeting.

One of these days, she decided, she would submit a poem or a short story to the magazine. It would give her a buzz to see her name in print, plus it would be something concrete to show Joseph. In the meantime, she listened to others talk of their work in progress, providing snippets of information about her own project only when asked directly. She endeavoured to fit in but had nothing in common with the mainly middle-aged women who were filling daylight hours with creativity now that their offspring had left the nest. The few men, timid types that stood in a huddle during the coffee break, never spoke to Anna and appeared overwhelmed by the voluble grey-haired women sounding forth on punctuation and grammar.

Anna would have preferred a younger crowd, but had no luck locating another writing group in either suburbs or city. Most of her contemporaries were fully occupied with work or bringing up children; she alone possessed sufficient time and energy to indulge her "nice little hobby". Typing hour after hour might be productive in one sense and was intellectually fulfilling, but now and then she felt a pang of guilt about the time stolen from household duties. Joseph rarely criticised, but she sensed from the occasional remark that he would have preferred a more conventional wife, the type that filled a home with the enticing aromas of home-cooked goodies rather than a fruit cake purchased from Coles. On the odd occasion she produced a batch of cakes or biscuits, he complimented her effusively, then chomped into half a plateful with such abandon, he couldn't have tasted a thing! Fortunately, Adam ate anything put in front of him with no concern for its origin.

When the oven timer sounded – she set it as a reminder to prepare a meal or hang out washing – Anna mused on past writers who were blessed with servants to carry out tedious household chores. She couldn't imagine Virginia Woolf cleaning the toilet or mopping a kitchen floor. Then, she would remember the modern aids that enabled her to race through housework in record time and berate herself for her ingratitude. Compared with those that had gone before, she had an easy life: access to a variety of healthy foods, excellent health-care, schooling for her child, the freedom to vote, speak her mind, read whatever she chose, limit her family. One small tablet enabled her generation of women to choose if, or when, and how many children to produce, without relying on husbands to practice birth control. And should a woman fail to conceive, the new procedure of in-vitro fertilisation could help create the longed-for foetus.

As Anna peeled potatoes, an image of Narelle slipped into her mind and she pondered the reason for her having so many children, especially a seventh, years after the sixth. Carelessness, a demanding husband, an inability or reluctance to take the Pill? She would never know. Narelle remained a closed book.

Slow Progress

Tall and skinny, with a mop of unruly black hair, twelve-year old Adam had become a good companion, his laidback temperament welcomed, particularly on days when Anna felt frustrated by her lack of progress.

'Cheer up, Mum,' he'd say, if she appeared downcast on his return from school. After tossing him a smile, she would rise from her office chair, follow him into the kitchen, switch on the jug and open the Tupperware box containing cake or biscuits.

Having already organised his own drink of cordial or a glass of milk, Adam would wait for her to make tea before taking his glass and the plastic box onto the screened-in patio – the mosquitoes were voracious in Elizabeth Park even during the day – and deposit them on the round polyurethane table in the corner. Seated on yellow plastic chairs, mother and son would spend half an hour enjoying afternoon tea and chatting about their respective days, before Adam retired to do his homework – which took up at least two hours a day, now he had graduated to High School – and Anna caught up on chores.

After a day spent in her study, Anna appreciated her son's company. Writing was a lonely business and she often wondered how professional writers coped, day in day out, with a solitary existence. At least she had an alternative for half the working week; not that she found her job particularly fulfilling. The solicitor's clients rarely exchanged more than a few words with her and the typing of conveyancing documents, wills and divorce papers had grown tedious after so many years.

Following Joseph's latest promotion, Anna had considered resigning and giving herself six months to concentrate on her new writing project before seeking another position, but a desire to retain her own income had stayed her hand. Although Joseph was generous to a fault, she had hated asking him for anything other than housekeeping money during her stay-at-home years. 'But it's *our* money not mine,' he would say when she tried to explain her reticence, her sense of being a 'kept' woman.

An unpaid period would have been acceptable had she found a publisher for her first novel. One or two had praised her efforts, but so far, none were willing to take a risk on an unknown writer. A few short stories and poems had been published in magazines but the payment, if any, was pitiful and apart from that long ago first prize, she had failed to win or even be short-listed for other writing competitions.

At the beginning of the year, she'd toyed with the idea of writing a romance novel. According to a woman she had met at an FAW meeting, these sold well, but inquiries to the recommended publishers revealed that authors had to write to a formula. Happy-ever-after with a handsome hero who rescued a peaches and cream heroine from the clutches of a cad, didn't appeal, so Anna had returned to realism.

Well aware that her first novel had evolved from an experience never likely to be repeated, for the second project she decided to focus on a young woman migrating to Australia on her own, against her parents' wishes and those of the boyfriend who wants to run her life. Her heroine would be a feisty woman determined to make her way in a new land. She would overcome numerous setbacks before emerging victorious. It would not be a tale of rags-to-riches, but a storyline designed to inspire, to show young women that in 1980s Australia, they could achieve their career goals.

The country was changing and women were no longer expected to forgo careers once a baby arrived. Since 1979, any woman employed by a company for longer than twelve months was entitled to fifty-two weeks unpaid maternity leave and unions were already lobbying for a limited amount of paid leave. Nowadays, childcare centres could be found in almost every suburb, such a difference from Anna's experience of only twelve years earlier. She recalled the cutting remarks about her pregnancy made by an old-fashioned supervisor, the directive to wear maternity dresses rather than an office uniform stretched around her stomach.

No doubt she would be branded a rabid feminist by some sections of society should her new book be published, but Anna didn't care about conservative opinions. Her objective was to provide readers with food for thought, as well as interesting narrative.

* * *

She was jotting down notes for a third chapter when the doorbell rang. Annoyed by the interruption, she crept into the front bedroom to see whether it was worth answering the door and saw the postie's motorcycle parked in the middle of the driveway, a sure sign he had a parcel to deliver. Probably a gift from England, as Joseph's birthday was in less than a week.

Before heading into the hall, she paused in front of the dressing table mirror to check for evidence of Milo smudges around her mouth.

'Parcel for Mrs Anna Fletcher,' the postie announced, as she opened the door.

'That's me.' She took the manuscript-shaped package and tried to sustain a smile. 'Thanks very much.'

'Have a good day.'

'You too,' she said automatically, her eyes fixed on the stamps she'd stuck to the self-addressed envelope weeks earlier.

Once hidden behind a closed door, she dropped the parcel onto the mat and aimed a kick at its unwanted contents. There seemed little point in reading yet another rejection letter. Back at her desk, she wrote out her frustration, finger and thumb stiffening around the biro, her mouth set like concrete. Aching joints and a numb foot – she was sitting with one leg tucked under her bottom – demanded a halt after half an hour, so she uncurled, stretching her digits and limbs until feeling returned to them. Hungry now, she got to her feet and wandered into the kitchen to make a sandwich, averting her eyes from the abandoned parcel as she padded across the hall.

As she carried a plate back to the study, her rule not to eat at the desk forgotten, she recalled the cover letter she had sent to publishers along with the mandatory synopsis and manuscript. In response to the question, "What inspired the writing of your novel?" she always wrote: "*Is No One Listening?* was inspired by personal despondency during an unplanned pregnancy and difficulties adjusting to motherhood following the birth of my son." It was a true statement, yet it omitted the real reason for embarking on her first novel. Reluctant to profit from another woman's misfortune, Anna did not mention her involvement in the Narelle White case.

Munching on a cheese and tomato sandwich, she pondered whether the time had come to tell the truth. *There but for the grace of God go I,* had been her immediate thought on learning a neighbour had reported Narelle for inflicting cigarette burns on baby Claire. The realisation that, under different circumstances, she, too could have been a mother on trial, had been alarming and this alone had triggered her novel of despair, misunderstanding and a miscarriage of justice.

She set the empty plate aside and brushed crumbs from her jeans before venturing into the hall to retrieve the parcel. Her cover letter lay beneath a generic rejection form; she plucked it out and took it into the study for editing, prior to retyping. Her sentences flowed easily, confirming the rightness of her decision and by the time she heard Adam's shout from the driveway, the finding of yet another publisher willing to accept an unsolicited manuscript was all that remained to be done.

'Coming!' she called, even though he couldn't have heard her as she hurried from house to garage to open the roller-door from the inside.

'Have a good day, Mum?' Adam asked, as he wheeled his mountain bike into the garage and leant it against a side wall.

'Fine, love, how about you?'

'Boring. We had double maths instead of swimming, 'cos Mrs Dawson was crook.'

'Couldn't another teacher have taken swimming class?'

Adam shrugged and, hoisting his backpack onto one shoulder, declared, 'I'm bloody hungry. Hope there's plenty of grub in the fridge.

'Don't swear,' she said to his retreating back, reflecting that within weeks, he would enter the teenage years when parents would find their influence waning as their offspring endeavoured to discard childhood. Mary and Roger's sweet-natured Katy had metamorphosed into a disruptive, moody girl for several years, while James, at eighteen, despite good school grades, refused to apply for university, maintaining he preferred working at McDonald's.

Anna recalled her own adolescence; the arguments with her mother about a ten o'clock curfew, her father's insistence on church attendance every Sunday morning when she would much rather have stayed in bed. Would Adam become sullen and spotty, his easy-going personality swamped by raging hormones? She tried to envisage her talkative son communicating with little more than grunts and shutting himself in his bedroom to listen to hard rock and heavy metal. Such a transformation seemed impossible. Adam always came bouncing back from illness or disappointment in record time. Even when reprimanded by Joseph – not known for patience when dealing with his son's misdemeanours – Adam would be whistling cheerfully minutes afterwards. She could only hope.

Success and Complications

Truth proved the catalyst for further consideration, as a contract was forthcoming several months after Anna had submitted her manuscript to a tenth publisher. The family celebrated with champagne followed by a weekend at the Gold Coast, Adam delighted with a visit to Seaworld plus the opportunity, rare in his household, to indulge in KFC and McDonald's meals.

The publisher, a small company with a good reputation, informed Anna her manuscript would undergo several editing processes, the first of which might require extensive re-writing. Even so, Anna was horrified by the amount of red ink adorning her pages, with the manuscript having already undergone numerous drafts before being submitted. Overall, her spelling and grammar were correct, the editor being more concerned with refining structure, character development and making the narrative more succinct. The initial acceptance letter proclaiming her book a fascinating read that stood out from others in the same genre, seemed at odds with the plethora of criticism; nevertheless, Anna acknowledged her inexperience and re-worked with diligence.

The manuscript arrived back for final edits halfway through '85, just small corrections previously overlooked, together with a request to complete and return it within the week as the release date had been brought forward by three months. Anna complied, although she wondered what had prompted the rush to publish a debut novel by an unknown author. Reluctance to appear anxious prevented her seeking an explanation, but an unexpected call from the publisher soon answered her question.

After thanking Anna for her prompt return of the manuscript, the well-spoken woman – Anna envisaged her as middle-aged, university educated and beautifully groomed – explained that the company wished to take advantage of current events to generate more publicity than a debut novel usually received. 'No doubt, as a feminist writer, you're fully aware of the recent raids on the Greenslopes Fertility Control Clinic?'

'Of course,' Anna answered, recalling the extensive media coverage following premier Joh Bjelke-Petersen's order for police to raid Brisbane's sole abortion clinic. 'Police confiscated patient files and medical equipment, interrogated patients and arrested two doctors.'

'Disgraceful acts, but now that the topic of a woman's right to abortion has been beamed into living rooms throughout the country, we believe readers will rush to purchase a novel inspired by the horrific aftermath of a harassed mother's unwanted seventh pregnancy.'

'A brilliant deduction!'

'I thought so, too.'

Anna imagined a self-satisfied smile. 'So, what can I do to assist with publicity?'

'Be prepared to answer the Abortion Question. Reporters and readers alike will want to know your opinion. Events in so-called backward Queensland might be on everyone's lips, but you can't risk putting too many people, particularly women, off-side.'

'I'll do my best to give a balanced response.'

'Thank you. We'll be sending out review copies prior to the launch date. Given the controversial subject matter, you can expect a call from one or two reporters. *Is No One Listening?* will be launched at the Women's Bookshop in Highgate Hill, which should generate further media attention.'

Anna had never heard of the Women's Bookshop. A small gathering of friends in the room adjoining the local library followed by afternoon tea had been her plan and she had already booked the space. 'I'm happy to do the catering.'

'No need. My secretary will arrange for wine and cheese. Your task is to give a ten-minute speech about what inspired you to write the book, why you decided on fiction rather than a factual account of the Narelle White case and anything else you feel is relevant. Can you manage that?'

'No problem. I have experience in public speaking.'

'Thank heavens for that. Some of our authors are so introverted, it's difficult to get a spoken word out of them. I'll introduce you. Book sales and signing will follow your talk.'

'Thank you so much for organising everything. I wasn't certain of the protocol, this being my first book.'

'It's my pleasure. And I hope you'll be submitting other manuscripts. If, as we predict, your debut novel is a success, readers will expect more in the same vein.'

'I do have ideas for a second novel.'

'Second, third, fourth, I foresee a glittering career for our newest author!'

Overawed, Anna could only murmur, 'I hope I can live up to your expectations.'

'Commitment to the written word is all that's required, Anna. See you at the launch.'

Long after the connection had closed, Anna held on to the handpiece as though reluctant to re-enter her study. Although flattered by the publisher's confidence in her abilities, she felt a level of anxiety not previously experienced when musing on a writing career. Press interviews and author talks had been at the back of her mind since signing the contract, but apart from a few notes scribbled in an exercise book, the pages of her second novel remained as blank as the ream of paper purchased the previous week. "Commitment to the written word" entailed more than hours of research and pounding typewriter keys. It could mean giving up her part-time job; taking a risk that the extra income she and Joseph had come to rely on could be replaced by royalties. Success or failure for a writer depended on the fickle reading public; what was popular one month could languish on bookshop shelves the next. The actions of a bombastic premier would be forgotten before long, the images of frightened women consigned to media archives.

Determined to focus on current tasks, Anna hung up the phone and headed into her study to prepare her launch speech.

* * *

Several weeks after the novel's release, sales were increasing steadily and the *Courier-Mail* had published a positive review plus a brief interview, so Anna readily agreed to the request for an interview from a popular women's magazine. The female reporter – blond, leggy, heavily made-up – arrived half an hour late, increasing Anna's pre-interview nerves, but she managed to adopt a confident expression when greeting her at the front door.

'Just ignore Harvey,' the reporter advised, indicating the long-haired photographer loitering on the driveway.

Anna nodded and ushered her inside and down the hallway to the family room. 'The light's better in this room,' she remarked, in response to a wrinkling of the reporter's neat nose as she perused the faded cane chairs and a rather garish sofa that converted into a bed.

'The patio room would be more suitable. A pool in the background will give our readers a sense of your circumstances.'

Anna frowned. She had assumed the questions would focus on her novel, not on her suburban status.

'Successful migrant family benefitting from the opportunities Australia has to offer,' the reporter continued, her gaze focused on Anna's bright sundress and shiny sandals. 'The image of a charming young suburban mother. Our readers will love your sense of style.'

Anna cringed, but the reporter appeared not to notice her change of expression.

'Remind me to ask for a family photo, Harvey,' she added, tossing the command over her shoulder while her scarlet high-heels negotiated the uneven brick step leading to the patio.

'Yep,' the formerly silent photographer replied.

Safe on level terracotta tiles, the reporter stood surveying the scene, hands on slim hips. 'Right,' she announced. 'We'll have Anna seated with her back to the pool with me opposite.' She waved an arm towards the chairs arranged around the patio table.

Harvey complied without further comment, dragging chairs into position with one hand, the other clutching his camera as if reluctant to relinquish his hold.

Suitably posed – hands folded in her lap, shoulders straight, face forward – Anna waited for an introduction similar to that given by the *Courier-Mail* journalist, which had focused on the juxtaposition of tragic suburban incident and debut novel. However, this reporter had other ideas, launching straight into the Abortion Question, her steel-edged tone revealing unexpected conservatism.

Anna's response, given in a sombre tone, dealt with women's rights and the importance of safe medical procedures. She also touched on the climate of fear generated by police raids and arrests and suggested governments should be focused on addressing the burgeoning AIDS crisis, rather than harassing pregnant women seeking terminations. Referring to her novel, Anna also stressed that a woman's mental health should be given greater priority by general practitioners and child welfare authorities alike.

'What about a woman's responsibility to her unborn child?'

'What about the father's responsibility?' Anna answered quickly. 'Many men simply walk away, leaving their girlfriends to deal with what they see as a woman's problem.'

'That's true, but the option of adoption should be considered instead of abortion, don't you think?'

'Surely we've moved on from the days when a girl who found herself in so-called "trouble" was sent away for the duration of her pregnancy and pressured into having the baby adopted out at birth?'

'So, you're in favour of unmarried women keeping their babies and expecting the government to foot the bill?'

'I believe a woman should have a choice and not be judged for the decision she makes. An unplanned pregnancy can devastate.'

'You're thinking of Narelle White?'

'Not particularly. I'm referring to any woman who finds herself in a situation she finds intolerable.'

'But your involvement in the White case led to the writing of your novel?'

'Yes, it did. Afterwards, I realised that my witnessing such a tragic event could be used to highlight the difficulties many women still face, despite the advances made in the area of women's rights. My primary concern, however, was the lack of support for vulnerable women and the bias, whether intended or not, of a male-dominated judiciary.'

The reporter raised perfectly plucked eyebrows. 'Do you intend to write further novels on controversial issues?'

Beyond caring what the editor of the women's magazine would think, Anna replied, 'I feel it's my duty as a feminist writer to explore controversial subjects. Contemporary Australian women want more than happy-ever-after romances to read.' She paused and looked directly at the camera, as an idea she had toyed with during days of writer's block surged to the forefront of her mind. 'My next novel will deal with the intimate relationship between two women that develops as a result of losing their partners, one male, one female, in a road accident.'

'Well, you have certainly given our readers plenty to think about, Mrs Fletcher. Thank you for your time and I wish you success with *Is No One Listening?* and any subsequent novels.'

* * *

'I suppose I can expect some hostility, this being conservative Queensland,' Anna remarked to Shirley the following afternoon, as they sat at the patio table sipping cold drinks and discussing the interview.

'Sure, but we need to think positive and celebrate victories, no matter how small. The self-righteous old farts that govern this state can't last forever.'

'The thought of many more years is enough to send me beetling down south.'

'Could you stand four-seasons-in-a-day Melbourne?'

'Probably not, but the city must have something going for it. I read somewhere that there are nearly three million inhabitants.'

Shirley glanced at the pool, where George and Adam were splashing one another. 'I wouldn't mind a change of scene one of these days. Brisbane's a great place to bring up kids, but the really good jobs are elsewhere.' She sighed. 'The trouble is, Sam would never agree to move.'

Anna reached out to touch her friend's arm. 'Same here. Joseph adores the Brisbane lifestyle.'

'Bloody men,' Shirley muttered, rising from her chair. 'No imagination.'

'Maybe not, but at least I persuaded Joseph to emigrate.'

Shirley smiled. 'Thank God for that. I can't imagine life without our friendship.'

'Same here.' She walked onto the patio to hide a blush. 'George, Mum's ready to leave.'

* * *

There was little opportunity for socialising over subsequent weekends, as Anna was busy signing books in suburban bookshops and giving talks about the inspiration behind her writing to FAW members and various women's groups. Sales exceeded the expectations of both publisher and author and a second print run was required six months after the first.

Anna basked in the sunshine of celebrity, so when the publisher suggested a pre-Christmas book signing and speaking tour encompassing Melbourne, Sydney and Adelaide, she readily agreed, even though it would mean taking leave from her job. So far, Mr Jephson had been most accommodating, arranging for his wife to cover Anna's absences to attend functions that clashed with work days and dismissing the suggestion he look for a new secretary. 'Make the most of your fifteen minutes of fame, my dear,' he'd said, following a client's delight on recognising Anna as the author interviewed on a recent TV programme. 'The public will soon lose interest, once the next controversial book is published.'

'Oh, I'm well aware of that, Mr Jephson. I just don't want to let you down.'

After reassuring Anna that he understood, the usually solemn solicitor had chuckled before confiding that his wife was relishing her surge of popularity at both golf and bridge clubs, owing, she believed, to her close proximity to Brisbane's newest popular author. All the same, Anna felt awkward asking for more time off and offered to use some of her holiday leave to cover the ten-day tour. Mr Jephson had no objection.

Joseph wasn't so co-operative, accusing her of abandoning Adam in her quest for celebrity. 'One bloody book and you think you can swan around all over Australia without a care in the world. You have responsibilities, for Christ's sake. You're a wife and mother first.'

Anna resisted the urge to say she was a writer first and foremost. Instead, she pacified, as women have done since time immemorial, promising an overseas holiday in the near future and suggesting she employ a cleaner.

'But what about after school? Adam can't be left alone until I get home from work.'

'I'll arrange a minder through the school if you insist, although I'm certain Adam won't like it. At thirteen, he thinks he's grown up.'

'Make sure you ask for references this time.'

Anna resented the allusion to Narelle. There was no way she could have anticipated the events of the previous year. 'Why don't I ask Gloria next door to keep an eye on him, maybe give him his dinner as well?'

'That would solve the problem.' Joseph sighed. 'I suppose I could buy a takeaway, or rustle up something when I get home.'

Anna didn't care what Joseph ate during her absence, but knew better than to make a snide remark, meals ranking high on his list of priorities. 'Try the new Chinese restaurant in Sandgate. Shirley and Sam went there recently and said the food's delicious.'

Joseph nodded and turned back to the television.

* * *

Southern book enthusiasts proved more critical than their northern counterparts. Some commented that *Is No One Listening?* should have been based on Narelle White's low socio-economic existence, rather than a fictional middle-class woman whose comfortable life gave her no excuse for her belligerent attitude and actions towards her son. Anna felt they had missed the point – child abuse and an aversion to motherhood wasn't determined by economic status – but she refused to be drawn into an argument, moving on instead to the next questioner.

Then, at a Melbourne literary function attended by mostly older women dressed in elegant outfits, a well-corseted matron maintained that Anna should not be benefitting financially from poor Narelle White's misfortune, a statement that drew applause along with shouts of disagreement. Argument erupted, many rising from their seats and pointing manicured fingers to emphasise opposing points of view. Alarmed by the uproar, Anna moved away from the lectern and walked over to the publicist appointed to oversee the southern tour. 'What on earth should I do now, Rachel?'

'Leave it to me,' Rachel reassured her, rising from her seat in the front row and heading for the lectern. A head taller than Anna and wearing high heels, she called the agitated audience to order, her cultured tones reverberating around the room.

The audience settled quickly as though reprimanded by a stony-faced headmistress. Handbags clicked open; lace-edged handkerchiefs were extracted to pat moist cheeks.

'Thank you, ladies,' Rachel continued, raising her copy of *Is No One Listening?* above her head. 'For those of you who have yet to read this thought-provoking book, the author will sign copies at the table in the foyer. But firstly,' she gestured towards Anna, 'a show of appreciation for our guest speaker, debut author Anna Fletcher.'

Much to Anna's astonishment, applause erupted like thunder and numerous women rose to their feet, calling 'Bravo' and 'Congratulations.' Uncertain whether to stand and smile her gratitude, Anna stayed perched on the edge of her chair until Rachel approached.

'A great success,' the publicist declared, bending to pat Anna's arm. 'Sales and signing now.'

Anna managed a smile, rose and followed her out to the foyer.

Changeable Weather

In between her job and household chores, Anna wrote steadily for the next two years, producing a second novel, *Feminine Company* and several short stories. The novel explored a year in the lives of two women friends following the sudden deaths of their long-term partners – one a gambling-addicted husband, the other a respected female academic – and the homophobia they experienced when grief unexpectedly led to a loving intimate relationship.

Published in mid 1988, this novel, like the first, evoked controversy, particularly from conservative Queenslanders convinced the AIDS crisis sweeping the world was punishment for what they considered deviant sexual acts. Several churches rebuked Anna for her pro-homosexual stance, one priest calling for public burning of the offensive book. Footage showing several members of his congregation setting light to books on the church steps was broadcast on ABC news, while the *Courier-Mail's* "Letters to the Editor" revealed varying degrees of disgust. As expected, Shirley's letter praising the book for raising important social issues did not appear in print.

Interviews followed and sales soared. Once more, Anna became a topic of suburban conversation, some expressing revulsion that a wife and mother could stoop so low, others praising her for tackling such a controversial subject. At work, the ever-supportive Mr Jephson proudly informed clients that his secretary was 'none other than that champion of maligned minorities, novelist Anna Fletcher.'

Anna considered the epithet a gross exaggeration. She might employ fiction to explore social issues that concerned her, but a novel couldn't alter attitudes forged over decades. Then, as Christmas approached, Mr Jephson's announcement that he had sold the business and would be retiring at the end of the year, proved the catalyst for decision-making, Anna having dithered for months over whether to resign.

The possibility of writing full-time had arisen after selling the film rights of *Is No One Listening?* to a Sydney production company. So far, the film hadn't been made but Anna had received a reasonable sum. *It's now or never,* she thought, convinced that mid-life – she'd turned forty a few months earlier – was the best time to pursue a writing career. She decided to give herself five years to prove her worth.

Discussion with Joseph followed her resolution, their financial situation the primary topic. Fortunately, the small mortgage taken out to build their second house had been paid off a year earlier. Expecting some opposition, Anna prepared what she considered a convincing case, but Joseph supported her decision wholeheartedly, maintaining she deserved some 'me' time, now that their son had left school.

A diligent student, Adam expected to be offered a place at university early in the New Year. His first preference was the University of Queensland, where he planned to follow in his father's footsteps and study engineering. Anna's fears of a troubled adolescence had proved unfounded, Adam having retained his laidback disposition and sense of humour. There had been the inevitable clashes over late nights, smoking in his room and swearing, but overall, the teenage years were passing without major incidents. On the single occasion when he'd arrived home from a party worse the wear for drink, Anna had managed to mollify Joseph, pointing out that although Adam was underage, at least the drinking had taken place at a friend's house and not in a pub or nightclub. Adam's subsequent hangover – two days of feeling like shit, with a diet limited to dry crackers and flat lemonade – cured him of binge drinking for years.

* * *

The University of Queensland occupied land seven kilometres south west of the city centre, in the suburb of St Lucia. Bounded by a bend of the Brisbane River, with parkland, lakes and beautiful sandstone buildings, the campus offered a tranquil study environment. However, for students like Adam travelling from outer suburbs by public transport, its location meant a lengthy commute.

Adam rejected the idea of living in a residential college for his first year, so learning to drive became a top priority, Anna using her car to teach him the basics. Lessons with a driving school followed and by the end of first semester, he had passed his test. Anna had no objection to Adam borrowing her car for the hour-long drive to uni; she rarely stirred from her study during the working week. Nevertheless, she encouraged him to save a portion of his earnings from a weekend job at a local restaurant for a future car purchase.

Meanwhile, a chance conversation with Roger led to Joseph's acquisition of a twenty-five year old Volkswagen that Anna felt should have gone to the tip. She suggested the wreck be stored in the concreted space alongside the garage.

'No way,' Joseph declared. 'I need the VW undercover, so I can work in all weather. Your car will be fine parked on the driveway.' He commenced restoration with typical efficiency, dismantling the vehicle until only a shell remained, each part suitably labelled before storage in a cardboard box. Weekends and the occasional evening were devoted to "Bertie Beetle", Adam having been granted naming rights in exchange for a specified number of hours assisting his father.

'Good training for the workplace,' Joseph countered, when Anna objected to the time taken from Adam's studies. 'Mechanics, auto-electrics, welding, panel-beating, spray-painting. What more could a trainee engineer ask?'

Bogged down in a first draft, Anna couldn't be bothered to argue. Once Joseph set his mind to a task, nothing could induce him to proceed at a moderate pace. Retreating to her study, she left father and son to their work, inserting ear-plugs to lessen the din of hammers and the whine of an electric drill. So far, the neighbours hadn't complained about the noise, male members of the households seeming keen to offer advice and assistance. Anna hoped their wives would remain equally tolerant.

* * *

Sunshine yellow Bertie gleamed at his unveiling early on a humid February evening. Neighbours and friends stood on the driveway, stubbies or wineglasses in their hands, to toast the rebirth of a vehicle once consigned to a weed-ridden graveyard at the rear of a farmer's paddock. Immensely proud of her boys' achievement, Anna made no mention of her forthcoming publication during the party that followed, scurrying instead from house to patio with trays of food, like a model suburban housewife.

Storm clouds gathered in the midnight sky, but no rain fell on the revellers – predominantly male – cavorting in the pool in their underwear, or swilling beer on the patio like there was no tomorrow. In the family room, Anna and several other wives sat fanning themselves with paper plates, the ceiling fan failing to stem the flow of perspiration from necks and shoulders covered by permed tresses. Anna's Lycra singlet stuck to her body; why had she worn it on such a humid night?

Summer temperatures had been higher than usual that year and she longed for respite. Nights were the worst; lying naked beneath a whirring fan with a damp face-washer laid across her chest, she struggled to sleep. A swim before bed helped, but unless she fell asleep quickly, body heat returned, along with a headache that throbbed for hours despite taking paracetamol. When the sun rose a little after four, flooding the bedroom with harsh summer light, there was little chance of catching up on sleep, so Anna would retreat to the still-dark family room and doze until movement from Joseph roused her. Adam slept like the dead, irrespective of temperature, so she didn't have to worry about a teenage son finding her sprawled naked on the sofa.

Twice that summer, she had suggested buying an air-conditioning unit for their bedroom, but Joseph maintained they were too noisy and that cutting a hole in the wall behind the bed would spoil the room. Like Adam, he slept soundly whatever the weather and had little empathy for the sudden onset of Anna's insomnia.

'Go to the doctor and get some sleeping tablets,' he advised her, following yet another round of complaints about the heat from his irritable wife. 'It's just a stage you're going through. It's nothing to do with the climate.'

Anna wondered whether insomnia and her increasingly low mood could be signs of imminent menopause, even though her periods remained regular, so she made an appointment at the local surgery. Her usual doctor, a youngish woman with whom Anna felt a certain rapport, was on leave, giving her no choice but to see old-school Dr Platt, who was on the wrong side of sixty-five. After listening to her description of wakeful nights and a sudden inability to cope with the heat and humidity, he prescribed sleeping tablets to restore a normal sleep pattern and sent her for a blood test to determine whether she was pre-menopausal.

A second visit, requested by Dr Platt, took longer than Anna had anticipated, as the doctor insisted on enquiring about the state of her marriage and her relationship with her son, prior to revealing that the test had proved negative. 'I conclude you're experiencing a bout of depression,' he declared, leaning back in the chair, arms folded over his protruding stomach. 'It's common in women of your age and situation. Think about it like this, Mrs Fletcher. For years, "mother" has been your primary occupation, but now your son is at uni, his focus is on a future beyond his childhood home. Your influence is waning and will continue to do so as Adam matures. A natural cycle, Mrs Fletcher, but one some women find difficult to adjust to. My advice is to take up a hobby or get a part-time job.'

Fury threatened to spill from Anna's mouth. How dare this puffed-up medico assume she fitted his perception of contemporary Australian womanhood? "Writer" had been her primary occupation for years; she had toiled long and hard to hone her skills, achieve her goal of publication. She didn't sit at home worrying about her diminished influence over a seventeen-year-old. Independence had been her maternal catchcry since Adam's early childhood. She had no time for children that clung to their mothers. They reminded her of juvenile magpies squawking for food when they were adult size.

'I am a full-time writer,' she said through gritted teeth, determined to remain calm. 'Three months ago, I resigned from my secretarial job to devote myself full-time to producing quality fiction. My workplace might be a home study, but, like other career women, caring for my family takes place outside working hours.'

Dr Platt frowned. 'Depression could be your body's response to a heavy workload.'

'Unlikely. I've been juggling work and home duties for years.'

'A holiday could restore your equilibrium. Is that a possibility?'

Anna nodded as images of a cool English spring flitted through her mind. For the first time in years, she no longer had to consider school holidays or fitting in with an employer's schedule. 'I'll mention a holiday to my husband.'

'I suggest sooner rather than later, Mrs Fletcher. A holiday is far preferable to my prescribing anti-depressants.'

'I agree,' Anna replied and took her leave.

As she drove home from the surgery, she envisaged spring flowers blooming in her parents' garden, walks in a forest burgeoning with new growth, bracing sea-wind clearing her head as she paced a sand-strewn promenade. A welcome respite from months of relentless heat and humidity.

The Consequences of Climate Change

Anna travelled across the world alone, Joseph having been unable to take leave at short notice. Concerned about her state of mind – constant mood swings despite improved sleep – he had no qualms about her leaving the family for a month. During the flight, she kept dark thoughts at bay by immersing herself in the movies shown on overhead screens. In between screenings and meals, she even managed a little sleep.

At Heathrow, parents, sisters and an assortment of nephews and nieces vied with one another for her attention, their delight in her presence bringing tears to the surface. The two-hour journey to her hometown – Anna in the rear of her youngest sister's car, an excited six-year-old nephew beside her – passed in a blur, constant questioning providing little opportunity to observe once-familiar forest and thatched-cottage villages.

Waking in her childhood bedroom after a night of deep but intermittent sleep, which she dismissed as jet-lag-induced, Anna felt weary yet content. Stretching her limbs, she encountered the edges of the narrow bed and relished the feel of empty space, the soft embrace of sheets and blankets. Her multi-layered life had been pared back to a single role. For the next few weeks, she would be simply a beloved family member, pampered by parents and siblings, a woman with no responsibilities.

The liberty of marriage, envisaged twenty years earlier, had proven illusory; within two years, she had succumbed to a woman's traditional role, the glorious adventure of a new land reduced to mind-numbing suburbia.

Determined not to waste the day, she slipped out of bed to draw back the curtains. Sunlight filled the room with pastel shades smooth as silk. No harshness here, no scrambling to locate sunblock cream and hat; these rays soothed. She stood at the window looking down at the garden, noting the dipping heads of daffodils beneath an apple tree awash with blossom. The promise of an English spring, April showers to nurture emerging flora, followed by delicate sunshine peeping through cottonwool clouds. Nature on an even keel.

* * *

Following a relaxing breakfast, she left her parents to enjoy their habitual second cup of tea, donned her rainproof jacket and headed for the sea. Her trainers squeaked on damp pavement; raindrops plopped from the overhanging branches of roadside plane trees and slid silently down her suntanned cheeks. She recalled crisp autumn mornings, scuffing through burnished leaves, her polished school shoes damp and grimy before she reached the bus stop.

Turning the corner, she increased her pace, powering up the slight incline as though training for a marathon. A shopping strip came into view, the familiar greengrocer's and baker's adjacent to the small supermarket built years after her departure from parental home and country. She stopped beside the kerb and recited the childhood mantra, "look right, look left, then right again", before crossing the road. A few hundred metres and she would reach the path that wound through public gardens to a clifftop café.

A pair of grey squirrels bounded across the path in front of her and she laughed out loud as they chased one another around a rubbish bin before scampering up the gnarled trunk of a nearby tree. Her laughter induced an urge to indulge in childhood actions, so she skipped to the end of the gardens, emerging breathless on the clifftop pavement. She had intended to retrace her steps at this point, rather than take the zigzag path down the cliff to the promenade and beach, but her buoyant mood demanded further activity. As she ran down the path, she almost collided with a man and his dog and murmured hasty apologies before continuing her race to the sea.

Few walkers were braving the windswept promenade and the row of beach huts hugging the cliff base stood shuttered against the morning chill. Warmed to the core, Anna turned her face into the wind and raced across the wide promenade and down a nearby set of steps to the beach, a narrow strip of yellowish sand washed by blue-grey waves. Giving a whoop of delight, she shed shoes, socks and inhibitions to turn cartwheels, her bare feet and hands leaving a haphazard trail in the cold, damp sand. Oblivious to stinging spray, she relished her anonymity. *Exuberant woman on a beach* was the only possible caption, should a photographer materialise.

Returning to her parents' home, she collapsed on a kitchen chair, exhausted but elated by the unaccustomed exertion. The lethargy of recent months had dissipated, left behind in a land of energy-sapping heat.

Her mother remarked on her rosy cheeks and sparkling eyes. 'I was worried when I saw you at Heathrow,' she continued, reaching out to brush a stray curl from Anna's forehead. 'You were so thin, I hardly recognised you. I sense there's more to your need for a holiday than just tiredness.'

Anna sighed. She should have foreseen this maternal concern. 'I've been a bit down lately. Nothing serious, just loss of appetite and occasional insomnia.'

Brow furrowed, her mother considered the admission. 'You would tell me if there was anything wrong between you and Joseph?'

'Yes, and no, there isn't. We're both extremely busy, that's all, the same as other couples our age. Since Joseph became area manager, he's rarely home before eight. I can't remember the last time the three of us ate dinner together during the week. I eat alone when Adam's working at the restaurant.'

'So why don't you defer dinner until Joseph comes home?'

'Eating late upsets my digestion and makes it even more difficult to sleep.'

'And weekends? I trust you two get together then.'

'Most Saturdays, we go out for dinner with friends or entertain at home,' Anna answered carefully.

Maternal lips pursed, a sure sign that censure disguised as advice would soon follow. 'I realise it's difficult, with Joseph's long working hours and Adam occupied with university and a part-time job, but you should try to set aside time to be a family. Going separate ways can lead to...' she hesitated, '... family breakdown.'

Reluctant to argue that Nineties' marriage and family life bore no resemblance to the Fifties'/Sixties' model, Anna changed the subject.

* * *

A carefree month catching up with family and friends, interspersed with solitary walks or strolls with her parents, worked wonders. Anna returned home eager to resume research and determined to include exercise in her daily routine. Relieved to see his wife restored to her former self, Joseph suggested visiting New Caledonia later in the year, just the two of them, as Adam, at eighteen, wouldn't want to accompany his parents. 'A sort of second honeymoon, my love, only on this occasion much longer and no need to worry about the cost.'

'A marvellous idea, darling!' Anna reached across the dining table to clasp his hand. 'I'll get some brochures from the travel agency tomorrow.'

Joseph beamed and lifted his wineglass. 'A toast to my beautiful wife of almost twenty years.'

They clinked glasses and red wine stained their smiling lips as their hands parted.

* * *

Anna worked hard throughout Brisbane's blue-sky cooler months, completing research for her third novel and making good progress on a first draft. Each morning, she left the house before breakfast to walk for an hour, varying her route to prevent boredom by exploring streets beyond the small estate. Sometimes, she ventured to the freshwater lagoon situated on the outskirts of Sandgate. Shaded by eucalypts, she walked the gravel path beside water ruffled by ducks and other waterbirds, soothed by the rustle of countless reeds. At peace with her world, she would return home ready to embark on the day's tasks.

Spring arrived in a burst of vibrant colour, garden shrubs producing exquisite blooms, sudden sharp showers reviving lawns grown thin over a dry winter. One beautiful September morning – cloudless sky, light breeze – Anna decided to revisit saltwater, so drove to Sandgate, parking beside the swathe of mown grass dotted with benches facing the bay. She had forgotten to bring a sunhat, but no matter; the air felt cool and her ever-present sunglasses would protect her eyes from the glare.

Setting off along the pavement, she power-walked for several hundred metres, then settled for a less exacting pace. Beyond grass and seawall, shallow water retreated on the changing tide, exposing mudflats pocked with dark mangrove roots. Seagulls arrived en masse, leaving foot and beak prints as they searched for food and squabbled like small children. Their antics amused her, although Anna could have done without the constant cawing. Determined to scatter the raucous gulls, she left the path and headed for the bay, leaping over the low seawall like an Olympic hurdler.

Her white trainers sank into brown sludge; she had overlooked the soft consistency of mudflats. She managed to extract her shoes but, with large mud extensions to soles and uppers, she struggled to make progress towards the still bickering seagulls. 'Bloody Mudgate,' she grumbled, stomping away from the water. Once she was safely perched on the seawall, she removed her trainers and, holding them at arm's length, attempted to detach the clumps of congealed mud. Repeated bashings against the stone wall achieved little, so she removed her mud-spattered white socks and made her way barefoot back to the car.

Her cheerful morning mood further diminished on returning home to discover the back of her neck was sore from sunburn. As usual, she'd scraped her shoulder-length curls into a pony-tail for her daily walk but, in her haste to reach the sea, had forgotten to apply sunscreen. 'Spring sunshine should be gentle,' she muttered, recalling a previous seashore walk that had required neither hat nor sunscreen. Something was changing and she didn't like it.

The climate continued to irritate her as September morphed into October and temperatures rose. Severe storms, unusual for the time of year, flattened spring blooms and soil oozed from garden beds to stain concrete paths and patio tiles. When would her menfolk learn to take their shoes off *before* entering the screened-in patio? Joseph didn't help, by remarking that she sounded like a broken record with her constant reminders.

Her early morning walks continued until November's rising humidity forced a retreat to the backyard pool, but Anna swam with ebbing enthusiasm once sun-strips struck the clear blue surface. As the days lengthened, she endeavoured to rise earlier in order to tackle exercise in muted pre-dawn light. The plan worked well until Joseph began to complain about her absence when he woke. Although they rarely made love during the week – at night, he fell into an exhausted sleep the moment his head touched the pillow and mornings were too rushed – he liked a few minutes' cuddle before the alarm clock shrilled its unwelcome command.

Reluctant to risk a return of marital disharmony, Anna decided to slip back into bed following her swim. Joseph seemed oblivious to her cool skin and damp hair, so she lay in his arms, grateful for a simple solution. Sometimes, she felt frustrated when he left to shower, but at least she could relieve the ache once she was alone in the house. Lying on rumpled sheets, she would conjure up an imaginary lover – usually a character from one of her novels or short stories – sense unfamiliar hands, lips, penis; gasp as waves of desire flooded her body. The consequence of what became a regular event that summer was a racy, fantastical short story, where Anna's writer-protagonist imagined her fictional hero into being. Alas, Anna's heroine paid the ultimate price for succumbing to the hero's skilful seduction, when he inserted her form into his preferred reality, the computer!

Anna had purchased an IBM 286 the previous year, so the story seemed appropriate. The new technology made a writer's task so much easier. Editing was a breeze and floppy discs were useful to back-up her work. Watching text emerge on the screen gave her a buzz; she blessed the touch-typing skills learnt in her youth.

The pre-Christmas holiday to New Caledonia had to be postponed due to a conference Joseph was obliged to attend. By way of compensation, he suggested that Anna should join him at Jupiter's Hotel and Casino, and spend the days shopping or enjoying drinks poolside while he was working. They could spend the evenings together, as no one would object to the area manager's wife attending conference dinners. Anna had no desire to play the corporate wife or visit shops catering for the gold shoe and gold belt brigade, so she simply stated that she would prefer to remain at home.

'No one in their right mind would turn down a three-day stay in a luxury hotel on the Gold Coast!' he retorted, his expression a mixture of exasperation and disappointment.

'I don't belong in that world, Joseph. I thought you would have realised that by now.'

A full-blown argument had erupted, with neither party willing to back down. Resolution came in the form of retreat, with Anna fleeing to her study, intent on spending the night on the fold-up bed stored in one corner.

Next morning, seated at the computer wearing old shorts and a baggy singlet, she contemplated the divergence of their lives. Once, they had held the same principles, their goal being to make good in a new land where hard work was rewarded, and nobody cared which school you'd attended or what occupation your father pursued. She didn't belong in Joseph's new world of corporate dinners, business class flights and a flash new company car every two years. A social conscience fired her writing career, not the pursuit of wealth and status.

In recent months, Joseph had mentioned that a move to a more up-market suburb would be in his best interests, as their house was too small to entertain inter-state clients. He envisaged a two-storey house with at least four bedrooms, an en-suite in the master bedroom and extensive landscaped gardens incorporating a large pool and spa. So far, Anna had managed to defer looking at properties, citing Adam's end of year exams, then Christmas, then the new university year, but she knew Joseph would soon tire of her excuses.

I don't belong were the words her fingers typed into the document, instead of the projected chapter heading. White letters against a sky-blue background, a statement easily deleted. But simple keystrokes could not expunge her deep-seated values or determine the future course of her life.

Unravelling

Her depression returned with the onset of winter; a deeper, darker cloud than she had previously experienced, and one that enveloped every waking hour and invaded the narrative of her dreams. Anna's doctor diagnosed clinical depression and prescribed a low-dose antidepressant. The pills helped, improving her mood and appetite, but insomnia remained a problem, taunting her attempts to restore her mental health. Permanently weary, she struggled to maintain her workday routine, the new novel advancing in fits and starts due to interruptions for snatches of sleep. Minor household issues began to irritate her – empty beer bottles left beside a family room chair, Adam's unmade bed, smelly socks left in shoes. Nagging became the focal point of her every conversation, with her husband and son trying to jolly her along with promises to mend their ways.

When stronger sleeping tablets failed to eliminate her insomnia, Joseph took matters into his own hands, insisting a change of scene was the recipe for recovery, not more pills. Too tired to argue, Anna spent Saturday after Saturday slumped in the passenger seat of Joseph's brand new Ford Fairlane as he drove to real estate offices in the western suburbs. The expensive houses left her as cold as the gleaming tiles in renovated kitchens and bathrooms; she stood silent in elegant living rooms, while Joseph enthused about thick carpet and quality curtains. Real estate agents soon abandoned any attempts to gauge her reaction, concentrating instead on her animated husband.

Spring brought the usual array of bright flowers and balmy weather, along with a "sold subject to the sale of" contract, as Anna had yielded to Joseph's wishes because she no longer cared where she lived. The twenty-year-old house in Chapel Hill – a prize-winning design for a house built on a difficult site – looked imposing from the street, with its white-painted bricks, terracotta tiled roof and wide stone steps leading to double front doors. 'The location's great, too,' Joseph told Roger. 'Close to the uni for Adam and only fifteen minutes to my work. What more could a family want?'

'Sounds wonderful, mate. Is there a pool?'

'No, but there's plenty of room for one in the front. Cut into the slope with palm trees all around, a pool would look most impressive.'

'You deserve it, mate. All those years of slogging away, spending weeks away from the family and working all the hours God gives. I couldn't have done it. I'm too fond of my own bed and a forty-hour week.'

'Each to their own,' Joseph replied, self-satisfaction engraved on his face. 'Besides, you've done pretty well for yourself and I'll never forget the help you gave me when I first arrived.'

Roger raised his beer bottle. 'To the best bloody country in the world!'

'I'll second that.'

In the far corner of the patio room, Anna lay on a sun lounger, re-calling the caress of cool water on her skin, her nakedness shielded from view by thick foliage and high fences. In Chapel Hill, she would have to wear swimming togs, as palm trees would provide no barrier to nosy neighbours or passing pedestrians. She mused on other pos-sibilities: a small flat near the ocean, a cottage on the periphery of a country town. Did she possess the courage to embrace freedom in all its myriad forms?

* * *

Anna left Elizabeth Park two hours after the removalist's truck had departed for the western suburbs. She tackled the final clean systematically, moving from the rear of the house to the front, vacuuming carpets, washing tiles and vinyl flooring, dusting the places where bookcases had leant against walls. Her housework ended at the front door, which stood open so she could step backwards onto the porch, the Hoover lifted into her arms.

After loading her cleaning tools into the boot of her car, she turned for a last look at the house the three of them had called home for almost a decade. So many experiences were locked within its walls, so many words spoken in its rooms, so many stories created in the small study. Most likely Adam would leave home once he finished university and move on to a house-share or a flat. It remained to be seen whether his mother could put down roots in a new place.

A move to the western suburbs meant more than a different home in a different street and unfamiliar shops. Anna's entire Australian life had been lived north of the river, a dividing line always mentioned when responding to location questions. Northern suburbs residents spoke of those in the south as if the Brisbane River were a Berlin wall separating two warring tribes. Southerners probably felt the same about their northern neighbours. The west seemed neither one thing nor the other; just a series of suburbs tucked into bends on both sides of the sluggish brown river that meandered through the city to Moreton Bay.

As she drove away from Elizabeth Park, Anna tried to focus on the future, rather than the friends she was leaving behind. At least, with five bedrooms and three bathrooms, there would be room for more than two visitors at a time. She could almost hear Shirley's reaction to the elegant guest rooms, divided by a gleaming bathroom complete with dusky pink bidet. 'Good Lord, Anna, you've gone all posh on me. Next thing, you'll be introducing me to the bloody servants!'

Feather-light, a smile brushed her lips and for the first time in months she sensed a glimmer of optimism. The new house wasn't to her taste, but a different working environment might provide the impetus she needed to regenerate her neglected career. The room she had chosen as a study – generous proportions, windows on two sides, ceiling fan and air-conditioner – should be a joy to work in, with its views of terraced garden beds filled with flowering shrubs. Dare she hope that her lingering insomnia would fade away once she slept in an air-conditioned bedroom, shielded from bright sunlight by a lush fernery planted in front of a two-metre-high retaining wall?

* * *

One year after moving to Brisbane's western suburbs, Anna finally acknowledged the real reason for her continuing, albeit less frequent, insomnia and the depression that seemed to surface whenever she considered the dark beast conquered. The answer lay not, as she had believed, in a wish to flee an unsatisfactory marriage, but in an altered emotional state that affected her entire life.

Enlightenment came as she sat at her desk, looking beyond the darkened computer screen to the shadowed shapes of trees and shrubs that moulded the contours of her hillside garden. Alone in the house – Adam was on holiday with friends and Joseph inter-state on business – she had continued working beyond the usual dinner hour, ignoring the rumbling of her stomach. Swift as the tropic twilight, a mantle of knowledge enfolded her, alarming, yet oddly comforting. Phrases churned in her head, demanding release; she grabbed pen and notebook and scribbled lines before they could dissolve. Twenty years had passed since she had chosen to express her adoration of Australia in language more suited to sonnets for a human lover. The remnants of her youthful exuberance lay concealed in a red folder; her Seventies stanzas would be eclipsed by elegy before that night ended.

Long strands of summer stretched behind her; breezes blowing perfumed petals high into azure skies, scarlet sunsets slipping over the rim as she sat sipping ice-cold shandy on a wide veranda. Her images of deep contentment were overshadowed by the passage of time. A present day portrait would reveal a feverish face spotted with specks of dust, brown blobs staining sun-damaged skin. Sprawled in a sweat-soaked patio chair, gulping glasses of iced water, she lacked the energy to swat the stinging insects that came zooming like zeppelins towards her defenceless limbs. And even when she had retired to bed, savage storms sliced through late evening calm and solid sheets of rain disturbed her brief slumber that had been a pleasant interlude of temperate dreams.

Beyond Australia's shores, more momentous events were shaping the end of the millennium days. A hated wall had tumbled; people-power had removed repressive regimes in central and eastern Europe. They were causes for celebration, yet Anna remained locked in her little life, impervious to global change. Interminable threads of summer stretched before her, compelling a swift return to a preferred reality where she alone controlled the storyline.

Currents of cooled air circled the room. Goosebumps erupted on her bare arms; a pen fell from her stiff fingers and rolled over white paper etched with melancholic idiom. A final stanza and then she must adjourn to the kitchen and find something to eat. She was no Thomas Chatterton, starving in a garret.

Falling, falling out of love
With my adopted land
Burning through the atmosphere
Like a shattered star
A love affair turned sour.

Retreat

A decade ended, along with a century and the millennium. Novels were written, published, reviewed. A son crossed the wide Pacific to take up an engineering position in British Columbia; a husband rose higher up the corporate ladder, relishing frequent business trips to Europe and Asia.

Cocooned within an air-conditioned space, Anna remained indifferent to a world of terrorist attacks, global financial crisis, increasing numbers of refugees and the dire predictions of climate scientists. Technology aided her withdrawal from reality. Her website and blog were available to readers 24/7 and Facebook friends were easy to contact on a daily or weekly basis. Brief text messages took the place of lengthy phone conversations, while the advent of FaceTime enabled her to not only see the magnificent Canadian landscape visible from Adam's Banff home, but also reduced the need for long lunches in noisy, overcrowded cafés. She felt certain Shirley preferred their bi-annual, girls-only weekends in refurbished country cottages to monthly gatherings in one another's homes, where husbands overindulged and spent Sunday sleeping off hangovers.

Spending additional hours alone also facilitated a change of direction she couldn't have imagined during her socially aware, controversial subject matter years. Writing fantasy novels for the YA market had come about almost by accident after Adam had sent her a book in the genre for a Mother's Day gift. Reading the novel out of a sense of duty, Anna had been surprised to find she enjoyed the exploits of youthful characters within a fantastical world and decided to attempt one herself.

Five years on, her change of genre was proving worthwhile, as readers were eager for fantasy set within a pseudo-medieval Australian landscape. A more regular income – she managed to produce one fantasy novel a year – facilitated an annual holiday spent in *her* preferred environment, Europe. Since her parents' deaths in 2012, she had spent most of her holidays in France or Italy.

Sometimes Joseph joined her, and they would spend pleasant days exploring picturesque villages and rural areas that bore no resemblance to their south-east Queensland home. There was little animosity between them now. For the most part, both of them were content to lead separate lives. Wisely, Anna had sloughed off her distaste of corporate dinners, having decided that wearing designer dresses and high heels occasionally was a small price to pay for her husband's happiness. Joseph always admired her attire but remained ignorant of its source, an upmarket Op shop she had discovered in a neighbouring suburb. He also approved of her donating the outfits to a charity that supplied smart clothes to disadvantaged women seeking employment.

Soothed by a calm relationship and a career that supplied most of her needs, Anna slid through her days like a diver weaving between colourful corals. The insomnia that had ruled and almost ruined her life for a decade had been cured years before by a young psychiatrist specialising in sleep disorders. He had advised continuing low-dose anti-depressants for life, to correct the chemical imbalance in her brain. Anna had no qualms about accepting his advice. She already took medication to control high blood pressure, so adding another tablet made no difference to her health regime. Relieved by her enlightened attitude – the stigma attached to neurological disorders remained, despite attempts by the government and the medical profession to eradicate it – the psychiatrist had said she had no need of further therapy and told her to go and enjoy the rest of her life.

Initially, the end of her love affair with Australia had provoked an overwhelming desire to run back to England, but in due course Anna settled into an emotionally detached relationship with the land. No longer entranced by beach or bush, she spent her days surrounded by suburbia, content to be labelled an urban writer. She learnt to handle climatic conditions by curtailing outdoor activities during hot weather. Swimming remained the exception; her daily plunge in a pool shaded by palm trees was always a delight.

Annual visits to what Anna considered her 'real' world, helped to eliminate the acute sense of entrapment she had experienced following the shock of love's demise. More than half her life had been spent in Australia, but she belonged in lands where history meant soaring spires and Roman roads, rather than ancient rocks daubed with handprints. Dreamtime tales held no fascination for her. They were simply a way for the First Australians to make sense of *their* world.

Likewise, she felt no connection to the Bible stories she had ingested as a child, or the prayers intoned alongside parents and siblings in a brick-box church built for pre-World War believers. Hers was a life led according to a set of personal principles, not commandments delivered to itinerant Israelites. Yet, despite her best intentions, failure surfaced with regular monotony, perhaps to remind her of a fundamental weakness.

At sixty-nine, she had given up asking herself why she'd found motherhood so difficult and unfulfilling, or why she'd developed depression when there was no family history of mental illness. The past was another country. She had moved on to a tranquil place and could coast towards the twilight years. Retirement, that stage of life welcomed by some and dreaded by others, did not figure in her thoughts. A writer could employ her skills anywhere, anytime; no age-limit applied. Only serious illness or death could put a stop to creativity.

Joseph had no intention of retiring yet. His health was excellent, his motivation undiminished. He talked of buying a property in northern New South Wales for their retirement, but beyond looking at a range of beachfront houses on the internet, he did nothing to further the matter.

During writer's block moments, Anna would contemplate restoring an old house in a French village, or a Cornish cottage – notions that quickly faded once the Muse returned. Permanent relocation might be feasible for a single person, but she had no wish to dissolve a long-standing marriage, despite its shortcomings.

Intrusion

A mid-evening nap in front of the television was a predictable occurrence when Joseph was home for dinner during the working week. Comfortable on her separate sofa, Anna paid no attention to the occasional snore coming from his half-open mouth. An almost empty wine glass sat within his reach on the small antique table he had inherited from her mother. Joseph enjoyed red wine with his evening meal, although Anna felt certain a third glass sipped during the late news contributed to the fit of sneezing that always followed his snooze. She had read online that red wine triggered hay-fever symptoms, particularly during spring, but her suggestions that he switch to beer for a few weeks had fallen on deaf ears.

The thump of bare feet on timber flooring alerted her to imminent explosions – Joseph never managed to reach the tissues in time – and she turned her head to avoid an unwelcome spray.

'God, that one nearly blew my head off!' he exclaimed, after blowing his nose.

Mine too, she wanted to add, but said nothing.

'Just going to fetch the bottle,' Joseph announced, heading for the kitchen.

So, I can expect snoring all night, Anna thought, wondering whether to sleep in another bedroom.

A fusillade of sneezes was followed by the sound of glass shattering on floor tiles and expletives that seemed to reverberate throughout the house. Anna leapt from the sofa and hurried into the kitchen. 'Are you alright?'

'Sorry,' he mumbled, staring down at the mess of glass and wine pooling around his feet. 'It just slipped out of my hand.'

'Don't move. I'll fetch a cloth and bucket.'

* * *

Re-settled on her sofa, Anna was surprised to see Joseph hadn't changed into his pyjamas. Instead, he wore a clean pair of shorts and t-shirt. 'Just going to fetch another bottle,' he said, pausing in the family room doorway.

'Whatever for? It's after ten!'

'So?'

'Surely you can wait until tomorrow?'

'I want another drink tonight.'

'Don't drive,' she called after his retreating figure.

'I'm not that bloody stupid.'

'Good. Enjoy the walk.' She turned back to the television and was soon engrossed in a favourite BBC crime series.

She surfaced at eleven, still alone. 'Joseph?' she called, thinking perhaps she hadn't heard the front door opening and he had taken a last glass of wine into the lounge.

There was no response.

Yawning, she reached for the remote control to turn off the television. Most likely he'd gone into the tavern near the local shopping centre rather than the bottle shop, met a mate and decided to drink there. After closing windows and checking that the doors were locked, she padded down the hall to the main bedroom.

* * *

Jolted awake by the doorbell, her first thought was that Joseph had left his keys behind, but a glance at the bedside clock confused her as she saw that the red numerals were flashing twelve-thirty. It was a ten-minute walk from the tavern to home; maybe five more minutes if you were slightly drunk. She must raise the subject of his drinking. His unwillingness to go without a third glass of wine for just one night implied addiction.

Irritated by her disrupted sleep and the assumption that Joseph had gone home with a mate for further drinking, she stomped crossly along the hall and down the three steps to the front door.

A middle-aged policeman stood on the top step. In the road below, car lights flashed red and blue. 'Mrs Fletcher?'

'Yes,' she muttered through clenched teeth, furious to think Joseph had been discovered drunk on the footpath. Would she have to assist the policeman in half-carrying him up twenty steep steps into the house?

'Senior Sergeant Keith Dodman and this is my colleague, Constable Glenda Schmidt.' He indicated the young woman who was climbing the steps behind him, before extracting his ID from a side pocket.

Anna hadn't noticed the woman before. She stared at the identity document as the truth dawned. 'Has my husband been involved in an accident?' She suddenly felt cold and a bit shaky.

'May we come in?'

She nodded and ushered them into the lounge. It seemed to take an age for the officers to choose a seat.

'Mrs Fletcher, I'm afraid we bring bad news,' Senior Sergeant Dodman began, shifting awkwardly in the plush lounge chair. 'Your husband was involved in an incident this evening outside Kenmore tavern.'

Anna frowned. 'A fight?'

'No. A witness said he was assaulted by two young men as he came out of the bottle shop.'

She could picture it; a snatched wallet... red blood pooling on grey pavement. 'Oh my God, is he in hospital?'

The sergeant nodded. 'We'll get them, Mrs Fletcher, there's CCTV around there.'

'Can you take me to the hospital?' She stood up shakily and took a step towards the door, knowing she needed to get dressed.

Dodman and Schmidt exchanged glances. 'The paramedics and the doctors at Emergency did all they could, Mrs Fletcher, but I'm afraid your husband passed away half an hour ago. We're so sorry.'

Constable Schmidt rose from her chair and hurried over to Anna, whose knees were buckling. 'Is there anyone we can call for you?' she asked gently, steering her back towards the sofa.

'Shirley Brown.'

'Your daughter?'

Anna shook her head. 'Friend. My son lives in Canada.'

The policewoman pulled out her mobile. 'Can you give me her number?'

'Of course, I can,' Anna snapped. 'We've been friends for over forty years.'

* * *

Anna stayed with Shirley and Sam until Adam arrived from Banff. She was grateful for their care and kindness, their ability to correctly anticipate her need for solitude or company. The funeral, held a week after the assault, seemed surreal. The celebrant spouted saccharine statements that bore no resemblance to Joseph the man and the Bible readings were irrelevant to life in 2017 BCE. The eulogy alone reached her heart, Adam's earnest portrayal of a loving, supportive father bringing a rush of tears to her eyes.

After the service, Anna stood with Adam, shaking hands with dozens of people neither of them knew, wishing she could return to the house and lose herself in a fantasy world where heroine or hero emerged scarred but intact from skirmishes with enemies, or fire-breathing beasts.

Days and weeks passed, with grief pushed into a corner as Anna dealt with piles of paperwork, scores of phone calls, visits to solicitor and banks; all necessary duties for the newly widowed. In between, she accepted invitations from close friends, aware she must make an effort to engage in ordinary life. The internet had proved a useful tool for learning about the different stages of grief, but nothing could supplant human to human contact.

* * *

One wet April day, Anna was having afternoon tea with Shirley when the subject of moving to a smaller property arose, more as a thought spoken aloud than a deliberate conversation topic. 'I've been trawling *realestate.com*,' she admitted, following Shirley's comment that it might be too soon to consider a move. 'The trouble is, I don't know what I want, or where I want to live.'

'Then stay put for a while. You have a reliable cleaner and gardener, so you've no problem looking after the place.'

'I know, but one person rattling around in an enormous house seems decadent.'

'Why? It's paid for!'

'I don't deserve it.'

'Why ever not? You and Joe worked hard to achieve your goals.'

Anna looked down at the plate that was balanced precariously on her knees. 'I didn't deserve Joseph, either.'

'How can you say that? You were a loyal wife who supported him in his career and didn't whinge about all the time he spent away from home.'

'I was a disappointment to him.'

'Bullshit, Anna. Joe was proud of you.'

'As a writer, yes, but not as a mother or a wife. He wanted more children, a wife who relished child-rearing, not –'

'We can't always have what we want,' Shirley interrupted. 'If it had been so important to him, he would have left – found a woman who would give him half a dozen kids.'

Anna raised her head. 'Do you really think so?'

'I do.' Shirley shifted in her seat. 'And I see little point in going on a guilt-trip. Or is self-deprecation one of the stages of grieving you were telling me about the other day?'

Anna considered the question, one hand resting on her chin. 'I suppose it could come under the Bargaining heading.'

'You can't believe every article you read on the bloody internet, Anna. Besides, I'm certain no one grieves according to a set pattern. Sure, I understand why you felt so angry with Joe going out to buy another bottle of wine, when he could have stayed at home and had a cup of tea or something. I would have felt the same if it had been Sam insisting on buying a packet of cigarettes. But you can't change what happened, or ask "what if" questions. Focus on what's best for *you* right now and if that means moving to a smaller place, go ahead.' Shirley took a deep breath. 'Bit of a lecture. Sorry!'

'A necessary one. I've been too focused on doing the right thing according to so-called experts, rather than proceeding at my own pace.' Anna took a bite of chocolate cake. 'Yum, this is great.'

'Thanks. It's George's favourite. He's coming over tomorrow.'

'How's his latest relationship going?'

'He's talking about moving in with Gemma, so I guess it's going well.' Shirley leant forward. 'Tell me I'm old-fashioned, but I do wish George would settle down. One year here, two years there isn't a recipe for relationship success in my book. No one's in it for the long haul these days.'

'Adam's the same. Just when I think he's ready to commit, there's a row and it's over.'

'At least he's bought a house. I keep telling George that if he doesn't get on the housing ladder soon, his father will be too old to assist with maintenance or renovation.'

Anna nodded, her thoughts turning to the contemporary log cabin with a stone basement, built into the side of a mountain, with large fir trees behind it and a view of Banff in front. She and Joseph had visited Adam for Christmas 2013, a welcome respite following two visits to England the year before to attend her parents' funerals. Sitting in front of a roaring log fire, Anna had envisaged future Christmases there, mulled wine and chestnuts roasting in a wire basket, perhaps a grandchild playing in the snow. She knew it was wishful thinking – at least the grandchild part – but there was nothing to stop her spending time in Canada. A month, three months, a year, forever... what did it matter? She was beholden to no one.

'Solution!' she declared, to Shirley's surprise. 'I'm taking your advice about focusing on what's right for me now. I'm going to rent out the house for a year, to go and explore Canada.'

* * *

Driving home through familiar streets, the windscreen wipers going full-pelt against a late afternoon downpour, Anna made plans that twenty-four hours earlier would have been unthinkable. She would work through the grieving process in her own time, aided by brand-new experiences in a land endowed with vast mountain ranges and sweeping prairies. She would learn to accept what fate had delivered, with no looking over her shoulder and no regrets.

The euphoria of enthusiasm sustained her for days as she pored over travel brochures and visited real estate agents to discuss leasing out her house. Adam was delighted to hear she would be visiting *his* adopted land and expressed no concern when learning that she planned to travel its length and breadth alone in a mobile home.

Only one question threatened to undermine her optimism. Could she risk forming a deep relationship with another country?

Dear reader,

We hope you enjoyed reading *A Question Of Country*. Please take a moment to leave a review, even if it's a short one. Your opinion is important to us.

Discover more books by Sue Parritt at

https://www.nextchapter.pub/authors/sue-parritt

Want to know when one of our books is free or discounted? Join the newsletter at http://eepurl.com/bqqB3H

Best regards,

Sue Parritt and the Next Chapter Team

You might also like:
Feed Thy Enemy by Sue Parritt

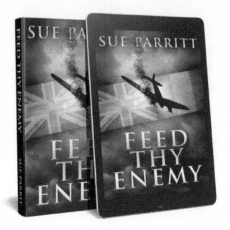

To read the first chapter for free, please head to:
https://www.nextchapter.pub/books/feed-thy-enemy

Dedication

To Mark, beloved husband for more than fifty years (November
1969-) and fellow migrant (July 1970)

Acknowledgments

Many thanks to Miika Hannila and the team at Next Chapter for having faith in my writing.

About the Author

Originally from England, Sue worked in university libraries until taking early retirement in 2008 to concentrate on creative writing. Since then, she has written short stories, articles, poetry, a short TV drama script and seven novels:

Sannah and the Pilgrim, Odyssey Books, 2014, first in a trilogy of a future dystopian Australia focusing on climate change and the harsh treatment of refugees from drowned Pacific islands. Commended in the FAW Christina Stead Award, 2014.
Pia and the Skyman, Odyssey Books, 2016. Commended in the FAW Christina Stead Award, 2016.
The Sky Lines Alliance, Odyssey Books, 2016.
Chrysalis, the story of a perceptive girl growing up in a Quaker family in Swinging Sixties' Britain. Morning Star Press, 2017
Re-Navigation recounts a life turned upside down when forty-year-old Julia journeys from the sanctuary of middle-class Australian suburbia to undertake a retreat at a college located on an isolated Welsh island. Creativia Publishing, 2019.
Feed Thy Enemy, based on Sue's father's World War II experiences, is an account of courage and compassion in the face of trauma as a British airman embarks on a plan that risks all to feed a starving, war-stricken family. Creativia Publishing, 2019.

A Question of Country explores the migrant experience through the protagonist's lifelong search for meaningful identity. Next Chapter (formerly Creativia), 2020.

Sue's current project, working title *Twenty-eight Days,* first in *The Doorkeeper* series, is set in Southern Australia in 2100. It deals with overpopulation and extended life expectancy in an increasingly climate-challenged world and the inhumane solutions adopted by a government determined to rid Australia of unproductive citizens.

Passionate about peace and social justice issues, Sue's goal as a fiction writer is to continue writing novels that address topics such as climate change, the effects of war, the treatment of refugees, feminism and racism. Sue intends to keep on writing for as long as possible, believing the extensive life experiences of older writers can be employed to engage readers of all ages.

A Question of Country
ISBN: 978-4-86745-873-0

Published by
Next Chapter
1-60-20 Minami-Otsuka
170-0005 Toshima-Ku, Tokyo
+818035793528
26th April 2021